SF Books by Vaughn Heppner

Visit VaughnHeppner.com for more information

Star Raider

By Vaughn Heppner

ISBN-13: 978-1530494477
ISBN-10: 1530494478
BISAC: Fiction / Science Fiction / Military

"The fixed determination to acquire the warrior soul and having acquired it to either conquer or perish with honor is the secret of victory."

-- George S. Patton Jr.

-Prologue-

"What's this?"

"Your orders, Tribune. High Command is sending several stealth boats to Avernus before the invaders get a foothold. The strike teams are to insert and snatch the smartest apemen, finding a way to get them back to Remus. If anyone can produce a tech miracle to save us, it's those furry eggheads."

"That's madness! The Coalition has swarmed into our system. By the time the boats reach Avernus, enemy space marines will be securing the planet. It's a suicide mission for whoever goes."

"I know that. It seems you do, too, now. That should make choosing who goes easier for you, yes?"

"What are you suggesting? That I send my troublemakers?"

"The stealth boats are prepping, Tribune. High Command is determined about this. You know what they're saying over there: 'We shall never give up.' Once the Coalition reaches Remus and begins dropping hell-burners, though, High Command will undoubtedly change its mind. But none of that matters today. Given the size and speed of the invasion fleet, few if any of the stealth boats will return. It's a long shot anyway. Your only decision is which thirty strike specialists you no longer want."

"I understand and I don't like it, but… Yes. At least, I know who will head the list. He was a sniper before he became a pilot. I'll say the strikers need his marksmanship."

"Your reasons don't matter. I just need thirty expendable men."

"The troublemaker is a plebian from the slums of Vesuvius, if you can believe that. He's one of those uppity types. He never seems to understand his proper station in things."

"I take it he's tough, though?"

"I suppose he had to be to survive his youth. What does anyone really know about those sewer rats, eh? Yes! Centurion Tanner heads the list. The others are going to be harder to choose, a whole hell of a lot harder. I suppose it's time to clean out the riffraff. We want to make sure none of those undisciplined killers are around to give us trouble after the war."

-1-

Centurion Tanner closed his eyes as his *Pilum*-class stealth boat dumped gravity waves in low Avernus orbit. It had been a harrowing journey from Remus. Two of the boats had bought it. Now, the last of them were going through with this folly.

Coalition battleships pounded the surface from orbit. The last defenders manned surface-to-space missile, or SSM, sites and mass accelerator gun silos. Enemy space marines had already begun to drop, securing the most important points.

Could the strike teams' handful of commandos insert, grab the brainiest apemen and get back upstairs? It was worse than doubtful. The mission seemed hopeless and frankly senseless.

The centurion's drop pod shivered inside its launch tube, causing his teeth to rattle. Maybe this was crazy, but so what? Two years ago, a Coalition raid on Cestus V had killed Tanner's sister and her husband-to-be. It had been at their wedding, annihilating everyone.

Tanner's eyes watered with anger. Growing up on the streets had taught him to pay back twice as hard as he got. There were Coalition troops down there, the same kind of space marines that would strut on Remus after the war, enforcing their hive-mind Social Unity system on the conquered. If he could kill a few more of them now, he would gladly accept the risks of a low-orbital insertion.

The shaking grew worse, making some of Tanner's equipment shudder. They were coming in hard.

"Get ready for ejection," the strike leader said through a speaker inside Tanner's helmet.

Officially, Decurion Pugio led them. Tanner outranked the man but that hadn't mattered to the tribune. Pugio had a rep as a strike leader and the patrician tribune had a grudge against Tanner. Pugio had gotten his nickname because the man loved using knives. Pugio was an ancient Earth term from Roman history, the knife a legionnaire used with his short sword.

Now, the shaking forced Tanner to tighten his muscles. The team had gone over this in a drop simulator many times, but none of them had ever done it in real time.

Then it happened. A loud clack preceded a slamming jolt. If Tanner's mouth had been open, the force would have snapped his teeth together hard enough to bite off his tongue. He heard something else and then there was silence. He was outside the boat.

The seconds lengthened—

A click in the interior speaker gave Tanner a second of warning. Afterward, a small explosion blew the pod apart, exposing him to space. Tanner hung over Avernus in low orbit.

The centurion looked around. Bright, boot flares showed him the rest of the team. Six men in special spacesuits had begun to fall toward Avernus. This would be the longest dive in history—the longest anyone on Remus knew about anyway.

From up here, Tanner could see the curvature of the hot, jungle world. The stealth boat was invisible to his naked eye and so were the Coalition battleships in orbit. He was alone in the darkness, able to see two of the planet's continents down below.

I'm going to die today, aren't I?

The tribune had only chosen lower-class strikers. Everyone on the mission had earned their way into the elite unit through sheer grit. The desperation of the war had shaken the regular social order. Maybe the bluebloods didn't want their types around after this was over.

The mood had soured on the trip to Avernus. Some of the men had talked about hijacking the stealth boat and leaving the system. Tanner had nixed that idea and made it stick. Some things were more important than life. Among them was

4

honor—and killing invaders while there was still a ghost of a chance of winning.

Soon, Tanner could no longer see the curvature of the planet. The starry darkness had already turned into a touch of blueness. The world below became fluffy white. Avernus remained under eternal cloud cover. One of the scientists had called it the Venus Effect.

Tanner watched the inside of his visor, keeping track of his G-meter.

To his right, he saw wild motion. Trooper Marcus had begun to spin faster and faster. If the man spun too fast, the blood would drain from his brain, causing irreversible brain damage. The ladies would surely miss Mr. Lover Boy.

A huge chute appeared on Tanner's other side. It was a drogue chute, meant to stabilize another man. A second chute appeared there, as the first had already ripped away. Ah, good, weasel-faced Gaius had stabilized.

Tanner looked in the other direction to see how Marcus was doing. No! The man spun so fast he'd become a blur. Marcus was as good as dead.

With bitter concentration, Tanner used his arms and legs as stabilization guides. He remained in a perfect skydiving pose. If he lost it, if he hit with a splat, his sister would give him a tongue-lashing he'd never forget when he met her in the afterlife.

He plunged into the clouds. Timelessness seemed to take over until he dropped through the bottom. The former blue above the clouds was muted light below. Far below him spread out the tops of the giant trees that grew on the jungle planet. Did any apemen remain at the depots? Had the natives already scattered?

According to the boat's intelligence officer, space marines were already prowling downstairs. Would the enemy capture the brainiest of Avernites? Did the Coalition even know the secret about the apemen's technical genius? Many thought them mere brutes, but some of them were brilliant.

Tanner studied his visor's instruments, gauging his height. He needed to deploy the main chute in three, two, one—

The centurion pulled a handle. A violent yank against his shoulders told him the chute bit the air. He began to float. As he did, Tanner began readying his jetpack. This would be tricky.

Working by rote drilled into him by hundreds of hours of training, he checked the intake valves, the fuel feed and the gyrostabilizer. Lastly, he snapped out the control-arm pad and tested the joystick. Everything seemed ready.

Tanner focused on the trees. They spread out below uncomfortably near. He had seconds to do this right. With a flick, he detached the chute straps. Instantly, he fell, dropping like a rock. That was good. He needed to be clear of the silk. With his control hand thumb, he turned on the jetpack so it purred into life.

The tops of the giant trees zoomed up to greet him.

Remember, you're falling hard.

Within his helmet, Tanner nodded. He twisted the throttle so more fuel squirted into the motor. A second later, thrust pulled at the harness around him. He lifted, twisted a little less power and floated through a tiny area between two huge tree canopies.

With the jetpack, Tanner guided himself past vast mossy branches and onto the dark jungle floor of Avernus. Once his boots touched dirt, he deactivated the jetpack. He'd made it. He was here, ready for the next phase of the operation.

***

Four space-strike team members hoofed it across the jungle floor. Two had died, Marcus spinning during the descent and Julius whose jetpack had failed. Poor Julius was a mass of protein and shattered bones on the ground. Tanner would miss the team jokester.

The centurion brought up the rear of the column. They all felt the planet's greater drag. It was slightly larger than Remus, meaning it had more gravity than their muscles were used to.

"Two more klicks," Pugio said through the helmet speaker.

"We should jetpack there," weasel-faced Gaius panted. He always got tired the easiest.

"Negative," Pugio said. "We might need the packs later."

"You really think there's going to be a later?"

"We're the best. If anyone can do it, we can."

"If you'll notice," Gaius said, "that isn't a freaking answer. We're all dead men, right?"

"What do you think, Tanner?" Pugio asked.

Before Tanner could answer, harsh static came through his interior speaker. He stopped, dropping to his knees, scanning the heavy foliage. The others did likewise.

Finally, the centurion chinned a helmet control that caused his visor to whirr open. The rotted vegetative stench hit him like a hot wall. It took Tanner several tries before he could breathe the stuff.

"Coalition space marines," Gaius whispered. He'd also turned off his helmet comm and opened his visor. "I wonder if they got a fix on us."

"You wait here," Tanner said. "I'm going to scout around."

Tanner slid a massive, material-destroying rifle from his shoulder. He worked his way to the left past huge damp fronds, soon leaving the others behind. The harsh static meant enemy space marines might be washing the area with radar. The intelligence officer had said only a few marines were in the immediate area.

Tanner looked around. There was nothing but fronds and trees—these giant trees that poked into the heavens. He shouldered the rifle and activated his jetpack. With a throttle twist, he lifted two hundred meters, landing birdlike on a massive branch. Shutting the pack down, he cradled the rifle again. With great patience, he readied the heavy gun.

If the few Coalition marines were out here, this was as good as place as any to kill them. He'd rather slip by to complete the mission, but that might not be possible. The enemy used power-armored suits, jumping like giant crickets with exoskeleton strength, and they had good sensors.

There, he saw one, a flash of dark metal against the green.

Hatred boiled in Tanner's brain. Despite his earlier resolution to stay stealthy, old instincts took over as he inhaled the heavy vegetative stench, relaxing his shoulders. If the enemy never saw him, they would think he was a native defender. He worked the rifle's bolt, putting a huge shell into

7

the firing chamber. Then, he focused the sights. Once more, a leaping, jet-assisted space marine appeared against the green.

Tanner squeezed the trigger. The gun bucked hard against his shoulder. The armor-piercing shell slammed through the enemy's helmet, no doubt splattering the man's brains inside it. The space marine lost his coordination, falling to the ground far below. Tanner fired three times in rapid succession, bringing down more enemy marines.

He then shouldered the long-barreled rifle, turned on the jetpack and dropped down to the ground. By that time, enemy chain-guns blasted his former perch, spraying explosive bullets that blew leaves and bark apart.

During the next fifteen minutes, Tanner killed five more space marines. The enemy butchered Gaius, catching him as he lifted into a new firing position. Pugio and con man Lucius took out the rest of the enemy platoon. However, it was clear the space marines had known they were here.

"We killed them," Pugio said with surprise, once they regrouped. "We might actually pull this off."

"Never doubted it for a moment," Tanner said. "Now, let's go get some apemen while we can."

***

Ten minutes later, the team crept out of heavy foliage to a burning storage depot. No one moved over there as flames roared. A sickly sweet smell like roasting pork filled the air.

A worried Pugio glanced at Tanner.

"I've got this," Tanner said. "You guys stay cool."

Pugio and Lucius's visors whirred shut as their suits' air-conditioners began to labor. Tanner did the opposite, stripping off his space-strike suit. The time had come to go low-tech. They wouldn't detect him this way.

The stench struck him and the planet's heat tried to leech his strength. He refused to comply.

Wearing combat fatigues, a senso-mask and a floppy-brimmed hat, Tanner raced toward the burning depot. He carried a pistol in one hand and a monofilament blade in the other. He knew what the smell meant: burning human flesh, likely the furry Avernites that those on Remus referred to as apemen.

The flames made it hard to close in. Tanner concentrated and rushed the final distance. The leaping flames blanketed shot-up bodies, apemen with only pieces of their heads or badly mangled torsos. Why kill them like this? The space marines had butchered civilians. It was as if the enemy had gone wild.

Something ominous popped inside the depot.

Tanner turned and ran before his mind started processing the noise as a booby trap to catch anyone investigating. A subsonic explosion erupted. With trained precision, Tanner dropped into a depression. Heat and blast flashed over him. He endured. After it passed, Tanner leaped up and ran again. A greater cauldron of flames billowed at the former depot, igniting some of the nearer branches.

Finally, Tanner reached the team.

"Turn around," Pugio said, sounding worried.

Tanner did, exposing a badly burned back. The blast had scorched away most of the fire-retardant camouflage material.

"How are you still managing to stand?" Pugio asked.

"Pain can be ignored," Tanner told him.

Pugio cursed under his breath and dug in his pack. He held up a bottle of a powerful narcotic cream.

Tanner shook his head.

"I know," Pugio said. "This stuff can play with your mind. But your back is bad. Believe me. You're going to need this."

Sweat slid down Tanner's face. It felt as if he might faint. "Okay," he said in a harsh voice.

Pugio sprayed Tanner's burned back with the healing salve. "That should start feeling better right away."

Tanner didn't answer. He was too busy enduring the pain. But Pugio was right. The intensity eased into something bearable.

"Did you see anything back there?" Pugio asked.

Tanner had to concentrate while the knife junkie asked a second time. In short, monosyllabic answers, Tanner told them about the shot-up apemen.

"The enemy is committing war crimes," Pugio said.

Tanner nodded.

Pugio clicked a map onto his visor. "There's another camp five klicks away." He cursed softly. "But guess what? The Coalition set down a lifter there. Space marines must be swarming the area."

Tanner began to don his space-strike suit and jetpack. His eyes fluttered and he moaned in agony as fabric touched his burned skin.

"What should we do?" Pugio said.

"We'll use our jetpacks and fly there," Tanner whispered. "We need a lifter, remember? This could work."

"If we fly, the space marines will spot us with their radar."

"If that lifter leaves without us, we're never going home."

"You think we can make it off this hellhole?"

The narcotic must have already started working. A tiny portion of Tanner's rage had slackened. His back didn't hurt as much now either.

"We grab some apemen and leave," Tanner said. "We stick it in the tribune's face."

"Stick what?"

Tanner grinned starkly. "The fact of our survival. Come on, let's do this."

-2-

The three commandos flew a meter above the highest canopies, their jetpacks hissing. They flew with radio and click silence.

Harsh static burst from Tanner's helmet speaker. The space marines were using their radar again. Likely, the enemy knew they were coming.

Tanner waved an arm, hoping the other two saw him. Then, he eased the joystick, flashing under the canopy, weaving past huge mossy branches. He would burn up the last of his precious fuel doing the weaving, but that would be better than presenting an easy target for any Coalition jets or battleships in orbit.

On his visor-map, Tanner saw that the next compound was almost in sight. Since the marines knew he was coming…

Tanner dropped down, dodging giant leaves. His back throbbed, he was almost out of fuel and the mission looked more impossible by the second. But there was something he'd learned a long time ago. A slight changeup done with extreme aggression could produce miracles. The prize often went to the man with balls. On the flipside, if he was going to see his sister today, he wanted to see the shock on her face as he told her what he'd done. He'd missed her shocked look for a long time already.

Tanner flew centimeters above the ground, which took perfect flying control. He burst out of the tree line, zooming over a carpet of fungus grass. The compound loomed ahead, as

11

did a 150-ton enemy lifter. Several suited space marines stood around the vessel with their chain-guns aimed skyward. At the same time, a line of handcuffed apemen filed up a ramp into the shuttle. So this time the Coalition was capturing them, huh? Well, he wasn't going to let that happen.

One of the space marines saw him at almost the same moment Tanner's jetpack sputtered, running on fumes. Several things happened at once then. The space marine lowered his chain-gun, trying to get a bead on the enemy legionnaire coming at him. Tanner's hands roved over the harness, shedding the buckles holding the jetpack in place.

The chain-gun spat explosive bullets. At the same time, the jetpack fell away from Tanner. Just like a rocket shedding a lower stage, the lost weight gave Tanner an extra burst of speed. The bullets shredded the jetpack, sending it tumbling backward as it bled metal and plastic hose.

Tanner flew a short distance with his feet barely touching the ground. He ran as hard as he could, using the final burst of forward momentum from the jetpack to gain some distance.

If only he'd had a little more fuel in the pack.

***

Several Avernites on the ramp witnessed the strange sight. One of them was named Greco. Like most of his kind, he was short and bow-legged, hairy, long-armed and thinking about a pleasure he'd missed for a long time already. In Greco's case that was a good stogie and brandy to help his gray cells do some deep thinking.

For the past weeks, Greco had realized that he was in the wrong place. The Remus flatfoots had wanted elders, the cloud thinkers, as his people called them. Lured by cigars and brandy, the flatfoots had gotten him. Greco wasn't really a cloud thinker, though, but a tinkerer. He could make the most fantastic toys with a whittling blade.

Greco had been feeling useless. He'd been bored nearly to death sitting around discussing philosophy and higher-level calculus with the cloud thinkers. He could do that as an old man when the strength left his muscles. What he really wanted was to wander the world to gain experiences so he could learn how to fashion a *koholmany*.

A *koholmany* was an Avernite expression, an ultimate invention that exhibited the wanderer's essence of being. Greco didn't know what kind of *koholmany* he would invent, but he had begun to have an inkling in what direction the ultimate invention would take. Greco was the best drummer of his tribe. After smoking cigs and drinking brandy, he loved nothing more than pounding the drums. He had concluded three months ago that something about the vibrations going through his body while he drummed delighted him. Besides, the ancient Tesla was something of a cult legend among his people.

As Greco stood on the ramp, feeling the space marine's chain-gun rip it up, inspiration struck. It must have had something to do with the trick sprinter flying across the ground toward them.

The Remus legionnaire must think he was trying to rescue the Avernites. It was something out of a comic book, which Greco loved to read. He imagined the running man should have been wearing a fluttering cape. That would have made it perfect.

A chain-gun fired again. Greco liked those, as he could feel the noise through his body. The ground spurted up as shells struck just behind the runner. The spurts closed the distance to the sprinter—

Abruptly, the gunner's helmet exploded. The chain-gun stopped firing, and the space marine toppled onto his back, dead.

Greco realized the flying runner had hidden friends. It was obvious now. Running man was the distraction.

While most Avernites loved peace, Greco had grown tired of these invading flatfoots. He didn't know about the murders in the nearby depot, but he didn't like how the exo-armored ones shoved them around. Even more, he hated these handcuffs.

Suddenly, all of these things combined in one drumming moment of time. Greco lifted his face toward the clouds and hooted wildly. With a surge of adrenaline strength, he burst the chain linking the handcuffs. Those of Avernus were far stronger than flatfoots, who often underestimated them.

"Let's fight!" Greco hooted. "Don't let our allies find us tied up like shrikes."

The hairy, bow-legged apeman of Avernus ran down the ramp and leaped onto the back of a space marine. Howling, Greco ripped away the marine's visor. As the enemy marine reached up to grab him, his servomotors whirring with power, Greco used his stiffened fingers to jab the flatfoot in the eyes.

The space marine went down, howling, clutching his face as he rolled across the fungus grass.

Other Avernites stared at the space marine in shock.

"Fight!" Greco shouted, taking up the fallen chain-gun. He was sure he could use this. Aiming at another space marine, Greco let it rip.

The gun nearly shook out of his grip. This was crazy, the vibration making his teeth chatter. At the same time, bullets drummed against space marine armor, finally breaking through and taking another enemy combatant out of the fight.

***

All this happened as Tanner's feet touched down, as he ran as hard as he could but slowed just the same through inertia.

Pugio and Lucius continued to use sniper-shots, taking out enemy marines. On and around the ramp, more apemen howled, attacking other armored enemy.

Tanner drew his monofilament knife. It was fashioned out of a special alloy and had an edge one molecule thick. He wanted to test it against space marine armor.

The monofilament knife worked like magic. With it, Tanner hacked through space marine armor. In the confined corridors of the lifter, he was like a man amok, stabbing, slashing and eviscerating the enemy.

In the end, with the apemen's help, Tanner, Pugio and Lucius did the impossible, overpowering the Coalition marines. Unfortunately, before all the marines died, they turned on the Avernites, killing many of them.

That made the surviving apemen angry.

"Why did you attack?" the oldest Avernite demanded of Greco. She was a bowed elder with more gray fur than brown. "You roused the others. You should have remained where you were and let the flatfoots fight it out amongst themselves."

"The space marines murdered others of your people," Tanner said.

The elder whirled on him.

"In the other encampment," Tanner said. "I saw them shot down in cold blood, and then burned."

"Why would the Coalition marines do that?" the female asked.

"Who can know the thoughts of a hive-mind thug?"

The elder cocked her head, considering. "What do you suggest we do now?"

"That's up to you."

Pugio cleared his throat.

Tanner looked at the knife-man.

Pugio shook his head.

"You're kidding, right?" Tanner asked. "We've lost the war. Do these people really want to come to Remus with us? Maybe they want to slink away and remain free on their own world. I doubt the Coalition is going to try to settle on Avernus."

"Our orders…" Pugio said.

Tanner knew these were special apemen, smart as hell and given to flights of fancy that often produced technological miracles. The monofilament knife was one of their inventions.

The narcotic cream must have done it. Tanner couldn't stop the words from flowing. "The war's over. We all know that, right?"

The Avernites listened to him attentively. "Why do you say this?" the elder asked him.

Tanner told them about the giant Coalition fleet that had invaded the star system. The Remus space force had fought back gamely but had been severely outnumbered. In a few weeks, the enemy fleet would finally reach Remus itself for the final siege.

"This flatfoot is a truth-teller," the elder announced. "I trust him. I will do as he suggests."

Everyone stared at Tanner.

He had to concentrate. He needed more cream on his burned back. "Here's my counsel," he said. "Come with us if you want to keep fighting. I'm never going to quit. But if you've had enough of bullets and blood, go hide in the jungle."

"Which of you will remain with the flatfoots?" the elder asked the others.

Only Greco came forward. He wanted to wander so he could fashion his *koholmany*. Maybe wandering off-planet would allow him insights he'd never find elsewhere.

"It is decided," the elder said. "The rest of us are leaving."

"Not so fast," Pugio said, fingering his weapon.

"No," Tanner said. "It's their decision. Let them go."

Pugio stared at Tanner. "When the tribune hears about this—"

"I'm not lying for that bastard," Tanner said with heat. "Besides, who's going to tell him?"

Pugio reddened, looking away.

After the other apemen left, leaving Greco with them, Pugio went into the lifter's flight compartment.

"That was amazing," Greco told Tanner.

"What part?" Tanner asked. "Telling your people the truth?"

"Don't all of you tell the truth?"

Tanner shook his head.

"Oh," Greco said. "Why don't you?"

"I do."

"All the time?" Greco asked.

"No, not all the time."

"Do all flatfoots lie some of the time?"

"I don't know all flatfoots," Tanner said.

Greco hooted with delight. "That's spoken like a true thinker. I like you, Tanner."

Tanner grinned, deciding he liked the hairy apeman in return. "We'd better get buckled in," he said. "We're going to lift off soon."

"Will the enemy allow that?"

Tanner shrugged. "We're going to find out real soon, now aren't we?"

"How do you mean?" Greco asked.

"Come on," Tanner said. "Let's find a seat."

-3-

They made it onto the stealth boat, and their boat was the only one that reached Remus. By that time, the main Coalition fleet began its final drive. They'd conquered, captured or destroyed everything else in the star system. Now it was Remus's turn.

The last of Remus's space fleet worked closely with the surface defenses. They scored kills, good ones, and that angered the Coalition.

The enemy dropped nukes. One of those slammed into Vesuvius, Tanner's home city. The final days slaughtered Remus pilots. They had never been that numerous. During the last week of the war, Tanner found himself a VTOL pilot again. He flew recklessly and remorselessly, deciding if Remus was going down, he was going to take as many of the enemy with him as he could.

***

The underground hangar shook from another surface explosion as Centurion Tanner saluted. Lights flickered, gravel fell from the ceiling and mechanics stopped to look up, seeing if the cavern would collapse this time to bury them.

No. The rock ceiling held. The war wasn't over for them yet. The bleary-eyed mechanics resumed working, readying the few VTOL fighters left for another sortie against the space invaders.

The centurion lowered his arm. He stood before a makeshift desk in a far corner, out of the way of scrambling legionnaires.

Tanner wore an oil-smudged Remus AirSpace Force uniform and had dark circles around his eyes. During the invasion, he'd become an ace, having obliterated an incredible *seven* Coalition dropships. He'd done it while they'd carried their hated cargoes of space marines, too, not after unloading the killers when their protection became lighter.

The Coalition had gained complete space superiority. Their heavy orbitals had systematically knocked out one Remus SSM site after another. At the same time, Coalition battleships had launched massive space-to-ground missiles. Vesuvius was gone, a radioactive graveyard for ten million citizens. Pilots like Tanner flew compact VTOL fighters. They were outgunned, out-armored and outnumbered ten to one.

Consul Titus Flavius Maximus of House Tarentum sat behind the desk. He was a squat man with a bloody rag around his head in lieu of a proper bandage. Since the nuclear bombardment of the capital, he had become the supreme leader for Remus's dwindling forces.

Tanner had no idea why Consul Maximus had summoned him. It made no sense. The great man had vastly more important things to do than talk to a lowly centurion. The war was almost over. He would have thought Maximus would have already spoken to the Coalition leader regarding terms.

The idea of surrender made Tanner scowl. After everything everyone had done…the hated Coalition had still reached the homeworld. All the years of sacrifice, all the lost lives, and now the oppressor would put his jackboot on their neck, trying to crush the soul out of a defeated people with their Social Unity ideology.

The consul studied a tablet in his thick-fingered hands. The older man seemed to wrestle with a thought.

Tanner glanced over his shoulder at a fighter being wheeled toward a launch pit. If he could get the interview over with soon enough, he might make one more sortie today. Despite his exhaustion, he yearned to climb back into the sky, to knock down another dropship.

19

"Centurion," the consul said.

Tanner faced forward, standing stiffly at attention.

The consul eyed him curiously before glancing at the fighter. Finally, he indicated the tablet. "It says here you never went to the Academy."

"No, sir," Tanner said.

"You have a sketchy bio. I can't tell if you have any advanced degrees or not."

Tanner didn't know what his bio had to do with anything. Had the head wound scrambled the consul's thoughts?

"I never attended a university or a trade school," Tanner said.

"Yet...you destroyed seven dropships with your fighter, only one of the kills made with a missile. You used your *autocannons* to knock down the others?"

Tanner nodded.

The consul tapped his chin. "You'd have to get awfully close to a dropship to penetrate the hull armor with cannons."

"I suppose."

The consul frowned at him.

Tanner almost shrugged. He was dead tired and surprised that he was still alive. He knew the war might end any hour. The overwhelming enemy force had embittered him. He could not foresee a life after the war. The Coalition was a vengeful organization with its Social Unity policy. There would be reeducation camps for many, enforced speech codes and deviant occupiers molesting their women to brutalize them into compliance. Instead of talking with the consul, he'd rather take a few more of the enemy with him before he died.

The consul had become curious. "Explain to me how you managed to destroy these heavily armored dropships with your cannons."

Tanner stared into the older man's eyes. He saw someone weighing him, judging his worth. That ignited indignation in Tanner's heart. Just like the tribune who had sent them to Avernus, the old man sat in safety while giving orders—

Tanner opened his mouth to speak. There weren't any fancy tricks to what he'd done. It had been the simple determination to take out a dropship any way he could. In his mind, that had meant ramming the bastard. He'd prepped each dropship with his autocannons first and they had each happened to come apart before he could smash through them.

Remembering whom he addressed, Tanner adjusted his words at the last moment. "A dropship's exhaust tubes lack hull armor, sir. If you fly right behind one—"

"That's suicide!" the consul said, interrupting. "Their coaxial lasers would have shredded your fighter in seconds."

A hard grin touched Tanner's lips. That might be true sometimes, but not if the Coalition gunner was too busy pissing himself seeing a Remus fighter crawling up the tailpipe.

"Timing helps," Tanner heard himself say. "So does the enemy's fear. Most of their gunners have never been in real danger."

The consul eyed him differently now. It seemed as if the older man had almost come to his decision. "Where did you learn to fly well enough to time lasers?"

"The best place of all, sir. The school of hard knocks."

The consul set the tablet on the desk, maybe the better to regard Tanner. "You drew a gun on a flight deck commander two hours ago."

So that's what this was about. "Yes, sir, I did."

"Why?"

"Isn't it all in your report?"

Instead of enraging the consul, the answer seemed to amuse the man. "I want to hear it in your own words, son."

Did the old man mean that?

"I think this is it, sir, the end of the war. That means any day could be the last day of aerial combat. The flight commander told me to wash up, get some chow and rest. I told him I wanted to go back up. He said I was crazy. Well, if I was crazy, then I might as well do what I wanted. I drew my gun and told him I'd kill him unless he let me into a ready fighter."

"Would you have killed him?"

"I like to think I would have come to my senses, sir."

The consul leaned back in his chair.

"I've been reading your bio, Centurion. You grew up in the Vesuvius slums, the worst on the planet. With minimal schooling, you picked up advanced concepts of electrical engineering. According to the bio, you were a hands-on practitioner and that made you important to certain criminal elements. When the war started, you gave that up and passed some tough entrance exams to join the AirSpace Service."

"I came from the wrong side of the tracks, but I'm no criminal, sir."

"I wonder about that," the consul said.

If the way the consul said that was meant to goad Tanner, it worked. His face heated up as he said, "I'll tell you something, sir. A fine pedigree and fancy schooling counts for less than nothing against Coalition drones and lasers. Only results matter. This street kid gets results."

The consul smiled without humor. "You have spirit, young man, and I think you have the right attitude. You might do."

Another surface explosion shook the underground hangar. The lights flickered worse than before. More gravel showered down from the ceiling, trickles of it raining onto the desk.

The consul stared at the grit before standing. He came around the desk, approaching Tanner. The older man held out his hand.

Tanner looked down. There was a small device there.

"Take it," Maximus said.

Tanner did, looking up questioningly.

"That will allow you to draw credits from the Markus Bank on Excalibur," Maximus said.

"One of the Sword Worlds, sir?" Tanner asked.

"Yes," Maximus said. "There are ten thousand Coalition credits stashed there. You will use them to keep your *Gladius*-class recon-raider serviceable."

"What raider, sir?"

"The one you're going to slip through the Coalition blockade. It's called *Dark Star*."

"*Dark Star*? But sir—"

"Listen to me, son. Remus has lost this round. The conventional war is almost over. The secret battle to restore our world has just begun. My secretary informed me a few hours ago that *Dark Star's* crew is dead."

Tanner nodded.

"I've been looking for a new captain."

"Me?"

"Son, this is going to be a long, hard slog. I need a fighter, a bitter man who refuses to quit. You seem like that. Drawing the gun on the flight commander was the kind of attitude I've been looking for. People are already making plans for the peace—for the coming subjugation. You aren't one of those, though, Centurion Tanner. You want to keep fighting."

A flush swept over Tanner. He couldn't believe this. It meant…he might not die today. Then, a sobering reality came over him.

"You want me to raid the Coalition planets after they find someone to sign a peace accord?"

"No!" Maximus said sharply. "That's not it at all. The Occupation Force would simply gather people to execute, killing twenty of ours for one of theirs. Besides, the Coalition would soon hunt you down or send bounty hunters after you. What I envision is longer-termed and more subtle. Firstly, you won't be the only one out there. There are others. More than anything else, your existence will help to keep our dream alive as you hunt for ways to free our beloved planet."

"But…"

The squat consul put a hand on Tanner's shoulder. "Listen to me, son. I've chosen a band of brothers, those who will never quit, who will never say die. You can take one or two people with you as your crew—"

"I want to fight here, sir. I want to make the Coalition pay."

"I know," the consul said softly. "I understand. You're like me. You have steel in your soul. The Coalition can kill us but they can't bend or break those like us."

Tanner studied the small bank device. What the consul was suggesting…the war would never end for him. Yet…keeping a spaceship running took lots of money and high-end upkeep.

"What happens once I run out of credits?" Tanner asked.

"Don't," the consul said. "I'll try to find ways to funnel you extra funds now and again. I wish we had squirreled away more, but money was simply too tight these past years. You're going to have to find ways to get credits, but I don't want you turning outlaw. You must extract the credits in lawful ways.

You're representing Remus out there, son. There's going to be a lot riding on your shoulders."

Tanner stared at the older man.

"Do you accept the charge?" Maximus asked. "Are you willing to fight for your world's freedom for the rest of your life?"

A burning anger mixed with love welled up within Tanner. Here was a higher ranked officer who thought like him. He didn't know those existed.

"I gladly accept the charge, sir. By the Lord's grace, I'll fight the Coalition until I die. I will see Remus free again."

The consul's fingers dug into Tanner's shoulder. "One lost battle doesn't lose a war. As long as one of us refuses to surrender, the fight goes on."

"One question, sir," Tanner said.

"I already know it. How do you get past the Coalition fleet?"

"That's right, sir. The Coalition has orbital space sewn up tight, to say nothing about the rest of our star system."

The consul took a deep breath. "Here's where the plan gets tricky…"

FOUR YEARS LATER

A heavy bump shook the *Dark Star*. The customized *Gladius*-class raider had dropped out of hyperspace back into normal space. For the past four years, the ship had served its tiny crew as headquarters for the Remus resistance, funded by their bounty hunting.

Captain Tanner took a deep breath. He sat in one of the two seats in the control chamber. There was some standing room behind him before an archway led into a bigger area with crash seats.

Stars glittered through the port window, one of them a little brighter than the rest. That was the Nostradamus System star, the raider's destination.

Tanner began flipping switches and tapping controls. The raider's diagnostics looked okay until a red signal caught his attention. He tapped a screen. Someone was scanning them. That was odd this far out.

The *Dark Star* was one hundred and fifteen AUs from the system's farthest planetoid, a frozen rock world. Hyperdrive physics meant a ship had to drop out of hyperspace before reaching a deep gravity well or risk sudden implosion.

There! He had a fix on the scanning object. It—

Tanner's jaw dropped as the object went into hyperdrive. It disappeared into hyperspace before he could fully scan it.

What had just happened? The scanning ship…it had to have been a spaceship, right? An automated device wouldn't have done something like that, would it? Could it be a Nostradamus device? He doubted it. The thing couldn't very well have gone in-system with hyperdrive. It would have used hyperspace to head to another star system.

Could someone have known he was coming to the Nostradamus System? Tanner didn't see how.

With growing misgivings, Tanner activated the fusion engine. Nothing happened.

"Now what?" he grumbled.

The intra-ship comm came on. "Sorry about that," Greco said. "I should have told you. I'm working on the atomic coil. Until it's running smoothly, the fusion core won't give you efficient service. I took the fusion engine offline."

"When did you do this?"

"I noticed the problem when you were asleep. I thought I could fix it before we left hyperspace."

Greco was the mechanic. He kept suggesting a complete overhaul. The *Dark Star* had seen four years of constant service already. Tanner wanted to know where they would get the money for this overhaul.

"I'm just saying," seemed to be Greco's favorite phrase, as that had been his answer each time.

Tanner peered out of the port window. The scan bothered him. If the object hadn't been waiting for the *Dark Star*, why had it jumped into hyperspace so fast after scanning them? He told Greco about it.

"That does seem weird," the mechanic said.

"Maybe we should leave."

"What about Jordan?"

Nelly Jordan was their computer wizard, financial coordinator, bounty job selector and all-around morale officer due to her cheerful nature. At the moment, she was down with Rigellian fever. At the start of the hyperdrive run, the fever had seemed to be leveling off and Tanner had figured she would be fine, but he was wrong. During hyperdrive, the fever had become steadily worse. Jordan needed a doctor fast.

"Doctors are supposed to be the best on Calisto Grandee," Greco said. "It's a luxury habitat."

"The best means the most costly," Tanner grumbled.

"We still have a few credits left."

"Yeah," Tanner said. "But did you happen to read the abstract on Calisto Grandee? Everything there costs money. And if you run too low, they confiscate your remaining assets. Then, they sell them off to pay any outstanding debts while giving you a one-way ticket elsewhere."

"What's your point?"

"I don't like getting boxed in."

"Meaning what?" Greco asked. "I'm too busy trying to fix this atomic coil to read your mind."

Tanner exhaled. "We have a possible client on Calisto Grandee. But it costs credits to dock there. Now, it's going to cost more credits to pay for Jordan's doctor. If the client discovers this, she can drop the fee by a considerable amount because we have to take what we can get."

"I have the solution to that."

"I'm listening."

"Don't let the client know how desperate we are."

"I suppose you're right. With Jordan's fever, we don't have a choice." Tanner straightened. "Get the atomic coil ready so we can begin the burn in-system."

"Roger," Greco said. "I should have everything ready in another hour."

***

Nostradamus System was a key refueling point on the long run from Coalition territory to Earth-controlled space. Most of the interstellar liners stopped here.

Humanity had burst from the mother planet a long time ago. There were thousands of colony worlds scattered throughout the Orion Arm. In the beginning, there had been an Old Federation. Then, a terrible war had rocked everything, bringing vast destruction and a dark age. Remus and others had eventually climbed back up to hyperdrive technology, finding other worlds in similar straits. In the last hundred years, Earth had begun expanding, creating a New Federation as it brought its wayward children back under its wing.

However, in this region of space, the Coalition of Planets was the great power, gobbling up worlds like Remus. Since that war, the Alliance of Worlds had arisen to counter the Coalition. Both powers had sent envoys to Earth in order to make sure their opponent didn't acquire a new, powerful ally. Instead of keeping Earth Force away, though, it was likely going to encourage the Earthmen to play the Coalition against the Alliance.

That was long-term. In the short term, Remus still groaned under the Coalition's Social Unity tyranny. That weighed on Tanner because he felt guilty. He had begun to get a reputation as a successful bounty hunter. Sometimes, he feared he might slide permanently into this new role and forget about the charge the consul had laid on him. Honor demanded he do something to help free his planet. Rage about his sister's death and Vesuvius's nuking had turned into a deep hatred against the Coalition. What he could do against his enemy, though, he had yet to figure out.

***

Greco finished his repairs.

"The atomic coil will hold for a few more weeks anyway," he told Tanner.

"Anything else I should know?" Tanner asked.

Greco shook his head.

"Okay. Get some shuteye, then. You look terrible."

"You're just jealous," Greco said. "You know all the girls on Calisto Grandee will run to me."

"Yeah, that's it. Better check your temperature while you're at it. I don't want you catching the fever."

"That's not going to happen. My genes are different enough the Rigellian fever can't touch me."

"Right," Tanner said.

The planet Avernus was hot and a little too close to the Remus System star. During the Dark Age when most worlds had collapsed into pre-industrialism, the few humans on Avernus had gone through what some said were rapid evolutionary changes. A man from Avernus rarely impregnated someone from a different planet, while outsiders could never get an Avernus woman pregnant. It was true that few had tried. There were academic, scientific debates about whether those of Avernus had mutated into a true subspecies or not.

One look at Greco's simian features should have convinced anyone.

The two parted company, Greco going to his quarters and Tanner back to the bridge.

With the atomic coil back online, Tanner plotted a course to the huge gas giant gleaming on his star chart. The Nostradamus System lacked any terrestrial worlds. Instead, vast domes dotted various moons. The biggest places, though, were giant space habitats called gigahabs. Calisto Grandee was the most luxurious and orbited a stupendous gas giant called Titan.

According to Jordan's collected data, atmospheric mining brought trillions of credits to the corporations on Calisto Grandee. They also serviced many of the space liners stopping at the Nostradamus System for fuel.

Soon, Tanner engaged the fusion drive. He decided to push it, adding extra acceleration, making it a 2 G ride. It was going to be uncomfortable during the journey, but the sooner he could get Jordan to a doctor, the better.

It took time accelerating, coasting and then decelerating at 2 G's. Nostradamus Corporation—it ran the system's security—hailed *Dark Star*, granting Tanner permission to head for the Calisto Grandee gigahab.

Tanner tried to contact his client. She was not accepting any messages at this time. He tried three more times with the same luck.

Jordan's fever worsened during the 2 G fusion burn. That left Tanner even less leeway in choices.

"What do you think about our client not accepting calls?" he asked Greco during deceleration. They played billiards in the rec room.

The apeman lined up a shot. "Don't like it a bit," Greco said, "seems screwy."

"Like a trap?"

Greco looked up. "Are you serious or are you just trying to mess with my concentration?"

"Maybe a little of both," Tanner said, smirking.

With his stick, Greco bumped the cue ball. It rolled in the 2 G's to touch the nine, which slowly eased into the left corner pocket.

Standing, Greco laid the stick over his right shoulder. He walked around the table, examining the green cloth. "The woman's a recluse, huh?" he asked, referring to the client.

Tanner nodded.

"It could be as simple as that, then," Greco said. "She's not ready to talk yet."

"Is that what you really think?"

"I'm the mechanic. It doesn't matter *what* I think."

Tanner looked away. Greco was still sore about something he'd said along those lines two years ago.

"I think we're walking into a trap," Tanner said.

Greco bent over the table, lining up his shot. "Do we have enough to pay for Jordan's treatment?"

"They're going to quarantine her, make us go through a thorough examination."

"Problem solved," Greco said. "Nostradamus Corporation will pay for it."

"Things don't work like that here. We're charged for whatever they do. I'm beginning to wonder if we should turn around and go back."

Greco straightened, looking worried. "Jordan won't survive that. She's been coughing up blood."

Tanner said nothing. For a split second, he wondered how important Jordan's life was compared to the mission to save Remus.

Maybe Greco saw that in his eyes. "You can't be serious, boss. Jordan is one of us. If we don't stand by each other, what do we have?"

Tanner almost said, "Honor." Greco didn't think like that, though. Everything was personal for those from Avernus.

"Yeah," Tanner said. "We pay to fix Jordan. We hope the client is playing it straight, and if not, we have to implement Plan B."

"What's Plan B?" Greco asked, as he lined up his shot again.

Tanner chewed on his lower lip. He was still working on that.

-5-

Three weeks later, the gamble had just about played itself out. There hadn't been a client on Calisto Grandee. It must have been a trap after all, an extremely clever one meant to draw a troublesome Vesuvius street kid to this system where credits were law.

What made everything worse was that Tanner didn't even know if Jordan was all right or not. She and Greco were in lockup because of their lack of credits, pending transportation out-system. The docking fees had been much too pricey. And to cap it all off, he hadn't been able to get any kind of work on Calisto Grandee, not even as a burger clerk. He'd tried twice to get work under the table. Each time, the person had looked aghast, as if Tanner had asked to have sex with their mother.

Now, Tanner's eyes ached from a lack of sleep. He'd been on the move for the past sixty-two hours. Maybe he wasn't thinking straight anymore. It had been four days since he'd eaten and he was almost out of water.

His legs felt like rubber. He needed to rest. He stopped, leaned against a stanchion and almost closed his eyes. That would be a mistake. Crowds passed him, either enjoying the star view or heading to the bazaar. If he wasn't careful, someone would notice his weariness. It would only be a matter of time then before a concerned citizen notified a member of the vagrancy squad. If the VS found his credit score was below the gigahab's minimum…

Tanner almost shoved off the stanchion to stagger away. Then, he noticed a woman eyeing him. She seemed suspicious, maybe understanding the strain in his eyes. He was exhausted.

Don't just stand here like an idiot.

Tanner reached back with what seemed like slow motion. He unhooked his water bottle, working to keep his hand from shaking. His weakness goaded him, giving him a spark of animation. He grinned at the matron as he flicked off the cap.

She looked away, blushing, hurrying past him.

Despite his thirst, Tanner only allowed himself a sip. He had to make the water last. The fountain was on the other side of the gigahab. It was a vast, wheel-shaped, slowly spinning habitat. It would take a good twelve hours of walking through public passageways to get back to the fountain.

Tanner wore a leather jacket and boots. The duty constables had made him check his gun and knife in before they'd let him onto the habitat to search for his client.

Maybe he could sell his gun to raise his credit score enough to give him another two days leeway. There was no way he was going to sell his monofilament blade.

Tanner rested on the S2 C5 promenade deck with a vast viewing port showing stars and the northern pole region of the gas giant Titan.

He stiffened. In the reflection of the viewing port, he saw a woman pointing at him. Two others nodded who looked like cops.

As Tanner hooked the water bottle onto his belt, he lurched toward the bazaar.

Walk steady, friend. Nice and easy does it.

In order to ease his nervousness, Tanner flexed his hands. If the vagrancy squad caught him, they would take him to a judge. The judge would see his only assets were his gun and the *Gladius*-class raider. The judge would put *Dark Star* up for auction to pay for Tanner's many fees. And that would be the end of his quest to free Remus and screw the Coalition. It was a brilliant plan on someone's part. To add to the insult, the Nostradamus Corporation would use the proceeds from the auction to pay for a starliner ticket to the next system, which held a rocky prison planet for people like him.

Thinking about losing *Dark Star* after all this time caused an inner rage to ignite. No one was going to sell his raider. He'd turn outlaw before that happened. But turning outlaw…would go against Consul Maximus's orders.

Tanner squeezed his eyelids shut before opening them wide. He needed sleep more than he needed food just now. His judgment was slipping.

"Hey!" a man shouted from behind.

Tanner's back twitched. It felt as if someone aimed a gun at him. He lengthened his stride, passing people.

"Stop, you!" the man shouted.

With a snarl, Tanner broke into a sprint.

A woman walking ahead of him looked back, seeing him charge toward her. She screamed, throwing herself out of his way.

That caused even more people to turn and stare.

Tanner ignored them as he sprinted for the archway into the bazaar. Shoppers under the brighter bazaar lights turned and stared. Many shrank from him as if he had a fatal, poverty-creating disease. The sprint and the stares seemed to shed the years from Tanner, to slough off the space service training that had helped transform a street ruffian into a space-strike legionnaire. In his mind, he reverted to the street punk that had survived many vicious incidents. He realized then that monitors would be watching him on cameras.

He passed under the arch, swung around a portly gentleman and slowed as he entered a shoe store. He had to act natural.

Several people inside the store looked up. One man noticed that those outside stared at Tanner. The man backed away from him.

Tanner realized he had seconds to change the situation. He hurried down an aisle and switched to another row. He was counting on regular Calisto Grandee etiquette as learned these past weeks: that it was best not to get involved with trouble.

No one in the shop had screamed or shouted yet, although several people rushed outside.

Changing rows once more, Tanner worked his way to the back. The aisles of display shoes blocked this area from the storefront. A clerk carrying several boxes headed toward him.

"Excuse me," Tanner said, forcing a smile.

The clerk looked up and raised his eyebrows. Did he notice how scruffy Tanner's clothes were?

"Is the manager here?" Tanner asked.

"I'm the manager."

"Right," Tanner said. "There's a problem."

The man focused on Tanner, and suspiciously asked, "What problem?"

Tanner took the shoeboxes, setting them on the floor.

"What are you doing?" the clerk asked, his voice rising.

"I need you to open the back door."

"What? Why?"

"I'm undercover," Tanner said. He sensed the clerk needed greater persuasion. "The capture of the forger is worth a large reward. Due to your assistance, the shop will receive twenty percent of the arrest bonus."

The clerk tried to look to the front of the store and the sounds of commotion. Tanner didn't give him the opportunity, as he grabbed the clerk's elbow and swiveled him toward the rear door.

"Prompt action is critical," Tanner said. "We've been working on the case for weeks. I don't want to blow it now."

"But...what are you trying to do?" the clerk asked, as he dug a key out of a pants pocket. "What does my store have to do with a forger?"

"You're in the clear, if that's what you're wondering. I've learned that much from surveillance. My boss doesn't agree with me, though."

"Your *boss*?" the man asked. That wasn't the way someone on Calisto Grandee would say it. The man had already inserted the key into the lock, but now looked up. Maybe he noticed the fatigue in Tanner's features. Maybe he realized that no one on Calisto Grandee looked anything like this dangerous vagrant.

Like a junkyard dog, Tanner sensed the change. "Do you want to live?" he asked.

The clerk's eyes widened with fear. He turned the key so the lock clicked open.

"Good," Tanner said. He tightened his grip on the elbow so the man squirmed.

"Please," the clerk whispered. "Don't hurt me."

Tanner shoved him into the storeroom and removed the key.

"I never did anything to you," the clerk whimpered.

"Where's the exit?" Tanner demanded, pocketing the key.

"Over there," the clerk said, pointing shakily into the gloom.

Tanner debated knocking him out. Otherwise, the clerk would run to the police the moment he left.

"Please," the clerk whimpered. "I've done what you asked."

That was a righteous point. Tanner pressed the key into the clerk's palm. He didn't want a judge saying later that he'd stolen anything.

"If I get away," Tanner said, "I don't have a reason to hunt you down later for ratting me out."

The clerk nodded fast.

Tanner bolted, striding into the gloom. He was sure cameras watched him. A glance around didn't show him any surveillance devices, but that didn't mean anything.

He kept walking, taking turns, hurrying down stairs, avoiding exits. He noticed it was cooler here. That meant something. Did the vagrancy squad patrol this area of the gigahab?

He took another flight of stairs, walked along an endless corridor and finally realized he didn't hear any sounds of pursuit. Had that been the vagrancy squad he'd seen on the promenade deck earlier or someone else?

Tanner rubbed his aching forehead. He'd lost the adrenaline rush. He slowed his step and then stopped. He realized it was darker here. Was this an abandoned area? No. He doubted that because…

He started with a jerk, blinking rapidly, realizing he'd almost keeled over. He was close to passing out.

After several more steps, Tanner's knees buckled. His back slid down the wall until he thudded onto his butt. That should have jarred him awake. Instead, it was the end of his sixty-two hour ordeal. Like an old, axed tree from a forest back home, Tanner fell sideways. His left shoulder struck the floor and the side of his head thudded next. His eyes opened and then fluttered closed.

For a moment, possibly longer, he knew blissful sleep. His aching body absorbed the healing process. His normally sharp senses failed to alert him of three approaching strangers. Not even a bright light shining in his face woke him up.

"That him?" the biggest of the three asked.

A woman wearing a silver jacket with an illegal coilgun holstered under her armpit checked a cellphone. It had Tanner's face on it.

"That's him," she said. "Wake him."

"Be my pleasure," the big man said, who drew back his right foot before driving a steel-toed shoe into Tanner's stomach.

-6-

Gasping from the kick, with his stomach still throbbing with pain, Tanner let them haul him down the dim corridor. The biggest bruiser gripped his right arm. That one was a head taller than him and had to outweigh him by eighty pounds. The man was built like a square slab and likely was either from a heavy gravity planet or took muscle enhancers.

Tanner sensed that the man toyed with him, would love nothing better than if he would resist. The bruiser was bald with a flat nose and cauliflower ears. He must be a wrestler or some other kind of exhibition fighter. What he wasn't was a Tong assassin or a Coalition Special Intelligence operative. Tanner would have recognized either.

The thug holding his left arm had garlic breath. As they'd hauled him off the floor, Tanner had noticed the man's belt buckle, a heavy piece of iron. No doubt, it seconded as a flail-type weapon.

The woman led the way. She was small and slim, a dancer possibly or a professional thief. She had shined a light in his eyes, grinning at him as he coughed and gasped for air. She'd thrust her fingers through his hair and jerked up his head.

"Tanner," she'd said. That was all except for an eloquent sneer.

Baldy and Garlic Breath marched him down the long corridor. Dancer shined her light on the floor. By their slow rate of advance, Tanner guessed she was looking for something.

The few minutes of unconsciousness had done nothing to wipe the ache from Tanner's eyes. It had felt good to close them, though. The kick had swept a few cobwebs from his brain. As his stomach stopped throbbing, Tanner began analyzing the situation.

These three did not belong to the CGPD Vagrancy Squad. Cops would have informed him of his crime by now. Thus, these three were not cops. He doubted they were bazaar security, either.

Think, Tanner. Use your gray cells before it's too late.

He squeezed his eyes shut and shook his head.

That caused Baldy to tighten his grip.

Tanner ignored the man. Had he ever seen these three before?

Suddenly, it dawned on him that these were the people he'd seen back on the promenade deck. He remembered Baldy's shiny dome and the man's obvious density. It had led him to believe the bruiser had been an undercover vagrancy cop.

I guessed wrong.

Tanner opened his eyes, glancing at Baldy.

The man had coarse skin and grinned, exposing heavy teeth. The look asked him to try something so Baldy could have some more fun. Tanner realized the bruiser must have been the one to kick him. He owed the man a beating for that.

Baldy's fingers tightened on his arm and the grin became sinister. The bruiser liked to inflict pain. Tanner had known thugs like that in Vesuvius.

Tanner looked down.

"That's right," the bruiser whispered. "Look away, pansy boy."

The woman turned back, raising an eyebrow.

"The flyboy and me are getting to know each other," Baldy told her.

The woman eyed Tanner. He felt her scrutiny. She swiveled around all the way, walking backward.

"You ever going to ask us what's going on?" she said.

Tanner didn't reply. He knew what was going on. Bad people had him. They must be bounty hunters wanting to collect on his price.

"Or are you too frightened to speak?" she said.

Tanner kept his head down. Bluster couldn't help him now. He was exhausted, hungry and outnumbered. They didn't want him dead or the bruiser would have already broken his neck. Would the Coalition pay for his corpse? He believed so. What did it tell him that these three had taken him alive? Did that mean they wanted to torture him first?

Tanner considered the implications. Besides the Coalition, a small number of very bad people wanted to make him suffer. The credits needed to keep the *Dark Star* running had meant he'd gone after some seriously tough hombres. Could these three belong to a criminal lord desiring vengeance against him? If so, that meant letting them take him to the secondary scene of the crime was stupid. He had to stop that from happening, but would have to choose his moment with care. Thus, if the woman wished to believe he was too frightened of them to speak, so much the better.

"Bah!" the woman said. "The mighty bounty hunter is highly overrated, I see. Without your gun and crew, you're a frightened punk. It's just what I thought."

He was right about these three belonging to a crime lord. He should have stayed in the public areas. Tanner almost groaned aloud as a realization struck. They had flushed him. They had *wanted* him to run down here. He had acted like prey without realizing someone other than the vagrancy squad was after him.

This was much worse than having Calisto Grandee cops grab him.

Tanner stilled his sudden impulse to resist. The men had him. Stomping on a foot likely wasn't going to work against Baldy. And if he didn't take out the bruiser right away, the fight would go against him fast. Maybe if he'd been well rested and in top condition—

The woman had spun forward again, shining her light on the floor, searching. "Stop," she said.

Tanner focused on the lit spot. There was a rung embedded in the floor.

She knelt, took out a small device and clicked it. The rung rose. With a small hand, she grasped the metal ring and heaved. A trapdoor appeared, swinging upward on hidden hinges.

The woman looked up at Baldy.

Tanner sensed the man nodding.

Without a word, she swung her feet into the opening and began climbing down steel rungs. Was this an emergency access hatch?

Soon, Garlic Breath let go of Tanner. The thug crouched and swung his feet into the opening, standing on rungs and beginning to climb down.

Tanner had kept himself neutral, waiting for the exact moment. *Now!* He lashed out with his left foot, stretching, aiming a kick at the man's head.

Baldy was alert and yanked Tanner, throwing off his aim and foot velocity. The boot only grazed the side of the thug's head, but it was enough. Garlic Breath shouted more in surprise than pain and lost his balance so maybe his feet slid off the rungs. He plunged into the opening, screaming.

The yell dwindled until a thud and a grunt told of Garlic Breath's likely impact with the woman.

Baldy snarled, swinging Tanner against the wall. The force knocked the wind out of Tanner, making him gasp like a stranded fish.

"I'm going to beat you, boy," Baldy said. He drew back a right, keeping hold of Tanner's arm with his left.

Tanner stomped with everything he had left—using his heel to smash the top of Baldy's left foot. It made the bruiser grunt, and loosened his grip a bit. It didn't stop the pile-driving right, though. Tanner dodged his head just enough to make it a glancing blow. His right ear flared intensely, and the force of the hit was enough to knock him free of the gripping hand.

Tanner maintained his balance, but he knew he would never beat Baldy down here, maybe never one-on-one on his best day. He wasn't going to outrun the bruiser, either. That left just one option.

Tanner took it. He jumped down the dark opening.

Baldy must have been expecting that. The bruiser was faster than he looked, too. A square, dense man like him should have moved like a glacier. Instead, he had cobra-like reflexes.

Big fingers latched onto the collar of Tanner's leather coat. That yanked Tanner hard, the jacket jerking up against his armpits. He dangled in midair for a fraction of a second. Then, he fell again, the bruiser's hand and arm going with him. Tanner jerked short once more. Baldy grunted just above him. The bruiser must have slammed his chest against the floor with his right arm thrust into the opening.

Tanner began sliding downward with Baldy hanging onto the collar. Then it all happened fast even though it seemed like slow motion. Tanner plunged feet-first with the bruiser coming after him headfirst.

Tanner had no idea how far the shaft went. He smashed against the sides as he fell, hitting a steel ladder some of the time. Despite his wretched condition, his training kicked in. He tried to relax, bent his knees and focused on Baldy. The bruiser was a stubborn bastard and refused to let go. Tanner realized that was good. The arm let him know where the man's central mass was. When he hit the floor, Tanner wanted to make sure Baldy didn't land on top of him, but beside him, hopefully, breaking his squat neck.

Maybe Baldy understood that. The bruiser released him. A roar of noise just above Tanner's head told him Baldy went for it. Something happened, because the dense body slammed against the sides.

Had Baldy snatched a steel rung, swinging his body so now his feet aimed down? Tanner no longer sensed the bruiser just above him.

A harsh surprise ended those thoughts as Tanner hit the floor. Bones snapped as he slammed to a halt.

Suppressing a groan, Tanner instinctively crawled. The floor shifted under him and he realized that wasn't the floor but a body, two bodies. Garlic Breath must have knocked out the small woman. They lay below him. What had his impact just now done to them? Whose bones had broken a second ago?

"Lacy?" the bruiser shouted. "Say something."

Tanner was dazed, confused, hurt and determined to stay alive. He had to rescue his friends. He had to get the raider back. He had to free Remus and make the Coalition pay.

His left ankle throbbed. He had no idea if he could stand or not. He tried to rummage for a weapon, finally sliding the man's belt with its heavy buckle.

"I hear you, Tanner," the bruiser said from several meters up. "If Lacy is dead, I'm going to kill you."

Tanner made a split-second decision. He heaved forward into a passageway, slithering fast. He needed to put distance between them and him.

Baldy landed hard on the floor and shouted angrily a second later. "Tanner!" he roared.

Tanner was on his hands and knees, crawling like mad. He saw a dim light in the distance. A moment later, brighter light illuminated him. A glance back showed him someone holding the woman's flashlight.

"Gotcha, Tanner," Baldy growled.

Heavy footfalls struck the floor and the light began nearing.

Tanner climbed to his feet. He groaned as he put weight on his left foot. It hurt badly, but it held. He began running.

"You lousy bastard, you ain't getting away from me."

Tanner's lips peeled back. He could damn well make a go of it. He would need room to swing the belt like a morning star. This passageway was cramped, barely high enough for him to stand. Every so often, his shoulders brushed against the walls.

The bruiser breathed hard. The squat giant was gaining on him.

As Tanner ran, he wrapped the belt around his right hand. He positioned the buckle so it would act like a pair of brass knuckles. He'd used those before on the street. As a punk kid, he'd been used to being outnumbered and outmuscled, but not outthought or outfought. His elite, space-strike training had taught him the best dirty fighting techniques.

He panted and his sides ached. He wasn't going to last much longer. A glance back showed that Baldy had almost reached him. Madness gleamed in those red-rimmed eyes. The bruiser wanted to kill him. This would be a lousy place to die.

Tanner's panting turned to wheezes.

"You're finished, meat," Baldy sneered.

Tanner silently agreed. Still he unwound the belt from his fist and dropped to the floor. He tried to kick out his feet and catch himself with his hands. He was too tired to do it right. He crashed onto the floor as pain flared in his left wrist. He must have sprained it. Then, Baldy's feet collided with his. The big man grunted in surprise, sailing over Tanner's prone and aching body.

If Tanner tried to do the same move a hundred more times, it would never have worked as perfectly as this again. Baldy thudded onto the floor ahead of him. The man was like a spring, though, and scrambled to his feet.

Tanner groaned. He moved too slowly, still trying to get to his feet. Baldy growled with rage, rushing him, stomping and kicking. Tanner rolled, rolled the other way and heard Baldy's shoe stomp twice in fast succession. Instead of rolling a third time, Tanner swung the belt in a short arc.

"What the blazes?" Baldy shouted.

The iron buckle swung around one of the bruiser's ankles. Tanner yanked as hard as he could. Maybe Baldy had been in the process of trying a kick to the face. It meant he might have already been off balance. With an "oof" sound, the big man landed on his chest.

A final impulse drove Tanner. He launched himself, landing on the monster's back. He had the belt in his hands and had no idea how he'd gotten it off the bruiser's ankle.

Tanner found himself on the man's back with the belt around the dense throat. He twisted the leather around gristle as hard as he could. If he failed, Greco and Jordan would surely die on a prison planet.

Baldy hissed like a rock snake while climbing to his feet. The man had incredible strength, much greater than Greco's. Thick fingers reached back and grabbed at Tanner's head. He ducked it, twisting the belt harder, choking the bruiser. Fingernails scraped his scalp. The two of them sounded like animals.

Tanner had no idea how long this lasted. Several times, Baldy pushed back, body slamming him against the wall. With grim determination, Tanner maintained the chokehold.

Another smashing hit proved too much. Tanner lost his grip. Baldy gasped as he ripped the belt from his throat.

"You filthy bastard," the bruiser whispered hoarsely. He flung Tanner onto the floor. "Now, it's my turn, boy."

Tanner fought but it didn't matter. The leather looped around his throat and tightened painfully. He couldn't breathe! He clawed at the belt.

Baldy laughed in his ear.

"Stop!" a woman said.

That didn't make sense to Tanner. Was he hallucinating already?

"You're killing him!" the woman shouted.

"Yeah," Baldy whispered. "The choker dies here."

"No," she said.

"Shut up, Lacy. He's a dead man."

"I said no."

A second later, Baldy collapsed onto Tanner. The grim constriction around his throat loosened.

Tanner gasped and shuddered, pushing the bruiser off him as he luxuriated in being able to breathe again. None of this made sense. What had the woman done to the bruiser to make him stop?

She picked up her flashlight, shining it on Baldy for just a moment.

Tanner wasn't sure. He thought he saw blood leaking out of the man's ears. Was Baldy dead? Tanner didn't recall hearing a shot. The woman had a coilgun, but she didn't hold it.

He focused on her. It seemed as if she put something about the size of a cellphone in her pocket.

She shined the light in his eyes, making him squint.

"You're a mess," she said.

He still gasped and shuddered, trying to think and doing a lousy job of it.

"Get up," she said. "We're on a tight schedule."

He didn't move, just breathed—just lived.

Lacy—if that was her name—grabbed an arm. She hoisted him to his feet with effortless strength. That didn't seem right. Nothing was making sense.

45

"Move," she said, shoving, making him stagger toward the distant light.

What was going on? What was this all about? Tanner tried to look back at the dead man on the floor. She shoved him again, making him stagger worse than before.

He'd heard bones snap when he'd landed. How had she survived the fall? She looked like the frailest one of the bunch, yet she seemed unhurt.

"Who are you?" he whispered.

"The woman who just saved your sorry hide," she said. "Now, shut up and walk. With that little stunt you just pulled our margin for error has all but disappeared. If the CGPD finds us the game is over for good."

Something about all this rang a bell in his memories. "Do you belong to Keg's crew?" Tanner asked.

"Not a bad guess, bounty hunter, but the answer is no."

"Then—"

A knife appeared in her hand, the blade less than a centimeter from his throat. "Do you understand what shut up means?" she asked.

Tanner didn't answer.

The blade touched his throat. "One slice and it's over for you, Tanner. No more games, no more fun. Just go where I tell you, huh? You can bargain with my boss but not with me. Got it?"

Maybe it troubled her having to kill the bruiser. Maybe she wasn't just a hard case. She hadn't let the man choke him to death, right? What did that mean, though?

"Sure," Tanner said, having trouble thinking straight.

Getting one's throat cut was better than being tortured to death. But being alive meant one could still hope for the best. The truth was that walking down the dark corridor was a gamble, one he might come to regret bitterly. It's not as if his luck had been good lately.

No, he told himself. *Don't rely on luck. You have to make something happen.*

For the life of him, though, Tanner couldn't think of what.

7

A lock clicked loudly.

Tanner stirred, blinking wearily. He raised his head off the table where it had lain. He'd been asleep—for how long he didn't know. It must have been more than a few minutes because he felt drugged with lethargy.

His stomach rumbled. Lacy had brought him to this cell, shoved him in and locked the door. The cell had contained a table with water, wafers and a chair. He'd eaten the food, drank the water and lain his head on his crossed arms.

Now, he blinked sleepily at the door. There was a subdued light in the ceiling, allowing him to see.

He must have been asleep for several hours, at least. His eyes no longer hurt, but his throat was sore to the touch where Baldy had choked him.

Lacy had prodded him for several hazy kilometers. He'd been thinking hard during that time. The dead bruiser had felt like one of Keg's crew.

Keg had been a vile man with a vile bunch of people. They had been kidnappers searching for young girls to sell to nasty sex emporiums. A certain consortium in the Lustra System had tired of Keg's antics because the man had gone pirate, raiding Lustra starliners for pretties. The corporate heads had hired assassins to kill Keg. Tanner had a growing reputation as a hunter. The corporate heads had offered him a deal, too. Killing for money wasn't his trade, though. Instead, Tanner had captured Keg and brought him to the consortium headquarters, collecting a hefty sum. What the consortium had done afterward to Keg hadn't been Tanner's concern. Besides, since an encounter with a Coalition picket boat, the *Dark Star* had needed more torpedoes. The best ones cost plenty, too.

The one negative to his "no assassination" policy was that people had seen him capture Keg. One of those had been Keg's primary lieutenant. Since then, members of Keg's crew had come after him, forcing Tanner to kill two of them in self-defense.

Lacy claimed she hadn't belonged to Keg's crew. Maybe that was technically true. Maybe she belonged to the people who used those like Keg and now wanted Tanner to pay.

One of these days, he had to figure out a way to make friends instead of so many new enemies.

Tanner inhaled through his nostrils. Despite his aching throat, he felt better for the few hours' sleep, more clearheaded. The wafers might have helped as much as the sleep. He sat back, crossing his arms, waiting for the door to open. Despite the anxiety in his gut, he kept his face impassive.

Had he made the right choice? Should he have resisted Lacy? How had she made Baldy's ears bleed?

The heavy door opened and—

Tanner sat straighter, shocked to his core.

A Remus praetorian entered the room. The praetorian was a big man. They usually were. The symbols on his jacket proclaimed the man a tribune. Two more praetorians filed in. Each wore a uniform of House Varus and wore a sidearm and shock baton on his belt.

Tanner rubbed his eyes.

Praetorians were house guards from Remus. Each house trained special men to guard the patricians of the extended family.

The two rankers flanked the open door, standing at attention with their hands on belted batons. The implication was clear: if Tanner did anything the tribune disliked, the rankers would beat him.

The three wore helmets, chest-plates, shin guards and forearm protectors. Without arms, Tanner could not possibly win a fight against three trained praetorians. Even with arms, he'd have a hard time of it.

"Stand in the presence of the Patrician Ursa of House Varus," the tribune said in a rough voice.

Tanner's body obeyed before he consciously thought about it.

A woman walked into the cell. She wore a flowing white robe that trailed on the floor. Demurely, she doffed a white shawl from her head, staring at Tanner. Patrician Ursa was tall, although not as tall as Tanner was. She had pale skin and long, blonde hair with the greenest eyes Tanner had ever seen. She was gorgeous.

"Lady," Tanner said, as he inclined his head.

The tribune stiffened, glancing sharply at the woman.

"Now, now, Tribune," Ursa said in a candy voice. "He cannot know proper protocol. He is a plebian, after all. I hear he grew up in the sewers."

"The correct word is slums," Tanner said. "Rats live in sewers."

That was too much for the tribune. "You will wait for the patrician to address you before you speak to her."

Because the tribune was from Remus, Tanner gave a single nod of acknowledgement. Did they know Consul Maximus? Had they come to help him?

"Are you…" Ursa said, frowning, turning to the tribune as if offended. "Must I stand while addressing the plebian?"

"No, Lady," the tribune said, snapping his fingers at the two rankers. "Please, forgive my oversight."

One of the rankers hurried around the table, taking Tanner's chair. The man brought it to the patrician's side, placing it behind her.

"Closer," she said, stepping to the table.

"Allow me, Lady," the tribune said, taking the chair from the ranker, setting it behind her as she sat.

The ranker returned to his position by the door. The tribune flanked the patrician. She fluffed her robes, making herself comfortable. Once finished, she looked up at Tanner. She scrunched her nose, made a face and looked at the tribune.

The big man seemed confused.

49

"He needs a bath," Ursa said.

"Ah, of course," the tribune said. Straightening, staring at Tanner, he made a shooing motion.

Tanner took a step back.

The tribune glanced at the patrician. She ignored him.

"More," the tribune said.

Tanner backed up against the wall.

Lady Ursa nodded. She had a silk handkerchief in her left hand and delicately held it under her nose.

"I have a proposition for you," Ursa said. "I would like to rent your boat."

Tanner frowned, not certain he'd heard correctly. Just what in the heck was going on?

"Naturally," she said, "I will return it to you once I've completed my voyage."

Tanner glanced at the tribune. The man faced forward, staring at the wall.

"I'm addressing you," Ursa told Tanner.

That made the tribune focus on Tanner again, giving him an obvious non-verbal message: act with utmost respect toward the patrician or else.

Tanner couldn't fathom the meaning of all this. It bemused him. He had assumed they came from Consul Maximus. Now, he wasn't sure.

"By, ah, 'boat,' do you happen to mean my raider?" Tanner asked.

"Yes," Ursa said. "That's right."

"I see. Yes, I might be persuaded to take you to your destination."

"No," Ursa said. "I want your boat, not you or your smelly crew. Surely, I've made that clear."

Tanner glanced at the tribune and the two door guards. Was this for real?

"I almost forget," Ursa said. "What is your rental price?"

"You're mistaken, Lady," Tanner said. "I won't rent my ship to anyone. I hire out if the contract is acceptable. Tell me what you want and I'll tell you if I'm willing or not."

She lowered the handkerchief, giving him a knowledgeable smile. "I understand men like you enjoy dickering, but I'm in a

50

hurry. My mission is urgent. Tell me your rental price so I can be on my way."

Tanner zipped up his leather jacket. It was all the armor he had against those batons. He had a feeling the guards were going to swing soon. The patrician was crazy if she thought she could bully him like this.

"There's been a mistake," he said. "If someone told you I would rent you my ship, they're dead wrong. You can hire me. I'll take you where you want to go. Otherwise, you can piss off."

The tribune's head jerked around. The two guards shoved off the wall, their batons hissing as they slid out of the leather holders.

"I'm just a smelly plebian," Tanner said, holding his hands palms outward, "a rude sewer-dweller, a rat, I suppose. What did you expect would come out of my mouth?"

"Lady," the tribune said. "I suggest you leave the room. This dog needs a lesson in manners. He'll speak more civilly once you return."

"I'm not sure," she said, putting the handkerchief against her nose. "He's a centurion, isn't he?"

The tribune's eyes narrowed as he reexamined Tanner. "Is this true?" he asked.

Tanner said nothing.

"I asked you a question," the tribune said.

"You can piss off, too," Tanner told him. "Either you're going to beat me or you're not. If you do, I'm never going to hire out to you."

"Tribune," Ursa said, "this is unacceptable."

"Yes, Lady," he said. "Please, if you would retire…"

"No," she said. "I want the boat now. We should already be on our way."

"He's stubborn," the tribune pointed out.

"I was told the centurion is a patriot," she said. "Why is he trying to thwart us, then?"

The tribune shook his head.

"Oh, this is impossible." Ursa focused on Tanner. "My mission is of the utmost importance. It will help free Remus from occupation. Do you love your world?"

51

Tanner got it, then. They were fishing. This must be a Coalition Special Intelligence trick. He was supposed to blurt out his contact, Consul Maximus. This was another setup and these people were traitors to Remus.

"I love my world," Tanner said deadpan.

"Then give me a fair rental price and I can be on my way," the patrician said.

That was too much. "Do *you* love Remus?" Tanner asked.

She lowered the handkerchief. "How dare you say that to me?"

"Yeah?" Tanner said. "Likewise."

Her eyes widened with outrage. "I will have you beaten."

"Go ahead."

"Do you doubt me?"

Tanner frowned as something seeped into his thinking. Why would Lacy have brought him in? What did the thief have to do with a Remus patrician?

"Why do you need my ship?" Tanner asked. "What makes it so important to your project? You could rent other spacecraft, so why come after mine?"

Ursa looked down at the table.

"You know I'm a centurion," Tanner said. "Few people out here know that. It's unlikely that one of those persons would be an airheaded patrician beauty. This is an act, a performance on your part. What do you hope to gain with such an act?"

"You're in no position to bargain," Ursa said, looking up, her candy voice changing to something harder. "Your ship is impounded and your crew is in lockdown. You're close to finding yourself on a one-way ticket to Shayol. Soon enough, the Calisto Grandee authorities will auction your boat. I can buy it outright then."

"Maybe," Tanner said. "The fact you're trying this proves it won't be so simple."

Ursa drummed her fingers on the table as she studied him. She no longer held the handkerchief under her nose. She no longer seemed like an airheaded princess.

"What do you think, Tribune?" she asked.

"Maybe Maximus is right about him," the tribune said. "Maybe he could be an asset to the mission."

So, they knew about Consul Maximus. That made everything more interesting.

"The centurion might be an asset if he can take orders," she said, staring at Tanner.

He realized this was his cue. He was supposed to assure her ladyship that he could take orders with the best of them. Tanner also realized that these two were trying to pull something over on him. But if they knew Consul Maximus, why go through this charade?

"Where do you want me to take you?" Tanner asked.

"Nowhere in particular at the moment," Ursa said, offhandedly. "I'd just like to use your boat."

That was a lie. This must be a setup so he would say yes to something he would never normally do. He couldn't think what that could be, not if Consul Maximus backed the plan. This was strange. Events were not adding up. Just what was going on here?

"Sure…" Tanner heard himself say. "I'll hire out to you. But you're going to have to front some heavy credits first."

"I will," she said, "but not to you directly. I'll pay the impound fees but you'll have to transfer the deed to me as collateral."

"Wrong," Tanner said. "Nothing will make me sign over the *Dark Star*, not even as temporary collateral. If you want my help, which I think you most certainly do, then you give me the credits outright. I'll buy out my own ship. Besides, I'm beginning to think you set up this situation."

"What situation?" she asked.

"Sure, Lady, I buy that."

She turned to the tribune. "Maybe a beating is in order after all."

The tribune hesitated before shaking his head. "I don't agree, Lady. He's just as Maximus said he would be. I doubt the centurion would have lasted this long out here if he was any other way."

She frowned.

"His cooperation might be important to us," the tribune added.

The patrician drummed her fingers on the table. She looked up at Tanner.

He waited.

"Very well," she said, primly. "I will assign you credits. But I expect prompt service. We will go together—"

"No," Tanner said, interrupting. "You give me the line of credit. Then, I'm going alone to free my crew. I want to talk to them before we begin."

The patrician's eyes hardened, but finally she nodded. "Yes," she said. "You will free your crew. But we must move quickly. Our time is limited."

"Why's that?" Tanner asked.

"You'll learn soon enough," she said.

8

An attractive clerk wearing moderate heels led Tanner down a narrow hall. She stopped before reaching the destination, indicating that he enter the office on his own. The hall was narrow, and Tanner had to brush past the woman to reach the entrance. She glanced up into his eyes as he did, smiling shyly before looking down. Then, she hurried away.

Tanner watched her go. Why hadn't she gone into the office to announce him to the adjustment officer?

Suspicion caused him to check his jacket pockets. The one still held the electronic credit voucher from Patrician Ursa.

The clerk turned the corner, taking her beauty from view. Tanner shrugged, knocking on the open door as he stepped in.

The adjustment officer behind the desk looked up. He had narrow, foxlike features and wore a blue robe and headband with earphones and a microphone jack before his lips. There were three computer screens on the desk with a single keypad between them and a hot cup of jasmine steaming to his left.

The officer pointed at a chair in front of the desk before resuming typing.

Tanner approached the chair, hesitating as he examined it. Compared to the adjuster's desk, the chair was ridiculously low. He thought about standing but decided that would be worse as it would make him seem like a beggar with hat in hand. He sat and found that his knees were propped up as high as his chin.

Was such an obvious psychological ploy necessary for the interview?

The adjuster continued typing while he spoke into the microphone.

Tanner waited, trying to be patient. He finally glanced at the plaques on the wall. That's when he noticed a large photo of the pretty clerk in a revealing two-piece posed provocatively in a botanical garden. She had long dark hair and a rather voluptuous shape.

Hanging such a large photo like that in a workspace seemed odd. Could that be why the clerk hadn't entered the room? Was she embarrassed of the photo?

Out of the corner of his eye, Tanner studied the adjuster. The man had to be three times the woman's age. Despite his vulpine features, the man had a receding chin and there seemed to be something unsavory about him as he bit the inside of his own cheek.

Tanner eyed the photo again. Was that a professional shot or did she have an after-work liaison with the man?

The adjuster abruptly stopped typing. He took a sip of jasmine, smacking his lips as he did. He noticed Tanner studying the large photo.

"Cost me three hundred credits to get her to pose like that," the adjuster said. "Mar Bree loathes the transaction now. At the time, she was about to be evicted from her apartment because of a lack of funds." The man grinned. "I tell her how men like you lust over the photo while they pay their fees. You'd think she would be happy how I've learned to take the sting from men such as yourself over the payments. She's beautiful, don't you agree?"

Tanner could barely see over the desk at the grinning adjuster. Clearly, the man enjoyed other people's pain. Tanner would be glad to leave Calisto Grandee.

The adjuster leaned back in his chair, taking another sip of jasmine before biting his inner cheek again. "I can't tell you the number of times she's asked me to take it down. I'm sure she hates the idea of men like you leering at her body." His grin widened. "Perhaps I originally gave her the impression the photo would remain in my studio…" He laughed. "The woman wants to advance. I give her credit for trying to use what assets she possesses. I'm still waiting for her to make me an offer."

Tanner stared at the man.

"I'm sure you think I'm talking about a sexual offer, and that would be acceptable. But I doubt Mar Bree would agree to such an exchange. She knows I could simply put up the picture later and ask for another, ah, *payment*." The adjuster laughed. "No. The offer I'm talking about is her trying to buy back the photograph and however many copies I've made of it."

Tanner kept his features blank, although he started envisioning himself getting up, reaching across the desk and yanking the smirking face into his fist.

"I sense your disapproval," the adjuster said. "That marks you as old-fashioned and prudish. You don't understand that I'm actually helping Mar Bree."

"Yeah?" Tanner said.

"Of course," the adjuster said. "I've educated her on the true ways of the world, that a woman of her charms must practice discretion in her monetary choices. I think she should pay for that education, don't you agree?"

Tanner finally realized what was going on. The adjuster was a small cog in a big wheel. The man tried to wrest the greatest amount of enjoyment he could from his job. Since the man was a pig, he delighted in inflicting the little amount of pain he could onto others. Did that mean the adjuster would try to cause him trouble? Yes, of course, it did.

"Well, now," the adjuster said, leaning forward, typing again. "You're Tanner, the owner of the *Dark Star*, is that right?"

Tanner grunted a "Yes."

The adjuster scanned a screen. "Oh, I see your ship has been impounded for quite some time, and two of your crew are in lockup. My, my, you've barely made it to my office in time. Your vessel had another fourteen hours to go before it went into auction. That's cutting it close."

Tanner nodded.

"Ah, look at this," the adjuster said. "This is going to be pricy. One of your crew is still in the quarantine ward. She

57

hasn't recovered yet from…is this Rigellian fever, I'm seeing?"

"I paid up front for medicine," Tanner said. "The fever should have broken by now."

"You did?" the adjuster said, typing, glancing at the most leftward screen. "No. You didn't pay anything. You pawned it off onto us, not even putting down a deposit. I'm afraid she only received the standard fare."

"What does that mean?"

"Sir, I would appreciate it if you kept a civil tone. This is Calisto Grandee. Everything here is done with the utmost decorum. If you find that you cannot keep your tone civil, I will add a discourtesy charge to your fees."

"What?"

The adjuster paused in order to look down his nose and past the almost intervening edge of the desk at Tanner.

Tanner looked away. Otherwise, he was going to surge up and slug the prick in the face.

"Hmm, let me see," the adjuster said, with bite to his words as he studied the middle screen. "Oh. I'm afraid under the rules of Nostradamus Law I cannot allow your feverish crewmember out of quarantine just yet."

"There shouldn't be a problem with that. I'm leaving Calisto Grandee."

"That has no bearing on the situation. She is extremely ill."

"What I'm trying to say—"

Primly, the adjuster held up a hand. "Let me make myself utterly clear. You are in the Nostradamus System. If I deliver the sick crewmember to you, you might visit another Nostradamus habitat or dome and infect them with your feverish victim."

"No. I'm heading out-system."

"I realize this is what you're *saying*, but to insure your compliance, we would have to send a warship all the way out-system to follow you. The fuel for such a journey out and back again would be prohibitive given the nature of the mission."

By sitting as straight as possible, Tanner could barely see the man over the front edge of the desk. That and the conversation were beginning to make him seriously angry.

Tanner balled his hands into fists, working to control himself. He had to reason his way out of this. He had to get Jordan back onto the *Dark Star*. But if they wouldn't release her just yet because of the fever…

Clearing his throat, Tanner asked, "What kind of treatment has she received?"

"I've already told you Calisto Grandee has paid the upfront cost out of the goodness of its collective humanity. But, the fever victim is a foreigner without funds. Thus, she received the minimum requirements. It has kept her alive so far. And for that, you should be grateful."

"Yes," Tanner forced himself to say. "How much will it cost for her to receive maximum treatment?"

The adjuster nodded knowingly. "That is a fine sentiment, sir. I congratulate you for it. I think ten thousand credits—"

"Ten thousand!" Tanner shouted. "Are you giving her a new body?"

The adjuster stared down his nose at Tanner. "That is a miserly tone, sir. We're discussing one of your prized crewmembers. You just told me you desired that she receive V.I.P. treatment. If you disagree with my interpretation of what you just said, I can play back your words."

"I just want her to get better."

"I suppose it's possible the fever will burn itself out. But…" the adjuster typed, studying the middle screen. "Too long of a burn-out could leave her permanently impaired. In her case, that could be with a twenty or more IQ point loss."

Brain damage, Tanner realized. "Okay. I want the best medicine but minimal facilities."

"The two do not coexist, sir, as the one is related to the other."

"Give me the best you can that matches my requirements."

"Hmm," the adjuster said, typing. "I have a five thousand credit—"

"No."

The adjuster glanced at Tanner. "Well, here is a three thousand credit—"

"Give me a five hundred credit plan."

The adjuster looked up in shock. "Sir. That is a niggling sum considering your friend's terrible and prolonged state."

Tanner studied his credit voucher. Earlier, he had believed the patrician generous. Now, considering the expenses of this luxury habitat, the amount might prove too little.

"One thousand credits," Tanner said, softly.

The adjuster closed his eyes as if pained.

"And a bonus for you if she pulls through," Tanner said.

The man opened his eyes, raising an eyebrow. "Are you trying to bribe me, sir?"

"Ah… No."

The adjuster appeared crestfallen, almost pouting. "One thousand credits in advance. Let me see what is available." He typed, studied the screens, typed some more and frowned at what he saw.

"I have a fifteen hundred credit—"

"Listen!" Tanner said, shooting to his feet. He'd had enough of this.

The adjuster's right hand flashed to a large red button on the desk, one that Tanner hadn't noticed earlier. "I can terminate the interview, if you wish. I should point out that if that happens, your ship will go up for auction and you and your crew will find yourselves on Shayol sooner than you can believe."

Tanner swallowed his anger, cursing himself for having come to Calisto Grandee. Slowly, he sat down again in the ridiculously low chair.

The adjuster watched him before going back to typing. "Hmm, it appears I missed an eleven hundred credit possibility. It would entail the second best medical plan with a stay in a Grade C Facility."

"Let me see it."

The adjuster nodded, pressing a switch. Soon, he tore out a small printout, passing it across the desk.

Tanner took it, but he couldn't make out heads or tails about any of this medical gibberish. Jordan always deciphered those things for him.

As Tanner stared at the various squiggles, he decided on a new strategy. "Do you happen to know what my profession is?" he asked the adjuster.

"I do not, sir."

"I'm a bounty hunter," Tanner said, looking up past the edge of the desk at the man.

The adjuster eyed him, pursed his lips thoughtfully and finally nodded. "I suppose you mean that as a veiled threat."

"A *veiled* threat?" asked Tanner. "No. It's not meant to be veiled at all." He laughed in a carefree manner. "You would never believe the ruffians I've had to deal with. A more thorough group of rascals—and the head cracking and finger breaking—I am highly trained at my task and have learned to enjoy it immensely."

A touch of color appeared on the man's cheeks. He shifted his right hand toward the button.

Tanner dropped his voice as he said, "Do you know that Mar Bree and I had an interesting conversation before I entered your office."

The fingers halted just before they would have pressed the button.

"She told me you have the most interesting living quarters," Tanner said, "situated in a prime housing tract. I was so curious about it, I asked her to show me the spot. I must say, Senior Adjuster, after seeing it on a map, I'd love to see your home in person. We would have such a grand time together. I can already envision the things we would do. No matter how long it would take me to make such a visit…"

The fingers that had reached for the button curled into a fist. The adjuster pulled his hand back. His cheeks had become pale.

"This…" Tanner said, raising the printout, shaking his head.

"Hmm, I may have miscalculated the estimate. Let me recheck." The adjuster typed, glanced at the middle screen, made a few keystrokes and soon ripped out another printout. He handed it to Tanner.

Tanner looked at it, frowning as he did. He couldn't tell what this one said any better than the first. The point, though, hopefully, was that the adjuster didn't know he couldn't read Calisto Grandee script.

"How much is this plan?" Tanner asked.

"This price is on—"

"I know very well the price is on here," Tanner said in a scathing tone.

"Oh," the adjuster said. "Yes, I forgot." He typed fast and gave Tanner a third printout.

Tanner barely glanced at it. "Yes. This is acceptable."

"I should think so," the adjuster said. "Now, let us go over your ship's fees and penalties. I want to finish here before lunch, as I have an appointment I need to keep."

"Fine, as I'm in a hurry, too."

"Excellent," the adjuster said, as he began to type furiously.

-9-

A little over an hour later, Tanner waited in the detention lobby.

An armored guard stood by a steel hatch. Something winked on the guard's belt. The man glanced at it, clicked it off and typed a code onto a box.

The hatch slid up. A long-armed, Avernus apeman walked out. Greco wore a soiled uniform and looked thinner than before.

Greco looked around and saw Tanner. "Boss," he called.

Tanner motioned him over.

Greco hurried near. They shook hands, with Tanner slapping the mechanic on the shoulder.

"Good to see you," Tanner said.

"I was beginning to wonder if you'd forgotten about me."

"Not a chance," Tanner said. "Let's go. We're on a tight schedule."

The two left the detention lobby, soon entering a narrow corridor. Tanner pulled out a small device, clicking it. Blinking lights appeared on the floor. They followed them, taking various twists and turns.

"Are we going to get Jordan?" Greco asked.

"No. She's still sick with fever."

Greco glanced at him. Maybe the apeman heard the anger in his voice. "We've been here a while. Jordan should be better by now."

"Should be," Tanner agreed.

Greco glanced at him sidelong. "Is she dying?"

Tanner shook his head. "I upgraded her situation and put her on prolonged medical care."

"I take it you finally found our client?"

"In a manner of speaking," Tanner said.

"Boss?"

"A client found me."

Greco glanced at him again. "You're making less sense than usual."

Tanner eyed the extended corridor. How likely was it that Calisto Grandee builders had put listening devices in the halls? How likely was it that anyone was listening to the two of them through such snooping devices? He hadn't survived four hectic years out here by being the trusting sort.

The other thing was Jordan. It bothered him she was still sick. Before hurrying to the detention lobby to get Greco, he'd seen her through a glass in the Grade C Facility. She'd looked gaunt and paler than he'd ever seen her. Jordan had been asleep with tubes in her arms. A nurse had assured him that he'd gotten her to them just in time.

That meant the Calisto Grandee people had almost let her die. If she had... Tanner would have never forgiven himself for not selling the *Dark Star* to pay for her medical bills.

Several minutes later, the blinking floor lights led Tanner and Greco to the hatch of a massive hangar bay, one bigger than Vesuvius's spaceport. Robotic carts pulled huge wagons full of luggage. Workers with lit batons guided spaceships of various sizes to docking bays.

An armored guard approached them. "State your purpose," he said.

Tanner showed the guard his ID slate.

"That way," the guard said, pointing in the distance.

Soon, the two waited behind a portable force screen. They watched a crane lower the *Dark Star* from an upper-level docking bay.

The *Gladius*-class raider was circular-shaped with a bubble area above and below. It had battered stealth plating and odd, anti-sensor angles here and there. The ship boasted two torpedo tubes, several point-defense autocannons and a particle beam emitter. The ship had more cargo area than one would suppose—the vessel was one hundred meters in diameter—and could comfortably transport ten people.

Tanner, Greco and Jordan had worked hard to keep the *Dark Star* running smoothly these past four years.

"Wasn't sure I was ever going to see her again," Greco said.

Tanner nodded. He had begun to feel likewise.

"I don't like this leaving Jordan behind, though," Greco said. "It seems like we should spring her."

"Just the two of us?" Tanner asked.

"Be hard, I know."

"Yeah," Tanner said. "It would be that."

Greco became thoughtful, scratching his side. "If you ask me, leaving her is bad luck."

"She has Rigellian fever. What am I supposed to do?"

Greco scratched harder. "You can feel the bad luck swirling around us, can't you, boss?"

"That's crap. A man makes his own luck."

"That's when I know something is really eating you—when you begin talking about making your own luck. That's always a dead giveaway."

"Whatever," Tanner said.

Greco hooted without humor. "I just realized you were paid a lot of dough upfront. Jordan's medical costs, freeing the *Dark Star*…" The apeman shook his hairy head.

"The people who fronted us the money know the consul."

Greco raised his eyebrows. "Boss, this is a setup. No one pays upfront like that. They're playing us."

"Maybe, but what else do you suggest I do? If I didn't take the money, you'd still be in lockup, Jordan would be dying and I'd probably be dead."

"That's a good question," Greco said. "But I'm just an apeman, so what do I know?"

"Would you drop that already? I said I was sorry for saying that over a year ago."

Greco's head snapped up. "You never said you were sorry."

"I must have."

"No. I'd remember."

"Well, you forgot this time."

"Boss, you never say you're sorry, especially if you really are."

Tanner scowled. He hated apologizing and didn't plan to start now.

"Hey, are those our employers?" Greco asked, tugging one of Tanner's sleeves.

Tanner looked where the apeman pointed. What he saw instinctively caused his gun-hand to drop onto the butt of his holstered weapon.

Patrician Ursa rode a cart with the tribune and the two rankers riding with her on one side. On the other side was a man in black, Lacy and two monstrous blue-skinned humanoids with tiny heads. Those two wore leather straps in lieu of clothing and were outrageously male. Behind the cart followed twenty others brimming with luggage and metal boxes.

"We're going to be seriously outnumbered this trip," Greco said.

"Yeah," Tanner said, not liking this one bit.

"What if they try to hijack us once we're in space?"

Tanner had an urge to draw his gun. He was going to miss Jordan with her hacking skills and deadly sub-rifle. Just what was going on, anyway, and what were those humanoid giants? Each looked as if it could rip the raider apart with its bare hands.

"Lithians," Greco said, with the snap of his fingers.

"What's that?"

"The two blue monsters," Greco said. "They're Lithians. They're supposed to be incredibly savage. They come from the planet Lithia. Earthmen colonized the planet ages ago. Lithians have even worse genetic drift than those of Avernus. I've never heard of a civilized Lithian. Usually, they tear regular people apart."

"Those two are sitting with no problem," Tanner said.

"Boss, this is weird. I mean, truly weird. Something ain't right."

"I agree. So we keep on our toes until we can dump this bunch."

Greco glanced at Tanner. "Go back on our word?"

"I didn't say that."

"But that's what you're implying."

Tanner studied the approaching vehicles. "We stay alert. If they do anything wrong that breaks the compact between us we can legally defend ourselves by getting rid of them."

"What if they get the drop on us before that?"

Tanner nodded slowly. "We're going to have to make sure that doesn't happen, now aren't we?"

-10-

As the crane lowered the raider onto the main deck, the ship extended landing gear. Once it had settled, a ramp in the middle of *Dark Star* lowered onto the hangar floor.

Shortly thereafter, a worker in a brown jumpsuit approached the portable screen. He shut off it from his cart.

"Tanner?" the man asked.

The centurion stepped forward.

"If you would sign here, sir," the worker said, holding out a slate.

Tanner took the manifest, written in regular script. He noted the routine checkups on the fusion core, the hyperdrive, the torpedo tubes and the particle beam emitter.

"What's this?" he asked. "It says here you took all the torpedoes off?"

"That's standard docking procedure, sir," the man said. "Your extra charge was added because you carried proscribed torpedoes. You can flip the screen to read the addendum on privately owned vessels and their legal munitions. Just to let you know, the particle beam emitter is also offline. Naturally, the point-defense cannons are primed and ready."

"When do I get the torpedoes back?"

The man shook his head.

A spot in the back of Tanner's head threatened to begin throbbing. He hated Calisto Grandee. "Okay. When do I get reimbursed for my torpedoes, then?"

"Your adjuster should have gone over that with you," the man said. "You signed the release form agreeing to our terms. You should already know Calisto Grandee doesn't reimburse a private traveler for any confiscated proscribed items."

"I didn't see any of that on the adjuster's form," Tanner said. Had the slick bastard gotten something over on him?

"No use getting angry at me over it, sir. I'm just the transporter. Now, will you sign the form or not? If not, I'm going to have to take your ship back to storage."

"Is this why Calisto Grandee is so rich?" Tanner asked with heat. "You rob your guests?"

The transporter frowned. "Those are rude words, sir. I'm supposed to report them. It would add to your departure fee, you know. This time, though, I'm willing to overlook the infraction, but please don't do it again."

Tanner was thoroughly sick of Calisto Grandee. He just wanted to leave this place. Yet, they had taken all seven of his torpedoes, making him substantially weaker against any attacker. The torpedoes had been expensive, too. Who would pocket the credits for taking them? He wondered if it was the senior adjuster.

"If you're not going to sign the manifest—"

"Give me that," Tanner said, taking the slate from the transporter. He signed with an angry flourish.

"Glad to be of service to you, sir," the worker said. "Here's your control unit to the ship."

Tanner pocketed it and motioned to Greco.

The worker cleared his throat. "Aren't you forgetting something, sir?"

Tanner looked back. "Why don't you tell me so I don't have to guess what it is?"

"At this point," the man said, "a gratuity is in order."

Tanner blinked, hardly believing what he heard. "Sure," he said. "I'd be glad to. Find the man who stole my torpedoes and tell him I told you to give him half the proceeds."

"I don't understand the joke, sir."

"I guess we're even, then, because I don't understand Calisto Grandee. Come on, Greco. Let's get out of here."

The two left the worker staring after them, as they strode for the *Dark Star*. They reached the raider at the same time as the carts parked.

The tribune jumped off his seat, giving Patrician Ursa a hand as she stepped down. The two of them approached Tanner.

She whispered into the tribune's ear. The big man nodded, approaching Tanner alone.

He was several centimeters taller than Tanner with broader shoulders and a thicker chest. Seeing him for the second time, it dawned on Tanner that the tribune was related to Ursa, cousins perhaps. They had the same nose and chin.

"Is everything in order?" the tribune asked.

"As good as can be expected," Tanner said.

The tribune eyed him. "I detect hesitation in your answer. What is the problem?"

Tanner debated with himself. Could the tribune retroactively withdraw the credits, or recommend to the patrician they be withdrawn? Tanner's innate honesty won out.

"One of my crew is sick with Rigellian fever. She's going to remain in medical."

"How seriously will that harm your efficiency?" the tribune asked.

"We'll make do."

"That isn't what I asked."

"Now that I think about it," Tanner said, "you're right. It isn't."

The tribune's face flushed. "You would do well to keep a respectful tone in my presence."

Tanner felt Greco's fingers plucking at his jacket from behind, but he ignored the mechanic as he stepped closer to the tribune.

"I'm the captain of the ship. You'd do well to remember that. Your fancy airs don't impress me, so don't bother blustering."

"Do you realize who I am?"

"The lady's lackey, I assume."

"Please, boss," Greco whispered from behind, "at least wait until we're off Calisto Grandee."

"You will keep your creature *silent* in my presence," the tribune said. "And if you fail to address my sister with the proper respect, I will have my men beat some civility into you."

His sister—Patrician Ursa is the tribune's sister?

Tanner's heated reply died in his throat. The insignia on the tribune's uniform finally penetrated. The man was the heir of House Varus, one of the most powerful prewar houses on Remus.

The tribune and Ursa weren't just patricians, then, but the *highest* patricians of Remus. Before the Coalition War, Remus had been a deeply stratified society. The war years had broken down some of that. Thus, a centurion like Tanner had rubbed shoulders with high-class patricians in the AirSpace Service. Still, most of the upper class always made sure he and others like him knew their place.

A host of conflicting feelings and thoughts warred for Tanner's attention. What were two of the highest-ranking patricians doing hiring *his* raider? Why would two like them have tried to trick him so crassly in the cell?

"I will speak to the heir of House Varus with respect," Tanner said, "and do likewise with his sister."

"That's better," the tribune said.

"However...Lord," Tanner said. "I will not tolerate anyone speaking to my mechanic with anything but respect."

The tribune frowned. "Mechanic?" he asked.

"I'm referring to Greco," Tanner said, indicating the apeman. "He is fully human and can speak to anyone on my ship as he wishes."

The tribune's eyes narrowed, as did his lips. "I have spoken regarding the creature," he said.

"So have I, Lord."

The tribune stared at Tanner. Tanner found it difficult to meet the stare with the same ferocity as before. A lifetime of training was difficult to overcome.

Tanner spread his feet in an effort to bolster his courage. Then, he set his hand on the butt of his holstered gun.

"Consul Maximus gave me a charge, Lord. I have fulfilled it to the best of my ability. I intend to continue fulfilling it.

That means I must back my crew, and on my ship and in my presence, no one had better treat Greco with anything other than respect."

"Bold words, Captain," the tribune said.

"Just so you and I understand each other, Lord."

"I understand you are rash, but that you possess a native cunning in small vessel maneuvering and fighting. Keep your...*crew* out of my way and we won't have any problems. That goes double for my sister."

"Marcus," Ursa said, having moved up. "We must speed the process. This is taking too long."

Tribune Marcus Varus nodded without turning to his sister. "I will make quick introductions, Centurion. Then, we shall be on our way, yes?"

"Yes, Lord," Tanner said.

"First, these are my lifeguards," Marcus said, as he snapped his fingers.

The two praetorians hurried near.

"This is First Sword Lupus and Second Sword Vulpus."

The two looked remarkably similar with thickset bodies and close-set, gray eyes. With a shock, Tanner realized they were guard clones, psychologically unable to raise a hand against House Varus patricians. There were rumors that some houses injected animal DNA into guard clones in order to give them speeded reflexes and heightened strength. It was possible these two seldom or never talked. Tanner understood then that Marcus's praetorian uniform was a disguise.

"Glad to meet you," Tanner said, holding out his right hand to them.

Neither ranker paid him any attention.

Marcus jerked his head to the side. The two lifeguards retreated to flank Ursa.

"Was the handshake test necessary?" Marcus asked quietly.

Tanner had heard before that the way to test full humanity with guard clones was to try to shake hands with them. Now, he believed it was true.

"They cannot speak?" Tanner asked.

"Given the right conditions," Marcus said, "they can speak just fine. I doubt they will ever say a word to you, though."

Tanner ingested that as he realized it was dishonorable to allow undermen to wear praetorian uniforms. Marcus and Ursa were playing dangerous games.

"Centurion Tanner," Marcus said, "this is Lord Acton. Lord Acton, this is our captain for the voyage, Centurion Tanner of Remus."

"Hello," the man said in an odd accent but with a rich, baritone voice.

Tanner shook hands. Acton had a firm grip, but his palm was greasy. Despite that, the man exuded a presence, a sense of age and wisdom. He had thick, graying hair and wore an expensive black suit with tails and heavy boots.

Tanner had no idea regarding Acton's planet of origin. It didn't seem to be from the local region of space.

He flexed his right hand, rubbed the palm against his pants and felt compelled to stare into Acton's eyes. For an instant, something like…cosmic awareness seemed to swirl there. It proved frightening, a growing force pressing against Tanner's mind. At what seemed like the last moment, he resisted the sensation. This was weird. He felt as he had back in the slums chased by bigger, stronger boys. He remembered the helplessness of his youth. He had vowed on many nights to find a way to protect himself for the rest of his life.

"No!" Tanner shouted.

The feeling of cosmic awareness fled from Acton's eyes. The pressure dissipated, and Tanner found himself before the man with his fists raised before his eyes like shields.

Tanner lowered his hands, feeling self-conscious. He found Marcus waiting for him, seemingly unconcerned with what had just happened. Greco had gone into the ship. Ursa was looking away.

Tanner dared to peer at Lord Acton again.

"Hello," the man said just as he had earlier.

Tanner opened his mouth, wanting to ask the man what had just happened.

"I do hope the Lithians won't be a problem," Acton said.

Tanner had to work to penetrate the accent. He was barely conscious of the man holding a small black device. "No," he said.

"Excellent," Acton said.

Was it Tanner's imagination or did the man tap the device with his thumb?

Farther away, the monstrous brutes grunted, lifting huge boxes, and approached them. The Lithians towered over Tanner. Their skin looked leathery and their bulkiness and density—they might have each weighted as much as a yearling bull on Remus.

"If you could show them where to store the equipment…?" Acton said.

"Of course," Tanner said. "This way," he told the Lithians. The ramp creaked under their weight.

After Tanner showed the blue giants the main cargo-holds, he realized that what had just happened had been strange. It wasn't just his response, but the lack of responses from Marcus and Ursa. Did Acton have mental powers or some strange force of personality?

Who was Acton and how did he control the two savages? What was in all those metal boxes?

Tanner was determined to go ask Marcus. It was only later as the *Dark Star* left the hangar bay he realized he'd forgotten to do that.

Did Acton do something to my mind?

Tanner was beginning to agree with Greco. This trip had the stink of very bad luck indeed.

-11-

Tanner piloted them out of Calisto Grandee, carefully obeying the flight instructions from the gigahab's Space Central.

A nagging doubt troubled him, and he wasn't sure why or what the doubt entailed. He certainly recalled the strange Lord Acton. The man's eyes had power. Later, the man had overseen the loading, seldom letting the Lithians out of his sight.

Lacy had nodded to him once and then locked herself in her quarters. Was she embarrassed because of her previous actions in the gigahab's halls, or was it something else?

Tanner didn't have time to worry about her.

Lord Acton was in his quarters now, too, and the Lithians were in theirs. Tanner had had his doubts about the blue giants being alone.

"They will hibernate until I wake them," Lord Acton had informed him, as if the man could read his thoughts.

Tanner seriously didn't like half his passengers. Brother and sister Varus—the verdict was still out on them.

Calisto Grandee slowly rotated. It was an enormous wheel with hundreds of spindly spokes connected to a huge central mass. Countless spacecraft orbited the gigahab. A few moved toward brightly lit docking entrances. Other craft began long fusion burns for various regions of Nostradamus space. Others headed out-system so they could begin a hyperdrive journey to another star.

Tanner glanced at the gas giant Titan. Vast storms swirled in its upper atmosphere. They appeared as multicolored circles from here.

"You are free to engage your thrusters, *Dark Star*."

"Thank you, Central," he said.

Tanner began to make his calculations. Why did he have a nagging doubt? He checked fuel. The capacitors were full. He studied the gauges to the fusion core and engine. Everything checked out there, too. The point-defense guns seemed fine.

He tapped a control, aiming the guns at the gas giant. A stab of a button sent red tracers at Titan. The point-defense cannons worked.

Space Central on Calisto Grandee called a minute later. They wanted to know what he was shooting at. Clearly, they were monitoring him closely.

"Checking my guns, Central," Tanner said. "I thought I'd spotted a glitch in the programming. Just wanted to make sure they were okay."

The flight operator told him to be careful with that.

"Roger," Tanner said.

He continued with the calculations. Was there a reason Central watched him so closely?

Tanner checked this instrument and checked that gauge. Finally, he couldn't delay anymore. He informed the passengers to get ready for the first fusion burn.

This leg of the journey, he would give the raider one G of thrust. Soon, he engaged the fusion engine. The thrust pushed him against his seat. The raider began to pull away from Titan, heading out-system.

What have I overlooked? What is my subconscious trying to tell me? I'd better figure it out soon. Otherwise, I think I'm going to have a nasty surprise.

***

The hours passed in continuous work. After the sixth heavy yawn, Tanner finally headed to his quarters. He wanted to sleep a good long time. He undressed, climbed under the covers and yawned once more.

It was good to be in his own bed again. His eyelids closed and his breathing evened out. Another few seconds and he would have been asleep.

His eyes snapped open and he cursed aloud.

Climbing out of bed, he went to the intra-ship comm. He tapped it. "Greco," he said.

The apeman's face soon appeared in the tiny screen. "What's up, boss?"

"Check the particle beam emitter, would you?"

"I already did. Everything is fine."

"You fired it?" Tanner asked.

"Well, no. I checked all the relays, though."

Tanner sat back, tapping his chin. Was there a reason other than Calisto Grandee's hearty dislike of spending one credit more than they had to for Jordan's continued sickness? Might someone have wanted the *Dark Star* to lack a computer expert? That seemed farfetched, almost absurd. Yet, maybe that was the source of Tanner's nagging doubt.

"Fire the emitter," he said.

"When?" asked Greco.

"Immediately."

The tiny face in the screen screwed up as if to argue. Then, Greco said, "Will do, boss."

Tanner waited by the comm. The minutes lengthened. Finally, he heard the engine build up. It was a subtle thing compared to the thrum that gave them one G thrust. He kept waiting for the particle beam accelerator to sound.

Before that happened, the comm blinked and Greco's hairy face appeared.

"What is it?" Tanner asked.

"We've got a problem," Greco said. "The particle beam accelerator isn't working."

Tanner's chest constricted. Had he been right, then? Was there more going on than he realized?

"Shut down the emitter and go to the accelerator," he said. "I'll meet you there."

"Everything on my board shows that it should work," Greco said.

"Yeah," Tanner said. "That's because someone has tampered with it. Now, go check it and figure out exactly what's wrong."

***

Two hours later, Tanner was back in his quarters. He spread grease removal cream on his hands and wrists, wiping them with a cloth.

Then he started pacing.

His cabin was small like most of them on the *Dark Star*. He walked four steps, turned around and walked four more the other way, turning again. The room held a bed, table and chair, with cabinets built into the bulkhead.

Finally, he stripped off his work clothes and put on his centurion uniform. On impulse, he added his holster and gun. He was going to wear it the entire trip along with the monofilament knife. Afterward, he headed into the corridor.

The corridors were narrow on the *Gladius*-class raider, with a single float rail for zero-G maneuvering.

Tanner marched to the heir's cabin and pressed a switch. After a minute, still nothing had happened. He pressed the switch again. Another minute brought no change to the situation.

What did this mean?

Tanner kept his finger pressed against the switch this time.

Thirty seconds later, the hatch slid up and a sleepy, angry-looking Marcus Varus glared at him. The heir wore a silk robe with a gun in his hand.

"You'd better have a good reason for bothering me," Marcus said. "I haven't slept for more than fifty hours."

Why is that? Tanner wondered. Aloud, he said, "We have a problem, Lord."

"Well? What is it? Spit it out."

"Someone on Calisto Grandee tampered with the raider's particle beam emitter."

"Then fix it, man!"

Tanner shook his head. "Maybe in one hundred hours if Greco can manufacture the part in his workshop—"

"You mean this is sabotage?" Marcus interrupted.

78

"That's the right word for it, yes."

Fear seeped into the heir's eyes.

"There's more, Lord," Tanner said. "The Calisto Grandee people confiscated my torpedoes. At first, I thought they were following their own greedy regulations. Now, I'm not so certain. I think—"

"You mean your space torpedoes?" Marcus demanded.

"I think you're starting to see the situation. We don't have a working particle beam emitter and lack any space torpedoes for our tubes."

"What does this bucket have for weapons?"

"Point-defense cannons," Tanner said.

"That tears it," Marcus said. "Someone knows. Someone is trying to interfere directly. I suspect the long arm of Coalition Special Intelligence, but it could be others."

"What do they know?" Tanner asked.

Marcus seemed not to have heard the question. "Right," he said to himself. "I'll have to wake my sister. Then, captain, we're going to have a council of war. We're going to have to anticipate our hidden enemy. Someone wants us unarmed. The obvious reason is so they can attack us without worry."

"Either that," Tanner said, "or capture us."

The heir's head snapped up, and now real fear shined in his eyes. "We can't let that happen."

"It hasn't yet."

Marcus stared at Tanner as if seeing him for the first time. Then the heir of House Varus did something Tanner didn't expect. He grabbed Tanner by the arm, yanking him into his quarters.

"Stay here," Marcus whispered. "I don't want..." He peered into the corridor, glancing both ways. Then, he ducked back within. "I don't want Lord Acton hearing about this just yet. I'll get my sister. You wait here. I'll bring her. We have to figure out what we're going to do before—"

The heir swore under his breath before dashing into the corridor, slapping the switch that closed his hatch with Tanner in his quarters.

-12-

Tanner looked around the room. Everything was neat and tidy. Two suitcases stood by the bed, which was made with military precision. He studied that, and realized that's exactly how he had made the bed, which meant Marcus hadn't been trying to sleep. Well, if he had been trying, it hadn't been under the covers or on the bed. Had Marcus lied about sleeping or about being up previously for fifty hours?

Why bother? Hmm, maybe as a reason for why he hadn't answered the buzzer right away. But if Marcus hadn't been sleeping, what had he been doing in here?

Tanner glanced at the hatch before approaching the suitcases. He tested each, finding them locked. So much for seeing what was in them.

The quarters were a little larger than his own. If…Tanner frowned.

Deciding there were too many mysteries, he drew his gun and stood on one side of the hatch. If Marcus was trying to trick him, the tribune was going to be in for a rude surprise.

The seconds lengthened into minutes. This was taking too long. He readied to push off the bulkhead and leave—

The hatch opened and Patrician Ursa stepped into the room. "He's gone," she said, not seeing Tanner to the side.

"What?" Marcus said, charging into the room and finally spinning around.

Tanner aimed the gun at his face. The heir's right-hand knuckles were white as he clutched a nasty little beamer.

"Drop it," Tanner said.

Marcus Varus stared at the huge gun barrel centimeters from his face. He seemed stunned.

"Do it," Ursa said. "We don't have time for theatrics. The captain is nervous. You know he has a right to be."

Marcus pitched the beamer onto the bed. Then, he backed farther into the room so the hatch slid shut.

Ursa took one of her brother's hands, guiding him to the bed, pulling him down beside her. "There," she said to Tanner. "Does that put you at ease?"

Tanner still aimed the gun at them. The room was small. Marcus could easily launch off the bed to attack him. He noticed that Ursa gripped her brother's right hand. Was she trying to assure him her brother wouldn't be able to try a sudden lunge?

"Push the beamer onto the floor," Tanner said.

With the back of her left hand, Ursa did so, making the compact weapon *clunk* onto the floor. She used the toe of her shoe to push the beamer toward Tanner.

He crouched down, taking the weapon, sticking it between his stomach and belt. Then, on impulse, deciding to test them, Tanner holstered his gun.

Marcus visibly relaxed as tension oozed out of him.

"He's sworn to protect me," Ursa explained.

Tanner frowned. Why would she tell him that? A thought struck. "Did he swear it to Consul Maximus?"

Ursa appeared surprised by the question. She nodded a moment later.

Tanner studied them. "Are you really the heirs to House Varus?"

A wintry grin appeared on Ursa's face while Marcus scowled.

"How dare you question our authenticity?" Marcus said.

"No, no," Ursa said, patting her brother's hand. "He's suspicious, and he acts quickly on his suspicions. Maybe that's why the centurion has survived when so many of the others are dead. We must applaud the consul's foresight and instincts. We have few cards remaining. The centurion may be our best bet left."

Marcus glanced at his sister, finally nodding. "I beg your pardon," he told Tanner. "I am the heir and Ursa is the heiress. Not that we have much left to inherit," he said. "The Coalition has either divested House Varus of its holdings or destroyed them. We have—"

"That's enough," Ursa said, quietly.

Marcus glanced at his sister again before looking down at his lap.

She gave Tanner a calculating study.

He tried to determine if this was another act or if this was how they really felt.

"You can trust us," Ursa said.

"You can't imagine how relieved I am to hear you say that," Tanner told her drily.

Marcus's head snapped up.

"Shhh," Ursa told him. "He's trying to goad us."

"The Fates may have cast us down—" Marcus said.

"Hush, I said," Ursa told her brother. "Let me do the talking."

Marcus glared at Tanner. "If you dishonor her—"

"Marcus!" she snapped. "Please."

"Yes, sister," he said, although he didn't take his eyes off Tanner.

"I have no desire to dishonor anyone," Tanner said. "I just want to know why Calisto Grandee stole my torpedoes and put a damaged main relay into my particle beam accelerator."

"That part is easy to understand," Ursa said. "Someone paid the Calisto Grandee people to do it."

"The other question is why they did it?" Tanner asked.

"Precisely," she said.

Tanner thought about that. "I imagine we'll discover the why before we reach hyperdrive territory. My guess is our hidden enemy will meet us somewhere at the edge of the Nostradamus System."

"That seems logical," Ursa said.

"Your brother seems to think Coalition Special Intelligence is behind this."

"They're the obvious candidate," Ursa said.

"Who else could it be?" Tanner asked.

Ursa's lips firmed, as if she didn't want to say.

"You just told me I could trust you," Tanner said. "That means you should start telling me the truth."

Marcus's shoulders stiffened, but he refrained from speaking.

"What's with Lord Acton?" Tanner asked.

Ursa smiled while Marcus seemed to become more alert.

"Whatever do you mean?" Ursa asked.

"He tried a mind trick on me when I first met him," Tanner said. "How did he do that?"

"Did you shake his hand?"

"Of course," Tanner said.

"Then I would guess he dosed you."

Tanner recalled the man's greasy palm. "Dosed me with what?"

"A mild mind-altering drug," Ursa said. "Likely, he was testing you, gauging your strength of will. My guess would be you surprised him."

"And no one thought to tell me the bastard would try something like that," Tanner said.

Both brother and sister looked away.

"Do you fear Acton?" Tanner asked.

Ursa looked up. "Most certainly we do."

"Listen," he said. "I'm tired. Lord Varus here said he's been up for fifty hours. No doubt, he'd like to get some sleep. I know I would. So, instead of having me ask one hundred questions, searching for the right one, why don't you tell me what's going on? Then, I'll begin to think about trusting you two."

Ursa released her brother's hand. She bowed her head and pressed her hands against her face. "Marcus, would you go patrol the hall, please?"

Marcus swung toward her. "Sister!" he cried.

"I'll be fine. Someone has to keep guard, though. We don't know if Acton will try to eavesdrop on us."

"I can't leave you alone in here with a strange man."

"Marcus, please, this is Centurion Tanner. If we can't trust him, if we can't trust Consul Maximus's judgment, this will never work anyway."

83

"I know that," Marcus said, "but it's another thing to risk the family honor."

"Oh, Marcus," she said, "sweet, brave, ferocious, Marcus." She touched his face. "You have nothing to fear. I will keep our family honor intact."

He rose stiffly, glaring at Tanner.

"Take this," Tanner said, handing him the beamer, butt forward.

Marcus accepted the weapon, opening his mouth, perhaps to give Tanner a warning. He glanced at the tiny, deadly beamer in his hand. He grunted softly, moving past Tanner into the corridor.

After the hatch shut, Ursa rose, walking onto the other side of the bed, putting more distance between Tanner and herself.

"Remus is dying," she said softly. "Coalition Special Intelligence knows their business too well. They've broken other worlds before ours, fitting them into the greater machine of Social Unity. The occupation forces hunt down the patriots, executing many and brainwashing others. We're running out of time, Centurion. You wouldn't recognize Remus if you dared visit your homeworld."

"Is Consul Maximus still alive?"

"He's in hiding, so I think so. But he could be dead by now. That's why Marcus and I are risking everything for the answer to the occupation. Our world no longer has the time to resist. Given another year, even if we could drive the Coalition Forces off Remus after that, too many people would accept the tenets of Social Unity: the lack of individuality, the antlike subservience to the Coalition's One Way Thinking. The enemy's psych people talk about our right to be free while enforcing strict speech codes and correct action policies. Anyone who deviates from the new norm is driven from their employment and home, forced to live in one of the so-called Liberty Sites, which are nothing more than reeducation camps. The Coalition psych and propaganda people are turning the meanings of words on their heads. In their lexicon, free means slave and slave means free."

"They're sucking the soul out of our people," Tanner said.

"Yes. That's why Maximus decided we must risk everything on one bold throw of the dice of fate. We must search for the weapon that none dare wield, take it, and destroy the Coalition before Remus is a soulless husk of its former self."

"What weapon is this?" Tanner asked, intrigued.

Ursa finally faced him as she hugged herself. "I dare not tell you yet, Centurion. Clearly, someone has seen to it that our spacecraft is disarmed. That must mean someone will try to capture us. If I tell you our goal, there is that much more of a chance they will learn our final gambit through mind-probes."

"How about I turn the ship around?" Tanner said.

"And go where?" Ursa asked. "No. I believe this voyage is Remus's last change for freedom. We must take the risk despite the wretched odds for success."

"You're going in circles, Patrician. That will put me to sleep soon. Either you tell me—"

She strode to him, taking one of his hands. "I implore you, Centurion."

He looked into her green eyes. She was beautiful and had an intoxicating scent. His loins reeled with sexual possibilities. Wait a minute. She'd told him about Acton's mind-altering toxins. Had she just put some on him now?

"Let's keep this platonic," Tanner said, marching her backward to her former spot. He disengaged from her, returning to his place near the door.

She studied him. As she did, the hatch opened.

Tanner stepped to the side, his hand dropping onto his gun-butt.

Marcus stared at him, with the beamer aimed at his chest.

Tanner wondered if the two had timed this. Was Marcus supposed to have come upon them while they touched each other? Would Marcus have declared that as defilement, as dishonor?

"We need a little more time," Ursa said.

Marcus searched her face. She nodded. He backed away, letting the hatch shut.

"There," Ursa told Tanner. "That should prove our good intentions toward you. Marcus just had the drop on you."

"How about you tell me something useful? Otherwise, I'm heading to my quarters and getting some shut eye."

Ursa inhaled deeply, maybe to give her an extra second to think. "We'll take one step at a time, but I will tell you this. Lord Acton is extremely dangerous, as is his niece."

"Why did Lacy come after me on Calisto Grandee?" Tanner said. "Who were the thugs aiding her? Were they also Lord Acton's relatives?"

"No. They were ordinary thugs."

Tanner remembered the bruiser's bleeding ears. How had Lacy caused that? Had she used some kind of sonic weapon? Yet, if she had fired a sonic weapon, why hadn't it made his ears bleed?

There were still too many unanswered questions for his peace of mind.

"Tell me this," Tanner said. "Were you my original contact on Calisto Grandee? Was that a ploy to get me there and then set me up for capture?"

"It's a long, complicated story," Ursa said. "I don't have time to get into now."

"That's it," Tanner said, turning to go. "We're heading back to Calisto Grandee."

"Wait! I can tell you this."

Tanner regarded her.

"Lord Acton is an Earthman," Ursa said.

"What?"

"It's true. He was born on Manhome. He knows the ancient legends and is privy to much of their higher understanding."

"The man's from Earth?" Tanner asked, bemused. "I guess that means Lacy is also from Earth."

"I don't think so."

"Then, how can she be his niece?"

"I don't know the precise situation between them."

"Is saying she's his niece a euphuism for she being his lover?"

"No," Ursa said. "Don't be absurd. Lord Acton is the danger and our great hope. He actually belongs to the Institute of Man."

86

Tanner shook his head. He had no idea what that was supposed to mean or why it should matter.

"The Institute is a powerful, semi-secret organization centered on Manhome," Ursa said. "They have many degrees of service or levels, many ranks. I've heard it said that within the Institute resides all of humanity's previous knowledge. It is the reason why Acton has poisons that can render an individual open to his suggestions. It's the reason he can control the Lithians. More to the point, it is how Acton has the knowledge Remus can use to free itself."

"Why would the Institute want to help us?" Tanner asked.

"I don't know."

"Acton hasn't told you?"

"No."

"Do you trust him?"

"No."

"Then why are you working with him?"

"Because our homeworld has no other choice," Ursa said. "The situation is dire and Lord Acton is our last hope."

"Why is your brother acting as a sentry?"

"In case Acton walks the corridors looking for you or us. I don't want him to know that you are aware of his identity yet."

"Why would that matter?"

Ursa seemed reluctant to say. She hugged herself, finally saying, "Because I'm certain at this point Acton would kill you in order to keep his identity secret."

Tanner laughed once, sharply. "Lady, instead of making things clearer, you've made them murkier. I still don't understand anything about this supposedly unique weapon that we dare not wield."

"None of that is going to matter if we can't get out of the Nostradamus System."

"Okay," Tanner said. "I can see that. It might help me though if you would give me the hyperdrive coordinates to wherever we're headed."

Ursa thought about that. "Yes, I can do that. Once we reach the hyperdrive region, you can lay a course for the Petrus System."

87

"Petrus!" Tanner exclaimed. "That's madness. It's a pile of rocks, a blasted system—"

"I know all that," Ursa said, interrupting. "But the system also has the Petrus Hideaway."

"You're kidding, right? The hideaway is a lawless port full of swindlers, cutthroats and pirates."

"Precisely," Ursa said. "It's the perfect place to buy new torpedoes as well as certain other refinements your raider is going to need."

"If we make it out of Nostradamus System alive," Tanner said.

"Centurion, you've been to Petrus Hideaway two other times."

"How do you know that? Never mind. Maximus must have told you. I was lucky to get away last time. Bounty hunters are not well loved at the hideaway."

"I understand. Bounty hunters are hated there, in fact. Those at Petrus call them weasels and have a de-weaseling organization to check each ship coming into port."

"Okay. You know about that. Now you realize why we can't go there."

"We must go there," Ursa said. "It's the only place you're going to be able to purchase a cloaking device for the raider."

Tanner became blank-faced. "Do you realize how much money a cloaking device would cost?"

"A vast sum," Ursa said.

"More than my raider is worth," Tanner added. "If we're carrying that kind of wealth…we'd be fools to take it to the Petrus Hideaway."

Ursa smiled. "Don't you understand yet? That's what this is: a fool's mission. That's why we chose you."

Tanner bristled.

The hatch opened, and Marcus stuck his head in. "You'd better wrap it up. Acton is awake and he's heading for the captain's quarters."

-13-

Tanner beat Lord Acton to his quarters. The centurion rummaged in his bulkhead drawers, finally pulling out a pair of leather gloves. By the time he slipped them on, the hatch chime rang.

"Okay," Tanner whispered to himself, squaring his shoulders. He took a deep breath and opened the hatch.

Lord Acton had added a cape to his attire and held an ivory cane. The Earthman seemed to take in Tanner at a glance.

Tanner felt as if Acton noted the gloves in particular.

The Earthman's head swayed the tiniest fraction. He raised the cane as if making a mental adjustment. The top of the cane had a golden lion head on it. He let the lion head tap against Tanner's chest.

Already keyed up, Tanner grabbed the cane, yanking it out of Acton's grip, tossing it into his quarters so it *clattered* onto the floor.

Acton's eyebrows rose, and he made to brush past Tanner, no doubt to retrieve his cane.

"Not so fast," Tanner said, blocking the way.

With a thrust of his arm, Acton shoved Tanner aside, hurling him against a bulkhead, making the centurion's back thump against it.

He's strong like Lacy, Tanner realized. The next moment, he drew his gun, aiming it at Acton.

"Touch the cane and I'll kill you."

Something in Tanner's voice must have convinced the Earthman. Acton halted, turning around, taking in the gun aimed at his chest.

"You have primitive emotions," Acton said in his odd accent, "much too easily engaged. I suggest—"

Tanner thumbed back the hammer. Every instinct screamed at him to gun down the Earthman in cold blood. There was something very off about Acton. He was more than dangerous. For this instant in time, he seemed like a virus out to destroy the galaxy.

Acton inclined his head in a smooth, polished manner. "I see I miscalculated concerning you. I don't often do that. Will you retrieve my cane for me?"

"Get out of my quarters! You have a second to comply."

Acton inclined his head once again, as if the threat didn't truly concern him. With a swirl of his cape, he moved to the hatch.

Tanner backed away to keep space between them. The impulse to shoot almost made his gun hand shake. What was wrong with him? The man had tossed him aside much too easily, that was true. Did that sting his pride so much that he was willing to murder the man?

"Captain," Acton said from the corridor. "If you will permit me—"

Tanner pressed the switch that shut the hatch. He locked it a second later. Holstering the gun, he went to the cane. Grabbing it where he'd seen Acton hold it, he raised it, carefully examining the lion head. He couldn't see anything resembling a spike.

Putting it back on the floor, Tanner unzipped his jacket, shrugging it off. He searched for a pinprick, but couldn't find one.

Tanner rubbed his chest where the lion head had struck. He didn't feel any different. He'd assumed that Acton had seen his gloved hands and tried to dose him with toxins another way. It appeared he had been wrong.

Putting his leather jacket back on, Tanner picked up the cane. He tested it. The lion head twisted with a click. He pulled a sword out of the ivory cane-case.

The chime rang.

Tanner shoved the sword back into its holder, twisting the lion head so it locked. The Earthman hadn't dosed him again, but the man was far stronger than he appeared.

The chime rang again.

Tanner had to make a fast decision. How was he going to handle Acton? Ursa said he had the antidote to the Coalition. It would appear he had overacted against the man.

The idea of someone trying to control him...enraged Tanner like nothing else could. Maybe the arm-swing toss had been a freak occurrence.

The centurion opened the hatch, handing the cane to Acton lion-head first.

The Earthman nodded, taking the cane, tapping the end on the deck. "I did not mean to presume, Captain. I have heard about some of your exploits. I imagine a man in your profession must have hair-trigger responses. Rest assured that I am no threat to you. The cane is an heirloom. I forgot myself and wished to retrieve it immediately."

"It appears we understand each other," Tanner said.

"Assuredly," Acton said. "You are a man of action, of purpose and with great pride. I will not forget that."

That almost sounded like a threat.

"Now," Acton said, "let us consider this matter forgotten. Otherwise..."

Tanner raised an eyebrow.

Acton moved his lips in the approximation of a smile. There was no humor or good will in it, though. A smiling puppet would have been more convincing.

"I have considerable...*assets*," Acton said. "Neither of us should presume concerning the other. If you should aim your weapon at me again..." The Earthman let his unspoken threat hang in the air.

"If you don't like having a gun aimed at you," Tanner said, "don't give me cause to do it."

"Yes," Acton said, as if speaking to himself. "You have received a fair warning from me. That will suffice for now."

91

Tanner itched to draw his gun again just to see what Mr. Big Shot would do. Sometimes, though, discretion really was the better part of valor.

The Earthman's eyes seemed to drink in Tanner's reactions or lack thereof. "We have settled the issue, I see," Acton said. "That leads me to the reason for my late-night visit. I have detected a problem."

"Yeah?" asked Tanner.

"Your particle beam emitter has malfunctioned."

A cold feeling blossomed in Tanner's gut. "How could you know that?" he whispered.

The Earthman showed his teeth. Maybe he thought it was another smile. "In your way of thinking, I am like the legendary Shand of lore. I have… techno-*miraculous* abilities that would astound you. Fortunately for you and Remus, I am on your side."

"That doesn't answer my question."

"But it does," Acton said. "I know because I am like a Shand. That is like saying a wolf knows a deer is in the woods because it can sniff the deer's scent. I have 'sniffed' out your dilemma, as it were."

"Let's say you were right," Tanner said, guardedly.

"If I were right, I would like to help you fix the weapon, particularly as the raider is without torpedoes."

"You can't—" Tanner was going to say, "You can't know that." But clearly, the man did know.

"My mechanic is working on a replacement relay for the accelerator."

"By mechanic you mean the Avernus apeman?" asked Acton.

"Do you have a problem with that?"

"I assume you are referring to the common Remus bigotry directed towards those of Avernus. I have none of those biases, I assure you."

"Fine," Tanner said. "What's your—" Again, the centurion cut himself off. The Earthman was speaking graciously. Maybe the man really was trying to get along with him. It was time for a new direction with Acton.

"I appreciate your thoughtfulness, Lord," Tanner said. "It is probable that Greco will fail to manufacture a new relay in time for combat."

"I have come to the same conclusion. It is why I am offering you help in manufacturing the relay."

"The workshop is small—"

"I have failed to make my meaning plain," Acton said, interrupting. He reached into an interior coat pocket, the one with tails, and withdrew a shiny main relay for an accelerator.

Tanner's jaw dropped.

"Please," Acton said, thrusting it forward. "Take it."

"How did you…?" Tanner asked, taking the relay.

"I have told you how, Captain. I am like a Shand. I have mysterious means. Normally, I keep this information to myself. The Varus twins do not know about it, but I'm sure you will inform them. I don't mind, as I understand the nature…well, I understand human nature all too well concerning these matters."

"Okay. If this relay works—"

"Captain, I ask that you do not insult me. The part works. It will be the last part in the accelerator to fail."

Tanner weighed it in his hand. It seemed heavier than the broken relay Greco had pulled out of the accelerator.

"I did not intend any insult, Lord."

"Your apology is accepted, Captain. Until tomorrow, then. I wish you a restful night."

Acton tapped the deck with the end of his cane, turned and headed down the corridor to his quarters.

Tanner clutched the part. He hadn't apologized because he hadn't tried to insult the man. He'd wanted to tell Acton that his words hadn't been an apology, but had decided that wouldn't help things between them.

He studied the part. Would it work? Why was it heavier than the original? It was time to see Greco and find out.

***

"It works all right," Greco said, later. "Do you want me to test fire the emitter to make sure?"

Tanner stood on the floor near a removed plate. Greco was lower down inside the accelerator. The centurion crouched so he could speak more easily to his friend.

"Doesn't that strike you as weird?" Tanner asked.

"Which part?" Greco asked.

"That Acton had the needed part."

"Not if he's a Shand," Greco said.

"I've never heard of whatever that is. What's a Shand supposed to be anyway?"

"They were a strange group of technologically advanced miracle-workers before the Great Break Up."

The Great Break Up had been the destruction of the Old Federation with far too many planets losing the science of hyperdrive. Some had fallen out of industrialism and back into bronze ages where champions fought with swords and spears.

"Their understanding of science seemed miraculous to ordinary people," Greco said. "They were instrumental in the final defeat of the cyborgs."

"Ancient history, in other words," Tanner said with a shrug.

"I wouldn't dismiss it, boss. The man did give us the right part. We might actually have a weapon now. That's huge."

"Or we may be putting a Trojan horse into our only real weapon."

"Why would Acton do that?" Greco asked.

"I have no idea," Tanner said. "I just know I don't trust him. I'm not sure I trust brother or sister Varus much either. But at least they're not freaks."

Greco shrugged. "At the moment there's not much we can do about any of that. We have—"

"No. We can do something."

"What's that?" Greco asked.

"I want you to finish making the relay in your workshop."

"Boss, are you serious? I'm exhausted. I want to crash—"

"I'm not saying do it right now. Get your sleep and then keep manufacturing the part. If Acton is going to spring a threat on us later, I want to have an alternative."

"You're making life hard on me," Greco said.

"The last four years have been hard on all three of us."

"I know. I'm just saying, with the part already installed—"

"Quit your complaining. I need to tell you a few things." Tanner proceeded to tell Greco the evening's incidents, including the mind-altering palm grease.

"So Acton is an Earthman," Greco whispered later. "Do you believe that's true?"

"If Acton is a Shand, he doesn't have to belong to the Manhome Institute. He already has crazy powers, right? He gave us this piece, and he knew the accelerator wasn't working."

"I just thought of something," Greco said.

"Yeah, I know what it is," Tanner said. "Maybe Acton was the one who paid the Calisto Grandee people to give us the bad part. That's the easiest explanation as to how he knew about it."

"Occam's Razor," Greco said.

"Say again," Tanner said.

"The simplest explanation of a thing is likely to be the best explanation as to why a thing is," Greco said.

Tanner thought that through. "Oh. Yeah. I can see that."

"So, why did Acton pay someone to do that? Why did he treat you badly when you guys first met? And is he really a strongman?"

Greco climbed out of the hold. The two men lifted the plate, putting it back in place. Greco used a power drill, putting the screws into their slots.

"What now, boss?"

"You go to the bridge and keep watch. I'll go to sleep and spell you in six hours. Everything should be okay for a little while at least."

"I hope so," Greco said.

"One thing," Tanner said. "Whatever else happens, don't let Acton touch you."

"I can't wear gloves like you, boss. I'm too hairy."

"You know what you can do."

"Act like a wild man?" asked Greco.

"No," Tanner said, "like an apeman."

"Ha-ha," Greco said. "You ain't funny."

"Gnash your teeth and hoot like crazy, make Acton back away if he gets too close."

"If Marcus sees me act like that, he's liable to shoot me."

Tanner stared off into the distance. "I'm beginning to believe Ursa."

"What about?" Greco asked.

"That we're headed to a crazy place all in order to try to find a weapon no one should use."

"Wonder what kind of weapon that would be," Greco said.

"Yeah," Tanner said, yawning. "We have a few hours grace, I think. Nothing should go wrong until we're near the outer region."

"Boss, you're jinxing us by saying that."

"No, I'm not. Trust me. Everything will be fine until then. See you in a few."

"In a few, boss," Greco said.

-14-

Seven hours later, Tanner changed heading by seventy degrees. The Petrus System lay seventy-four degrees from their present course, but he didn't want to give away the precise destination so far out. In case anyone had watched them make a 1 G burn from Calisto Grandee, he increased acceleration to 2 G's. In these ways, he hoped to disrupt anyone attempting to map and time the raider's exact arrival in hyperdrive territory.

He endured the greater acceleration in the control room, spending most of his time in the pilot seat. The few times he moved around, he did so slowly and carefully. It was easy to pull a ligament or tendon in the heavier gravity.

Four hours later, his intra-ship comm light blinked. Tanner tapped the unit.

Patrician Ursa appeared in the tiny screen. "How much longer do we have to endure this?" she asked.

Tanner checked the flight schedule. "Another two hours," he said.

"And we'll have to decelerate at this rate later?"

"Not necessarily," he said. "I've been thinking about entering hyperdrive at this velocity."

Ursa looked worried. "Is that wise? Hyperdrive—"

"That isn't my first choice. I'm just saying if the need arises, we have an option."

The worry increased. "Have you spotted anything suspicious?"

"Not yet," Tanner said. "But that doesn't mean much. If it is Coalition Special Intelligence that's after us, they could have had someone near Calisto Grandee observing us and reporting to a warship in neutral territory."

Neutral territory was anything outside a star system. The distance varied from place to place. Usually, it was fifty AUs beyond the last planet. Some like the Nostradamus Corporation claimed a lesser area because they didn't want to enforce their laws so far out. Others like Coalition-run systems claimed much greater regions and often patrolled the greater range with warships.

"Does a waiting enemy have to be in neutral territory?" Ursa asked.

"I suppose not. But it's good to remember that the Coalition is distrusted out here. Would they risk an interstellar incident just to destroy us?"

"Capture us, Captain. They want to capture us, not destroy us."

"Are you sure about that?" Tanner asked.

"Oh, yes, very sure," she said. Ursa signed off a moment later.

Tanner checked sensors, scanning in all directions. He spotted various spacecraft. Most made hard fusion burns like the *Dark Star*, making them easy to see. The gas giant Titan was already in Nostradamus's outer system, with only two other planets beyond it. Those two were terrestrial ice-rocks, not worth much to Nostradamus industrialists or interplanetary traders.

In time, Tanner opened a ship-wide channel. "This is the captain speaking. I'm about to turn off thrust. We will be entering a weightless period as we coast to our deceleration point. I recommend that you check your quarters and secure any loose items."

He flicked on a clock. "I will shut down the thruster in ten minutes. That is all."

Ten minutes later, Tanner did just that. Immediately, the ferocious 2 G's quit. It no longer felt as if an invisible giant pressed against his body as weightlessness took its place.

The bigger starliners and warships had gravity control. The *Dark Star* did not.

He leaned forward and clicked on the comm. Greco soon appeared on the small screen.

"How's the manufacturing going?" Tanner asked.

"You're kidding me, right? I haven't done anything yet."

Tanner stared at the apeman.

"First, I went to sleep. Second, the ship was under high gravities. I'm not about to use the workshop under high G's."

"You have in the past."

"It was an emergency in the past," Greco said.

"This could be an emergency."

"Do you hear yourself, boss? Do you understand the operative word? It's 'could', which is radically different from 'is' an emergency."

"Get your butt down there and start working on the part now."

"Roger," Greco grumbled.

Tanner unhooked himself and floated through the corridors to the ship's galley. He brewed some coffee, ate a nutrient stick and used a nearby head. While floating along a corridor back to the control room, using a rail to pull himself, he noticed Lord Acton down a different corridor. The Earthman gripped his cane, trying to pull himself with the other hand. Tanner wondered if Acton had ever been in zero gravity before. It sure didn't look like it. The tails to his suit floated upward, making him look slightly ridiculous.

"Captain," Acton called, "if I can have some assistance, please. This floating is most unnatural."

Tanner hesitated. He had his holstered gun but he wasn't wearing gloves. They were in a small compartment in the control room. Finally, he headed down the corridor, stopping a ways from Acton.

"I would appreciate it if you could guide me to the galley," Acton said.

"It's that way," Tanner said, pointing.

"Very good," Acton said. "If I could hold onto your arm while you guide me—"

"No."

It took Acton a moment to straighten himself. "I am a paying customer, am I not?"

"I'm not your servant."

"Is that a sore point with you, Captain?"

"Maybe—no," Tanner said. "I'll tell you what is a sore point, though."

Acton waited.

Tanner exhaled. He wasn't supposed to say anything about the greasy palm, as he wasn't supposed to know about the psychedelic substance. "Forget it," he said.

"Just a moment, young man."

Acton tucked the cane under an arm, using that hand to hold onto the rail. He used his free hand to reach inside his coat. But whatever he was trying to do must have been beyond his capabilities. Finally, he let go of the rail to grab his coat. The cane slipped out from under his arm, floating away, although he didn't see that. The Earthman began to rotate in the air, however, turning upside down.

Tanner reached out to grab the cane. As he did, he noticed a shiny area on the stick. It was where Acton had been holding it.

Is that a smear of grease?

Tanner pressed his back teeth together in outrage. The Earthman had planned to dose him again. He couldn't believe it. He'd been right to keep away from Acton.

Tanner grabbed the lion head top, alert to any sign of moisture or grease there.

By now, Acton had made a complete weightless summersault. He used a foot on the rail, pulling himself into a proper position. The other hand held onto a slate that shined a blue light in his eyes.

"Ah," the Earthman said, as he studied the slate. "This is unfortunate." He looked up. "I suggest you return to the bridge, Captain. A foreign ship is scanning us. I believe it is a Coalition cruiser."

"You want me to believe that little device can tell you all that?" Tanner asked.

"How I know is immaterial. Whether I am right or not is the critical issue. The quickest route to satisfying your curiosity is to check your sensors."

100

"I just did a few minutes ago."

"I see. That would indicate you have inferior equipment. I hadn't foreseen that." Acton tapped the blue-glowing slate. "Hmm, in your terminology, I suggest you study the coordinates 54-C-32. Oh, wait. There are—emergency! This is a Class 1 emergency. Captain, you must attend to your duties at once."

Without further ado, Acton took his cane, shoved it through a belt loop and used both hands to pull himself down the corridor. He no longer seemed clumsy, but moved with grace.

He was acting earlier, the bastard. He was trying to trick me.

Could the man be right about a Coalition cruiser, though? What else had Acton seen on the slate? Something had frightened him. Did the man truly possess the legendary powers of a Shand?

Tanner flew up the corridor to the control room. If a Coalition cruiser was in position 54-C-32 then the journey to the Petrus System might already have failed.

-15-

Tanner buckled into his seat and began tapping controls. He couldn't detect any scans directed at them.

Hmm. It would seem Mr. Greasy Hands had been wrong about that. That was a comfort, at least. There was no way the little slate could have detected a scan when the raider did not.

What about the coordinates 54-C-32? Was there anything to that, anything at the position?

That region of space was half a million kilometers behind them given their direction of flight. That meant a time delay even at the speed of light. Light traveled three hundred thousand kilometers per second. Therefore, half a million kilometers was almost a two second delay.

Tanner leaned forward, studying the sensor board. He didn't spy any Coalition cruiser out there. What a load of manure. He didn't—

What was this? An anomaly of some kind. It had a low sensor signature. If he hadn't focused on the region, the computer wouldn't have brought the slight anomaly to his attention. How could Acton's little slate have spotted this?

"You idiot," Tanner whispered. The blue-glowing slate hadn't necessarily been the instrument doing the scanning. The giant humanoids had carted hundreds of huge boxes onto the ship. Those could have carried sensor equipment that relayed information to the slate.

Tanner bet that was what Shand's did. Like any stage magician, practicing sleight of hand and deception tricks,

Acton simply gave the illusion of being a mind reader, a mind-controller.

Still, the Earthman had spotted an anomaly. That was impressive no matter what it turned out to be. Was the man easily spooked, though? It would seem so.

The comm light blinked.

Tanner tapped the screen. Lord Acton appeared.

"Captain, a drone has drifted uncomfortably near our vessel."

"You're seeing drones now?" Tanner asked.

"Check...24-X-12," Acton said. "I would suggest you hit the coordinates with a strong radar signal."

"All right, all right, I'll check it out."

The screen went blank. Tanner began manipulating the scanner. As he'd expected, there wasn't anything out there. This time, the raider's sensors didn't even spot an anomaly.

"The guy panics at wannabe ghosts," Tanner muttered. That was good to know. Acton had his tricks, sure, but in the end, he lost his nerve too easily. Keeping one's nerve under hard conditions was the first rule of a good bounty hunter.

Tanner sat back. He had time now to figure out what the distant anomaly was, but until then...until then...

He cursed softly, leaning forward again. What had Acton said, "Use a heavy pulse radar."

Most of the time, a raider used passive sensors. That helped to keep one hidden from those one scanned. In space, if someone spotted you, he could hit you with nasty weapons. But the *Dark Star* hadn't tried to sneak anywhere. They'd used a fusion drive, which lit the raider up like a Solstice light on the Eve of Birth Night. Using radar gave a ship away ninety-nine percent of the time. So one only used radar for short targeting ranges or if you didn't care that the enemy would spot you in turn.

Tanner put in the coordinates 24-X-12. That was a little more than one hundred thousand kilometers in front of them. He tapped *scan* and waited.

The radar results caused a klaxon to wail and made Tanner start. If he hadn't been strapped in his seat, he might have pushed himself out of it.

He slapped off the klaxon and studied the results of the radar scan. He felt cold at the sight. That was a Coalition Falcon Five Stealth Drone. It carried a one-megaton warhead. If it came within twenty thousand kilometers, the nuclear blast would destroy the raider. At forty thousand, the blast could fry many sensitive ship systems.

At one hundred thousand kilometers—

Tanner went into action, manipulating the weapon's board with practiced skill. The particle beam emitter had better work. Normally, he would have launched a torpedo at the drone as back up. He didn't have any back up now. The point defense guns wouldn't hit the drone that far out. This was a nuclear-tipped drone. He couldn't believe it. The Coalition was as good as flipping off the Nostradamus government. Exploding nuclear warheads in a neutral star system was a good way to drive that system into the hands of your enemy.

Lately, the Coalition had been trying to keep a lower profile out here. No doubt, the leaders wanted to dissipate the fear their wars had spread. The Alliance of worlds against the Coalition was small and young, barely three years old. If the Coalition exploded a nuclear warhead this deep in Nostradamus space, it would likely cause a diplomatic incident.

The fact of the warhead showed Tanner how badly the Coalition wanted to stop this mission. That meant more than ever that the mission must succeed.

Tanner put in the targeting code. One hundred thousand kilometers was a longshot all right. He didn't expect to hit the drone the first time. That didn't mean he wasn't going to try.

If the *Dark Star* had used a laser, he wouldn't have tried such a long shot. Lasers dissipated over range just like a regular flashlight beam lost luminosity over distance. Besides, the raider was small as warships went. It wouldn't have generated a very powerful laser. That was for big battleships. Now, a particle beam was different. Sure, it didn't fire at the speed of light. But it charged particles in its cyclotron and sent the electrons out as a ray at near-light speeds. Those particles hit with tremendous kinetic energy, inducing near-instantaneous, catastrophic superheating even against an object one hundred thousand kilometers away.

What made the idea of hitting the drone possible was that it wasn't under power. It drifted or coasted at a constant rate. Nor did it seem it would jink into a slightly different heading anytime soon, thereby nullifying the shot. The drone was trying to remain hidden. Sure, the radar would alert someone. But if that someone was at the location 54-C-32, that meant a little more than six hundred thousand kilometers separation between the two objects. That gave Tanner a few seconds grace.

If the drone sent out a signal that it had been spotted, that signal would take two seconds to reach the possible cruiser half a million kilometers behind the *Dark Star*. Someone on the cruiser had to make a decision then as to what to do. The human decision would take several seconds at least, maybe a minute or two at most. Whatever the case, the order to the drone from the cruiser would take two more seconds to reach it. Then, the drone's computer would have to activate engines or defensive procedures. Before that happened—

Tanner checked. The particle beam emitter was fully charged. "Here we go, bucko," he said, tapping the firing switch.

The fusion engine quit whining and a loud hum indicated the shot. A knot of charged electrons sped through space at near-light speed.

Tanner turned on the radar, watching—

"Hit!" he shouted, grinning so wide his mouth hurt. "You thought you could sneak up on us, did you?" he shouted. "You wanted to play your filthy games against Centurion Tanner of Vesuvius. Well, I got news for you, sicko, you lose."

A bloom on the scanner screen showed him the death of the nuclear-armed drone.

"Ha!" he said, pumping his fist into the air.

The comm light blinked. He tapped it on.

"What's going on, boss?" Greco said. "It sounded like you just fired the emitter."

"That's right. I just destroyed a Falcon Five Stealth Drone."

"Out here?" Greco asked, alarmed.

"One hundred thousand kilometers in front of us," Tanner said.

The apeman's eyes widened. "That's good shooting, boss."

"Yep."

"How'd you spot it so far out?"

Tanner told him about Acton's sensors.

"But boss, if there was a drone ahead of us, in our path, that means—"

"Hold it," Tanner said. "I have an incoming message." The signal came from the direction and region of the anomaly.

-16-

Tanner opened channels, putting the incoming image onto a larger screen.

A second later, he stared into the face of a Coalition deputy superior. The woman looked old, with a wrinkled face and a cap situated low over her forehead. Tanner doubted she had any hair left. The woman definitely looked as if she'd used extended life treatments. When she opened her mouth, her teeth seemed metallic. Behind her moved the bridge crew.

Tanner drank in the details. It was a Coalition cruiser all right. He'd only faced their destroyers before. A cruiser was much bigger, possessing laser cannons. Was the cruiser here alone or did it have escort vessels with it?

It would appear that Acton had been dead right about a cruiser being back there. That was deep in Nostradamus territory. There was no doubt the Coalition was playing hardball.

"You have just destroyed Coalition property," the deputy superior said. "Worse, by your profile and raider markings, you once belonged to the Remus AirSpace Service. Almost five years ago, they unconditionally surrendered to Coalition Forces, making all their former members subject to our laws. You have broken Coalition law—"

"Wait a minute," Tanner said. "I'm innocent of all charges. How was I supposed to know the drone belonged to you? No one warned me. I believed it a danger to my ship. Under interstellar law, I am allowed to defend my ship from all unknown objects."

"So you're a space lawyer, are you, Centurion Tanner?" the woman said.

She knew his identity.

"I am engaged in legal business," Tanner said. "Unless you state your name and purpose, I am cutting communications between us."

"Have a care, puppy, lest you anger the Coalition and bring about your destruction."

Tanner slapped the switch, cutting communications with the woman. He turned on the intra-ship comm. "This is the captain speaking. We are about to make a slight course correction. I will begin the burn in ten seconds. Please find a safe location and secure yourself."

He timed it, hating the idea that a laser beam could already have targeted his ship and be on its way. He would only know as it struck, as there was no way to see a light-speed beam coming at you.

Ten seconds later, the fusion engine thrust them at 0.25 G's. Tanner stopped the thrust after fifteen seconds, having given the ship a slightly new heading.

The comm light blinked once more.

"Let's see if you've learned some manners," Tanner whispered, seeing that it was the cruiser again. With a tap, he accepted the message.

"That was rash, Centurion," the deputy superior said, her features having tightened.

"Who am I speaking to?" Tanner asked.

"You may call me Deputy Superior Pallis. Now, I demand that you decelerate and await my ship. We will be there—" She checked a screen to her left before looking up at Tanner again. "We will arrive in thirty hours."

"I am about to call Calisto Grandee Space Central," Tanner said. "I'm sure they'd be interested in your piratical threat against a registered vessel."

"You are incorrect," Pallis said. "Your ship must follow Coalition law and procedures."

"Negative," Tanner said. "I do not recognize your authority over me, especially not in the Nostradamus System."

"Do you or do you not belong to the Remus AirSpace Service?"

Tanner wanted to take a deep breath. Here it was; the big question. He tried to speak boldly and forcefully. Instead, he said as if winded, "I do not."

"That is a curious statement, Centurion. My speech meter tells me you are conflicted."

"How about that," Tanner managed to say.

The old woman scowled, leaning forward. "I suggest you speak to your employer, the former Patrician Ursa Varus."

They knew about Ursa, too? This was bad, very bad.

"Former patrician?" Tanner asked.

The deputy superior showed her metallic-colored teeth. "Remus no longer recognizes such outdated social hierarchies. She is now *Citizen* Ursa, no more."

"I know no such person."

"You lie!" Pallis said.

Tanner's back stiffened. It wasn't because the Coalition officer called him a liar. He didn't care what she thought. It was because of what he saw on the sensor board. The cruiser had just begun a 3 G burn toward him.

He concentrated on the deputy superior. She did not seem discomforted by the hard acceleration. So the cruiser had the latest gravity dampeners. It must be nice.

"Give me a moment, Deputy Superior," Tanner said. He muted her, freezing the picture. Then, he turned on intra-ship communications. "This is the captain speaking. I am sorry to inform you that a Coalition cruiser has begun hard acceleration toward us. It is presently five hundred thousand kilometers away. I will check soon, as I believe that puts us in range of their heaviest lasers. No doubt, they will soon launch interceptor missiles. Before that happens, I will call Calisto Grandee. At the moment, though, we will restart our own acceleration at two gravities. That is all."

Tanner engaged the fusion engine, readied the thrusters and waited. Once everything was ready, he began acceleration.

Immediately, it felt as if a giant pressed against his body, forcing him against his seat.

He tapped the comm. "What were you saying?" he asked Pallis.

"I imagine you have begun acceleration," the deputy superior said. "That is a mistake, compounding your penalty."

"Listen, lady, I don't take orders from you. I despise your government. You would do well to stay out of my way. I am seconds away from informing Calisto Grandee about your threats."

"I don't think so," she said.

"Yeah? Well, you think wrong."

"You will refrain from calling Calisto Grandee unless you wish to see your friend, hmm, *punished before your eyes*," the deputy superior said in a triumphant tone.

Tanner's eyes narrowed. If they had Jordan—

"Permit me to show you," Pallis said. She snapped her fingers. Her picture moved leftward so the camera could center on two large marines. They held a wide-shouldered but short old man wearing an orange jumpsuit. His skin was a sickly gray and his head slumped forward with a weird metal band around it. One of the marines used the old man's hair as a grip and yanked up the head.

Despite the old man's blank, bloodshot eyes and slack features, Tanner whispered, "Consul Maximus."

"Ah, you recognize him," the deputy superior said. "That is good, as it will help expedite the situation. Now, unless you wish me to—"

"What's around his head?" Tanner snapped.

"That," the woman said in a silky voice, "is a re-trainer."

The metal band didn't touch the consul's head. Instead, prongs jutted inward from the band to press against Maximus's skull.

"Let me demonstrate," Pallis said. The deputy superior held a clicker and pressed a switch.

The effect proved immediate. The old consul stiffened, his head jerking up. His eyes bulged outward and his mouth opened as wide as possible. He didn't speak, but croaked with dismal pain.

The woman clicked the device again.

Maximus slumped forward, kept from falling onto the floor by the marines.

"Do you see what I mean?" the deputy superior asked. "Unless you do exactly as I say, you shall watch the consul wilt into nonexistence as he attempts to resist the re-trainer."

-17-

Tanner seethed against the Coalition. Social Unity fouled whatever it touched. They claimed to help and heal but always hurt and destroyed.

He was about to utter fateful words when a hand latched onto his shoulder, squeezing hard.

Tanner twisted around to stare into Patrician Ursa's stunned features. She didn't look at him, but at poor Consul Maximus on the screen.

"Citizen Ursa," the deputy superior said, as if savoring the bite of her favorite meal.

"I am *Patrician* Ursa of House Varus," she said proudly.

Deputy Superior Pallis sneered. "That is such a noble title for a *privileged* individual. I'm curious. Do you truly believe yourself better than the rest of us?"

"I am proud of my heritage. My forebears built a strong civilization."

"An exploiting system that devoured wealth and energy from the poor," Pallis said.

"Wrong on both counts," Ursa said. "My forebears enriched Remus through hard work and intelligent decisions. It was our sweat, our thinking—"

"That weighed down the poor with your enforced sense of shame," the deputy superior said.

Ursa shook her head. "If you hate the taint of privilege, give up your rank, Deputy Superior. How is it possible for you to give orders to anyone? You exploit those lower-ranked than you, do you not?"

"You are a snake-tongued devil," Pallis said. "You delight in arrogantly repositioning yourself—"

"Why don't you answer the question, Deputy Superior? I'll tell you why, because you don't have an answer. You're a hypocrite following a lying creed."

"Enough!" the deputy superior said. She raised the black unit. "Surrender at once or I shall cause the ex-consul to plead for his life to you."

"Oh, Maximus," Ursa whispered. "You must forgive me."

Tanner looked at her. There were tears in Ursa's eyes. Her fingers tightened against his shoulder. She took a deep breath as she bit her lower lip.

"Have you decided on wisdom, Citizen Ursa?" the deputy superior asked.

"We are in Nostradamus System territory," Ursa said weakly. "The Coalition has no jurisdiction here."

"You deluded fool. We know your plan. Stop this foolishness at once and come home to Remus. You belong on your planet, not racing throughout the galaxy on some fool's errand."

Tanner saw the tears leak out of Ursa's eyes, sliding down her cheeks. Had Coalition Special Intelligence interrogated Maximus? Yes, of course they had. How much had he told them? Likely, Maximus had told them everything.

Tanner slapped the switch, putting the deputy superior on mute. He turned around, prying the patrician's fingers from his shoulder.

"Now what do we do?" he asked.

Ursa had to blink several times before she could look at him. She seemed confused, stunned, close to broken.

"They tortured him," she whispered.

Tanner said nothing. The look in Maximus's eyes would surely haunt him for the rest of his life.

"They must have broken him," Ursa said. Her left hand flew to her mouth. "What has he told them about the plan?"

Tanner shook his head.

"We're finished," Ursa said. "If they know the plan, Remus is done."

"We can't surrender," Tanner said.

"Nor can we watch them torture our friend. If they know our plan...it will never work. It's over. The great plan is finished. I can't believe it."

"Lady," Tanner said softly. "Maximus is finished. I admired the man—"

"We can't let him die!" she shouted. "Not now, now that nothing matters."

"It does matter, and we can't surrender to the enemy. We must fight no matter the cost. This is the hard road, the hard choice."

"No," Ursa whispered.

"Consul Maximus would do the same thing in our place," Tanner said.

"I don't believe that."

Tanner realized he would have to do this himself. It was a dirty, foul task. He loathed it, but someone had to take matters in hand.

"I suggest you return to your quarters, Patrician," Tanner said. "You'll pull a tendon if you remain on your feet during heavy acceleration."

Her eyes were shiny with growing horror and despair. "We can't outrun a Coalition cruiser."

"We may not have to," Tanner said. "We just have to get to the hyperdrive region fast enough."

"And go into hyperdrive at this velocity?"

"No," Tanner said. "We'll go in even faster."

"That will destroy us," she whispered.

"Maybe," he said, "maybe not. I'd rather die a clean death than fall into their hands. But that's not even the point. As long as we have a chance, we have to take it. We have to free our world from these monsters."

"You shouldn't throw that into my teeth now, Centurion. This is..." The tears began to fall more freely.

Tanner faced forward, tapping the comm, bringing the deputy superior back online.

Deputy Superior Pallis took them in. After examining Ursa, the woman smiled triumphantly.

"The truth is always difficult," Pallis said, "but you will be better off accepting it. Shut down your engine, turn the ship and begin deceleration. You must submit to social justice. You have flaunted the conventions too long. After you list your failures in committee and beg for reinstatement into the fabric of public life—"

"*No!*"

Tanner heard the agonized cry and saw Consul Maximus rip a hand free from one of the marines. The old man took something from a pocket. It looked like a glassy object. He stabbed the object into the thigh of the second marine. It all happened fast.

The second marine howled, releasing Maximus. Freed from restraint, the consul lunged at the deputy superior. Pallis shrieked, trying to leap from her chair. Maximus knocked her back against it. The once powerful old man made a horrid strangled sound. He might have tried to choke her, maybe bash her face. Maybe Maximus realized his time would be incredibly short. As the sick sound rose from his throat, Maximus ripped the black control unit from the deputy superior's shaking fingers. The consul pushed back from her and thus saved himself from the first rush of a marine. The big soldier slammed against the deputy superior so they both collapsed on the chair.

"What's he doing?" Ursa whispered.

Maximus whirled around, facing the camera. His eyes shined crazily. "They don't know!" he shouted. "I kept the secret from them!"

The second marine, the one with a shard in his leg, clamped huge hands onto Maximus shoulders.

Maximus's eyes became wide and staring. "Go with the Lord!" he shouted. "Remember your oaths! Remus must be free!"

The consul jabbed his thumb against the black control unit. Immediately, his head jerked upright and his mouth opened wide. At the last moment, he made a wretched gurgling sound as smoke curled from his head.

A marine ripped the control unit out of his nerveless fingers. The big man pressed buttons.

At the same time, Consul Maximus collapsed onto the floor as if his bones had simply vanished. He twisted several times and then his air expelled. A second before someone froze the scene Tanner saw the peace of death settle onto Maximus.

The consul was dead.

Then, someone severed the connection between cruiser and raider, leaving the screen blank.

Tanner exhaled and found that he was shaking. He couldn't believe it. Maximus had…had… He looked up at Ursa.

She dried her eyes with both hands. "He's dead," she whispered. "He's dead. He killed himself in order to save the plan, to save Remus."

"He died for us," Tanner said. "He killed himself so they couldn't hold him hostage over us."

The comm light began to blink.

With a trembling hand, Tanner turned it on.

A new person faced them. He was lean and tall with stooped shoulders. He had wisps of hair on an otherwise bald dome. The man had a hooked nose and eagle-like eyes. He wore the black uniform of Coalition Special Intelligence with an interrogator prime's insignia.

"Where's the deputy superior?" Tanner asked.

The man seemed to lack emotion except for his eyes. "You must surrender at once," the man said in a low-pitched monotone. "Otherwise, the consul will continue to suffer."

"You're a bastard," Tanner said. He realized the man was trying to pretend that Maximus still lived so the man could have an advantage over them.

"Decelerate at once," the man said.

Tanner gave the interrogator a one-fingered gesture of contempt.

The man reached up, letting the tip of his right index finger—a long finger—slide across his lips. "I urge you to stifle your emotions, Centurion, as the next few moments will prove vital to you and your people."

"I'm about to call Calisto Grandee," Tanner said.

"It is a baseless threat," the man said, "as we have purchased the right to hunt you in the Nostradamus System. Or do you not realize that everything is for sale here? That is the weakness of a pure capitalist system. They will always sell the rope that hangs them. The lust for profit knows no bounds."

"We'll see."

"Yes, we shall," the interrogator said in his monotone.

Tanner cut the connection and called Calisto Grandee Central. They refused to accept his transmission.

"It's true," Ursa said in horror.

"Just a minute," Tanner said. He made another course correction, applying thrust to change their heading slightly. Afterward, he regarded Ursa again.

"Can we beat the cruiser to hyperdrive territory?" she asked.

"It's questionable," Tanner said, "but I don't see that we have any other option than to try. We can't let Maximus's sacrifice go in vain."

"Yes," Ursa said. "You're right, of course."

"There are several problems, however," Tanner said. "One, the cruiser can accelerate much faster than we can. Two, it can launch torpedoes either to destroy us or to try to incapacitate our engines. Finally, they have lasers. I'd imagine they can't fire the lasers with a high probability of hitting us until they're within two hundred thousand kilometers range."

"What about your particle beam weapon?"

Tanner shook his head. "Against pirates and drones, we would have a chance. Against a Coalition cruiser, forget it. We're outgunned twelve ways to Mayday."

"Then, it's over no matter what we do."

"Hold that thought," he said.

Tanner typed on the controls, engaging a two-move randomizer. The first would initiate thrusts at random intervals in order to slightly alter their heading and the direction and strength of the change.

Once finished, Tanner opened a compartment and pulled out a pair of leather gloves. Unbuckling from the seat, slipping the gloves on, he said, "It's time to talk to Lord Acton."

"But, the cruiser—"

117

"You let me worry about that. Besides, that's one of the reasons I need to see Acton. I have a request to make."

"We can't tell Acton about the consul."

"My guess is that he already knows," Tanner said. "The man has a few too many toys not to know. I'm sure he hacked into our transmissions."

"How can Acton possibly help us against the cruiser?" Ursa asked.

"That's what I want to find out. Come on. If we're going to survive the next few hours, we're going to have to start now."

-18-

Acton opened the hatch to his quarters. A powerful odor exuded from the room as well as wisps of dark smoke.

Tanner's original question died in his throat, as he had a new one. "What are you doing in there?"

Acton stepped forward.

Tanner automatically stepped back, pulling Ursa with him.

The hatch shut behind Acton as he held onto his cane. His skin tone was different. It had a tinge of blue now. Small strips of cloth were individually wrapped around his fingers although not around his palms.

"Are you okay?" Tanner asked, bemused.

"Hush," Ursa said, as she tugged one of Tanner's sleeves. "Don't worry about those things. They don't matter compared to…"

The randomizer took that moment to jink the raider. There was a simple clarion call and then the raider abruptly switched heading and velocity causing each of them to stumble.

Acton bumped against a bulkhead. Tanner bumped against Acton and Ursa crashed against Tanner's back.

Without a word, Acton shoved Tanner off him with considerable strength. That caused Ursa to catapult off Tanner against the other bulkhead, hitting the back of her head against it hard enough to make a thumping noise. Her eyelids fluttered and she slumped onto the deck.

Tanner crouched by her, checking her head and then pulling an eyelid back. She was unconscious.

"What's the matter with you?" he shouted at Acton.

The Earthman straightened, peering down at Tanner. "Don't ever touch me again," the man said.

"I didn't touch you, you freak. I bumped against you. In case you didn't notice, you stumbled, too."

Acton appeared to consider that. "Yes. You are correct. Still, do not touch my person unless I give you express permission."

"Yeah? Well, the same holds for you, buddy."

This was the problem with doing anything while at 2 G acceleration. Even a stumble and a bump could cause extra harm. Normally, Tanner would have carried Ursa to her cabin. She would be too heavy for that now, though.

"She will revive soon enough," Acton said. "While you are here, we can discuss the present situation."

Tanner didn't like looking up at the Earthman. This was also the second time Acton had shoved him. He knew for sure now, the man was incredibly strong. The centurion stood, letting his gun hand fall onto the gun.

"Your primitive gestures are noted," Acton said. "You dislike me and respond with simian actions. Why then should I help you?"

"I haven't asked for your help."

"Why are you here?"

"Okay. You have a point. I need your help. But you're also in the same boat with us."

"I thought you preferred to call this a ship."

"Never mind," Tanner snapped. "We have to work together."

"I'm sure I could receive reasonable terms from the Coalition people if I spoke to them."

"I'm sure you couldn't," Tanner said. "They don't like us. So, they're not going to like you, especially as you're supposed to help us find a wonder-weapon to beat back the Coalition from our world."

"What did she tell you about me?" Acton asked sharply.

"I can't remember." Tanner said, realizing he wasn't supposed to have let that slip. "Does it matter?"

Acton blinked several times. "At present, it does not. Let us engage the situation as you originally suggested. You fear the cruiser's weaponry, is this not so?"

"Have they launched any missiles yet?" Tanner asked.

Acton reached into his coat, pulling out the blue-glowing slate. He tapped it several times, studying it. "That's a well-reasoned question, Captain. The cruiser indeed launched a missile one point eight minutes ago."

Tanner cursed under his breath. "Listen, we have even less time than I thought. That missile will begin hard acceleration soon, making our progress look as if we're standing still."

"Explain."

"The missile will likely jump to fifty or sixty gravities of acceleration," Tanner said.

Acton stared at Tanner, becoming motionless. Suddenly, he twisted around, opened the hatch and disappeared into the smoke-hazy quarters. The door shut behind him.

Tanner crouched beside Ursa, feeling the back of the patrician's head. A lump had begun to rise. How bad was she? If he went to Marcus—

The hatch opened. Acton stepped out minus his cane. He held onto a brown unit. "Meet me at Cargo Hold Two in…" The Earthman blinked rapidly. "Meet me there in eleven minutes."

"Sure."

Acton used one hand against the bulkhead to help steady him. Then, he started down the corridor.

***

Marcus helped Tanner carry his sister. The heir kept telling Tanner to tell him what happened.

"I know you're angry," Tanner said.

"Acton hurt my sister, didn't he?"

"Why's the Earthman so strong?"

Marcus looked across at Tanner. Each of them had one of Ursa's arms over his shoulder as her feet dragged on the deck.

"He's strong?" Marcus asked.

"A whole lot stronger than me," Tanner said. "Are Earthmen normally stronger than others?"

"I've never heard that."

"It must be something else then."

"He doesn't look stronger than average," Marcus said.

"Looks can be deceiving."

"Don't seek to lecture me! I'm sorry," Marcus said a few moments later. "The circumstances have left me disoriented. Consul Maximus a Coalition prisoner and then committing suicide to save us…the possibility the enemy knows what we're after."

"What exactly are we after?" Tanner asked.

Marcus stared down the corridor as he breathed heavily. "I want to tell you, believe me I do, but I don't dare. That's up to Ursa."

"She's in charge of the mission?"

Marcus glanced at Tanner. "She's smarter than me, and she keeps her cool better. Yes, she's in charge as much as any of us can be."

"You're suggesting that Acton is in charge?"

"How can we think otherwise?" Marcus said. "He has the Lithians and Lacy."

"Lacy is strong like him," Tanner said, remembering how she'd effortlessly pulled him off the corridor floor in Calisto Grandee.

"That's strange," Marcus said, seeming to ponder this for a moment. "As I was saying, Lord Acton has the secret knowledge and abilities that have continuously baffled my sister and me. He's dangerous, Tanner. I don't trust him. But it is beyond doubt that we need him."

"That's always a dangerous position to be in," Tanner said, "to need them more than they need us. We could use a few cards of our own."

"We do have a little leverage, your vessel for one thing, and I'm beginning to believe your wits and courage are two other key ingredients toward the success of our mission."

"Thanks for the vote of confidence, Lord. I appreciate it. But don't sing my praises too soon. The only things that I count are victory points."

Marcus frowned, perplexed. "Whatever does that mean?"

"In the space-strike teams," Tanner said, "we used to play all sorts of war-games. Land combat games, space games and even naval games."

"Oh, the kind with plastic pieces and a board?" Marcus asked.

"That's it. One of the things I quickly learned is that a player can do all sorts of things on the board and still lose. The secret to winning was reading the rules and studying exactly how to win. Each game was different. Once I knew the victory points to a game, I worked to achieve those alone. Nothing else helped me to win, so nothing else mattered."

"Did you win more games after that?"

"You bet I did."

Marcus nodded shrewdly. "What are the victory points this trip?"

"Getting our hands on this secret, dangerous weapon or weapons and using them to destroy the Coalition and free Remus," Tanner said. "Besides *that*, nothing else matters."

They neared Ursa's room. At the hatch, Marcus glanced at Tanner. "That kind of thinking helps clears the mind, doesn't it?"

"Yes."

Marcus slapped the switch. They carried Ursa into the cabin and carefully laid her on the bed.

"Thanks again, Centurion."

"Yes, Lord," Tanner said.

"No, call me Marcus. In this adventure we're comrades, not patrician and plebian."

"I would stay, Lord...Marcus, but I have to meet Lord Acton at Cargo Hold Two. An enemy missile is heading our way fast. Unless the Earthman has an antidote, our mission may be short lived."

-19-

Tanner's step slowed as he saw the two Lithians waiting by the cargo hatch. They hulked even bigger in the narrowness of the corridors. For the first time, he noticed a musky odor emanating from them.

Acton stood behind the Lithians, with a brown control unit in his hands.

"We must move quickly, Centurion," Acton said. "The missile has begun accelerating. It is coming at us at seventy gravities."

"Right," Tanner said. He tapped in the code, wondering if Acton could have broken it and already entered the hold.

The Lithians lumbered into the large, cold chamber. At Acton's direction, they began to unload metal crates.

"There," Acton said.

The bigger Lithian set a huge crate on the deck and pried off the lid. Afterward, he reached in, pulling out a short tube. The second Lithian pulled out an even bigger tube. At the Earthman's directions, the giants put the tubes together to make a small torpedo.

Acton faced Tanner. "How many missiles will the Coalition fire?"

"The one for sure," Tanner said. "If this one misses us maybe they'll fire one more."

Acton eyed the boxes. Finally, decisively, he nodded. He began tapping the control unit. The Lithians took down more boxes and began to build a second torpedo.

Tanner eyed the weapons. "What kind of munitions do those torpedoes have?"

"Ah," Acton said, "I've triggered your simian curiosity. These are not counter-missiles as you surmise. They are decoys. Now, cease your chatter while I calibrate them."

The Earthman sat cross-legged beside the first decoy. He opened a small hatch. With tiny, glowing-tipped tools, he reached inside, making adjustments. From time to time, he checked his slate.

When the Lithians finished putting together the second decoy, they crouched around Acton like massive gorillas, watching him.

"There," Acton said. He put the hatch back onto the decoy and welded it into place with one of his tiny tools.

Tanner couldn't fathom how that little tool generated the needed energy to do what it was doing. Maybe Acton really was a Shand. That was fine with the centurion, as long as they could survive the approaching missile.

Acton chattered gibberish words to the biggest Lithian. The male grunted, climbed to his feet and picked up the first decoy, cradling it in his giant arms.

"He will follow you and place it in the firing tube," Acton said.

"Right," Tanner said. "This way," he told the Lithian.

"You do not need to speak to him," Acton said. "The beast will know what to do. I have instructed him."

Beast? Did Acton think of the Lithian as an animal?

***

Halfway to the torpedo tubes, with the giant trailing him, Tanner looked back. "Is it hard working for Lord Acton?" he asked the Lithian.

The giant man-creature focused dull eyes on him. They were gray-colored with black, pin-dot pupils.

"Do you even understand me?" Tanner asked.

The Lithian pursed his lips, nodding his giant head up and down.

"Does that mean yes?"

The Lithian did the same thing as before.

125

Tanner didn't get the idea the Lithian knew what it was doing. "I guess your nods really mean for me to hurry up, that you want to do whatever the master has told you to do."

Tanner continued guiding the giant. What would cause—wait a minute! Acton had used a control unit on the creatures. What exactly did the control unit signal?

The centurion stopped and approached the giant. The musky odor grew stronger the closer he came. The Lithian eyed him, making nervous sounds. Tanner reached up as if to touch the decoy. The giant bent lower, maybe understanding that he was supposed to let Tanner do that. Instead of touching metal, Tanner reached past the missile and brushed some of the shaggy hair from the Lithian's neck.

The giant hooted with fear or anger. It lurched away, making the upper back of its head slam against the ceiling. The jerking motion almost caused one of the massively muscled arms to knock against Tanner. The centurion darted back just in time, stumbled and slammed his shoulders against a bulkhead. That hurt. If the creature had knocked him with an arm—the force of the blow might have killed Tanner in the heavy Gs.

The Lithian groaned, sagging to its knees. Tanner noticed a dent in the ceiling. The thing must have a skull several centimeters thick to have withstood that.

The heavy eyelids blinked and it groaned again. Then, it slumped forward, releasing the decoy as it crumpled onto the floor. The decoy must have been heavy. It hit hard, rolled and slammed against a bulkhead.

Tanner went to the decoy and tried to lift it. No, that wasn't going to happen. Had dropping the decoy damaged it? Oh, this was a fine fix.

While debating what to do next, Tanner approached the snoring Lithian. He swept back the hair, feeling on the head. Finally, he found a hard nodule on the back of the skull. Tanner pressed it. The nodule didn't strike him as skin or bone, but a piece of embedded metal. He had no doubt this is what received Acton's transmissions from the control unit.

How deep did whatever Acton had put in the Lithian's skull or brain, go?

I don't have time for this now.

He went to the decoy and tried to roll it. No. It would take far too long to reach the torpedo room this way.

The answer came to him a second later. Tanner had to do this as fast as he could, but he couldn't risk walking too fast in the two gravities or he'd pull something for sure.

***

Tanner reached the control cabin, informing the passengers that he was going to turn off the thruster for a few minutes. As soon as weightlessness returned to the *Dark Star,* Tanner floated back to the snoring Lithian.

Now, he could move the decoy, but he'd have to do so carefully. It might not weigh anything at the moment, but it still had plenty of mass. If he tried to stop it too fast, and got in the way of it and a bulkhead, the decoy would pulp his skin and crush his bones.

By careful maneuvering, Tanner finally brought the decoy to the torpedo room. He maneuvered the thing into a tube, shutting the hatch.

As he floated back to the control room, Tanner wiped sweat from his brow. It was harder working in zero G than a person would believe.

Tanner strapped himself into a seat, pressing the blinking intra-ship comm unit.

"Where have you been?" Acton demanded.

"Getting the decoy in place," Tanner said.

"I've been trying to hail you for some time."

"Everything is ready."

"My Lithian is unconscious in the hall. I want to know what you did to cause that."

"Me?" Tanner said. "He's the one that bumped his head."

"Will you force me to play back his memories?"

"You can do that?" Tanner asked.

"I can do many things."

Tanner believed that. Yet, he also had a stubborn streak. He would let this one ride.

"I'd love to chat, chief," Tanner said, "but I have a decoy to set."

There was a pause. Then, Acton said, "Yes. I have one quick question then."

As Tanner spoke, he readied the torpedo decoy for firing. "I'm listening."

"How did you know the cruiser would fire a laser?"

The cruiser fired at us? Tanner played back images from camera one. He started from his seat as a streak of coherent, dangerous light flashed several kilometers past the raider. The Coalition people had decided to play deadly, firing their main laser. Luckily, he had turned off acceleration in order to move the decoy. That lack of acceleration had changed their position—of where the raider would have been if they had still been accelerating at 2 G's.

"I've been in the Remus AirSpace Service a long time, Lord. I was highly rated then and still am now."

"Are you claiming instinctive intuition?" Acton asked.

"I don't like to brag about my special knacks," Tanner said, "especially when we're still under fire."

"I suppose it is possible that this is a positive and useful display of your primitive senses."

"Yes," Tanner said. "My senses are very primitive. But they worked this time, didn't they?"

"I cannot refute that. Perhaps we shall survive the cruiser after all. I am sending the second decoy to the torpedo chamber."

"I'll have Greco meet the Lithian there."

"That will suffice," Acton said.

After Tanner shut off the comm, he concentrated on what he was doing. The laser had missed because he'd shut down the fusion drive at just the right time. Likely, the cruiser had advanced sensors. But the enemy was still a long way off. It was time to start silent running, trying to drift and sneak away to the hyperdrive zone.

He pressed a switch.

On the main screen, he watched the torpedo launch from the tube. He applauded whatever Acton had done, because the torpedo matched their velocity but only slightly changed its trajectory.

While it was still in visual range, Tanner watched antenna and other instruments emerge from the decoy. Shortly after that, it began to emit signals, matching that put out by the *Dark Star*.

Tanner typed fast on his controls. By the time the Coalition missile reached them…yes, the decoy and the ship would have enough separation. By the time the missile reached the decoy, if it went after the decoy, its blast wouldn't hurt the raider that killed the decoy.

There were too many ifs to this, though. Were they about to die or did Acton know his craft? One more decoy would push the odds in their favor, giving them a thirty-three percent chance of dying instead of a fifty-fifty chance.

The trip had hardly begun and it had already turned into the worst voyage of Tanner's life.

-20-

The next several hours proved tedious and tiring as Tanner remained at the controls. The cruiser tried hailing them. Tanner refused to acknowledge them for the simple reason that it would fix their position.

The enemy missile no longer raced at seventy gravities. It coasted now, having built up tremendous velocity.

The hailing became more urgent.

"Maybe they want us to surrender," Greco said. The apeman sat beside Tanner in the control room.

Tanner shrugged. His eyes had become red-rimmed from a lack of sleep.

"Let me spell you, boss. You look terrible. Go get some sleep."

"Soon," Tanner said.

Greco shook his head. "When you say it like that soon means three days from now. Come on, boss. How does being half-awake help you at a time like this?"

"It doesn't, but I wouldn't be able to sleep anyway. So, I might as well be up here making the right decisions."

"Not that many to make at this point," Greco pointed out.

Tanner fiddled with the controls. "Oh-oh," he said, indicating the sensor screen.

Greco leaned forward. "The missile has increased gravities again, building fast. Look at that, 50 G's. That thing has legs."

"That's what I was afraid of," Tanner said. "At fifty G's…" His fingers flew over a keypad. He cursed under his breath at what he saw. With the latest acceleration, the missile would reach them even sooner.

"Bad?" Greco asked.

"Not if you like radiation poisoning," Tanner said.

"Better have everyone wear a suit then."

Tanner kept staring at the screen. If the missile went after the decoy but reached it soon enough, the blast would reach them with hurtful results.

"Suits won't be enough?" Greco asked.

"Maybe for you," Tanner said.

Greco nodded. "My race will survive long after the rest of you have passed on."

Tanner glanced at the apeman before returning to staring at the numbers. With the increased velocity, there wasn't going to be enough separation between the decoy and the raider—even if the enemy missile went for the decoy. They should soon know the missile's target.

"Radiation pills, suits and lying in the shield room should protect us from a near miss," Greco said.

"Look at the numbers," Tanner said.

Greco leaned forward to give the numbers a glance. He hooted sadly after scanning it. "That's bad, boss."

The next thirty minutes seemed to take forever. Tanner rubbed his eyes constantly. He made a calculation and slouched back as if he'd suddenly lost strength.

"What is it now?" Greco asked.

"We're not going to have to worry about radiation suits."

"That's good news, right?"

"No. The missile is heading for us instead of the decoy."

"Oh," Greco said. After a moment, he added, "Lord Acton failed to produce a miracle."

"Maybe."

"What else could it be?"

"When we were transporting the decoy, I caused it to hit the deck in the corridor. I might have broken an interior circuit that caused something to go wrong."

Greco thought about that. "You'll have to tell Acton and launch the second decoy."

Tanner glanced at Greco. A second later, the centurion shook his head, growling to himself. He slapped an intra-ship comm switch.

"Captain Tanner?" Acton asked.

"We have to launch the second decoy."

Acton shook his head. "If the first failed to—"

"I might have broken it on the way to the torpedo room."

Acton became still, his eyes fixed on Tanner. "That must have happened when you caused my Lithian to fall unconscious."

"I suppose so."

"Tell me what you did."

"Does it matter now?" Tanner asked.

Acton waited several heartbeats. "It matters," he said at last.

Part of Tanner wanted to argue. The stupidity of wasting any more time convinced him that telling the truth would be better. So he told Acton exactly what had happened, how he'd searched the back of the Lithian's head.

"Simian curiosity," Acton hissed under his breath. "Always, your kind touches what it shouldn't. It will be the death of my mission, the end of—"

Acton straightened. "Yes, launch the second decoy without delay. It may already be too late, though." The man brooded before saying, "Listen carefully. Here is what we'll have to do…"

Tanner listened to the man talk before signing off. Soon thereafter, he launched the second decoy. It acted much as the first had.

"I have to time this just right," Tanner said. He set up the controls—

The ship accelerated at 0.65 G's. At the same time, the same strength of thrust caused the second decoy to separate from them. The two objects veered away from each other fast, at a greater angle than the first decoy had done.

"Three, two, one…zero," Tanner said, shutting off the ship's thruster.

"What's the Coalition missile doing?" Greco asked.

Tanner hunched over the scope, watching, waiting and mentally urging the enemy missile to follow the second decoy. Maybe the corridor bump hadn't done anything to the first decoy. That would mean Coalition electronics was more powerful than Acton's gear.

"Yes!" Tanner said. "The missile has changed heading. It's going after the decoy." He ran some rapid calculations. "Well—"

"Look, boss," Greco said. "The missile has increased velocity again."

Tanner studied the screen. "The commander over there must have come to the same conclusion I did. If the missile arrives soon enough, the blast will hurt us either way. They're making the right choice."

"Seems like it's time to for us to swallow the pills and don the suits," Greco said.

"I think you're right."

***

The insulated bay was a tight fit. Worse, it lacked room for the Lithians. Each of the regular-sized people took a blue radiation pill, put on an insulated spacesuit and carefully fitted into a cubicle. Lastly, Tanner pressed a switch. A heavy insulated plate slid into place over them.

The *Dark Star* ran on automated. According to Acton, the Lithians had returned to their room and gone into hibernation mode.

"I wish there was something more I could do for them," Tanner said from his cubicle.

"Do not concern yourself," Acton said through a suit-comm. "Each of them should survive long enough to complete their task on Planet Zero."

"Where?" asked Tanner.

"Planet Zero," Acton said. "Surely, that should stir your simian curiosity to a fever pitch. During our confinement together, you will undoubtedly desire to know more. But I will tell you no more. You will have to wait, Centurion. And waiting, as I have discovered in my travels, is the worst torment to inflict on one of your kind."

133

"What's that supposed to mean?" Tanner asked. "Are you saying you're not human?"

"Your reasoning capacity is quite limited," Acton said.

"That doesn't answer the question."

"Nor does the question bear answering. I am fully human; more so than your first mate."

Tanner inhaled, ready to launch into a heated reply.

"Leave it, boss. I'm used to it."

"I meant no insult to you, apeman," Acton said.

"Maybe we should try to sleep," Greco said. "We're stuck here lying next to each other. Arguing and fighting isn't going to help us."

"Fine," Tanner said.

The others seemed to agree, as no one commented during the next hour.

"The missile is nearing its detonation range," Acton informed them later.

Tanner snorted and smacked his lips. He couldn't believe it. He'd actually fallen asleep for a time.

"Do you happen to know the warhead's size?" Tanner asked.

"This one is two megatons," Acton said.

"Will the blast radius reach us?"

"By us, do you mean us in here or the ship in general?"

"In general," Tanner said.

"We will know in another minute," Acton said.

They waited in the insulated hold. Tanner took out a hand unit linked to the raider's sensors. The missile wasn't visible to teleoptic sight. The decoy showed as a green dot against the background of space. Suddenly, an intense white light appeared in the hand unit's screen. The white grew, expanding rapidly. Heat, x-rays and gamma rays reached the decoy, destroying it in a flash. The destroying circumference and EMP kept expanding.

"Here it comes," Tanner said.

The gamma rays, X-rays and heat washed over the raider's armored hull—the raider was too small to boast any kind of force screen. The weakened but still deadly rays swept through the ship. In some places, they burned out systems. In others, they merely irradiated things. The Lithians each received hard dosages of radiation. How much the blue giants could take would be another matter.

The insulation bay and suits protected the others from the worst radiation. Even so, each person received rads.

"Anybody feel sick?" Tanner asked.

"I have an icky feeling on my tongue," Ursa said.

"We'll have to take treatments," Tanner said. "But I have to tell you: I've been hit with worse than this and survived. We're going to make it."

Marcus sighed heavily.

"It's time to get up and find out the damage," Tanner said. "Lord Acton, do you feel well?"

The Earthman stared at his slate, the blue-glowing light shining on his helmet's faceplate. "We must hurry," Acton said. "I detect another ship. It is bearing toward us on an intercept course."

"That's foul luck," Greco said.

"What kind of ship?" Tanner asked.

"I'm uncertain," Acton said. "I think the blast damaged my sensor box."

"That tears it," Tanner said. "I have to get back to the control room."

***

Still in his suit, Tanner hunched over the scanner. He saw the other ship easily enough. It came at them from the other side as the Coalition cruiser. It was still many hundreds of thousands of kilometers away but was faster than the cruiser.

"Is it another Coalition warship?" Greco asked over the suit speaker.

"Can't tell that yet," Tanner said. "I don't think so, but I can't be sure."

"If it's not a Coalition ship—" Greco quit talking as the comm light began to blink. "Message from somewhere," he said needlessly.

Tanner checked the signal. It came from Calisto Grandee.

"They ignored us before," Greco said. "Why would they want to speak to us now?"

"I'm thinking it's our turn to ignore them," Tanner said.

"What if the call is about Jordan?"

"Exactly," Tanner said. "If I don't talk to them, they can't threaten me with her, now can they?"

Greco cocked his helmeted head. "I never thought of it like that."

Tanner made some calculations then sat back, thinking. The comm light began to blink again. He checked the heading and realized this one came from the Coalition cruiser.

"They launched another missile," Tanner said.

"I wonder why they don't fire their laser at us."

"We still have a lot of separation from them. It would be a difficult shot at this distance."

"But if they wanted us badly enough, they should go ahead and fire," Greco said.

Tanner studied the apeman. "Are you suggesting they're not really trying to kill us, just making it look like they are?"

"No..." Greco said.

"What then?"

"The situation..." Greco waved a space-suited hand. "The situation feels wrong to me."

"The Coalition attempts against us feel wrong or Lord Acton actions do?"

"Lord Acton feels wrong."

"I agree. I'd like to know why Acton is way out here. What does he hope to achieve?"

"Probably the same thing as Marcus and Ursa," Greco said.

"You know what I think? Marcus and Ursa are trying to use Acton and Acton is trying to use them. I have a feeling that Acton is doing a better job of it."

"Why does his niece stay in her quarters all the time?" Greco asked.

"Yeah. That's another thing, and the Lithians, the way Acton calls them beasts and us simians."

"You don't like that?" Greco asked, sounding amused.

"I guess not."

"Welcome to my world, Centurion."

Tanner was silent for a time. "Are you sorry you came with me?"

"No. I always came in order to learn how to make my *koholmany*. I haven't had much luck yet, but I'm always collecting data."

"Are you sorry your people allied with us on Remus against the Coalition?"

"Maybe, but maybe we never had a real choice. The weaker cannot dictate to the stronger. The weaker must take what they can get."

"You're not weaker," Tanner said.

"Physically, I'm the strongest man aboard ship."

"Stronger than Acton?" asked Tanner.

"I have begun to believe he's not a man."

Tanner inhaled, nodding shortly, ingesting the idea. "Okay. If that's true, then what is he?"

Greco grinned, showing his teeth through the faceplate. "If we knew that, maybe we'd know his ultimate plan."

Tanner noticed something new on the sensor screen. He tapped the board, made a few adjustments and sat back in thought.

"The new vessel is a Nostradamus destroyer-class warship," Tanner said. "It's racing at us at 5 G's."

"I wonder why?"

"I bet someone paid the Nostradamus people. My guess is the commander of the Coalition cruiser had discretionary funds. They're using those funds to try to capture us."

"You have a plan, though," Greco said hopefully.

"I do indeed. You can listen while I tell the passengers what we're going to do."

***

For the next three hours, the *Dark Star* accelerated near its limit of 3.5 G's. It was an exhausting strain on everyone. Every few minutes, the craft made the slightest of adjustments. Every twenty minutes, a laser beam shot past the ship. So far, the Coalition cruiser had missed each time.

From three hundred thousand kilometers away, an enemy missile burned at seventy gravities, straining to reach them.

The Nostradamus destroyer continued to race for a collision point with them. That point was at the very beginning of the hyperspace region.

Lord Acton presently stood behind Tanner and Greco. The so-called Earthman made rapid calculations on his slate. Tanner had no idea how Acton could remain on his feet for so long in 3-plus G's. He doubted he could do it, and he was much younger.

"I have it," Acton said quietly.

"I still say it's impossible," Tanner said. "At the velocity we're going, this will destroy us, implode the vessel."

"Are you ready to accept data?" Acton said.

Tanner hesitated. What other choice was there? None, he realized. The Coalition, with Nostradamus' help, had them unless this worked. He recalled Consul Maximus's last horrible moments aboard the enemy ship.

Tanner tapped a control. "Ready?" he said, hoarsely.

Acton tapped his slate, downloading his calculations into the flight computer.

Tanner wished Jordan was here. She could have set it up so the data didn't go directly into the computer, but sat in a receivership in case it carried a virus. He had every anti-virus element running. Was Acton trying to take over the ship by a backdoor method?

Tanner ran the Earthman's data. "Get a load of this," he said. "The computer says it should work."

"We are out of other options," Acton said. "Haste is critical. I suggest you engage now."

Lord Acton had just given him a program that should allow the raider to enter hyperdrive ten AUs sooner than normal and at a greater velocity than anyone thought possible. Both were incredible breakthroughs. Together, this might be revolutionary. And the Earthman had seemingly done it off the cuff. That was more than weird. It should have been impossible.

"If we enter hyperspace even one degree off from my calculations," Acton said. "the raider will implode."

"Everybody ready?" Tanner asked.

Acton put a gloved hand on the back of each seat, bracing himself. "I am ready, Captain."

Tanner blew out his breath, squeezed his eyes shut and opened them wide. He rechecked his calculations. Everything should work. If that was true, why did he have to keep blinking sweat out of his eyes?

"Engage," Acton said, "engage now. The cruiser will aim to kill next time. They must."

Tanner let his space-suited finger hover over the switch. With a silent prayer, he stabbed down, engaging the hyperdrive.

-21-

Dark Star began to shake. Tanner had never felt anything like it when entering hyperspace. A sound like a sea-beast groaning vibrated through his helmet.

"What's happening?" Tanner shouted. The words sounded garbled to his ears. A sense of disorientation struck him. With seeming slow motion, he twisted around in his seat, looking up at Lord Acton. The Earthman seemed frozen in shock.

"Can you hear me?" Tanner shouted.

Acton made no sound or sign that he did.

The ship's beastlike groaning grew worse. It seemed as if the entire raider twisted and that was metal shifting, the hull and the bulkheads in particular.

Tanner faced the flight board. The shaking made the instrument panel blur. The calculations hadn't worked just right. That had to be the problem.

Then, Tanner heard hooting in his comm-link. He twisted to his left. The apeman hooted again. Greco lurched at the board, tapping on it. The apeman withdrew his hands from the blurring panel, unlatched suit seals and hurled the constricting gloves from his hairy hands. With seemingly great patience, Greco tapped, waited and tap-tapped again, studying the board each time.

That didn't help at all, though. The shaking around them worsened and the groaning made Tanner certain the raider was about to tear apart and spill them into hyperspace.

"All or nothing," Greco said, as if to himself. "Every drummer knows this." The apeman's fingers began to tap faster. He looked at the results and tapped another quick sequence.

The groaning sounds lessened, as did the shaking.

Greco hooted with apeman laughter. He continued the process, tap-tap, wait, tap-tap-tap and wait longer.

The shaking abruptly quit and so did the metallic groaning.

At that point, it seemed as if all of Tanner's muscles gave out at once. He collapsed against his seat, breathing raggedly. He was alive. They'd made it into hyperspace. What in the heck had just happened?

He was too tired and relieved to ask just yet.

Greco adjusted the controls once more. "We're in hyperspace," he announced.

Tanner managed to move his eyeballs just enough to glance at the screen. It showed a grayish universe with streaks of darker color. Yeah, this was hyperspace all right. It was a dreary realm, allowing a spaceship to cross light-years of distance without any time dilation. If the calculations were correct, they would come out of hyperspace just outside the Petrus System in about eighty hours. They would leave hyperspace at the same speed they entered. That should give them an advantage there.

The thought started Tanner's mind functioning again. "Are we going to have this problem coming out of hyperdrive?"

Greco glanced back at Acton. The Earthman still wasn't talking. "I think it likely," the apeman said. "I believe we hit a chrono disturbance coming into hyperspace and will probably pass through one leaving it, too."

"What did you call it?" Tanner asked.

Greco sighed. "I doubt I can explain it so you can understand. You know I'm engaged in a serious study of Tesla vibrations, don't you?"

"Ah...no," Tanner said. "I had no idea."

"It's why I originally agreed to join you, in order to fashion a *koholmany*."

"How could I forget?" Tanner said.

"I'm fascinated with Tesla vibrations. It's why I suspected we'd entered a chrono disturbance. The time between pulses was wrong. They moved too slowly. If they had moved at regular speeds, the vibrations would have shattered the ship."

"Okay..." Tanner said.

Greco unbuckled, standing. "I must assess the ship's damage. There could be complications from the overdue stresses. The chrono disturbance might have struck unevenly."

Tanner's mind felt sluggish, but he finally got it. Greco didn't want to say too much in front of Acton. That made sense.

"You did well," Acton said, suddenly. "Your quick action saved us all. I did not realize you understood Tesla vibrations or chrono disturbances. That is remarkable."

"We're a remarkable people," Greco said, sounding stiff.

"Indeed," Acton said. "I shall not forget that. Captain, I must check on my Lithians. If you will excuse me?"

"Sure," Tanner said.

Acton pushed off in the weightlessness. They no longer accelerated. No one had figured out how to do that in hyperspace. The speed was always the same no matter how fast you entered. The difference in flight times was affected only by the distance from one object to another in regular space.

Tanner understood none of the hyper-physics of it, but Greco and Acton likely did.

"What just happened?" Tanner asked his friend.

Greco watched the Earthman disappear down the corridor.

"Hey," Tanner said.

Greco faced him. "Let me check the ship. You should get some sleep. Afterward, we need to figure out what Lord Acton is and why he needs to go to Planet Zero."

***

After getting lots of sleep over the past thirty-six hours and feeling much better for it, Tanner made sure everyone finished out the anti-radiation treatments. Then, he checked up on Greco's progress in repairing the ship.

Afterward, they sipped coffee in the galley. Greco's eyes were bloodshot and his fur lacked its normal luster.

"When did you sleep last?" Tanner asked him.

"Can't remember," the apeman said.

"I'm ordering you to quarters once we're done talking."

Greco nodded as he raised his cup.

"Better put that down," Tanner said, regarding the sealed coffee container.

The apeman stared at the cup, finally lowering it. "My mind is fuzzy. But everything on the ship is working again. I know the Calisto Grandee people went over the equipment, but we're going to need a real overhaul sooner than ever."

"Did the Calisto Grandee people screw us?"

"No. Their mechanics did genuine work. I suppose that means the mechanics weren't on our enemy's payroll except for whoever removed the main accelerator relay."

"That's good news," Tanner said.

Greco stood.

"I'm still curious," Tanner said. "What was that you said before about the Tesla vibration and chrono disturbance?"

"I'm tired, boss."

"I know. And you should head straight to your quarters. But I've been thinking—'

Greco hooted tired laughter.

"What was that for?" Tanner asked.

"Your simian curiosity is showing," Greco said in an imitation of Lord Acton.

"Yeah, yeah. Are you going to tell me or not?"

Greco sighed. "It's very technical with a lot a mathematical understanding needed. Let me say this instead. We Avernites often have a quest, an area of study that absorbs our thinking in a life-effort. I'm sure I've told you about it before."

"Maybe you did. It does sound a little familiar."

"You probably weren't listening."

Tanner knew his friend was probably right about that.

"It's why I love drumming," Greco said, "or part of the reason. Vibrations fascinate me. I want to make a machine to study Tesla vibrations. I want to see if I can crack a planet in half."

"What the heck?" Tanner said. "Why would you want to do that?"

"It's an ancient boast made by the original Tesla. No one has ever accomplished it. I would like to be the first."

"I didn't think Avernites liked making weapons of mass destruction."

"We don't."

"What you're talking about would be a planet buster, an ultimate weapon."

Greco blinked rapidly. "Yeah. You're right. I had not foreseen that. This is terrible."

It was Tanner's turn to laugh. Leave it to an apeman to forget about something so obvious. They really were a bunch of eggheads.

"I'm never going to be able to sleep now," Greco complained.

"Yeah, you will," Tanner said. "You look beat. Now go on, get. I need to talk to the patrician."

Greco gave him a sly wink before pushing off for his quarters.

Tanner finished his coffee. The patrician had been avoiding him ever since the insulation room. He was sure it had to do with Planet Zero. It was time to get some facts straight. If brother and sister couldn't start leveling with him, he wasn't sure he wanted to continue playing their secret game.

-22-

Tanner approached Ursa's quarters, finding First Sword Lupus floating in front of her hatch. The praetorian underman watched him closely, with a hand curled around a belted baton.

"Do you plan to hit me?" Tanner asked, floating nearby, with one hand on a float-rail.

The underman said nothing nor did he look away.

Tanner found he didn't like that. "Get your mistress. I want to speak to her."

The underman didn't move.

"If I have to draw my gun—"

The hatch opened and Ursa stood there. She wore a silver one-piece that did little to hide her charms. She'd put her hair up, which helped to show off her lovely neck.

"I wish you wouldn't harass my guard," she said.

"He's blocking my way."

"He's merely doing his duty, protecting me."

"Okay, I can see that. We need to talk, though."

Ursa yawned. "Maybe later, I'm tired now.

"That's not going to work. I have grave concerns—"

"Must I call my brother?" she asked, interrupting.

Tanner shoved off the bulkhead. The underman drew his baton with a growl, swinging in the same motion. Tanner had already anticipated that, hunching his right shoulder, taking the hit. It hurt, and the blow slowed his forward momentum. The force of the hit also shoved the underman backward so he floated away.

Lupus croaked in dismay.

By that time, Tanner reached Ursa. He grabbed her right wrist.

That enraged the underman, and he shouted incoherently.

"He's not trained for zero-G combat," Tanner said. "Your brother should be using this time to rectify that."

"Let go of me this instant," Ursa said.

"I have some questions for you," he said, keeping hold of the wrist.

By this time, the underman seemed to have figured out what he needed to do. He grasped the nearest float-rail, with his gaze fixed on Tanner.

"If you don't let go, Lupus will never stop coming at you," Ursa warned.

Tanner twisted her wrist, making her cry out softly. That allowed him to shift her position. He maneuvered Ursa in front of him so he could whisper in her ear.

"Why do you have to make this difficult?" Tanner asked. "I have a right to know what's going on. My hide is at stake as well as Greco's. I owe it to my crew and my mission to know what I'm getting into."

"Lupus," Ursa said. "Stand down."

The underman had gathered himself to fly at the two of them.

"Obey me," Ursa added.

Sullenly, the underman shoved the baton back into its holder.

"You must let go of me," Ursa told Tanner. "Otherwise, Lupus will call my brother. Then, we will have a true situation on our hands."

"Will you talk with me?" Tanner asked.

"Before I answer, you must let go."

Tanner debated options. He recognized the growing fury in the underman's eyes. He could feel the patrician stiffening, getting angrier by the moment. Part of him wanted to keep doing this. The other part realized he was taking out his anger at Acton on Ursa. That wasn't fair to her.

Tanner released her wrist, pushing away until his back bumped gently against the bulkhead opposite her hatch.

She regarded him, and she finally seemed to realize that what she wore was too revealing. "I will speak to you in fifteen minutes. I must first settle down my guard."

"Sure," Tanner said. "Why not meet me in the galley. We can have lunch together. Maybe keep your pet in your room, though."

"I do not appreciate any insults directed at my guardian," Ursa said. "You can apologize to Lupus anytime."

"Thanks for the update. I'll see you in a few." With that, Tanner turned away, using the float-rail to shoot down the corridor.

***

Tanner checked his watch as Ursa floated down the corridor. She was ten minutes late. She did look good, although not as stunning as she had in the tight coverall.

She wore yellow slacks and shoes with a frilly white blouse and white cap. He liked the way her hair curled underneath the hat and noticed she'd put on a touch of makeup.

"Do you have trouble apologizing even when it's warranted?" she asked, as she settled into a chair.

"Nice hat," he said, ignoring the question. "You look good in it."

She touched the hat and seemed to work to keep her lips from smiling. "Marcus bought it for me on Cestus IV."

Tanner scowled, his fingers tightening around the saltshaker he'd been fiddling with as he waited.

"What happened on Cestus IV?" she asked, noticing his reaction.

Tanner shrugged moodily.

"A tragedy, it would seem," she said. "Do you consider my asking about it prying?"

"No. No. That's okay. My sister—the bloody Coalition killed her during a missile attack. They killed her and her groom on their wedding day. Nice guys, those Coalition bombers."

"I'm sorry," Ursa said. "I know what it's like losing family to the terrible war."

He nodded, staring at the saltshaker, finally moving his head side-to-side. "The past is the past." He looked up and forced himself to smile. "It's still a nice hat, though. You look good in it."

"Thank you, Centurion. How good of you to notice."

His smile became genuine. "Look, earlier, I just wanted to talk, right? I wasn't looking—well—forget it," he said, ending bitterly.

"Lupus doesn't hold grudges for long if there isn't any blood involved. But I wouldn't turn your back on him for a while."

"I never planned to in the first place. Hey, what would you like to eat? Or would you rather have something to drink?"

"Do you have orange juice?" she asked, hopefully.

Tanner thought about it. "I think I might have a thimble full. Would you like it?"

"Oh, yes, absolutely," she said.

Tanner got up and checked and there was indeed a little frozen concentrate left. He made it and brought the orange juice to the table in a sealed container.

"I appreciate this," Ursa said, accepting the cup. "I haven't drunk orange juice—" She put the straw to her mouth and pressed a button with her thumb. She sipped, savoring the juice as if it was the choicest wine.

"Excellent, sir," she said.

Tanner smiled, feeling absurdly glad she liked it.

He cleared his throat, deciding this would be a good time to get her talking. "I never did find out if you set me up with a fake Calisto Grandee client. Not that I'm asking you. I already assume you did."

"You know what they say about assuming."

"I've heard it, sure," he said, making a slicing motion in the air. "But that isn't what concerns me. I'm not even going to delve too much into Lord Acton. There's too much that doesn't make sense with him."

"For instance…?" she asked.

"You're smart, Patrician. You'd rather get me talking about him so I don't ask you what I know you dearly don't want me to ask you."

"Oh?"

"Planet Zero," Tanner said.

"Acton was having a joke with you. I wouldn't take it seriously."

"That was no joke."

"I assure you—"

"Don't," Tanner said. "I don't want any false assurances. I want to trust you. But every time you start lying to me, I ask myself why I should bother."

"We're on the same side," Ursa said. "We each worked with Consul Maximus at one time or another. We can't let his horrible death go in vain."

"I can agree to that. But if we're on the same side, then you need to start trusting me by telling me what's really going on."

Ursa seemed to think about that, finally saying, "After we leave Petrus I'll tell you everything. I promise you. I can't risk it now."

"I hope you're not going to say that if I don't know, I can't let anyone torture the information out of me."

"You see," Ursa said, earnestly. "You already know my reasoning. That's exactly right. The Coalition seeks to learn our plan. There may be others who have discovered bits and pieces and desperately wish to pry as well."

Tanner leaned back, eying the beautiful woman. Between Markus and her, she was definitely the smartest. This earnest manner, the asking for orange juice and the wearing of a pretty hat, the makeup and outfit—

Tanner snapped his fingers. "Oh. You're good, Patrician, very good."

"Pardon?" she asked.

He smiled crookedly. "I'm a hard case. I always have been. I grew up on the wrong side and I have an attitude. You must have decided by now that an attractive woman is one of my weak links. You want to use that against me. I doubt you showed me the one-piece by accident."

"Whatever are you talking about?" she asked.

He leaned forward on his elbows. "No more blowing smoke in my face. I want to know about Planet Zero. I want to know what we're after. Why is the Coalition breathing down our necks so hard? Why would they spend money in the Nostradamus System? That isn't the Coalition way. They don't like buying anything from capitalists. If there's one thing I know about Coalition people, it's that they're purists when it comes to their Social Unity doctrine."

Ursa drained her container slowly and slotted it into a table holder. Finally, she regarded Tanner in a thoughtful manner.

"You're not an ordinary centurion, are you? You bluster and act like a common legionnaire, one quick to fight and draw his gun. There's more to you, though. You have a brain behind that cocky grin, and I imagine you've melted many a girl's heart with your roguishness."

"You're going to make me blush if you keep talking like that."

Ursa turned away and sucked on her upper lip. Her brows drew together. "I'm not sure you can understand."

"Uh…which am I then, the rogue or the smart plebian? You're confusing this simpleton with your bait and switch."

She smiled. "You can understand what I'd say in the technical manner, but not the possibilities for Remus. It's a subtle plan, a very clever plan that will take a sure hand to implement. Consul Maximus came up with it a long time ago. Believe me, he worked on it the entire time the AirSpace Service fought the Coalition in our home system. It was the most secret project of all, the ultimate weapon that none dare wield. Now, our Remus is almost gone, throttled by secret police tactics, Social Unity propagandists and masses of new Coalition colonists. We have to give the old Remus life before it dies forever. That has given me the courage to attempt to reach for the ultimate weapon. The other reason is Acton. I've never met anyone like him. His knowledge about Planet Zero dwarfs my own."

"Where is Planet Zero? How come I've never heard about it?"

"But you have heard," Ursa said.

"I don't remember, then. Enlighten me."

"You do remember," she said.

"Look. We can play cat and mouse all afternoon. But what's the point, eh? Either you're going to tell me or you're not. If not, then I have to go to plan B."

Ursa raised her eyebrows. "What's plan B?"

"Show me yours and I'll show you mine," he said suggestively.

Incredibly, the patrician blushed. Tanner found he liked that.

Ursa studied the table. After a time, she shook her head. "Long ago, all humanity lived on Manhome, on Earth. Those first humans invented space travel but knew nothing about the hyperdrive. Soon, humanity lived on every moon and asteroid in the Solar System. They lived in kilometer-deep cities on the homeworld. They had colonized Venus and Mars."

"Where are those places?" Tanner asked.

"If you knew your ancient history, you would know those are the second and fourth planets in the Solar System."

"By Solar System, you mean Manhome?"

Ursa nodded.

"So…?" Tanner asked.

"Humanity expanded in the mother system and reached overpopulation levels. Wars began as they fought over resources. Someone decided their side needed better soldiers. Those people made the first cyborgs."

"I've heard of cyborgs," Tanner said.

"Yes," Ursa said. "The cyborgs brought about the terrible Dark Age to the Old Federation. My point about earlier ancient history…" She shrugged. "Maybe that doesn't matter. The humans of that time barely defeated the worst menace people have ever faced. The machine-flesh men proved to be deadly opponents. Unfortunately, those oldest, Sol humans didn't stamp out all the cyborgs in the mother system. Some of the terrible enemy got away into the greater universe. It time, humanity found the hyperdrive. They expanded everywhere on a thousand planets, a thousand star systems. When the Old Federation came into being, humanity expanded more and more. Then one day, they bumped into the ancient enemy, the cyborgs.

"The cyborgs had gone far, far away. They had built their own empire. They had cultivated human slaves for their tissues. Once the Old Federation found the Cyborg Empire, the two clashed. It brought about a galaxy-wide war."

"I've never heard that," Tanner said. "I thought it was confined to the Orion and Perseus Spiral Arms."

Ursa sighed. "Yes. That's true. I was being poetic. I should have known better than to use that on a centurion."

"You mean on a plebian," Tanner said.

Ursa sighed again. "The cyborgs converted billions of humans on hundreds of worlds into their kind. They grew more powerful. The cyborgs prospered, but in the end, the Old Federation managed to defeat them. Unfortunately for our distant ancestors, the vast war drained the spirit from the Old Federation. The galaxy-wide dominion fell apart. Even worse, mankind's drive failed. Too many technicians had died on too many worlds. All over the Orion and Perseus Spirals, planets fell into bronze ages or worse. Men fought with swords and spears instead of nuclear-tipped missiles and ray guns."

"A real tragedy," Tanner said.

Ursa's nostrils expanded. "The Old Federation had burned every world where the cyborgs had dug in. On some planets, radioactive fires still roar due to the hell-burners the cyborgs or humans dropped. As the last Old Federation starships retreated, they set up sentinels on some planets. On others, they landed grim, automated defenses."

"Why?" Tanner asked.

Ursa looked up. "They had learned the hard way that some cyborg devices tunneled deep into a planet's mantle. There, the devices would wait for a different era to emerge. The cyborgs had learned from the first Solar Wide War. Always prepare for defeat so you can rise again. That was one of their great powers. The cyborgs always rose again to renew their war with humanity. All the cyborgs have to do is win one time and they will win forever."

"Uh… you're not going to tell me Planet Zero is one of these ancient cyborg worlds, are you? I mean, I know about one or two places like that. No one goes there because wicked crazy defense systems still operate to obliterate anyone foolish enough to…"

Tanner stopped speaking. He could see that's exactly what the patrician was thinking.

"That's crazy," the centurion said.

"The places you're thinking about won't help us in the slightest."

"Why not?" Tanner asked.

"Because they're devoid of any ancient cyborg devices," Ursa said.

"And we know that… Oh. I get it. Lord Acton told you all this, right?"

"Yes," she said in a soft voice.

"How does he know?"

"He's a Shand."

"They're just a fairy tale. You know that, right?"

"No!" Ursa said, reaching across the table, grasping one of his hands.

He pulled his hand free, making a fist with it. "Look, I know Acton talks about being like a Shand. Greco likes to think that, too. But they're not real as you guys are thinking about them."

"I've studied ancient history," Ursa said. "The Shands helped the Old Federation defeat the cyborgs. If humanity hadn't stumbled onto them in the distant past—"

"Hold on," Tanner said, interrupting. "You're making it sound like Shands aren't human."

"They're not," Ursa said. "Acton certainly isn't."

Tanner's face grew cold. "Wait, wait, wait," he said. "You're telling me I took an alien aboard my ship?"

"I suppose that's true."

"He's not an Earthman then?"

"He may have been born on Earth."

"But he's no man, right? I mean, that's what you're telling me, right?"

"I guess."

"No. I don't want any guesses. Either it's true or not. Is Acton human?"

"No."

"He's an alien then?" Tanner asked.

"One that can mimic human ways quite well," Ursa said.

Tanner shook his head before staring at Ursa. "Why did Shands help the Old Federation against the cyborgs?"

"The cyborgs absorb everything in their path, or they did. I'm sure in the distant past they tried to turn Shands into cyborgs. Humanity was the lesser of two evils for the Shands. Thus, they aided our side for their own good."

"I see," Tanner said. "I suppose that makes sense. Now tell me this. Why is Acton aiding us this time around?"

"He fears that hibernating cyborgs on Planet Zero are about to break out of their ancient cocoon. If they do, they could restart the ancient war. That would be the best outcome for us."

"If that's the best, what would be the worst?" Tanner asked.

"That the cyborgs would run away and hide and rebuild until they're very powerful," Ursa said.

"So you're telling me that Lord Acton is doing this out of the goodness of his alien heart?"

"You make it sound silly saying it like that, but the answer is yes."

"Ah," Tanner said.

"You don't trust him, I take it."

"You take it right, Patrician. I think you may be insane for trusting him."

"I'm not, you know."

Tanner searched her eyes. "Okay. I take that back. You're not insane. You've been tricked, though."

"No I haven't. I know this is a risk."

"What are you hoping to gain on Planet Zero, an ancient weapon?"

Ursa nodded grudgingly.

"What kind of weapon?" Tanner asked. He was interested in spite of himself.

"I don't know yet, as I don't know what's on the planet."

Tanner laughed. "That's rich. That's just great. We're supposed to sneak past super-powered ancient Federation defenses in order to land on a crazy weird planet with hidden cyborgs ready to pop up and restart war with humanity. But we'll land and find these super-weapons without a hitch or without getting killed or turned into a freaking cyborg or—"

"If you're frightened—"

Tanner laughed harder, and he slapped the table. "You're damn straight, I'm afraid. This is a lunatic's dream. Do you realize how crazy your idea is?"

"You haven't thought this through like I have," Ursa said.

"Okay, Patrician, explain to me what I'm missing."

"If the cyborgs are indeed stirring as Lord Acton believes, who will stop them?"

Tanner kept staring at her.

"You see that I'm right," she said.

"I see you're twisting things around so that you think—"

"You know I'm right," Ursa said, interrupting. "Think about it. The Coalition attacked Remus before we were ready. The Social Unity ideologues defeated us, but at least they're human. If the cyborgs hit the Backus Cluster before anyone is ready for them, we won't all become socialists, as bad as that is, but machine-flesh beings attacking the rest of humanity."

Tanner scowled.

"We can stop that possible nightmare," Ursa said. "And while we're at it, we can find a weapon to drive the Coalition from our world. So, not only are we saving humanity from a horrible fate, but we're rescuing Remus from socialist slavery."

Tanner stared at her while in his mind he searched for flaws in her reasoning.

"Do you really think Acton is legitimate?" he asked.

"I have no reason to think otherwise so far," she said. "Besides, we'll all be watching him."

"Watching him on a planet full of sleeping cyborgs," Tanner said.

"No one said saving our world would be easy. I imagine saving humanity is going to be even harder."

Tanner finally looked away, drumming his fingers on the table. "If this is all true, we should gather a hundred battleships—"

"You mean tell others," Ursa said, interrupting once more. "I've thought of that. Firstly, I think that's too risky. It's hard to trust people with power. What if others believe they can use the cyborgs for their own ends? Many people have made that devilish bargain in the past."

"According to you," Tanner said, "*we're* going to try to use the cyborgs."

"No. We're. Not," Ursa said firmly. "Using them is letting the cyborgs come back to life. We're going to destroy any waking sleepers and take the greatest weapons for ourselves. That's a different thing altogether."

"Hmm…" Tanner said. "Okay. What's the second reason why we shouldn't get a bunch of battleships together and destroy Planet Zero?"

Ursa looked away.

"Well," Tanner said, "what is it?"

She licked her lips. "Planet Zero is far from here."

"The way you say that makes it sound like I'm not going to like what you say next."

"Planet Zero is on the galactic rim," Ursa said. "It's the last planet before leaving the Milky Way Galaxy."

"Is this more of your poetic license?" Tanner asked.

Ursa shook her head.

"We're pretty far out as things go," Tanner said. "But we're not at the galactic rim. That would take some traveling."

"Yes."

"More than a raider like mine can do comfortably."

"We have plans for that."

"What kind of plans? I hope you're not going to say we should all enter hibernation."

"Maybe you don't want to hear our plans just yet."

"Great," Tanner said, "we're supposed to race to the galactic rim, Planet Zero, the last planet in our galaxy." He shook his head.

"The Old Federation chased down the cyborgs to the very end. It was a long and brutal war. Planet Zero was the cyborgs' last stand, a fortress world meant to survive mighty armadas. If ever there was a war-world, a vault world containing many fantastic treasures, Planet Zero is it."

"And we're supposed to be able to land on it just like that?" Tanner said, while snapping his fingers.

"No. Not just like that," Ursa answered.

Tanner sighed. "I think I'm beginning to understand. This is why we need stealth equipment."

"Of course," Ursa said. "We're going to have to sneak past the worst, or best, I suppose, guardian devices in the galaxy."

Tanner snorted. "I'm hearing a lot of big talk. One, are we sure about this Planet Zero, that it still exists? Two, are we sure the vault system has these workable deadly devices in storage after all this time? And three, if those powerful weapons are stored down there, can we figure out how to use them?"

"Do you remember Tribune J. M. Majorian?"

"More by name than sight," Tanner said.

"His raider and crew—"

"Let me guess," Tanner said, interrupting. "He found Planet Zero."

Ursa nodded.

"But when he attempted to land on the surface, the old defenses destroyed him and his crew?"

Ursa nodded.

"And you know this…" Tanner laughed grimly. "No doubt you know this because you watched them from a safe distance."

Ursa nodded once more, although more slowly than before. "Centurion, our time to act is fast running out. Those of Remus that remain free are almost all gone. The Coalition was and is too powerful for us. It always was too strong. Once we're gone, who is going to go in to stop the cyborgs while it's still possible to stop them from wakening?"

"The Shand can do it," Tanner said.

"I'm not sure he'll care to try if we fail him. Acton doesn't like working with humans. He finds it tiring."

"I find Lord Acton tiring," Tanner said.

"That's the wrong way to view him. Acton is a priceless opportunity for us and for Remus. We have to do this, Centurion. We have to move before the Coalition captures us."

"Let the Coalition destroy the cyborgs."

"What if they do?" Ursa said. "Then they'll have the exotic weapons. That's not as bad as revived cyborgs, but it's still very bad. The truth, though, is that I think Planet Zero is too far away for the Coalition to send a battlefleet there. They'll wait until the cyborgs have built up again and are too strong for anyone in the Backus Cluster to defeat."

Tanner stared down the corridor. "I have to talk to Greco about this."

"You're evading the issue. Do you believe me or not?"

They stared into each other's eyes. Slowly, Tanner nodded. He realized that he did believe her.

This is crazy. This is absurd. I'm agreeing to do something that will get us all killed.

"I still don't trust Lord Acton," he said.

"Do you trust me?" Ursa asked.

"A little more than I trust him."

"Then do this. You already agreed to it back on Calisto Grandee anyway."

"Yeah, I agreed in order to get my ship back."

"Tanner—"

He swore under his breath. "Okay. I'm in. I'm crazy for saying this, but you've convinced me. Now, I have to think about it and make sure we get what we need at the Petrus Hideaway. I don't think we're going to get a second chance at doing this, right?"

"True," she whispered. "If we fail the first time, we'll all be dead as the best possible outcome."

-23-

The remainder of the hyperspace voyage from the Nostradamus to the Petrus System proved uneventful until the very end. Everyone was too busy on their particular projects to worry about the others.

Lord Acton ministered to the Lithians, nursing them back to health from their radiation poisoning.

"I'd like to know how he's doing that," Tanner told Greco.

The apeman worked on the transfer nodule. A bright light and a hiss showing he welded two tiny pieces together. Greco wore dark goggles and delicately used a slender fuser rod.

"Is the Shand withholding a critical process from us?" Tanner wondered.

The hissing and bright light quit. Greco looked up. "Boss, I have to concentrate or I'm never going to get this done in time."

"Sure," Tanner said.

The centurion left Greco, floated past the junction to the Varus's corridor and considered knocking on Lacy's hatch. She was still staying in her cabin. Was she really Acton's niece, another alien or was she human and controlled in some manner like the Lithians? What if Acton was a cyborg in disguise? That would be a neat turnaround, them helping their enemy wake up the rest of his people. How did they really know Acton was a Shand and not something more sinister?

Tanner finally went to his room. He made a list of the things he wanted from the hideaway. They were going to travel a long way to reach the rim. He still didn't like the idea of hibernating for most of the voyage there in hyperspace. Maybe Acton had a plan to wake up and fiddle with the raider while the rest of them slept.

Tanner stared at his list. He was remembering Maximus's death. He imagined the Special Intelligence people would have gladly had Maximus live. All the consul had to do was spill his guts about everything. Sure, Social Unity theory produced an awful system of mind control with a world police state. In the end, though, the Coalition would fall as every human institution eventually did. Having the Coalition win didn't mean the end of humanity. If the cyborgs won, though…

Had Maximus made the right decision killing himself to keep the plan secret?

Tanner snorted. When Maximus had made his decision, had he been in full control of his own mind?

The centurion shook his head. There was too much about the enterprise he didn't know or understand. If this was so terribly critical to human life, why stake everything on a small *Gladius*-class raider? That didn't ring right.

Tanner picked up his list, staring at the words but seeing Acton's emotionless features in his mind's eye. Could the Shand have mind-controlled Marcus and Ursa Varus? It sure seemed like a possibility.

Tanner slapped the list onto the table. This was insane. He was just a centurion from a small planet.

Maximus had asked him once if he'd gone to the Academy or had any advanced degrees. Tanner smirked. Him go to school? Right! He was the street kid with too much curiosity, with too much bone in his skull so he slammed his head into wall after wall. He'd lived by his wits or fists for a long time. He wasn't a deep thinker like Acton or an airy-fairy intellectual like Greco.

You're it, Tanner. If you screw up, it might be good night for humanity.

He frowned. Did that sound right? Could the stakes be that astronomical? It seemed farfetched.

He drummed his fingers on the table. Who was Ursa Varus? Did she work for Remus Intelligence? Was her tall tale a cover story for what was really going on—whatever that happened to be?

Yeah, Acton's speech and behavior made him seem like a freak. Did that necessarily mean he was an alien though?

Throughout humanity's spread across the galaxy, Tanner never remembered hearing about real aliens. Humans made their own aliens like the cyborgs or small human colonies were cut off for thousands of years. During that time, the people changed enough with genetic drift to become…well, like the apemen of Avernus. But true-to-life nonhuman aliens, no sir, Tanner had never heard of those before this.

"That doesn't mean aliens can't be real," Tanner told himself.

He stood up. He examined the list of goodies on the table. Then, he headed for the exit. It was time for a showdown with Lord high and mighty Acton.

The one thing I'm going to do is play this game for keeps. If everything depends on me, then, by the Lord's grace, I'm going to give it my all.

∗∗∗

Tanner found Acton in the rec room.

The sound of billiard balls clacking had stopped the centurion in the hall. The *Dark Star* did not have artificial gravity nor did the raider accelerate to produce pseudo-gravity. How then could anyone be playing billiards?

Tanner found Lord Acton floating around the green-cloth table, lining up a shot as he floated. Acton struck the cue ball. It rolled across the table and hit the five ball. The five rolled into a pocket, sinking out of sight.

Acton should have floated back just a little. He did not. He remained in his horizontal shooting position.

"How are you doing any of that?" Tanner asked.

Acton glanced at him. "Captain, your curiosity is showing. You positively wear it on your sleeve I believe is the correct idiom."

"No one likes a smart-aleck, Your Highness."

Acton cocked his head. "Ah. You are indulging in your personal witticisms."

Tanner shook his head. "Look. Maybe you're trying to get me angry." He shook his head again. "How are you getting the balls to stay on the table? Did you magnetize them or something?"

"That is correct."

Tanner pushed toward the table.

"Careful, Captain," Acton said. "I urge you to avoid floating *over* the table."

Tanner reached out, catching himself on the edge of the pool table. "Are you telling me you have localized gravity control?"

"I did not tell you, but you have guessed it."

Holding onto the pool table, Tanner pushed himself to the floor. He saw a low, bulky object under the table that normally didn't belong there.

"It's humming," Tanner said.

"Once it ceases to hum, the game ends."

Tanner straightened himself vertically to regard Acton. "You should have set this up sooner. Greco and I love to play. It helps pass the time."

"You distress me, Captain."

"Are you trying to make a joke?"

Acton regarded him.

"You're saying it distresses you because that makes you just a little bit like us," Tanner said.

"How remarkable," Acton said. "Your mind is more agile than one is at first led to believe by your mannerisms."

Tanner figured it was time to cut the dilly-dallying. "You're not human, are you?" he asked.

Acton stared at him.

"You're not a bad mimic, though. I'll give you that. One piece of advice: don't tell people they have simian curiosity or call the Lithians beasts. That's kind of a dead giveaway you're not human."

Acton shifted his horizontal position, lining up another shot on the table.

"Is it hard for you to spend time with humans?"

"Your objective is obvious but futile, this trying to needle me," Acton said. "I do not react in the ways you expect. If I become truly tired of you…I will not make snappy phrases in reply but react with deadly intent against you."

"Maybe we can work together after all, as that's how I respond, too. You're just like me, Acton."

The Shand gave Tanner a dead-eyed stare.

How did I ever think he could be human? He wears his face like a mask. Another chilling thought struck Tanner. Maybe the greasy hand before was a natural alien process. He'd thought Acton had pre-slimed his hand with mind-grease. Maybe the slime automatically oozed from Acton's pores like a bug squirting a defensive spray.

"Is there a secondary reason for your presence here?" Acton asked.

"Yeah. I have a question. Is Lacy human or one of you?"

"Lacy is no concern of yours."

"If she's human with a control unit in her brain like you've put in the Lithians—"

"Captain, perhaps it is time for some ground rules between us. I have need of your vessel and a limited use of your expertise. That expertise is not vital, however. In case you have missed my meaning—"

"I get it. You're threatening me."

"Merely because that seems to be the kind of behavior you desire. The Lithians and Lacy are outside your…your need of concern. They belong to me. Hmm. Perhaps you can understand it better this way. They are my property."

"You're saying they're your slaves?" Tanner asked.

"I spoke in Remus terminology for your benefit. You were capitalists, I believe, with a profound concern for private property. Consider Lacy and the Lithians as my private property."

"We call that slavery, which I abhor."

"While I abhor useless chatter," Acton said. "Yet, sometimes, for the sake of the greater good, I allow myself to enter the maelstrom of idle talk."

"Is Lacy human?" Tanner asked again.

It hardly seemed possible, but Acton's features grew stiffer. He set the cue stick onto the table. It lay there as if in the grip of gravity. With a slight push, Acton straightened his body vertically.

"Your hectoring has become tedious," Acton announced.

"Why can't you answer the question? It could solve—"

A klaxon began to blare. Both Tanner and Acton turned toward the noise. A click sounded over the rec room comm.

"Tanner," Greco said over the comm. "I need you in the control room. You'd better hurry, boss."

"Saved by the bell," Tanner muttered under his breath. As he propelled himself down the corridor, he wondered which one of them the alarm had saved.

-24-

"What's the problem?" Tanner asked, as he slid into his seat from above. He buckled in as Greco pointed at the flight screen.

Tanner looked up at Greco. "We're half a minute from coming out of hyperspace."

"Yes."

"That can't be right."

"Not according to our previous calculations," Greco said.

"What happened differently?"

"You already know the answer, boss. We entered hyperspace at speeds greater than anyone has knowingly tried before."

Tanner absorbed the information in silence. "Are you suggesting our greater speed has propelled us faster through hyperspace? I thought it didn't matter how fast one went into hyperspace."

"What other hypotheses do you have?" Greco asked.

"None."

"I only have one other theory," Greco told him.

"Let's hear it."

"It's too late. Get ready, boss, as I didn't have time to get everything right yet for reentry into normal space."

Tanner understood the problem. They'd had a tough time coming into hyperspace and would therefore likely have a tough time coming out. Greco had been working to change

165

that. Their sooner than expected reentry had thrown off the apeman's timetable.

Tanner swore softly under his breath. With a flick of a switch, he opened ship's channels. "Sorry for being so abrupt, but we're about to come out of hyperspace. This could get dicey. So get ready, captain out."

The moment he shut off the intra-ship comm, *Dark Star* began shaking horribly and making the same metallic groaning noises as before.

Tanner hung on. This was crazy. He'd never heard of anyone having trouble entering and leaving hyperspace. Could there be speed settings to entering the strange realm? Maybe no one had entered hyperspace as fast as the raider had.

For the next minute, Greco played with the controls, tapping, waiting and tapping more. By degrees, he lessened the rattling and hull stresses. Finally, it stopped altogether.

"We made it," Tanner said.

"We're out of hyperspace. That's true. Did we make it to the Petrus System, though?"

"Right," Tanner said. He began studying the constellations, matching them on the computer. Finally, he focused on the nearest star.

"G-class star dead ahead," Tanner said. "There's only one gas giant in the outer system. I see two inner planets and one vast asteroid field." He grinned at Greco. "We did it. We're here, just outside the Petrus System."

"Do you realize what this means?" Greco asked.

"That we can start on the next phase of his crazy mission," Tanner said.

"No, well yes," Greco said. "This is a new discovery."

"What do you mean?"

"We've found a way to travel faster through hyperspace. No one thought that was possible."

"No humans did. It would appear the Shands have known for some time."

Greco grew thoughtful. "I wonder what else Acton can do that we think is impossible."

Tanner told the apeman about the pool table and localized gravity control. He'd already spoken with Greco about the talk

166

with Ursa. The centurion then told him about the exchange of threats between Acton and him.

"I don't know, boss. I don't think I'd screw around with the Shand like you do with most people. For one thing, he's not people. Acton is something different with different responses. Usually, you know when to back down. You probably won't recognize the danger signs with Acton. I think you should stay away from him for now."

Tanner didn't respond. This was his ship. He didn't like the idea of having to stay away from anyone on his ship.

"Maybe Acton had better keep out of *my* way," Tanner said.

"Can you do impossible things, boss?"

Tanner grinned. "Did you ever see me fly across the ground and take out a crap-load of Coalition space marines?"

Greco studied him. "I did, and I thought you should have been wearing a cape at the time. Okay. Maybe Lord Acton should stay out of your way."

"Damn straight," Tanner said.

Greco glanced at the flight screen. "So how should we do this, boss? Are we going in at this velocity or should we slow it down some so our burn isn't as massive at the end?"

"Good question," Tanner said. He considered the various factors. "Let's slow down a little first, and then a little more once we're in the system. They'll be watching us soon enough. We don't want them to think we entered hyperspace faster than ordinary. That will make them suspicious."

"If I remember last time right, everything makes these Petrus people suspicious."

"Yeah," Tanner said. "But I guess they have a good reason to be." He opened intra-ship channels to begin explaining the situation to the others.

***

They decelerated hard for a time and then decelerated at half that speed later.

"We're running dangerously short of fuel," Tanner noticed.

"Petrus System is expensive, boss. If we have to purchase fuel here, too—"

"It would be good to know what we have for currency," Tanner said, interrupting. "I'm going add that to my list of things to know."

Dark Star continued the process of coasting toward the inner asteroid belt. The Petrus System was closer to the rim than any of the other star systems they'd been to so far. All sorts of vagabonds, romantics, crime lords, drug dealers, chop shop artists—pirates in space terms—and other nefarious people gravitated to the Petrus Hideaway. One of its chief defenses was its distance from the habitable systems. The other was the asteroid field, with its unusual density. The reason why the various rocks were so close to each other was that they used to all belong to one giant planet. Before man had ever ventured into space, a disaster or a disastrous war had taken place out here. No one knew what had happened. Could Acton know the reason for the destroyed planet?

Tanner asked Ursa about that, bumping into her in the galley.

Lupus waited nearby, his gaze glued to Tanner.

"No hard feelings, hey fellow," Tanner said to the underman.

The hand gripping the belted baton whitened.

"Please, Centurion," Ursa said, "don't harass my guard."

"It's a reflex, I guess," Tanner said. "If you grew up where I did…you know what I'm saying."

"I suppose so," she said, sitting down with a tray of food. They were under one G declaration at the moment.

Tanner grabbed a cup of chili, raising his eyebrows as he stood at the table waiting.

"Please, join me," Ursa said. Lupus had positioned himself behind her.

Tanner sat down and soon stirred his chili. It needed extra spice, but he didn't feel like getting up to get it. As they ate, Tanner asked her about Acton knowing the reason for the dense Petrus asteroid belt.

"That's an interesting thought," Ursa said. "I don't know the answer. I wouldn't ask Acton, though. He's become more reclusive lately. Have you noticed?"

"Maybe I have."

She gave him a closer study. "Tell me what happened between you two."

Tanner figured this was more of a request than an order, so he told her about the rec-room incident.

Ursa shook her head afterward. "You have a destructive streak, needling a Shand like that."

Tanner shrugged.

"You have to watch yourself with Acton. Please, no more needling."

"What if he's a cyborg?" Tanner asked suddenly

"What? No. He's not."

"How do you know he's not?"

"Because he's a Shand," Ursa said, smiling. "That explains his more-than-human strength and his strange manners."

"Being a cyborg would explain that too," Tanner said.

"You're right, of course, but I happen to know he's an alien."

"And Lacy," he said, "what is she?"

"Lacy is whatever Acton is," Ursa said. "Why, do you find Lacy attractive?"

"You know," Tanner said, as if thinking about it for the first time, "I do."

Ursa stiffened the slightest bit and pushed her food away. "I believe I'm done." She made to get up.

"Wait a minute," Tanner said, reaching for a hand.

Lupus reacted without any sound. At the last second, Tanner saw something out of the corner of his eye. He threw himself backward. Thus, the swinging baton only struck him a glancing blow instead of a killing blow to the skull. The baton-knock sent Tanner tumbling sideways off the chair onto the floor.

"Lupus, no!" Ursa shouted.

The underman wasn't listening this time. Lupus leaped onto the table and jumped at Tanner. The centurion rolled as the booted feet hit the floor. The baton hissed in a downward stroke. Tanner tried to dodge. The baton struck his shoulder, numbing that arm.

"Lupus!" Ursa screamed. "Back! Go back! Stop this at once."

With a roar, Lupus kicked Tanner in the stomach. It made the centurion groan in pain. The underman snarled, raising the baton for another head strike.

Sensing the immediacy of death, Tanner groped for his gun only to find that he wasn't wearing it today. Instead, his fingers curled around the hilt of his monofilament knife. The blade came free with a jerk. Tanner slashed as the underman swung down. The monofilament blade struck first, slicing through Lupus's left ankle as if it didn't exist. Then the baton struck, although it had lost most of its power. The knock dazed Tanner just the same, making it hard for him to see.

Both men shouted and raved as Lupus fell onto Tanner. The centurion tried to surge up, but the weight of the underman slammed him back down. Tanner thought Lupus was trying to grab the knife. As Ursa screamed at her protector to stop, Tanner hacked with a will, gutting the underman as he opened the praetorian up. He killed Lupus and drenched himself in blood doing it.

Ursa stopped screaming. Painfully, with his eyes struggling to focus, Tanner managed to climb to his feet. His bloody hand gripped the monofilament knife with all his strength. It was a killing weapon par excellence. He dared not let anyone else get a hold of it.

The centurion saw the bloody underman on the floor. He could see that Lupus was dead. The praetorian's blood soaked his clothes. Tanner stepped back, careful not to slip in it. Finally, he looked at Ursa.

She stared at him in horror. "You killed my Lupus," she said.

Tanner opened his mouth to tell her the underman had tried to kill him first.

"He's protected me all my life," she whispered.

The words he wanted to say wouldn't leave Tanner's mouth.

"You're a monster," she said.

"What…" He wanted to ask her what else he was supposed to have done. The underman had come at him. Maybe he should have apologized to the praetorian earlier.

Ursa Varus was shaking, with tears dripping from her eyes. "Don't ever speak to me again," she told him. Then, she turned away, staggering down the corridor weeping.

-25-

Marcus Varus solemnly spoke to Tanner in the circular area just before the bridge.

Greco and Tanner had already cleaned up the mess in the galley, putting the hacked-up body into a plastic body bag, zipping it shut. Neither man had said much then.

"The Lady Varus is angry," Marcus said in a low voice. The big heir wouldn't meet Tanner's eyes, but there was no sense of fear in the avoidance, just barely suppressed rage.

Tanner didn't know how to handle this situation. He hadn't intended to kill the guardian, but the underman had come at him hard. What else could he have done?

"This…this will make the mission more difficult," Marcus said. "The pair…has been with us for a long time. I can't tell if Vulpus knows who killed his brother. If he finds out it's you…"

"Keep him far away from me," Tanner said.

Marcus breathed a little faster as color tinged his cheeks.

"Lupus attacked me," Tanner said.

"You…needle people, Centurion. I…" Marcus's lips closed, pressing together.

Tanner wondered if saying he was sorry would help. He doubted it. No one ever believed that. What had happened had happened. He couldn't take it back. How would a few useless words help change things? They couldn't. Brother and sister were determined to hate him. That was fine with him. He knew

172

how to deal with hatred. He had been doing that for a long time already.

"I am not going to hold you to blame," Marcus said.

Heat built up in Tanner. Did Marcus realize the guard had just come at him? Was he supposed to let himself die so a patrician didn't lose her murderous guardian? Who did these people think they were? They should be grateful he wasn't charging them, or stranding them in the Petrus Hideaway.

Then it struck Tanner. The patricians would double-cross him because of this. *Maybe it's deeper than that. Maybe Acton set this all up.*

The realization of the possibility shocked Tanner. Could the Shand have done that with his ability to control minds?

"Wait a minute, Lord," Tanner said. "I just thought of something."

Marcus shifted his gaze enough to glance quickly at the centurion before looking away again. "Yes?"

Tanner explained his thought about Acton.

"Are you trying to evade reasonability for killing my guard?" Marcus demanded.

Tanner turned away, mentally counting to five. He had to control his anger. He had to reason with the heir. Working to keep his voice neutral, Tanner faced Marcus.

"I killed Lupus while defending myself from his attack. I had no malice against your underman."

"Go on," Marcus said in a tight voice.

"I had a run-in with Acton earlier. I might have made him angry."

"You appear to have a knack for that."

Tanner let that go. He had to. "We're getting closer to the big prize. Maybe Acton doesn't like me knowing so much. Maybe he has more to hide than we think. Maybe I just pissed the hell out of him in the rec room. He wanted to strike back but not in a way that might jeopardize the mission. Okay. So what does he do? Maybe he has listening bugs all over the ship. He knew how…how I needled Lupus before. So Acton decided to use that against me. I tell you, Lord, there was no reason for Lupus to come at me the way he did."

"You were trying to grab my sister's hand. He saw that and reacted as trained. I don't think you realize just how responsible you are for all this."

Tanner scowled. "I thought you said earlier—"

"Centurion!" Marcus nearly shouted.

Tanner stiffened, getting angrier.

Marcus swallowed twice and nodded slowly. "I did not mean to shout at you just now," he said. "I am...troubled by these events. I am angry. I don't think you can imagine how much. Now, this blame-shifting on your part—"

"I'm using my head," Tanner said. "I'm not letting emotion cloud my judgment."

"And I am?" Marcus asked in an ugly voice.

Tanner almost replied, "Yes, you jackass. That's exactly what you're doing." He hesitated, and in hesitating, he decided not to answer the question.

Tanner found himself breathing heavily. Could he be right about Acton, or was this one of those stupid problems that crops up at the worst times with people? Could he really have been at fault with Lupus?

"I respect your anger, Lord," Tanner forced himself to say. "I have shed the blood of one of your people. I understand if you resent, even hate me."

Marcus was staring at him now.

"I...I..." Tanner found that his lips were dry. His heart pounded.

"You what?" Marcus said.

Tanner rubbed his eyes. Why was this so hard? It hadn't been his fault. The underman had attacked him. Why couldn't these damned patricians keep their guards under control?

The centurion balled his hands into fists. "Look," he said, hoarsely. "Killing Lupus wasn't my intent."

"You've already said that."

"Yeah. I have. Now, I'm saying it again. I did not want to kill him."

Marcus frowned, and the stare had changed. It seemed as if understanding dwelled in the heir's eyes. "Are you trying to say you're sorry for killing my man?"

Tanner couldn't get the words out. They simply would not come. His nostrils flared. He warred with himself. Finally, with the barest of motions, he gave the barest of nods.

"I see," Marcus said. "Yes. I think I'm beginning to understand. I don't know if this will help with my sister...but I—"

Marcus Varus held out his beefy, strong hand to Tanner.

Tanner examined it to see if he could spot any alien grease on the palm. It didn't seem like there was any. He gripped the heir's hand in return.

"We won't talk about this again, Centurion."

"Yes, Lord," Tanner said.

"We had a terrible misunderstanding," Marcus said. "It's over now, behind us. We have to work together if we're going to free Remus."

"Yes, Lord."

Maybe Marcus would have said more. Before he could, the red alert began to blare.

-26-

Tanner reached the control room, sliding into his seat.

Greco tapped controls before turning to him. "I think we should stop our deceleration, boss, and head in-system at our present velocity."

The centurion saw the sensor board. A vessel using a hard fusion burn had barely left the extensive asteroid belt. While the spaceship was a long way from them, it was on an intercept course with them at its present heading.

"First," Tanner said. "What is that, a giant missile?"

"It's worse, boss. That's a destroyer-class vessel."

Tanner studied the sensor readings. "That's a Coalition destroyer."

Greco nodded.

"Has it been waiting out here for us?" Tanner asked.

"I'd give that a high probability."

"Maybe it's a coincidence," Tanner said.

"Why is it accelerating for us then?"

"Because it can read our dimensions as easily as we can read theirs," Tanner said. "They have to know this is a Remus raider. They've laid traps for us all over the place in the past."

"Yes," the apeman said. "That could be right. Or they could know the plan."

"You mean...Maximus's death was a fake?"

"We have to accept it as a possibility," Greco said. "Maximus might have told them everything, and they programmed him to kill himself in order to fool us as to what they know."

Tanner tapped a keypad, running numbers. "The destroyer will still reach us under those conditions, or reach close enough to use their particle beams on us."

Coalition destroyers didn't have lasers because the ship class wasn't large enough to make them effective. The destroyer had three times the raider's mass and many more personnel aboard.

Greco nodded.

"The destroyer must have been watching hyperspace territory closely to have spotted us this soon," Tanner said.

"That is one possibility."

"There's another?"

"Maybe the manner of our dropping into normal space gave a larger signature than ordinary," Greco said. "Maybe anyone would have spotted us because we entered normal space like a flashing beacon."

"Yeah. That could be right."

"You must speak to Lord Acton," Greco said. "He might have more…more surprises in those boxes."

"Yeah," Tanner said, recalling the interrupted talk with Marcus Varus. He stood and opened a small compartment, removing a pair of leather gloves, shoving his fingers into them. He buckled on his gun belt next. As he turned to go, Greco spoke up:

"What about our deceleration? I think getting to the belt faster might be better. If we survive the first pass with the destroyer, we can run into the belt and hide as we repair the damage."

Tanner considered that, finally saying, "Drop the deceleration to point five Gs. We're simply traveling too fast. If we save too much of our deceleration for the end, we risk entering the asteroid belt at high velocity. There's too much dust in the belt for us to do that and survive."

Greco nodded again, beginning to manipulate the flight panel.

***

Tanner didn't have to ring the buzzer to Acton's quarters. The Shand waited for him in a junction. It told Tanner what he'd already suspected: the alien monitored at least some of their conversations. Probably all the conversations on the bridge had been recorded.

"The ship is in danger," Acton said.

Tanner took a wide stance, keeping his hands on his belt instead of one of them on the gun-butt. "The destroyer outclasses my raider. If you'll remember, the Calisto Grandee people stole my torpedoes—not that I'd want to trade torpedo shots with the destroyer. Having the torpedoes would have given us more options, though."

"Your vessel cannot outmaneuver the destroyer?"

"Maybe if we could slip into the asteroid belt ahead of them I could," Tanner said. "But not out here in the open. They're heading for us. We could veer sharply away from them and run back to hyperspace territory. We could jump somewhere else and jump back here later, slipping into the Petrus System at that time."

"No. Our window of opportunity at Planet Zero is too small for that."

"I didn't think you'd like the idea," Tanner said. "Do you happen to know if the Coalition knows our plan?"

"How would I have gained this information?"

Tanner shrugged.

"You must not think I possess fantastical powers," Acton said. "I am merely wiser and more intelligent than you are. I am not truly magical as some simple people believe."

Tanner gripped his belt tighter. It was time to control his tongue, not give it free reign. "Do you have some torpedoes perhaps in your boxes?"

Acton shook his head.

"I'm going to need something extra against the destroyer," Tanner said.

"You must use your innate cunning. In order to stifle your curiosity, I will tell you that the majority of my boxes contain triton."

Tanner's eyebrows lifted. Triton was worth far more than gold or even platinum. "If most of those boxes hold triton, are you thinking about purchasing the entire hideaway?"

Acton said nothing.

Tanner hesitated, finally blurting, "What about gravity control? I saw that device under the pool table. If you had something bigger, we might be able to boost our velocity, outrun the destroyer along the curvature of the asteroid belt and then slip in when we're beyond their line-of-sight."

"I do not possess such an artifact," Acton said.

"Right. Thanks anyway, Lord." Tanner decided to bide his time for once. This wasn't over between them, not by a long shot. He headed down the corridor. Maybe Marcus had an idea.

***

Tanner explained the situation to Marcus. The heir put his hands behind his back, hunching his thick shoulders.

"I'll be honest," Marcus said. "I'm the fighter between us. My sister is the thinker. We have to talk to her about this."

"I don't think she wants to talk to me," Tanner said.

"Leave that to me. I'll convince her. Where should we meet?"

"Let's meet in the rec room," Tanner suggested, deciding to spare Ursa from the bad memories of the galley.

"Give me…twenty minutes," Marcus said.

"Sure. I'll be waiting."

***

It took one hour and twenty minutes. Tanner finally racked the pool table and knocked down all the balls nine times before he put everything away.

When Varus finally showed up, it was just Marcus. The big man said, "You're right, Centurion. She's not ready to speak with you yet."

Tanner crossed his arms, nodding after a moment. "Well—"

"She did have an idea, though," Marcus said.

"Yeah? What's that?"

"It involves the Petrus Hideaway."

"Okay," Tanner said hesitantly.

179

Marcus told him the idea.

Tanner looked disappointed. The idea sounded complicated and hard to do right, but he didn't see that they had many more options.

"I'll give it a try, Lord. But I'm not making any promises."

"I only ask that you give it your all," Marcus said.

***

It took some time to get everything ready, which included having Lord Acton loan him several triton bars. Surprisingly, that was the easy part.

"Do you think you can hit the communication satellite at this distance?" Tanner asked the apeman.

"At this range," Greco said, "it will be touch and go. It's a possibility we'll lose the connection at the worst moment."

"Can you do it or not?" Tanner asked.

"Let's find out."

For the next two hours, Greco manipulated his board and ran computer programs. Finally, the apeman said he was ready.

"About time," Tanner muttered.

"Firing the transmission link," Greco said.

An invisible laser speared from the *Dark Star* at a comm-satellite just outside the inner system asteroid belt. That was many billions of kilometers away. The laser-link wouldn't speed up the communication. The voices would still travel at the speed of light. That meant hours of separation between each location. That made dickering difficult but not impossible. Plus, using a laser-link made for a tight message, audible only to those linked to the satellite, so it couldn't be heard by the destroyer's comms.

As Tanner and Greco waited for the laser-link to hit the satellite and send their message, the centurion explained some of the plan's reasoning to the apeman.

"Ursa doesn't think the destroyer went all the way to the hideaway. Likely, it's been prowling on the outskirts of the asteroid belt. Since it's a warship, the pirates in the hideaway might have decided to leave it alone. Maybe they think the destroyer is a precursor to a major assault and are gauging its actions."

"I understand the reasoning," Greco said. "Yet that seems like a dangerous game for the destroyer."

"No one said Coalition people lack courage. It's partly what makes them so bad. If they were cowards, they never would have attacked Remus or Avernus."

The hours passed while they waited. Finally, the laser reached the satellite. It would take just as long to see if the laser had been on target and if the pirates would reply.

In any case, Tanner made his pitch. He showed the triton bars on the screen. He ran an analysis on them, showing the hideaway people these really were what he claimed them to be. Afterward, Tanner waited.

Greco left to get some shuteye.

Tanner remained at his post. Many hours later, with his eyes droopy, a signal lit the comm board. He snapped up and slapped the switch, opening the comm.

An unsavory individual with tattoos on his cheeks, a ring in his nose and long stringy hair stared out of the comm screen. His glassy eyes made him seem high.

"You have triton, beautiful triton," the man said. "Yes, I think you are showing me real triton. Therefore, I agree. We will do it. But it is up to you to reach the location. You don't have to send a return signal. I will know by your raider's actions. It should be interesting. And if you fail...I can send my scavengers out to your destroyed craft later to grab the triton. But I like your style, bounty hunter."

Tanner's stomach twisted. They knew he was a bounty hunter. That was bad. They hated bounty hunters at the Petrus Hideaway. Yet, he could deal with that when the time came—if it did. First, he had to get past the destroyer. He was surprised the Coalition people hadn't tried to hail him yet.

Tanner turned off the comm. He sat up, flexing his hands. It was time to begin, as this was going to be very hard to do right. Could they pull it off? Would the pirates really act at the right moment to help them? The only way to find out was to do it, so here he went.

-27-

Now began a long hard chase between the Coalition destroyer and the old Remus raider. It included most of the Petrus System, as the *Dark Star* started just outside the star system while the destroyer began in the inner system.

The asteroid belt was stationed in its star system in a similar place as between Earth's old orbital path and that of Mars in the Solar System, while Tanner had started at something just beyond Neptune's old orbital path around the Sun. The chase involved long distances, billions of kilometers, and it involved hard acceleration instead of deceleration aboard the *Gladius*-class ship as they increased velocity.

"We're going to be running on fumes by the time this is over," Greco told Tanner.

The centurion had gone into combat mode. His talkativeness had disappeared. He spoke in a monotone now as he concentrated on the situation.

A combat run this long, however, meant hours and hours of watching and waiting. The hours turned into half a day. The *Dark Star* didn't only accelerate. They stopped, accelerated again, stopped more and coasted for long periods before accelerating further.

The destroyer followed suit. It had longer legs, meaning it had greater powers of acceleration. The *Dark Star* had an advantage, however, as it had entered the Petrus System at much greater velocity than the destroyer traveled.

The raider curved away from the destroyer. The destroyer took that heading, making a new intercept point. The *Dark Star* kept this up for a day. Then, it decelerated hard as the raider made a shallow turn in the other direction, heading for the lone gas giant in the system.

"Will they figure out our plan in time?" Greco said.

"If they try to hail us, we'll know," Tanner said.

Greco drummed his fingers on a panel, playing a beat for enjoyment. "Why haven't they launched a missile at us yet?"

"That's easy. They want to capture not kill us."

"They're not going to capture us if we pass near each other at high velocity."

"I know," Tanner said. "But it will give them point blank range to knock out our engine. Then, whatever our velocity and heading, they can match it because we'll no longer be able to change it."

"Elementary space tactics," Greco said.

Two hours later, Tanner told everyone on the ship to lie down. They were going to decelerate at the ship's maximum. Once everyone checked in, including Acton telling Tanner the Lithians were down, the centurion engaged the hardest thrust of the trip.

The small raider shifted at a tighter angle, straining to reach the gas giant. Maybe the destroyer understood their plan. The Coalition people turned the destroyer one hundred and eighty degrees so its exhaust aimed in the direction it traveled. Then, the destroyer thrust as hard as it could at five gravities, braking their velocity.

In time, the *Dark Star* reached the gas giant's gravitational pull. At a tightening curve, the raider headed deeper into the gravity well, meaning the ship headed toward the giant planet. Tanner began to use the gas giant as a running man would use a pole in his path. By grabbing the pole, a man running fast could violently change his direction without tripping and falling. The raider used a similar tactic, using the planet's heavy gravity. The small Remus ship wouldn't circle the gas giant completely, but Tanner used the gravity to violently change their heading. They no longer headed to the left portion of the asteroid belt, left in relation to the system's star. Now, they went toward the right side of the asteroid belt. The destroyer would have to stop its leftward velocity completely. Once it did that, then it would have to accelerate again, this time heading for the asteroid belt's right.

Finally, after the shaking quit, the raider moved away from the gas giant, quickly escaping its gravitational pull.

Greco ran the new numbers. "We could do this, boss."

"Yep," Tanner said.

Five hours passed. Finally, the destroyer commander attempted to communicate with them.

"Do we talk?" Greco asked.

"I think we'd better." Tanner opened channels with the Coalition destroyer. The distance had closed considerably since they'd first seen each other. It made communication possible because now there was only a short time delay between them.

A bald woman appeared on the screen. She wore the blue Coalition uniform with the star and comet patch on her collar. She was pretty in a hard way, with thick kissable lips.

"You must decelerate and match heading with us," she said.

Tanner glanced at Greco before he said, "I decline your invitation, Sub-superior. I suggest we end on a peaceful note. Why should we fight, you and I? It will only damage your ship, as we shall never surrender."

A few seconds later, the sub-superior smiled. "You are a braggart. Your profile already shows that, but it is good to know our intelligence people pegged you correctly. You must surrender according to the terms of the Remus peace accords."

"Yeah, well, I don't hold to those," Tanner replied.

Once more, the transmission took time as the light-speed message took the time to cross the distance between them. She nodded afterward. "So be it, Centurion. You have decided your fate. I will not allow you to reach the hideaway. Long before that, you and your rebels will cease to exist."

"If you launch torpedoes at me, Sub-superior, I will launch all our torpedoes at you."

"You lack torpedoes. Thus, your threat is meaningless."

Tanner squinted at her. How could the destroyer commander know that? It would indicate the Coalition plan had been formed some time ago. Could Coalition people have put the fake Calisto Grandee client on the luxury habitat? Had that been bait for a trap?

"I will meet with you, Sub-superior," Tanner said. "But I will do so on neutral territory, in the hideaway."

The sub-superior laughed. "I decline your wretched offer. We both know the pirates hate Coalition people. No, I shall destroy your craft and end this farce unless you surrender at once."

"I already told you my answer."

"So be it," the sub-superior said. "If you change your mind, you'll know where to reach me."

She cut the connection.

Tanner sat back. "Maybe it's just a bluff," he told Greco. "Until they actually launch a torpedo—"

"Boss," Greco said. "Look." The apeman pointed at the sensor screen.

On it, a missile began to separate from the destroyer image. The sub-superior had launched a torpedo.

"It's not a bluff, boss. They're playing for keeps."

"Okay," Tanner said. "It looks like we're going to have to do this the hard way."

***

Tanner declined Greco's idea about going to Acton for another decoy. This time, the raider was decelerating too hard for a decoy to simulate.

"We'll use our particle beam," Tanner said.

"You think we can hit a torpedo far enough away from the raider to make a difference?"

"Do you have a better idea?" Tanner asked.

The apeman shook his head.

"That's too bad," Tanner said. "I was hoping you did, you being a genius and all."

Later, the torpedo leaped into high acceleration, reaching forty-eight gravities.

The raider had the advantage over the destroyer now, even though the destroyer still had much less distance to travel. Given its initial speed and with the pivot around the gas giant, the *Dark Star* had zipped like a stone from a slingshot toward the far right end of the asteroid belt. The raider moved fast in comparison to the destroyer. The smaller ship would reach its destination point near the asteroid belt far ahead of the destroyer, too far for the Coalition vessel's particle beams to reach the raider accurately.

The farther a target was from a beam's launch point, the easier it became to jink out of the beam's path. Distance shots took fantastic targeting anyway, so the slightest deviations upset the precise calculations. It was one of the reasons missiles were critical in space combat and why most of the damage took place at very short ranges—short in terms of stellar distances.

Tanner's idea was to race around the asteroid belt far ahead of the destroyer, slow down while circling the outer edge and finally zip into the protective dust and rocks of the belt.

The torpedo changed all that.

Finally, after many dreary hours of watching the torpedo close the distance, it reached the raider's outer, particle beam range.

The *Dark Star* turned to face the torpedo. Greco adjusted the emitter, recalibrated and sighted the torpedo once more.

"Has the computer figured out the torpedo's jinking code yet?" Tanner asked.

"No," Greco said.

"That's too bad," Tanner said. "Okay. We have a few minutes to destroy this thing. Then, it enters its detonation range."

Torpedoes, drones and missiles seldom struck their targets, but exploded their nuclear warheads in close proximity. The heat and X-rays did most of the damage, while EMP knocked down any electrical systems.

The raider's fusion engine thrummed. The accelerator sounded as it cycled the particles and Tanner tapped a control. Charged electrons shot out of the emitter near the speed of light.

"Miss," Greco said a moment later. "The torpedo must have shifted its position just enough."

The torpedo no longer accelerated, but coasted at the raider at high velocity. It had side jets and jinked at random intervals.

"Let's try again," Tanner said.

Once more, the process repeated.

"Another miss," Greco said as he stared at a targeting scope.

Tanner tapped the comm. The light had been blinking. As expected, the sub-superior appeared on the screen.

Her bald forehead was shiny with sweat. She was nervous, it would seem.

"You have two minutes to surrender," she said. "If you fail to surrender, the torpedo will detonate. I assure you, your ship will not survive the explosion."

"We possess priceless knowledge," Tanner told her. "That knowledge will die if we die."

"While this may be true," she said, "it is immaterial, as I have my orders."

"I can offer you triton," Tanner said.

The sub-superior laughed coldly. "Why do I need triton? I am a Coalition officer, bound to my command by an oath of office. Mere wealth cannot tempt me."

"Still," Tanner said. "Triton can buy a load of luxuries. Have you enjoyed life to the fullest, Sub-superior? Has your bridge crew? Maybe they'd like triton. All they have to do is shoot you and take over the ship."

Her eyes seemed to shine. "How dare you attempt to bribe me and my loyal crew? It shows a lack of morals in you, a serious lack of character."

"Another miss," Greco whispered. "The torpedo is like a slippery tom-eel."

"Think about this carefully, Sub-superior," Tanner said. "I have enough triton to buy off your entire crew. If my ship is destroyed, you will lose it all."

Greco glanced at him. "She's a fanatic," the apeman whispered. "She's not going to budge."

"I know," Tanner whispered back out of the corner of his mouth. "I'm not talking to her."

Greco checked the comm link. "But you are, boss. Look." The apeman pointed at the link feed.

"I know that," Tanner whispered to Greco.

"Do you think her crew will try for her?" the apeman whispered.

"I doubt it."

"Then who are you talking to?" Greco whispered a little louder than before.

"It will be a pleasure watching you die," the sub-superior said. "You think that proud socialists such as us will succumb to your base tactic of—"

At that point, a laser beamed from one of the larger outer asteroids. The laser beam struck the torpedo, destroying it in milliseconds.

Greco blinked in astonishment. "What just happened, boss?"

Tanner clicked off the connection with the sub-superior. Let her beg to talk to him if she wanted to now.

"The comm light is blinking," Greco said.

"I see it."

"Aren't you going to answer?"

Before Tanner could say, another laser flashed from the asteroid. It shot across the *Dark Star's* exhaust port, which presently aimed in the direction of the raider's travel. The laser missed by a mere ten kilometers.

"Yes," Tanner said. "I believe I will answer the comm. I think the pirates really are going to bargain with us after all. Now, we're going to find out the true cost of doing business with them."

-28-

The same unsavory individual as before appeared on the comm screen. He had tattoo swirls on his sunken cheeks and an oddly shaped cross on his forehead. The ring in his nose shined golden, while he shook his long stringy hair. This time, the dark eyes were clear instead of glassy.

"You must stop immediately," the space pirate said.

"I can't do it at the moment, sir, due to physics and inertia," Tanner said. "I will stop, though, on my second circuit around the asteroid belt."

The pirate shook his head harder. "You will not do that. You are merely seeking to escape the range of my laser and thus break our bargain."

"I would have come in slower," Tanner said, "but the destroyer launched a missile at me. I had to maintain a high velocity to survive this long."

"Oh, I get it," Greco said quietly to Tanner. "You were talking about the triton for the pirate's benefit. You must have known he'd tapped into our transmission. You goaded him to act out of greed."

Tanner didn't acknowledge Greco, but the apeman was right. He hadn't expected the pirate leader to be at that laser turret, though. He'd thought one of the man's lieutenants had been listening in to the communication between the sub-superior and him. Tanner had been trying the old divide-and-conquer tactic against the pirate leader and his men.

"You owe me triton," the pirate said.

"I pay my debts," Tanner told him.

"That's what every crook says to those he plans to cheat."

"I'm not a crook, though. I'm Centurion Tanner of Remus. Maybe you've heard of me."

""I have," the pirate said. "You're the lousy bastard who took out Keg. He was a friend of mine. Knowing this, why shouldn't I smoke you now?"

"One word, Lord," Tanner said, "triton."

"You're a cagey one, ain't you?"

"I like living the same as the next man."

"That's not how I hear it," the pirate said. "Honor is your game, right?"

"Oh, Yeah. That's right, now that you mention it. And that's how you know you're going to get your triton. Centurion Tanner has given his word."

The pirate stared at him as if judging his worth. Finally, the pirate thumped his chest. "I'm Ottokar Akko. I'm one of the notables of the hideaway. If you deal me dirty I'll hack off your head."

"I deal fairly with everyone," Tanner boasted.

"You're a cocky scoundrel, if you're nothing else. Yes! I'll let you live. As I said, I like your style, bounty hunter. You go on into the belt. Get safely into the hideaway. I'll meet you there in a few days. Then...you're going to pay me what's mine."

Tanner decided he didn't need to say more. He'd made his pitch and it looked as if it would work. Would Ottokar take care of the destroyer for him? It's possible the sub-superior wouldn't risk giving the pirate the opportunity.

"It's been a pleasure," Tanner said. "I just hope they never give me a contract for your head, Ottokar. I'd hate to have to come after you now."

Ottokar Akko studied him with cold eyes. The pirate nodded before signing off.

"Why did you have to add that?" Greco said. "You just made him mad."

"I know," Tanner said. "But he expects that from me. I have to give him what he expects or he'll start to think things through carefully."

"Think things through in what way?" Greco said. "As far as I've ever seen, you've always been honest with everyone."

"I try to be," Tanner said. "But one, I don't own any triton. Two, I don't know how much we'll need to buy the right and no doubt expensive equipment to land on Planet Zero."

"You're planning to cheat Ottokar?"

"Not yet anyway," Tanner said. "Let's concentrate on the battle. We're not out of trouble yet. It's also more than possible Ottokar has more outposts. He just acted the way he did to throw us off our guard."

The apeman didn't seem to like that. "I never did enjoy the Petrus System," Greco grumbled.

"Me neither," Tanner said. "But here we are." He focused on the scanner, wondering what the Coalition sub-superior would do next.

***

The *Dark Star* continued around the asteroid belt. So did the Coalition destroyer. The destroyer was much farther behind, nearly seven hundred thousand kilometers so.

"It would be good to know what Ottokar is going to do next," Greco said.

Tanner had been thinking furiously. He furrowed his brow, trying out various ploys in his imagination. He was beginning to see only one way through this. It would be one thing reaching the hideaway and another leaving the place with the needed supplies.

"We're not going to do this by ourselves," Tanner announced.

"What's that?" asked Greco.

"All this," Tanner said, sweeping a hand through the air. "We can't make it on our own. We're going to have to bend a few people to our will."

Greco gave him a dubious look. "It's one thing bending objects and matter to your will. They have constant states. Humans have too many variables to gauge correctly."

"I'd agree that luck comes in handy."

Greco eyed him. "Do you consider yourself lucky?"

"Most of the time," Tanner said.

"Now?"

"Yep."

"I don't believe I care to hear that," Greco said. "It implies you're about to engage in risky behavior."

"Why should we quit now?" Tanner asked.

"Because the odds continue to lengthen against us," Greco said.

Tanner opened intra-ship communications, telling everyone to buckle in tight. Afterward, he applied hard thrust, as he slowed down the raider's velocity.

***

As the hours lengthened, the *Dark Star* moved around the asteroid belt's outer curvature. It wasn't like going around a planet's horizon, giving protection from a chasing enemy. A laser or missile could conceivably pass through the asteroid belt without hitting any debris. The likelihood of that happening, however, was very small. Through the middle areas of the asteroid belt that would be all but impossible. The belt was thicker with debris in the middle than on the edges, but even on the edges, there were clusters of denser areas. Ottokar's asteroid was one among millions of larger bodies. There were trillions of smaller pieces and even more pebble-sized particles and dust motes.

If the *Dark Star* attempted to turn into the asteroid belt at its present speed, the outer hull wouldn't last long. Dust motes and pebbles would pepper and critically pierce the hull long before a boulder ever destroyed the craft. Tanner took a risk flying this near the belt—thirty thousand kilometers from the so-called edge, as there would be more debris out here than in normal space.

The comm light came on later. Greco had left for some sack time. Tanner was alone, sipping coffee, working to stay awake.

He tapped the screen as much out of boredom as anything else. The sub-superior appeared.

"You have won this round, Centurion," she told him. "But you will lose the final contest."

"You could be right," he said.

"I have recorded your smugness. Special Intelligence will have a field day with you once you're captured."

"They'll never catch me," Tanner said.

The sub-superior studied him. As she did, the image became fuzzier.

Tanner decided this was a good time to cut the link.

He finished the coffee, thought about Ursa and found his eyelids drooping. Finally, his eyes shut and his head fell forward. He slept in his seat for six and half hours.

"Boss," Greco said, shaking him. "Boss, wake up."

Tanner started awake. He lurched up, only to have his buckles catch him and slam him back down.

"You fell asleep," Greco said.

Tanner rubbed his eyes. His neck was sore.

"You should go lie down in your bed," the apeman said.

"I'm not sleepy anymore." Tanner sat up as he checked the situation on the sensors.

The *Dark Star* had lost more velocity as the raider continued to brake at 0.75 G's. In another three hours, he could think about entering the asteroid belt. That would mean—

A klaxon began to blare. It surprised Tanner, making him twitch, which yanked at his sore neck. He groaned, rubbing the spot.

"What's the klaxon blaring about?" he asked.

Greco slapped off the switch. He studied the controls and finally pointed at the scanner. "Look, boss, isn't that a Stealth Five Missile?"

"Where?"

"There, coming out at us from the asteroid belt."

Tanner saw it. The sub-superior had shot a torpedo through the edge of the asteroid belt. It must have gone fast to reach them now. And it hadn't struck any pebbles or dust motes. Talk about getting lucky.

"Emergency, emergency," Tanner said through the ship comm. "A stealth missile is approaching detonation range. Everyone head for the insulation room. Don the suits and lie in the cubicles. I will attempt to destroy the missile before it can detonate near enough to kill us."

"You can't hit the torpedo in time," Greco said. "Remember last time?"

On the sensor board, a flare of heat showed off the torpedo's nosecone.

The apeman glanced at Tanner. "You just got your chance, boss. A stone must have struck it. The cone is heating up from friction. It has a bigger signature than before."

"Start up the accelerator!" Tanner shouted. "We have to do this *now*."

Greco tapped controls while Tanner targeted the approaching stealth drone. The stealth five model was bigger than Coalition destroyers normally carried.

The engine thrummed, the accelerator roared. "It's all yours, boss."

"I've got you," Tanner whispered. He pressed the firing tab as he watched the targeting scope.

The charged electrons traveled at near-light speeds. The target was thirty thousand kilometers away. The torpedo had good electronic warfare systems. It might jink now—

A white flare showed on the targeting screen.

"Direct hit," Greco said.

Tanner's muscles seemed to melt away. He sagged against the seat. That had been too close. If the pebble hadn't hit the nosecone... He didn't want to dwell on it.

"What do we do now, boss?"

Tanner forced his sluggish might to engage. "Now, I think it's time we headed into the asteroid belt. We want to reach the hideaway fast and get out fast."

"What's your reasoning? You believe the destroyer headed out system to go get reinforcements?"

Tanner shook his head. "I have no guesses as to that. Maybe the sub-superior is back there. Maybe she's trying to slice through the edge of the belt right now in order to get to us. Maybe she's headed out for reinforcements. I think we have to move before everyone thinks out every angle, and that includes the pirates and the Coalition."

"We're gambling, in other words," Greco said.

"Likely, we always have been," Tanner said. He clicked on the intercom to tell the others the good news. Then, he began the calculations for the precise instant they should head into the mass of asteroidal debris.

-29-

The *Dark Star* slowly negotiated the dense asteroid belt. The raider had shed most of its velocity by now and had answered three different robot challenges. Ottokar called once.

"Have you forgotten our bargain?" the pirate demanded over the comm.

"You want triton," Tanner said. He'd slept in his bed for twelve solid hours. He felt much better and more upbeat, although the problem with Ursa nagged at his conscience.

"I want *all* your triton, bounty hunter. How much do you carry?"

"You want me to broadcast that?" Tanner asked.

Ottokar laughed, showing he had several metal teeth. "You're a sly young devil, aren't you?"

"Just a man making a living," Tanner said.

Ottokar spat at his feet. "I give you that for your making a living. You're a wage slave."

"Hardly that," Tanner said.

"A grubber like the others," Ottokar said. "Only we pirates are free."

Free to rob and pillage, Tanner wanted to say. He had learned to despise their kind, but he doubted it would be good form to let the pirate know that.

"Do you doubt me?" Ottokar demanded.

Tanner shook his head.

"You be a fearing us, bounty hunter?"

"No, I just fear you, Ottokar," Tanner said.

The pirate smirked. "All I demand is that you don't forget what you owe me. I'll be there to greet you, bounty hunter. If you play me false, everyone gets to know who you are."

"I'm surprised they don't already," Greco said, once the pirate had signed off. The apemen gave Tanner a shrewd appraisal. "It's possible you're dead if we dock at the hideaway. They hate bounty hunters with a passion."

Tanner stood up. "That's why I have plan."

"What plan, boss?"

Without answering, Tanner headed down the corridor.

✳✳✳

Tanner found Acton inside one of the cargo holds. That made him angry. The Shand didn't have a key code. That meant the alien had broken into the hold.

"What are you doing in here?" Tanner said. He strode into the hold, and noticed a shadow move a second too late.

From behind, a Lithian grabbed him by the arms, effortlessly hoisting him so his head lightly bumped against the ceiling.

"Easy, my pet," Acton said. "We don't want to harm the captain too soon."

The Lithian grunted, lowering Tanner a few centimeters.

Tanner glared at Acton. The Shand wore his fancy black suit with tails. He held his cane and wore a black top hat. Somehow, it all fit, although it should have seemed ridiculous.

"You can be so troublesome at times," Acton said. "Do you realize that?"

"We're heading for the hideaway," Tanner said.

"I already know this."

"Ottokar Akko is expecting all our triton in payment for his services."

Acton's eyes glittered. It wasn't just an expression; they truly sparkled for just a moment.

"Just how much triton do we have on board anyway?" Tanner asked. "Ottokar wants to know."

"You can't have planned it like this," Acton said quietly, as if to himself.

Tanner tested the Lithian's strength. It was iron-like, unbreakable. Finally, he ceased his struggles.

"Did you plan this?" Acton asked.

"Have you ever played poker?" Tanner asked.

"Answer my question."

"I am, although in my own way."

Acton tapped the end of the cane against the deck. "Very well, continue."

"In poker," Tanner explained, "each player is randomly given a hand of cards of various values. The player combines the cards into various suits or hands of precise but different values, each outranking the other."

"I understand the concept," Acton said.

"The interesting thing is betting. The poker players each wager that his hand is the strongest."

"Why would anyone do something so foolish?" Acton asked. "They can surely see the cards before them."

"Oh. I forgot to tell you. Each player keeps his cards hidden from everyone else."

Acton tapped the deck once more. "Yes, I perceive the game. It is one of blind chance."

"That's not entirely true," Tanner said. "There is also human psychology involved. We call it bluffing."

"Explain the concept to me."

"Bluffing is when a player possesses a weak hand but acts as if it's a strong one."

"How does this help him?" Acton asked.

"The other players might fear his act enough to fold, to throw in their cards and accept defeat. They do this so they don't have to bet higher still and possibly lose more money."

Acton raised the cane, scratching his chin with the lion head. "I see. Yes. It is a game of wits as well as chance. How does this answer my original question?"

"I've had to play the hand I'm dealt, not the one I'd like."

"This is an idiom?" Acton said.

"No, it is an analogy. The cards represent my situation. I'm bluffing Ottokar Akko."

"I don't see why the pirate should fold. He will have the stronger hand all the way down the line."

"Maybe not," Tanner said.

"What could you possibly do to change his mind?"

"Me?" Tanner asked. "I can't do a thing."

"Then…" Acton became still. "This is why you have sought me just now, isn't it?"

"Yes, Lord," Tanner said.

"I wondered how you happened to stumble upon me at this precise moment. It is merely stupid simian luck on your part."

"Then you agree to help me?" Tanner asked.

Acton shook his head, turning away. "Put him down, my pet," the Shand told the Lithian.

Tanner felt his feet touch down. The vast warm hands let go of his flesh. He stumbled, and had to fight to keep from drawing his gun and shooting the Shand. He no longer believed the creature was on the same side as the Varus twins and him. What did he hope to gain from all this?

Acton regarded him. "You think yourself clever but in reality you are easy to read and predict. That is why I'm willing to keep you. The others are even more predictable and useful to me. This surprise—it was chance, nothing more."

"It must be nice being so smart," Tanner said.

"Like everything else, it has its advantages and drawbacks."

"What drawbacks are there to great intellect?" Tanner asked.

Acton smiled in a strange way. "I understand that you seek to probe for a weakness in me. I have none that you can use. The drawback concerns knowing too much, in seeing the futility in so many events. That doesn't concern you. You are too elemental and emotive, too driven by your urges and surface desires. Still, you can fight, and therein lies your true use."

"At least I can do something," Tanner said. "I was beginning to wonder if I was any use at all."

"I had not thought to detect self-pity in you." Acton cocked his head. "That diminishes you. I urge you to scrub self-pity from your mind."

"Why not grease me and make me do it."

"That would harm your utility to the project. I cannot have that."

"Not after hearing about Ottokar Akko, in any regard."

"Well said. In a small way, you have forced my hand. Yet, I already sense that this is for the better. I hadn't wanted to…never mind about that. We shall proceed. Go, Captain, complete your rounds. We will be at the hideaway soon enough."

Tanner paused before leaving.

"Is something wrong?" Acton asked.

"Did the Coalition destroyer stay or head for hyperspace territory?"

"Why do you think I know?"

"Because your equipment has proven superior each time," Tanner said. "I'd be more surprised if you didn't know."

"The destroyer launched the stealth drone and headed for deep space."

"You didn't think to tell me about the drone beforehand?"

Acton's eyes widened minutely. It made him seem more human, more likeable. He pulled out the slate, tucked the cane under his arm and tapped the technological device. After a time, he lowered the slate and stared at Tanner.

"You figured the drone would never make it through the dust and debris, right?" Tanner asked.

"The odds seemed low," Acton admitted.

"It almost ended your mission."

Acton's lips drew back as if making a silent hiss. He tapped the slate further. Finally, he put it away and gripped his cane.

"Go," Acton said, pointing at the cargo-hold hatch.

Tanner massaged one of his arms where the Lithian had held him too tightly. He walked around the giant creature, heading for the hatch.

He was more certain than ever that Acton had a hand in Lupus's death. The Shand played a deep game. The grimace just now had signified something. Tanner would love to know what it had meant. He didn't think it was anything good for his mission. What was Acton's mission? Tanner was convinced it was different from theirs and the cyborgs'. What would an alien want on Planet Zero?

As Tanner hurried for Greco's quarters, he decided the better question was how Acton planned to handle the pirate leader. Because if the Shand didn't have something up his sleeve, the rest of them were likely toast in a most gruesome and prolonged manner once they reached the hideaway.

-30-

The hideaway was the largest piece of the ancient shattered planet.

"I should be taking notes," Greco said at one point.

"Notes?" Tanner asked.

"About the pieces, to see if I can understand what shattered the planet."

"Why?" asked Tanner.

"Because of my *koholmany*," Greco said. "Every Avernite has a task, a life goal that gives him a sense of purpose. I seek to understand vibrations, everything about them. I would like to succeed with Tesla's boast."

Tanner had grown bored of the topic, although he did find the asteroid belt interesting. Throughout the years, various enterprising people had maneuvered large asteroids, adding them to the biggest ones that made up the hideaway.

The extra chunks made for a conglomerate of asteroids, most of them hollowed out and rebuilt with living quarters or industrial sites. No individual or group ruled here. Instead, powerful individuals or groups of people owned certain parts of the whole. The Dog Nobles were among the most powerful, a group of pirates that raided hundreds of light-years away. Keg the Slaver had headquartered on one of the smaller asteroids, although he'd only been a small time crime lord.

Any perversion, delight or vice could be found in the hideaway. The protective asteroids, the trillions upon trillions of drifting pebbles and vast dust fields meant any enemy battlefleet would have a dangerous time maneuvering close to the hideaway. This protection came at a cost, though. Each year, a number of pirate vessels met a grim end due to debris collisions.

The hideaway's benefits outweighed these disasters, though. The hideaway didn't possess a normal, restrictive government. Instead, the strongest or most cunning imposed their whims by fist, club or raygun. The jungle law of tooth and claw reigned throughout the hideaway.

Tanner guided the *Dark Star* toward the main asteroid. The tiny raider would have to pass underneath siege guns and particle beam emitters.

"Look at this," Greco said, indicating himself. "My fur is on end."

Tanner was too busy and too worried to look at the apeman. He guided the raider following the precise instructions Ottokar Akko gave them to ensure the particle beams and siege guns remained silent.

"Bring her to an all stop," Ottokar said over the comm.

Tanner used maneuver thrusters. He'd already had to turn off the fusion engine. That wasn't something he did often. The lords and ladies of the hideaway did not want suicide bombers taking out any of their fortresses. A madman had exploded his fusion engine once. Now, the underworld had a new law in the hideaway regarding docking procedures. It was one of the few rules everyone enforced.

The sights bewildered Tanner almost as much as they had the first time he'd been here. That had been a year and a half ago. Between the major asteroids was a vast area lit by a hundred lights, maybe more. In the area floated ships of many sizes: Coalition tramp haulers beside ex-Remus strikers and old orbital tugs. There were several Nostradamus luxury yachts and a big starliner. There were even some military vessels including two frigates that had once belonged to the Vaster Corporation. There were many more vessels of the raider's size or smaller. Most hideaway pirates used tiny craft to land on far larger prizes. Then, they boarded and took them over from the inside. Apparently, that was the historical pirate model going all the way back to the seas on Manhome.

"Bounty hunter," Ottokar said over the comm.

"I'm right here," Tanner responded. He hated the pirate using that name over the radio. But if he complained about it, Ottokar would surely do it even more.

"Do you see the large cube to your…left?" the pirate asked.

Tanner visually scanned the lit area. Greco pointed. The cube was to their right.

"He must have meant his left," Tanner said quietly.

"I heard that, mate," Ottokar said. "And you have that right. You're a quick one, aren't you?"

"Quick enough, pirate," Tanner said.

Greco shook his head and closed his eyes.

"You're docking over there in the cube," Ottokar said.

"Are you already there?" Tanner asked.

"If you fire at the cube, you're a dead man."

Tanner smiled. The pirate had just answered his question. He was there all right and worried about a vengeance shot.

For the next fifteen minutes, Tanner used the maneuver jets, bringing them closer to the cube. The cube's outer surface was pitted. It must have been a mobile docking cube stolen from the faraway Orion Conglomerate. The asteroid field had given it a thorough abrasion.

"Gun ports," Greco said, pointing out the window.

Tanner nodded, giving the guns a quick glance. He was too busy using the jets to study the guns any closer than that. The docking location Ottokar gave them was almost the same size as the raider.

"Are you any good as a pilot, bounty hunter?" Ottokar laughed.

"If I'm not, say goodbye to your prize."

It took several beats before Ottokar spoke again. "That little joke is going to cost you, bounty hunter."

"A man can only die once," Tanner replied.

Ottokar laughed in an ugly manner. "That's where you're wrong little man, dead blasted wrong."

Greco muted the comm. "Why do you keep antagonizing him? He's angry enough with you already."

"I can't help it," Tanner said. "His kind brings out the ugly in me."

The comm light flashed. Greco unmuted it.

"What are you trying to pull?" Ottokar said angrily over the tiny screen. "Who did you just signal?"

"No one," Tanner said. "My first mate needed to tell me something."

"Don't lie to me, bounty hunter."

"Never," Tanner said.

Ottokar somehow found it within himself to give them the rest of the docking instructions. Ever so slowly, the raider eased into the tiny chamber. The hull clanged from time to time, but not too hard. Finally, a final bang and a lurch ended it. They had docked in the cube. They'd made it. Now, the fun began.

* * *

Tanner led the way through the docking tube. He wore his Remus AirSpace Service dress uniform with jacket, brown with black trim. He wore boots, a gun holstered low on his hip and the monofilament blade tucked in a harness under his arm.

Lord Acton followed, still wearing the top hat and tails with the lion-headed cane. He moved erectly like a born aristocrat. Behind him, Lacy lugged a suitcase of something heavy. She had a tight smile and wore closefitting garments with a small jacket. Lacy hadn't spoken to Tanner, nor had she acknowledged him at all the entire trip.

"What's wrong with her?" Tanner asked Acton.

"Eh?" the alien said.

"Did you mind scrub her?" Tanner asked quietly.

"Don't be absurd," Acton said.

"I'm not. I can see it in her eyes."

"I suggest you concentrate on your primary role," Acton said under his breath. "Leave the rest to me."

Tanner glanced back at Lacy once more. She gave him a cold glance in return, nothing more. Feeling uneasy about her, wondering what she had been doing in her quarters all this time, Tanner marched down the snaking tube.

Finally, they reached a hatch. Tanner went to it, but it stayed closed.

"I could gas you if I wanted and take the triton," Ottokar said over a speaker.

"Where's the enjoyment in that?" Tanner asked.

"It's called 'playing it safe.' I know your reputation, bounty hunter. You're a little too resourceful if one can believe all the stories."

Tanner laughed, holding up his hands. "Are you afraid of me?"

"Put your gun on the deck," Ottokar said.

"Disarm myself in the hideaway?" Tanner asked. "I don't think so."

"Then we gas you."

"Yeah, and then you only get *some* of the triton instead of all of it."

The speaker clicked off. Tanner figured the pirates were arguing among themselves. The hatch clicked. Tanner tried it again. It opened this time. They marched through a solid looking corridor. Soon, they reached another hatch. This one opened on the first try.

Tanner walked into a large room with scruffy looking gunmen aiming hand cannons at him. They had earrings in their earlobes and nose, and expensive jewelry on their throats, fingers and a few in their lips.

"May I introduce Lord Acton of Manhome," Tanner said, indicating the alien Shand.

Acton bowed at the waist, doffing his top hat to the crowd.

The gunmen eyed him dubiously.

"Who is she?" the biggest pirate said. He clattered forward, Ottokar Akko. He stood almost as tall as a Lithian with black sheaths of plasti-armor on his legs, torso, arms and neck. He didn't hold a gun, although there was a big holster on his right wrist with a tube attached to it and the bottom of the gun butt in the holster.

"She is my aide," Acton said in his strange accent. "Are you the leader of these men?"

"I am," Ottokar said. "Are you in charge or is this bounty hunter the man?"

"I have hired his services," Acton said.

Ottokar leaned forward as if he was having trouble understanding Acton. He grinned a moment later. "Oh, you have, have you? You're a fancy pants from Earth, is that right?"

"I am from Manhome," Acton said.

"What are you doing out here near the rim?" Ottokar asked.

"I am an archaeologist."

"What's that?" Ottokar asked.

"He digs," said one of the gunmen. "He searches for ancient artifacts for a museum or a rich patron."

"Is this true?" Ottokar said.

"It is accurate enough," Acton said.

"You dig for people's junk," Ottokar said. "That sounds stupid. Are you stupid, Earthman?"

"Since that is a rhetorical question, I shall refrain from answering it."

"What? Rhetorical what? You're not making sense. Answer the damn question before I blow your head off."

"I am wise beyond your understanding," Acton said.

Silence descended upon the chamber. Several of the gunmen glanced at Ottokar.

"Now you've done it, fancy pants," the pirate lord said. "You went and pissed off Ottokar Akko. That's going to be your last mistake ever. Let me show you why."

With a clatter of plasti-armor, Ottokar raised his right arm, moving his hand into a shooting position. The big gun whipped out of the holster and slammed against his fist. In the tight confines of the chamber, the massive gun discharged twice, booming each time.

Lacy flew off her feet, the rounds slamming her in the chest. The suitcase went flying, tumbling over the deck. She lay motionless.

"Do you see what I mean?" Ottokar asked. Smoke trickled out of the pitted barrel.

Acton looked back at Lacy and then regarded the pirate lord.

The big gun shifted, aiming at Acton. "Do you want some of this?" Ottokar asked.

"I do not," Acton said.

Ottokar smiled evilly. "Didn't think you did, but I wanted to make sure."

Several of the gunmen chuckled.

There was a sound of tiny servomotors. Tanner heard it along with everyone else. Like them, he tried to locate the source of the sound. That's when he saw it. Lacy sat up as black fluid dribbled out of the gunshot wounds. She had a small compact pistol in her hand. The tip glowed red, and a smoking hole appeared in a gunman's forehead. That pirate fell down dead.

The rest of the guns began to boom. They fired at Lacy as the pirates roared or shouted in terror. Her torso, neck, head and arms jerked each time a heavy slug slammed into her. During the fusillade, she beamed two more pirates in the forehead. Finally, flesh and servomotors blew off her head. Lacy toppled backward onto the deck. From there, she arched up. The rounds continued to pummel her as pirates shouted incoherently.

Finally, Tanner reacted. The horror of what he'd seen had stilled him. Lacy was a cyborg. She had to be. Another synapse in his mind fired, and Tanner realized Ottokar Akko was going to kill him as a matter of self-defense.

Tanner drew and fired, trying to finish what Lacy had started. None of the pirates had bothered with him because their terror had caused them to fixate on her. Tanner shot the big gun in Ottokar's grip. By that time, the centurion was among the surviving pirates, as they had clumped together in horror.

Tanner drew the monofilament blade, as he didn't have time to reload his gun. Most of the remaining pirates had emptied their hand cannons against a thing that wouldn't die.

With a shout, Ottokar leaped at him. Tanner twisted to meet the attack, lunging, piercing the plasti-armor. The body slammed against him just the same, knocking Tanner backward. He lost hold of the monofilament knife as he fell and slid across the deck on his back.

When Tanner stopped sliding, he saw Acton unfold from where he'd hidden in a corner. The alien or cyborg, whatever he was, had retreated during the firing. Acton had made

208

himself a tiny target to an unnatural degree. Now, Acton moved surely, reaching the blood-coughing pirate lord.

A quick strike with the cane knocked the techno-knife out of Ottokar's hand.

"What are you?" the pirate shouted. "What did you bring onto the hideaway?"

Acton knelt beside the bleeding Ottokar, touching a check with a glistening hand.

The pirate twitched, moaned and began blinking wildly. Acton spoke low tones into the pirate's right ear. Soon, the bleeding pirate spoke back in a quiet tone.

"Excellent," Acton said. He took out the slate, tapping it. Then, he spoke into the slate. Lastly, he put the slate in front of Ottokar. The pirate lord spoke solemnly, giving what sounded like code words.

At the end, Acton aimed the slate at himself. "I affirm the agreement," the alien said. He shut off the slate, put it away and picked up his cane.

"Now what?" Ottokar asked in a wheezing voice.

Acton stood, twisted the lion head of the cane and withdrew the narrow-bladed sword. "Your use is at end, I'm afraid."

"No!" Ottokar wheezed. "I kept my agreement. I helped you."

"You destroyed my key," Acton said.

"Please."

Acton stabbed with the tip of the sword, and the pirate shivered once, a wretched gesture. Afterward, Ottokar Akko died. The alien picked up his top hat from the deck, inspected it and put it back on his head. Then he turned.

Tanner stood there with his reloaded gun aimed at Acton.

"We must leave at once," Acton told him.

Tanner used both hands to hold the gun and made sure to put plenty of distance between them. "What are you, Acton?"

"We do not have any leeway for this. My voice activation codes are extremely time sensitive. We must leave."

Tanner shook his head. "You're a cyborg."

Acton stood motionless before saying, "I perceive your dilemma. Lacy was a cyborg, certainly that is factual. I am not, though."

"So you say. I think there's only one way to find out quickly."

"You need me in order to reach Planet Zero," Acton said.

"And release all the cyborgs there to attack mankind—no thanks."

"Did you not hear me say that she was the key?"

"Yeah. What about it?"

"How does one unlock a cyborg vault?" Acton said. "The simplest way is with a cyborg, of course."

"Why would she help you destroy her kind?"

"You do not understand cyborgs well, do you?"

"Just answer the question, Acton."

"I reprogrammed her. I've done so several times. After all, I am a Shand."

"Why didn't you tell any of us she was a cyborg?"

"Your present reaction shows me the wisdom of my plan. Do you wish to die at the hideaway?"

"Prove to me you're not a cyborg," Tanner said stubbornly.

Acton stared at him, and it seemed as if his eyeballs might launch twin lasers. Finally, the lord looked away.

"You are a wretched creature," Acton said. "I will remember this."

"If you're still alive," Tanner said.

"Take your knife. Cut the edge of my hand. You will find it is flesh and blood, not composed partly of cyborg circuitry."

Tanner pondered that as he took in the dead within the gory chamber.

"Decide, human, before our time runs out."

"Grab the knife, Acton. You're going to slice your own hand. I'm going to stay back here in case you try something clever."

Once again, Acton watched him motionlessly. It reminded Tanner of a hunting bug as it waited for prey. At last, Acton retrieved the monofilament blade.

"Are you ready?" Acton asked.

"Just a minute." Tanner went to Lacy. He knelt as he kept the gun aimed at Acton. Then, he lifted one of her hands. She had circuits within her hands all right. "Okay. Cut."

Acton raised his left hand. His lips drew back in a silent snarl. Then, he cut the fleshy part of his left hand.

Tanner eyed it. He didn't see any circuitry. As he watched, green blood turned into red, dripping onto the floor.

It felt as if someone hit him in the stomach. There was no doubt about it. Acton was an alien, but it seemed he was not a cyborg. Tanner lowered his gun.

Acton threw the monofilament knife. Tanner shouted wildly, raising the gun. Before he got it all the way up, the knife stuck into the deck centimeters from his feet.

Tanner looked up at the alien.

"I could have killed you just now," Acton said, "but I didn't. Are you ready to leave?"

"Okay," Tanner said.

"Then help me carry Lacy. We're taking her back to the raider with us."

-31-

Tanner balked at the command.

"Surely you realize I must fix her if I can," Acton said.

"She's dead!"

"Cyborgs don't die the same way humans do."

"She partly made of living tissue," Tanner said. He hated this conversation. "That part must be dead by now."

"Correct."

"Correct? Don't you understand what that means? She'll be retarded if you revive her now."

"Are you a cyborg expert?" Acton asked sharply.

"Of course not," Tanner shouted.

"Then do not seek to lecture me about things you know nothing about. We have more than one reason to hurry."

"Oh! So I'm right about the dead tissues."

"There is some merit in your thinking," Acton admitted. "But if we remain here to argue, all of that will be moot."

Tanner took one last look around at the bloody, gory chamber with all its dead pirates. He hadn't expected it to go like this. "Okay. Let's go."

He wondered about a double cross from Acton as they hurried back to the raider. The Shand kept his bargain, though.

The next several hours proved exhausting. After depositing Lacy's remains in her quarters, and doing something in there for ten minutes, Acton joined Tanner in the control room.

Tanner tapped the comm controls as Acton spoke first to one pirate lord and then another. Finally, Tanner backed the

Dark Star out of the cube. There were arguments with various pirates. Over the comm, Acton showed them the slate with Ottokar Akko's statement. Grudgingly, Ottokar's people let them go, sending a large amount of supplies to the ship.

"They're going to be furious soon," Tanner said. "They're going to check the chamber despite Ottokar's so-called command to leave him in privacy."

"You are correct," Acton said.

"What will we do then?"

"It shouldn't matter at that point. Ottokar is a small fish in an ocean of criminals. He was cunning in a lowbrow manner, but he was essentially a stupid man. We are about to deal with truly dangerous individuals. We can longer rely upon animal luck, but must act intelligently."

Tanner glanced at the insufferable alien. "You mean like Shands?"

"That is correct."

The *Dark Star* was halfway through the vast lit area when Ottokar's people found their chief in the chamber.

As it had eleven times already in the past few hours, the comm light blinked. Tanner tapped the screen. An angry, tattooed pirate glared out of the screen.

"You shall deal with this one," Acton said quietly.

"What's up?" Tanner asked the pirate.

The man launched into a tirade of curses and threats. He demanded they return to the docking cube or face their considerable vengeance.

"Do I have to say anything to him?" Tanner asked Acton out of the corner of his mouth.

"Not unless you desire to gloat," the alien said.

Tanner tapped the screen, disconnecting. "You heard the man. They want revenge in the worst way."

"Before we're through, many here will have similar desires."

Tanner couldn't help it. He grinned. "You're a right royal bastard, Lord Acton."

The alien regarded him, cocking his head. "Is that an insult?"

"No. It's what we call a backhanded compliment. It doesn't mean I trust you, but you do have style."

Two hours later, Acton finished his dealings with Magnus Shelly. The woman owned the two frigates they'd seen earlier, among other vessels. She also owned one eighth of the floor space on the central asteroid.

"She is among the most powerful of the hideaway notables," Acton said.

"Do you think Ottokar really was a notable?"

"No. He was a thief, one who managed to turn guard duty on the belt's perimeter into a death sentence. If he had succeeded gaining our triton, though, he would have been wealthy beyond his understanding."

"Did you always know he was just a perimeter guard?"

"No. I learned it fifteen minutes ago."

The comm light blinked again. Once more, Tanner tapped it. This time, an orange-skinned woman peered out of the screen. She had silver hair and red-colored eyes. It was Magnus Shelly.

"Greetings," Acton said in a formal manner. "It is a great honor to speak with you, Lady."

"Yes," she said. "Is it true you have triton?"

"Would you like to see a sample, Lady?"

"I would indeed," she said.

The onscreen haggling as to protocol for the coming meeting took three hours. By that time, Tanner had docked the *Dark Star* in a more spacious area alongside expensive space-yachts.

Soon, Acton went to a meeting on the main asteroid. This time, he went alone, leaving the others in the raider.

Tanner hurried to Marcus's quarters. He informed the heir of everything that had taken place. The big man scowled at the news.

"This is accurate?" Marcus asked. "In particular, you're certain his niece was a cyborg?"

"It's all true," Tanner said.

"We must talk to my sister at once about this."

"We need to meet, all of us, to figure out what we should do next."

"Yes," Marcus said. "I agree. Where should we meet?"

"Somewhere that hasn't been bugged. We'll go to Cargo Hold Four."

"Why there?"

"You'll see." Tanner checked his chrono. "Meet me there in one hour.

"Surely, we should meet sooner."

"No. I'll need some time to move a few things around. One hour, Lord."

"We'll be there," Marcus said.

***

Tanner and Greco shifted heavy boxes and bulky duffel bags into the corridor, freeing enough space in Cargo Hold Four to set up a folding table and chairs. Lastly, the apeman set a pitcher on the table and four cups along with sandwiches.

Tanner sat and tilted his chair back. He poured himself some orange juice and threw it down his throat. He'd found more in a storeroom. He was thirsty after all that moving.

Ten minutes later, Marcus poked his head into the hold. He smiled, glanced significantly at Tanner and entered, holding out his hand. His sister took it, entering afterward. She kept her gaze lowered.

Tanner had almost forgotten how pretty Ursa Varus was. It had been soon time since the Lupus incident. She had avoided him since then. He stood abruptly, causing his chair to fall.

Ursa's head snapped up in surprise. Her gaze brushed his, and held.

"Lady Varus," Tanner said. "I appreciate your presence. We have important matters to discuss."

"I didn't want to come," she said, while still holding his gaze.

Marcus cleared his throat. Neither Tanner nor Ursa paid him any attention.

"I…" Tanner said.

Ursa raised her eyebrows.

"I'm sorry Lupus died," Tanner managed to say. His lips felt stiff as he spoke. "You have my condolences. I wish it had ended differently."

Ursa nodded curtly.

Tanner motioned to the table. "Would you sit, please?"

Ursa turned to her brother. "The ruffian has learned some manners. How quaint, don't you think?"

"I think Centurion Tanner is genuinely sorry for what occurred earlier," Marcus said. "You must remember his life was at risk. He is a fighting man. He reacts harshly because that is his training and inclination."

"Will he attack us if we move too suddenly?" Ursa asked archly.

"That is not worthy of you, sister. I wish you to retract your last statement."

"She doesn't have to," Tanner said.

"And I request the centurion to let my sister and I have a discussion in peace," Marcus said.

Tanner opened his mouth. Greco laid a gentle hand on his wrist. Tanner frowned, looked at the hairy hand and finally nodded.

Ursa had thrown her head back and squared her shoulders. She shivered, perhaps with anger. "If you think, brother—"

"Would you rather that Lupus had slain the centurion?" Marcus asked. "Given Lupus's rage, that could have easily been the outcome. If you don't know that by now—"

"How dare you?" Ursa said, as her hands clenched into fists. "How dare you say that?" she shouted, striking her brother's chest several times. Finally, Marcus staggered backward, catching her wrists so he wouldn't have to endure more blows.

Ursa bent her head, but she didn't weep. She shuddered, seeming angrier than ever.

"We must discuss our present situation," Tanner said. "It's urgent. We must put aside our differences for the good of mankind."

Ursa tore her hands free and whirled around, glaring at Tanner. "You've suddenly become noble minded?"

"No," Marcus said. "Centurion Tanner has always been noble minded. Those with eyes to see have already witnessed that."

Ursa's shoulder's sagged. "My coming here was a mistake."

Greco cleared his throat. "May I speak, Lady?"

Ursa shrugged.

"The situation is grim," Greco said. "We need your good consul. Humanity everywhere needs it. Please, forgive the centurion. If you cling to your bitterness, it could have dire consequences throughout the galaxy."

"You overstate the case," Ursa said quietly.

"I don't believe that," Greco said. "And I am equated as something of a genius, so I should know."

A sad smile appeared on Ursa's face.

"I beg you to forgive the centurion," Greco said. "I have known him for over five years now. He is brave, loyal and stalwart."

"You make him sound like a good dog," Ursa said.

Marcus hissed.

Tanner's features hardened.

Greco pursed his lips in a simian manner. "Your anger will destroy everything, Lady. Do you want that on your conscience?"

"Are you going to lecture me now?" Ursa asked.

"I think I will," Greco said, "as it seems you need it."

Ursa's cheeks colored. She took a step toward Greco. Suddenly, she turned and bowed her head, rubbing her face. A mournful sigh escaped her. Slowly, she looked up, turning to face them. Quietly, she moved to the nearest chair, sitting down.

"I'm thirsty," she said.

Tanner moved faster than anyone else did. "Allow me, Lady," he said, pouring her a glass, handing her the juice.

She accepted it with a nod, sipping, setting the glass on the card table.

Tanner sat back. At last, he put his hands on the table. Marcus quietly took a seat.

Tanner began to talk, telling them exactly what had happened in the docking chamber with Ottokar and his gunmen.

"A cyborg," Ursa said. "Who would have believed it? How can Acton have kept it quiet all this time?"

"There's another problem," Greco said. "Where did Acton acquire the cyborg?"

No one seemed to have any idea.

"The cut hand," Marcus told Tanner. "That was well thought out."

"Yes," Ursa agreed.

"Are you certain about what you saw, though?" Marcus asked. "Could Acton have tricked you regarding his true nature?"

"There's always the possibility," Tanner said, "but I don't think he tricked me. I took every precaution."

Ursa kneaded her forehead, seemingly deep in thought. The others fell silent. She looked up after a time as if surprised. "What are you waiting for?"

Tanner smiled softly. "I don't know what they're waiting for, but I'm waiting to find out what you see that I've missed."

"I have several thoughts. First, that was clever using Acton to climb out of your hole with Ottokar. We had been with the Shand for several months before meeting with you at Calisto Grandee. While Acton's suggestive powers are amazing, he seems disinclined to use them much."

"Maybe it costs him physically to do what he does," Greco said. "Maybe having his body manufacture the drug is a taxing process."

"I think you might be right," Ursa said. "In any case, Acton formulated a plan against Ottokar. Maybe he had several plans. The pirates' murderous ways disrupted some of that. I doubt Acton thought any of them would murder or be capable of murdering Lacy."

"Is killing a cyborg murder?" Greco asked.

"Who cares?" Tanner asked. "That seems like the least of our concerns."

"Not to me," Greco said. "I want to approach the Deity with a clean conscience when I die."

Ursa nodded. "That is a commendable thought, one not often considered by soldiers and warriors."

Tanner felt his face heat up. Had Ursa directed that at him? He suspected so.

"However," Ursa told Greco, "I'm not sure any of us are able to make that call."

"That troubles me," Greco said.

Tanner couldn't believe his friend sometimes. "Let's call it murder for now," the centurion said.

Ursa raised a single finger. "Lord Acton *had* a cyborg. Do you believe it's dead?" she asked, referring to the mangled form he and Acton had brought back to the raider.

"I do," Tanner said. "But Acton indicates that he can bring her back around, and that she wasn't fully dead in the same way a human would die."

"That is troubling," Ursa said. Her single finger was still upright. "Let us suppose Acton can revive Lacy—if she was ever truly dead. The only question that matters is what does Acton hope to achieve on Planet Zero with her? If his goal is to revive the rest of the cyborgs, we must kill him at once."

"How can we tell what he plans?" Tanner asked.

"We have to figure that out," Ursa said. "If we can't confirm the answer in some manner—either yes or no—we must kill Lord Acton and destroy Lacy out of prudence."

"Cold-blooded murder," Greco said. "I cannot agree to that."

"Perhaps you should leave the meeting then?" Ursa told the apeman.

Greco made to rise.

"Wait," Tanner said, putting a hand on one of Greco's wrists. "We only have a little time to figure this out. We need every insight. Greco should stay."

Ursa considered that, soon nodding. "Forgive me. I spoke in haste."

Greco reluctantly sat back down.

Tanner leaned forward. "There's one thing I feel firmly about: we can't let Acton bring anyone else onboard."

"Does he plan on trying?" Ursa asked.

"He hasn't indicated that he is," Tanner said. "I'm just saying. He already has the Lithians. We can't allow him yet more allies."

Ursa was quiet a moment. "Yes. That's a good point. Should we storm the room and destroy Lacy?"

"That all depends on Acton," Tanner said. "If he's on our side, we need him. If we need him, we need his cyborg key, don't we? That means keeping Lacy's remains for the moment."

"Perhaps you're right," Ursa said. "Too much hangs on Lord Acton, and we don't know enough about him."

Tanner glanced at the others. "I'm out of ideas at the moment. I'm tired, and I'm more than a little bewildered at everything that's been going on. I say we keep our eyes and ears open and start soaking up information. Maybe we should buy some useful cyborg-killing weaponry while we have a chance."

"What do we use for currency?" Ursa asked.

Tanner grinned. "That's the easy part. We put it on Acton's bill. He has the triton. A few extra purchases should go unnoticed."

"Don't count on that," Ursa said. "Acton is supremely aware of just about everything going on around him. He's uncanny."

"I'd agree to that," Tanner said. "Is there anything else to consider?"

No one came up with anything.

"Greco and I will clean up," Tanner said. "Remember, this game will likely go to the one who strikes first. Guard yourself and be ready to strike."

"Do we strike while we're still at the hideaway?" asked Marcus.

"No," Tanner said. "First, we get our ship modifications. I'm talking about later once we're in space again. We may not have another opportunity to talk like this any time soon."

They stared at each other, the importance of the centurion's words sinking in. This was a treasure hunt, possibly the most important in human history.

-32-

Several hours later, Lord Acton returned in a hurry. As soon as he stepped out of the airlock, he pointed the lion head of his cane at the waiting Tanner.

"We have serious trouble," the alien said. "It's worse than I'd foreseen. These humans are more than greedy. They are thoroughly corrupt and vicious. I suspect Magnus Shelly wants to double-cross me. It is most distressing."

The *Dark Star* had moved yet again and now waited in a main hangar bay inside the central asteroid. Greco had noticed guards an hour ago outside the raider, bringing it to Tanner's attention.

"What's the problem?" Tanner said.

"They are multiple," Acton said. "For the success of our enterprise, I must overcome them all."

"What's the first problem?"

Acton rubbed the lion head against his chin. "We must modify the raider. Otherwise, the sentries circling Planet Zero will destroy us before we can land on the surface."

"Okay. Why's modifying the raider a problem?"

"It seems I must trust you. Worse, I must arm you with suitable weapons."

"Whoa, whoa, whoa, what are you talking about?"

"Perhaps that isn't important," Acton said. He began to pace with his features blank as if he was deep in thought. "We only have a little time," the alien said. He stopped abruptly. "The pirates ruined the easiest path. I never expected such wanton destruction on their part. This destructive streak seems epidemic among you hominids."

"You've got to settle down," Tanner said. "I don't understand a thing you're saying."

Acton looked up. "You must come with me. Hurry. We don't have much time." He moved back to the airlock hatch, opened it and looked back. He frowned seeing that Tanner hadn't moved.

"What is your objection now?" Acton asked.

"Look," Tanner said. "Come on. Are you serious? You come in here huffing and puffing and expect me to just race out after you? Yours is an act, not a bad one, but an act just the same."

"Why would I pretend anything?"

"To get me off the ship and alone," Tanner said.

"No. You place far too much value on yourself. You are a cog, a mere cipher." Acton snapped his fingers. "It would be simplicity to eliminate you from the calculations. This self-insistence on your importance has become taxing."

Tanner grinned. "Don't forget that my quick wits have brought us this far."

"Negative," Acton said. "Your sloppy procedures have almost seen us killed several times already. I am appalled at your techniques. But you're all I have at the moment. Now, hurry, this delay is only making our situation more difficult."

Tanner shook his head. "What's your plan? Where are we going? I have to know what you're thinking."

"I have already told you the plan. We need powerful weapons to help us persuade Magnus Shelly to uphold her end of the bargain."

"How can I trust you enough to leave the ship in your company?"

"What do suspect I will do to you?"

"Have thugs grab me, allowing you to smear grease on my skin so you can control my thoughts."

Acton's lips peeled back in the silent hiss. "You speak about sacred acts as if they are common occurrences. It is difficult to speak to you for extended periods. It tires me."

"That's interesting," Tanner said. "Because you give me a pain right here," he said, rubbing his butt.

"If you won't go, I'll demand Marcus comes with me. You are better suited, however."

"Yeah? Why's that?"

"It should be obvious. You are more dangerous than the tribune."

Tanner sighed. "All right, I guess. We're already in a fix. Let me get my gun and gloves. Then, I'll be ready. But if this is a trick, Acton, I'm going to shoot you before they take me down."

"Your threat is noted. I have been warned."

Tanner hurried down the corridor. The hangar bay had artificial gravity, and thus so did the *Dark Star.* He told Greco where he was going, and gave the apeman instructions about how to test him once he'd come back.

"That's devious," Greco said.

"Let's hope it will work," Tanner said. He buckled on his gun-belt, checked his pistol and hurried to the airlock for the waiting Lord Acton.

***

The guards around the ship hadn't been a problem, although Tanner had seen one of them speak into a communicator.

At the moment, Acton and he moved through a crowded bazaar. The centurion carried the suitcase Lacy had carted earlier. It was heavy. No doubt, it held triton bars. The asteroid half-reminded Tanner of Calisto Grandee. It had the feel of heightened capitalism but lacked the luxury habitat's polish. Here, beggars cooked kabobs while slick operators beside them in booths sold jewelry or high-tech gadgets.

Several times, cutpurses bumped against Tanner as they hurried through the area. He chopped one youth on the wrist, grabbed a woman's hand trying to slip into a pocket—she began to shriek—so he let go and disappeared into the crowd. The centurion kept his hand firmly on his gun-butt after that.

Few tried to steal from Acton. The one who did sucked on his knuckles. The alien had rapped the man's hand with his cane.

They passed under a man-sized scanner, walking into a different area. Hard-eyed guards in body armor stood everywhere. They held heavy combat rifles, watching the various people. The crowds had thinned, but they wore fancier garments and bought expensive items.

Finally, Acton and Tanner entered an elevator with two guards.

"Weapons room," Acton said.

The elevator went up. Soon, they strolled in a quieter atmosphere. No beggars lined the passageways here. No booths stood anywhere. All the sellers had shops. Most of those showed weaponry: rifles, mortars, combat vests, grenades and portable plasma cannons among others.

"We could have used some of these weapons in the space-strike service back on Remus," Tanner said.

The alien didn't respond.

Tanner noticed a lack of guards, which seemed strange. This place should need them more than others. He pointed out the lack to Acton.

"The explanation is simple," the alien said. "Everyone up here is armed."

They passed shop after shop, the wares becoming increasingly more interesting.

"Is there any place in particular you have in mind?" Tanner asked.

Acton pointed at the second to last shop. The sign read, BELTER'S SUPPLIES. The shop only had a small, dingy entrance.

"The place doesn't look like much compared to its neighbors," Tanner said.

"Agreed," Acton said. "It doesn't have to be gaudy, though. His reputation draws in the customers."

"You've heard of Belter?"

"It is why we're here." Acton paused and looked back at Tanner. "I suggest you let me do the talking. I have a specific item in mind. If you talk...it could ruin everything."

"Mums the word," Tanner said.

"Make sure you remember that."

The store looked just as unappealing inside. A small old man with rheumy, sad eyes watched them as he sat on a three-legged stool. He wore a brown smock and had stubby little fingers. Glass cases held various plasma rifles and neat little heaters like those Lacy had used against the pirates. They were costly, high-tech items, but nothing out of the ordinary.

Acton gazed upon the various items. Once, he snapped his fingers, staring fixedly at Tanner and pointing at the ground behind him. The centurion finally complied, moving until he stood in the exact spot.

"He reacts as if he's been mind-chopped," the small man said in a high-pitched voice.

Acton nodded.

"Interesting," the clerk said. "There's a mulish look on his face. Is he stubborn?"

"At times," Acton said.

The small man considered the information. "Does he still have his sex organs?"

"He does," Acton said.

"Ah," the clerk said. "Therein is your problem. You should have him gelded. It will gentle him considerably."

Tanner almost went for his gun. Who was this little creep?

"I find that a gelding lacks combat aggressiveness," Acton was saying.

"Yes," the clerk agreed. "There is that to think about."

The two glanced at each other, and something seemed to pass between them. It made Tanner's hackles rise. He let his gun hand drop onto the butt of his weapon.

"He understands me," the small man said.

"True," Acton said.

"You are daring indeed."

Acton shrugged.

It began to don on Tanner that the little man on the stool might actually be another Shand. The desire to draw and fire grew stronger.

"He has become agitated," the small man said.

"Heel," Acton said, snapping his fingers.

Tanner forced himself to look down and step to where Acton pointed. Maybe he could learn more by acting dumb. If the little clerk thought of him as an animal, the man would likely say more than he should. Convinced of that, Tanner strove to act as the Lithians usually did.

Acton spoke again, but rapid-fire and in a language Tanner had never heard before. Maybe it was Shand cant. Whatever the case, the two spoke faster yet to each other. He wasn't learning anything now.

Finally, the little man hopped off his stool. He sauntered behind a case and pressed something on it.

"This way," the little man said.

Acton led the way and Tanner followed. A trapdoor had appeared at the spot. The two followed the little alien down a spiral staircase into a cool chamber. Lights brightened, revealing more glass cases. These held strange looking weapons.

Acton spoke more of the alien cant. The little man studied him. Acton spoke faster. The alien in the brown smock seemed troubled. Finally, with a start, he led the way through some curtains, into a smaller area.

Acton gave Tanner a significant glance before leading the way. They entered an alcove with a single stand. On it was a display case with a thick, rather longish gun inside.

"I would see your wares," the small alien said in Basic.

Acton snapped his fingers at Tanner, indicating a table.

Surprisingly, Tanner understood what Acton meant. He set the suitcase on it and stepped back. Acton handed Tanner his cane. The centurion took it in a reverent manner.

The small alien chuckled at that. "He's better trained than I realized. He instinctively recognizes a relic."

Acton didn't respond. Instead, he clicked open the suitcase, opening it, extracting three bars of gleaming triton.

The small alien's eyes shined with avarice as a lizard-like tongue darted between his parted lips. "I may touch?"

"One," Acton said.

The small man waddled near, picking up a triton bar, running it against his cheek.

"The gun is a genuine Innoo Flaam?" Acton asked.

226

"From the Third Period during their ascendancy," the small "man" said.

"It still self-charges?"

"It isn't a museum piece but a functional weapon. I would have you field test it, but…"

"I understand," Acton said. "I do intend to turn it on, though."

The small alien looked up in alarm. "Is that wise?"

Acton smiled. So did the small "man" after a moment.

"Yes," the small alien said. "I suppose it is wise. Please, turn it on."

"I won't," Acton said. "I'll let my man have the honor."

The small alien shook his head. "That is rash and to me seems unnecessarily trusting. Remember, he still has his balls. What if a testosterone rush causes him to go kill-crazy?"

"I have a murder switch in place," Acton said.

"Ah. I should have realized. In that case, yes. Let the human hold the blaster."

Acton turned to Tanner. The small alien waddled to the display case, inserting a key, turning it. The display case whirred with sound as the protective cover slid into the stand.

Tanner hesitated.

"He knows it's highly lethal," the small alien said. "How very remarkable that is."

"Some of them are sensitive to power," Acton said.

"I've noticed," the small alien said. "Heed me, Acton Indomitable, geld him or you will have trouble with the human in the future."

"I doubt that," Acton said. "But your concern is noted. Go on, Tanner, pick up the gun and do exactly as I tell you."

Tanner found that his hand trembled as he reached for the Innoo Flaam blaster. *Stop that*, he told himself. He let his hand drop onto the cool metal. Gripping the big, over-longish gun, finding it a perfect fit for his hand, he took it off the special cloth. The blaster was heavy. He looked to the right and left on it—

"The switch is to your right," Acton said. "Flick it with your thumb but do not pull the trigger."

Tanner flicked the switch.

227

Immediately, the blaster purred with power, vibrating in his hand. The end of the barrel glowed with a sinister red color. A sense of potent destructive force filled Tanner's being. He wondered what kind of damage this thing could do.

"Keep it aimed it at the floor," Acton said.

"That won't matter if he pulls the trigger," the small alien said. "We'd all die in the blast. It takes half a minute to recharge after each shot. You could take down some spacecraft with that and every terrain vehicle I know. It's a monster gun. No one makes weapons like that anymore."

"How do I disarm it?" Acton said.

"Two flicks of the same switch."

"Did you hear that?" Acton asked Tanner.

The centurion nodded.

"Then click it twice at once," Acton said in a commanding voice.

Tanner did so. The vibration immediately ceased. Ten seconds later, the red color deepened to black and then altogether disappeared from the end of the barrel.

"It's seems fully functional," Acton said.

"Yes," the small alien said. "It's worth five triton bars—"

Acton turned abruptly to the other and spoke in their fast, Shand cant. The two haggled. Finally, Acton won the Third Period Innoo Flaam blaster and several other weapons upstairs. He left behind all three triton bars.

As they exited through the small door onto the main corridor, Tanner turned to Acton.

"I can't believe you gave him three bars," the centurion said.

"We have the bargain," Acton said. "Do you know what you're carrying?"

"An Innoo Flaam special," Tanner said.

Acton shook his head. "It's sad to witness such profound ignorance among your species, Captain. The weapon you're carrying is over twenty thousand years old."

"What?" Tanner said. "No way is that true."

"The Innoo Flaam were aliens in the truest sense."

"Shands aren't aliens?" Tanner asked.

"They cracked sciences beyond our understanding," Acton said, ignoring the question. "As far as we know, the Innoo Flaam fought a series of wars against an energy race of beings. These energy creatures destroyed entire worlds, and they were immune to any form of attack while traveling through space. Finally, the Innoo Flaam invented these special blasters. The records indicated they could slay the energy creatures with several direct shots." Acton shook his head. "No one knows what happened in the end. It would seem likely that the energy creatures perished, but it is also possible that they emigrated out of our galaxy. One thing we do know is that they destroyed the Innoo Flaam. Yet, such was the science needed for these weapons that they outlasted their creators. Such a blaster as you possess is difficult to find anywhere. I had heard there was one in the hideaway."

"That man was a Shand?" Tanner asked.

"What does it matter to you? We have the blaster, and we have several other potent weapons. Now it is time to make sure Magnus Shelly doesn't cheat us as she upgrades your wretched raider."

"How is one gun going to do that?"

Acton smiled, and for once it seemed genuine. "That little gun could probably destroy the entire asteroid. Once it's armed, people pay attention."

"Big deal, I draw a super-gun. All this Magnus Shelly needs is a sniper to blow me away. Bam. That's the end of the threat"

"I'm sure she'll try that. At that point, she'll realize that she has to deal fairly with us after all."

"What does that mean?" Tanner asked. "I don't like the sound of this."

"You will," Acton said. "Of that, I assure you."

-33-

The meeting with Magnus Shelly proved uneventful except for one pregnant moment. Acton and Tanner stood in a sealed room, facing the orange-skinned lady as she stood behind protective glass.

"You will notice," she said, "that I have sniper guns pointed at you."

"I saw them immediately," the Shand said.

"How fortunate for you," the woman sneered. "I'm disappointed in you. I thought you were better than this, Lord Acton. I find—"

The Shand raised a hand. "Please, Notable, before you say something you might regret later. Let me show you something." He nodded to Tanner.

Tanner flicked the switch on the Innoo Flaam holstered at his side. At the same moment, Acton took a step nearer him.

"What's that?" Magnus Shelly asked. She stared at something on her side of the glass. "These readings just went off the chart."

"He has a nuclear weapon," a man said on her side.

"Are you insane?" Shelly asked Acton.

"On the contrary," the Shand said. "I am the most fully sane person on the asteroid save perhaps for one other individual. We do not have nuclear weapons. My associate has an Innoo Flaam blaster."

"Those are myths, old wives tales," Magnus Shelly said.

"No," Acton said. "They are quite real if very rare. If I ask my associate to draw and fire, you in the other room will all perish."

"You'll die with us," the woman said.

"You are misled in thinking so," Acton said. "As I said, this is an Innoo Flaam blaster. The guns were constructed to survive dangerous energy creatures of potent offensive capability. If you think I'm lying, fire your sniper guns at us. However, if you do so, our deal is suspended."

"Make your meaning clear," she said.

"My associate will kill you."

Tanner shot Acton a sharp glance. What in the heck was the Shand talking about? He had an old energy blaster. That didn't make him invincible. Why would anyone think so?

Magnus Shelly seemed undecided. Finally, her shoulders sagged just a little. "We will proceed with the deal."

"Excellent," Acton said. "One of the reasons I chose you was that you seemed rational."

"I despise gloating," she said.

"A small flaw, I assure you. It doesn't bother me."

Her manner became flinty as her lower jaw moved from side to side.

"Let us meet in person," Acton suggested. "I find this higher threat level taxing. Why should we interact this way, eh?"

"Yes," she said finally. "Let us talk in person. Just have your gunman turn off his weapon. I don't like it."

"No one does," Acton said just loud enough for Tanner to hear.

***

The work on the *Dark Star* began several hours after the meeting.

Everyone exited the raider, including Vulpus and the two Lithians. Everyone carried a gun or a weapon of some kind. The Lithians wore body armor and carried huge iron bars.

"Why do I have to wear this?" Greco complained. He had one of the new guns belted around his hairy waist.

"Vigilance is the requirement for safety in a place like this," Acton told the apeman. "We will remain together. I suggest none of us leaves except in the company of another. Truthfully, no one should stray from the captain. The notable fears the blaster, and for good reason."

"Why would Tanner destroy the asteroid?" Greco asked. "He dies too then."

"Possibly," Acton said.

They were in a hotel room overlooking the small shipyard. Acton had tested the room for listening devices, having found a dozen already.

"How could he survive the asteroid?" Greco asked.

Acton smiled coolly.

"What does that even mean?" Greco said. "A grin isn't an answer."

"No," Acton said. "But it leaves a question in your mind. That's all I need."

"Need for what?" Greco asked.

"To mold Notable Shelly's thinking," Acton said. "They believe the captain will act with revenge if something happens to me or stops our deal."

"Mind games," Greco said, shaking his head.

"Psychological manipulation," Acton corrected. "It is something I excel in. And that is good for all of us."

Greco glanced at Tanner. "I think you should ask him."

"Ask me what?" Acton said, becoming alert.

Tanner faced the Shand. The alien's actions in the asteroid had surprised him. Could Lord Acton be one of the good guys? It seemed hard to believe.

"We're worried about you," Tanner finally said.

"That is my lot in life," Acton replied.

"How can we trust you?"

"You wear the Innoo Flaam. Doesn't that count for something?"

Tanner nodded. "What do you hope to achieve on Planet Zero? You have a cyborg—"

"I've already told you why I had her," Acton said. "She was a key."

"Can't you see how having a cyborg would make us nervous?" Tanner said.

"Yes. It's why I've armed you with the blaster."

"Fair enough," Tanner said. "We'd still like to know what you hope to achieve there."

"The same as you," Acton said. "I want to throttle the cyborgs in their crib. If we fail, there will be ruinous war."

"Why should that bother you?"

Acton looked away. Finally, he said, "I cannot tell you my exact wish, for that would expose the essence of the Shands. We're not ready to reveal that secret yet." He turned to the others. "I have acted in good faith, I assure you."

"You've acted peremptorily at times," Marcus said.

"Yes. That's true. My heightened intellect and ultra-rational nature causes me to act before slow-witted creatures such as yourselves can think to do so. It is a burden knowing so much and having such resources. I am on the same side as right-thinking humanity. All I ask is that you do not get in my way when you fail to understand my higher goals."

Ursa stepped up. "Do your higher goals have anything to do with reviving the cyborgs?"

"By no means," Acton said.

"I wish I could believe you," she said.

Acton turned to Tanner. "Do you believe me yet?"

"I want to," Tanner said. "But you're so different. That makes you hard to trust."

"Yes. It has always been so." Acton glanced at each of them in turn. "It is not in my nature to disclose my secrets." He focused on Ursa. "As well should I expect to watch you rut with the centurion on the deck before an audience."

Marcus reddened, stepping closer.

"See," Acton said. "Even mentioning the sex act makes your brother froth at the gills. Can you imagine how I feel when asked such barbarous questions? Yet, I maintain my decorum. Truly, that makes me more rational than you."

Brother and sister Varus glanced at each other.

"Let's call a timeout," Tanner said. "I have this gun. Acton bought it for me. I saw him purchase it with three triton bars. I can only imagine what they're going to do to the *Dark Star.*

"You do not have to imagine," Acton said. "Your retraining will begin in an hour as you learn the new functions."

"What retraining is this?" Tanner asked.

***

The next few days were exhausting and mind numbing. Each of them used stimulants to stay awake the entire time.

Tanner and Greco learned the new systems put into the *Dark Star*. Notable Magnus Shelly's people attached special, nonferrous, sensor resistant material to the entire outer hull. Several holds lost their cargo. Tanner suggested they try to sell the goods on the open market. Acton said they lacked the time. Into these holds went stealth equipment, jamming gear and battery power sources.

Technicians installed entirely new computer equipment. Greco oversaw the transfer of data from the old into the new.

"We sure could have used Jordan," Tanner said.

Greco could only nod. His eyes were thoroughly bloodshot.

The techs installed various torpedoes. They upgraded the emitter and added a thruster multiplier to give the raider greater speed. Two more holds lost their cargo. Gravity dampeners took their place. That meant more training for Tanner and Greco. One of them used a hypnotic-trainer while the other watched. The watcher listened in from time to time to make sure the techs weren't slipping something unwanted into their minds.

Tanner's hands shook constantly. His eyeballs felt gritty. He ate so much that his gut ached most of the time.

"When is this going to end?" Greco complained.

"Soon," Acton told him. "We must remain alert until we're safely away from the hideaway."

"I know, I know," Greco said. "Vigilance is the price of freedom."

"It has always been so," Acton said.

"I'd agree to that," Tanner said.

Ursa wanted more data on the cyborg in Lacy's room. Acton wouldn't comply with her wish.

The raider's transformation took five days of constant work to complete.

"Money is the true magic," Acton told them toward the end of the ordeal. "It can do more than my tricks have ever been able to achieve."

"Where did you get all that triton?" Ursa asked.

Acton stared at her.

She turned away, blushing.

The notable's people worked fast even as Acton pushed them. Tanner's mind hurt, he'd learned so much in such a short time.

"Acton is hiding something from us," Ursa said on the fifth day.

Tanner and she sat before a window overlooking the repair yard. The centurion leaned back in a chair, having just removed a hypnotic-band from his head. It felt as if his eyes were swollen.

"Did you hear me?" Ursa asked.

Tanner knew they had all become irritable. Vulpus watched him closely, the underman never far from his mistress.

"I heard you," Tanner forced himself to say. He'd found that the longer he took the stimulants, the less he liked to talk.

"The Shand is too secretive," Ursa said. "The—"

Marcus barged into the room short of breath. "Go," he panted. "Get your things…We're leaving."

"You're not making sense," Ursa said.

Marcus shook his head violently. "Go!" he shouted. "Get your things! The Coalition…" He put his hands on his knees, wheezing for air. He must have sprinted for a ways.

"Yes, yes," Ursa said. "The Coalition is doing what? Why are you out of breath?"

Marcus shoved off his knees, straightening, with his eyes wide. "A Coalition fleet has just dropped out of hyperspace. We have to get out of here before the hideaway explodes with panic and turns on us."

-34-

Tanner led the way onto the repair yard with the barrel of the Third Period Innoo Flaam glowing with an evil red color. The gun vibrated with an audible hum. It *felt* dangerous—

Shots rang out. Greco hooted with fear. And the air sizzled before Centurion Tanner. As it did, the Innoo Flaam vibrated worse than ever in his hand.

"Fire back," Acton said. "Show them the folly of shooting at you."

Tanner saw two riflemen rise from their locations. Each of them wore body armor and cradled a heavy assault rifle with smoke trickling from each barrel. The guards seemed surprised.

The guards stood before the main repair yard building. The two men spoke to each other. One nodded, aimed the rifle at Tanner—

The centurion aimed the ancient blaster and began to pull the trigger.

"Level two!" Acton shouted. "Switch it to level two, or you'll take out our ship with them."

The words penetrated Tanner's thinking even as the air sizzled before him again. A force field devoured the slugs the two guards shot at him. The blaster was vibrating wildly now, so he clutched it with two hands. Before he pulled the trigger, he switched its setting to two. Then, he aimed and fired.

The blaster hummed louder than ever before discharging a red ray. It beamed the two guards. They flashed and

236

disappeared in wisps of smoke, along with part of their guard booth.

"You'll lack the full force field until the blaster fully recharges," Acton said. "That doesn't mean you can't threaten with it. Threaten, man, threaten."

Tanner was both elated and appalled at the gun's power. This thing was amazing. It had a force field, it seemed. That's why the air had sizzled. The force field had stopped the bullets from killing him and killing those inside his protective sphere.

No wonder the Shand had moved closer to him when they'd been talking to Magnus Shelly five days ago. The ancient weapon didn't make him invincible, but it was incredibly powerful when loaded for war.

The other guards scattered after witnessing the death of the first two, some of them pitching their rifles onto the floor in order to run faster. The next few minutes were a blur of shouts, running and charging onto the raider.

"We'll have to wait for the lifter to take us to the hangar bay," Marcus said. "Until then, we're trapped in the repair yard. How does getting aboard the raider help us anyway?"

"Go to your quarters," Acton said to the Lithians. The giants lumbered down the corridor to their room.

"You haven't answered my question," Marcus said. "How does it help us being here? After our gunfight, I doubt Magnus Shelly is going to order a lifter to the yard."

"Must I answer every dull-witted question when the fate of the universe hangs in the balance?" Acton asked.

Marcus scowled thunderously.

"No," Ursa said, tugging one of her brother's arms. "We're all tired. We're in danger. Let the Shand produce his miracle."

"But the lifter…" Marcus said querulously, while allowing Ursa to drag him down a corridor.

"The tribune is right," Tanner said. "Until the lifter arrives—"

"You blind dolt," Acton said. "This is it. The Coalition has cornered us at last. Do you want to end your days with a re-trainer jolting your mind for wrong answers?"

"Of course not," Tanner said.

"Then you must do exactly as I say," Acton told him.

237

"Okay. What's the plan?"

Acton pointed at Greco. "Go. Start the fusion engine. Make sure it is running at full capacity."

The apeman didn't argue. He dashed down the corridor leading to the engine room.

"Have you already called Magnus Shelly?" Tanner asked. "Are they bringing the lifter after all?"

"To the control room," Acton said.

Tanner hurried there, propelled even faster by a shoving Lord Acton. "How do you know the Coalition entered the star system?"

"They haven't," Acton said.

"But Marcus said they did. He burst into our hotel room to announce it."

"He did not say any such thing. The tribune said they dropped out of hyperspace. That is just outside the star system, not inside it."

"You're arguing over semantics," Tanner said.

"On the contrary, it is all the difference."

"Whatever," Tanner said. "Just tell me how you know they showed up. How about that?"

"I have a running order with Ottokar's people. They still serve on the asteroid belt's perimeter. They were to inform me regarding any vessels dropping out of hyperspace."

"Why would they do anything for you? We killed their leader, remember?"

"They are not doing so knowingly."

"Oh. Okay. That makes sense, I guess." Tanner slid into his seat buckling in out of force of habit.

Acton sat down beside him.

"I don't see a lifter," Tanner said, leaning forward, looking outside the window into the repair yard.

"We're not going to employ a lifter."

"Then how are we getting out of the repair yard and to the hangar bay?" Tanner asked.

"The most direct way possible," Acton said, "through the raider's propulsion."

Tanner turned toward the Shand. "Hey, buddy, I have some news for you. We're inside an inhabitable area. We can't just

238

use fusion power to blast out of here. It would kill hundreds, maybe thousands of people."

"A regrettable loss, I realize," Acton said. "Still, that is better than being captured and tortured, which is what will happen to us once the Coalition's demands are made known."

"What demands?"

"The ones that are coming through even now," Acton said." He withdrew the slate from his suit and shoved it in front of Tanner's face. With a tap of his thumb, the Shand turned it on.

Tanner listened to an ugly woman. After the officer made her demands, a different group appeared. This group sat at a long table. Among them was Notable Magnus Shelly. She spoke for the others.

"And if we hand them over to you?" Magnus Shelly asked.

When no reply was forthcoming, Tanner looked at the Shand. "Well, what did the Coalition officer say after that?"

"Everyone is waiting for the return transmission," Acton said.

"How many ships are in the fleet?" the centurion asked.

"Enough to defeat the hideaway given a prolonged siege," Acton said. "Before that happens, I'd imagine the Petrus notables would see it in their hearts to capture us for profit. That would surely be superior in their thinking to protecting us for destruction and loss of their asteroid port."

"Yeah," Tanner said dryly. "I can see that."

"Hence, the need for speed," Acton said.

"Indeed," Tanner agreed.

"Ah. Look. The fusion engine is ready," Acton said, while indicting a green light. "We must leave."

Tanner stared at Acton.

"Come now, Captain. It should be an easy decision."

"Easy for you maybe," Tanner said. "I'm human, remember?"

"It seems no one ever lets me forget. What is your point?"

"Maybe you don't mind murdering innocent people. I'm different."

Acton became thoughtful, finally shrugging.

"That's it then?" Tanner asked.

"Yes. I will slip off the raider and find another means to Planet Zero." The Shand unbuckled his restraints.

"Wait," Tanner said. "The Coalition people will find you too in time."

"That's doubtful, as I know how to hide."

"You mean that other Shand in the weapons area will help you?"

"He has no bearing on this," Acton said. "I will merge into the herd. It will be easy."

"The Coalition might murder everyone in the hideaway to find you," Tanner said.

"Possibly true, but I will slip away nevertheless."

Tanner stared out the window. He didn't want to die. He didn't want to fall into Coalition hands. It would be worst if Special Intelligence caught him. Yet, just blasting off in here would kill people. He couldn't have that on his conscience, could he?

"I don't know what to do," Tanner said.

"I realize this." Acton held out his hand. "I would like the Innoo Flaam back."

Tanner moaned, closing his eyes. He would fight against the best of them, but to just— He swore under his breath and began turning on the thruster and side jets. "Maybe I can do this without killing too many innocents," he said under this breath.

Acton sat back down, watching him.

"We're talking about cyborgs," Tanner said. "If we fail, millions possibly billions of people could die."

"That is true," Acton said.

"I have to do this."

"That is also true. I did not realize humans could be so coldly rational at the right time."

Tanner glanced at Acton, muttered some choice curses under his breath and said, "Hang on, you royal bastard. We're about to leave this place."

The *Dark Star* lifted off the repair yard floor. Cables snapped off the raider, metal rods splintered and cranes crashed onto the floor as the small spaceship began to float through the air.

"I hate doing this," Tanner muttered.

"You'd better fly faster," Acton said. "The Coalition admiral will give her reply in less than ten minutes."

Tanner glanced at the Shand.

"If the admiral's offer is high enough, the notables might agree to capture us for the Coalition. We have to not only leave the asteroid but be well on our way through the belt."

"I never signed up for this," Tanner said.

"I think you'll find that saving the galaxy for others is a thankless task."

Tanner scowled, trying to pilot the raider in such a way as to do the least damage possible. They were out of the building and now moving through the built up area.

"What are you talking about?" the centurion asked.

"Having to do the hateful task no one ever understands," Acton said. "Such as us are a people alone."

Tanner gave the Shand a second look. He hadn't expected something like that from Acton. Then, he remembered the control unit in the Lithian's skull. He recalled Lacy, and he remembered the blood leaking from the bruiser's ears back in the Calisto Grandee corridor. It felt as if too much of this didn't quite make sense.

"Are there are lot of Shands in the galaxy?" Tanner asked.

Acton shrugged.

"Do you people have a special purpose?" Tanner asked.

"It would be better to increase speed," Acton said. "Our escape is taking too long."

"If I just plow out, I'll wreck the raider."

"Have you forgotten your retraining already?"

Tanner thought about that, and he brightened, realizing the small ship could project a force field for limited periods.

Lights began to flash in the large passageways. People raced in terror on the streets away from the raider.

"If the notables agree to capture us," Acton said. "They can employ the siege guns in space against the raider. Nothing we possess will protect us from those guns."

""I haven't forgotten about the siege guns. That's why I'm not going crazy in here. If I do the least amount of damage here, that might make the least number of notables angry at us."

"Speed is our best guarantee," Acton said. "This excessive tepidness will ruin our mission."

"It's not always winning the game that counts but how you win that makes the difference."

"That is a quaint notion," Acton said. "I suspect you are saying this because of your extreme fatigue. Perhaps if you allow me to pilot the craft—"

"No," Tanner said. "I have this."

For the next ten minutes, Tanner guided the raider through the passageways, destroying as little as possible. Finally, he reached a huge hatch. It was open. He took it. The hatch began to close behind him.

"We are in the main hangar bay area," Acton announced.

"They'll surely train their guns and missiles on us once we're outside. I don't see how our actions have escaped the notables' attention."

Acton checked his blue-glowing slate. "I assure you, it has not. The admiral's message is no doubt several minutes away. We must escape now, Captain. You must employ full cloak and ram through the outer hull."

"Their outer weapons will lock onto to us if I do that."

"You do not realize what kind of cloaking devices we have."

"It won't make us invisible."

"It will to their targeting sensors until they rectify the matter. That will take time. During that time, we will accelerate out of the worst danger zone."

Tanner leaned back in his seat. "If I ram the bulkhead, it will damage our ship."

"You must first beam the bulkhead, of course. Do you see the new green switch on your board?"

Tanner glanced down. "I see it, but I don't remember learning about it."

"It is connected to a new ship gun. That emitter works on a similar principle as the Innoo Flaam blaster. I took the liberty of adding it to our craft. We now possess the means to take out a Coalition cruiser at extremely short range."

"Great," Tanner said. "Can this blaster take out a battleship?"

"The weapon is good, but it's not that good." Acton checked the slate. "You have the means, Captain. Do you have the will?"

Tanner took a deep breath before activating the raider's new blaster. With a tap, he fired.

A red bolt of raw energy struck the hangar bay bulkhead, vaporizing it. Open space beckoned, even as a hurricane-force wind blew out of the gaping hole.

"Hang on," Tanner shouted. "Here we go."

-35-

Interrogator Prime Clack Urbis approached the conference chamber hatch. He was tall and lean with stooped shoulders. He had wisps of hair on an otherwise bald dome and had a hooked nose with eagle-like eyes.

Clack wore the black uniform of Coalition Special Intelligence with the atom sign on his shoulder tabs indicating that he was an interrogator prime.

He had been on the Coalition cruiser *Bela Kun* in the Nostradamus System. He had spoken to Centurion Tanner, and he had witnessed the *Dark Star* escaping from them. The vessel had come to the Petrus System as he'd foreseen, although there were others who hadn't believed him.

Now, Clack and the *Bela Kun* had joined the Expeditionary Fleet. It was not a conquering fleet such as had annihilated the Remus AirSpace Service. No. This was a fast fleet meant to chase a dream, a will-o-wisp that had long eluded Special Intelligence. This fleet lacked battleships or even battle cruisers. The biggest warship was the Cruiser *Bela Kun*.

In the fleet were four cruisers, seven destroyers, nine escort vessels and eleven raiders similar to the Remus *Gladius*-class raider. It wasn't a necessarily intimidating fleet. Several battleships could easily scare it off. But the Petrus System did not possess battleships or even battle cruisers. Likely, the paradisiacal scoundrels didn't even have cruisers or destroyers. They did have the asteroid belt and strongpoints with laser turrets. Coalition Special Intelligence knew that much.

The marines on duty before the conference chamber hatch stood at attention. Clack Urbis knew better than to try to barge past them. He was above such petty displays, especially as the marines might well attempt to bar his path. That would be a loss of face. Special Intelligence interrogators deplored any loss of face.

Instead, Clack stood before the two marines, waiting.

At last, one of the marines cocked his head. The earpiece in his ear glowed red. The hatch slid open, and the marine nodded to Clack.

The Special Intelligence interrogator strode through, entering a large conference chamber. Two commodores sat on the left side of the table. The admiral was at the head of the table. Each commodore was a large man with excessive braid on his uniform. The admiral was different.

Admiral Sensei May was taller and leaner than the interrogator prime. She had gaunt features and a plain uniform. The only wrinkles were around her eyes. They were the only concession to her extended life treatment.

"Ah, Interrogator Prime," she said, "please, come sit down."

Clack Urbis knew a moment of uncertainty. He was a hard man who had done many foul deeds. He had listened to many people blubber for mercy, telling all their secrets lest they feel more pain. He believed that he could break anyone. But that was no mean feat. Many others could do the same. In his humble opinion, he also possessed one of the keenest minds in the Coalition. Another of those minds was here before him, Sensei May, the Chairman's daughter.

In a slow gait, Clack moved to the indicated chair. He sat quietly, ignoring the commodores who watched his every move.

The Chairman's daughter regarded him. "You had the Remus ship in your sights, Interrogator. Yet, you lost the ship in the Nostradamus System."

"We trailed it here, Admiral."

"Have we?"

Clack did not allow himself to frown or become agitated. He knew the Golden Path, the Stalin mind trick that allowed him to purge all emotions from his senses. It left dark rationality in its place, a razor intellect.

"So," the admiral said. "They speak truthfully about you, Interrogator. You do not fear me."

"I respect you, Admiral."

"I would rather have your fear."

Clack dipped his head. "I understand. Fear is a great motivator. Yet…I will work diligently in your service, Admiral."

"In *my* service?" she asked.

"As I serve the Party and the Chairman," Clack said in his monotone.

The admiral studied him in silence. She was a grim figure, often called the Chairman's Hatchet, cutting out the dead wood in order to protect Social Unity purity.

"Do you know what these so-called notables have dared to tell me?" she asked Clack.

"I do not."

"*Dark Star* has escaped from the hideaway," she said. "They have flown the star system. What is even more interesting is that my sensor officers have confirmed the information."

"That's impossible. There hasn't been enough time for them to enter hyperspace."

The admiral's features tightened, increasing her ugliness. "Do you dare to question me?"

"No," Clack said. "I rescind my words."

"You cannot, as I have recorded them."

"Ah. Of course. Then yes, I did say—"

"Never mind," she snapped. "I don't care about that. I want the *Dark Star*. I want the crew and I want to know where they're going."

"Admiral, despite your sensor officers, I believe the Remus raider is still in the Petrus System."

"Yet my officers have scanned for hours since the message. No one has spotted anything."

"Still, I believe the raider is in the system."

246

"What do I care what you *believe*? You failed in the Nostradamus System, and now, your vaunted destroyer that you'd stationed here has proven tardy in its news."

Clack put his slender hands on the table. "May I speak frankly, Admiral?"

She glanced at the beefy commodores before regarding him. "Do you think your Special Intelligence affiliation will protect you from my wrath?"

"I am uncertain regarding that."

Her mouth opened in surprise. "Do you think I enjoy those who say whatever thought enters their head?"

"I do not."

"Do you think you are special?"

"Yes," he said.

A slow and terrible grin slid onto her face. "Indeed, this is news. You are so special that I would gain from listening, even *heeding* your views?"

"Yes."

"Ah…" she said. "You are brave, and thus, I should be impressed with you, is that it?"

"No."

"What then?" she snapped. "I grow tired of these word games. I grow tired of your sly glances and emotionless manner. You are dull, Interrogator Prime. I abhor dullness in any form."

"I believe we are close to a truth, Admiral. I believe the hideaway is critical to that end."

"How?" she asked. "Once again, we have lost the *Dark Star*."

"Merely for the moment," Clack said in his monotone.

"I do not understand your trite statement."

"Admiral, this is the perfect instance to employ my skills. I will go to the hideaway, trace the prey's path and learn his objectives. He has taken a Shand with him."

"Why do you state the obvious? If the raider lacked a Shand, I would not be here. What do we care about the *Dark Star* except that it carries one of the ancient scourges?"

Clack nodded patiently.

247

"And another thing," the admiral said. "How do you think you're going to the hideaway? It could cost half my fleet to fight my way in."

"It might well cost all the fleet," Clack corrected.

The admiral studied him balefully.

"Thus, we should deal with them," Clack said. "We can besiege the asteroid belt easily enough. I do not believe the notables possess enough ships in common to be able to come out and challenge us."

"Challenge *me*," the admiral said.

Clack inclined his head.

"Well?" she demanded. "You still haven't explained yourself."

"Threaten or cajole them," he said. "Either way, force them to accept a raider into the hideaway. I will join the vessel with a few marines. Once at the hideaway, I will retrace our prey's steps—"

"You are willing to go into the hideaway alone?" she asked.

He nodded.

"You are an Interrogator Prime. I cannot allow you to fall into enemy hands, even into criminal hands. You know too many State secrets."

Here it was—the great gamble. Would she see through his offer, though? It might mean an ugly death if she did so.

"Rig me with an explosive," Clack suggested emotionlessly.

The admiral's eyes narrowed as she sucked in her breath. "What you're suggesting goes against a direct dictate of Chairman Malakind. If I agreed to it—it might mean my head."

Clack said nothing.

"You are a deviant to suggest such an idea," she said.

"We chase a Shand. Special Intelligence knows two things about them. One, they are filled with ancient secrets. Those secrets can build empires or overturn them. Two, Shands are extraordinarily difficult to run to ground and capture. To do so we might have to bend or even break a rule or two."

"Oh, that is bold, very bold, Interrogator Prime. Perhaps you are not dull, after all. You are a veritable…" The admiral sat back, studying him through half-lidded eyes. "Yes," she whispered. "My own people will rig you with the cortex bomb. Or do you want to withdraw your suggestion now?"

"No. I am ready to serve Social Unity no matter the cost."

"Oh, that is well said, well said, Interrogator. First, however, I will have to haggle with these parasites. If they agree to my terms, you will go to this asteroid fortress. If they decline…well, for your sake, let us hope they do not decline."

***

The Coalition fleet accelerated for the asteroid belt. As the Coalition cruisers, destroyers, escorts ships and raiders bored in, the admiral spoke via screen to Notable Magnus Shelly.

The talk took time, as each transmission traveled at light speed. A day passed. The fleet no longer accelerated, but coasted at its present velocity for the belt.

The talks resumed. The admiral felt the notable had become nervous. Finally, the Coalition fleet began to decelerate. They made the appearance of being willing to enter the asteroid belt at a crawl and battle their way all the way in.

Finally, the admiral summoned Interrogator Prime Clack Urbis to the conference chamber.

The same two commodores were there at the exact same locations. They watched Clack with the same hostility.

The Special Intelligence interrogator no longer believed that was their true rank. They were guards pure and simple. They might even be the ones who would torture him if it came to that.

"The notables have agreed," the admiral said. "You will leave in two hours. Are you still willing?"

"I am, Admiral."

"The cortex bomb has already been affixed?"

Clack might have smiled glumly if he'd allowed himself emotions. He did not. Thus, he merely nodded. His head still ached where they'd done the drilling.

"Do you have any last words?" the admiral asked.

He did not, so he said nothing.

"You are a cool operator," the admiral said. "Perhaps you will succeed. I give you three days, no more."

He stared at her.

"If the Remus people truly have a Shand, we cannot allow them anymore headway than that."

Clack silently disagreed, but she was the Chairman's daughter, so he kept his mouth shut. If she had been a mere admiral—well, she wasn't.

"Three days," he said. "It will be as you say."

***

The Interrogator Prime reached the hideaway with very little time to spare. He knew the bomb in his brain was on a timer. He had to get back to the flagship before the last tick. Otherwise, his brains would splatter the walls of whatever room he happened to be in at that moment.

He believed the admiral had blundered. Once he ran out of time—almost out of time so he had to go—he would make up what he had to in order to survive. Clack Urbis wasn't going to leave his brains in a parasitical pesthole like the hideaway. The trip back through the asteroid belt could give him the time to come up with a good story.

First, though, he would do one of the things he was best at: solving puzzles.

Clack met the Notable Magnus Shelly. He asked her a series of questions and jotted down her answers. He believed she was angry at the Shand. A glance at the damage the raider had made leaving showed the interrogator why she had reason to be.

After the interview, he tracked Lord Acton and this Centurion Tanner's journey through the asteroid. He studied the weapon shops and tried to figure out where the Shand could have bought the mythical Third Period Innoo Flaam blaster. What a quaint, even preposterous name.

Clack went into several weapons shops. He did not find a small old man with stubby fingers, however, as that weapons shop owner had departed two days ago.

After scouring the trail, he watched videos of the crew. The patrician was pretty. He would like to get his hands on her. He would know what to do before he broke her, oh yes, Clack would know exactly what to do with Ursa Varus.

After he calmed down from his sexual fantasy, he continued to watch the videos and question others. He checked his chrono often. Time was ticking down for him.

The Interrogator Prime learned about the modifications made to the *Gladius*-class raider. He studied the specs to the nonferrous material patched onto the hull. He spoke to those who had spoken to the crew. He listened, considered and studied star charts.

What interested him most was the sleep chambers put on the raider. Why would the Shand install those onto the tiny vessel?

The conclusion seemed obvious. They were going to make a very long jump.

At last, the Interrogator Prime realized his mission was over. He had to leave, which he did, entering the Coalition raider and wending his way through the dusty asteroid belt. Finally, he reached regular space and accelerated hard. To his dismay, Clack found that the main fleet had accelerated back for hyperspace territory.

He went to the comm officer and demanded she put him through at once to the admiral. That took an entire thirty minutes. Finally, however, the Interrogator Prime spoke to the admiral via screen.

"I have discovered the answer," Clack said with a slight tremor to his voice.

"Excellent," the admiral said. "You may tell me at once."

He cleared his throat as a stir of emotion touched his heart. He did not like the feeling. "Before I speak—"

"Interrogator Prime," the admiral said in a stern voice. "I order you to tell me. We can worry about your personal problems later. Or are you like the capitalists? Do you worry first about yourself and the state second?"

"I do not," he whispered. Even though he tried not to do so, Clack had just glanced at his chrono. He had very little time left.

"I am waiting," the admiral said with a smirk.

"Please," he heard himself say.

"Please?" she asked. "An Interrogator Prime has said please. Will wonders never cease."

The admiral was a callous bitch, Clack realized. He found that he hated her, and maybe it showed on his face.

"Oh, settle down," she told him. "Before you know it, you'll say something regretful and I'll have to order you shot. You have three extra days. You're quite safe."

Extreme relief washed through him. "You swear this is true by…by the Chairman?"

"You wanted me to swear by a deity, didn't you?" the admiral asked.

"No," he lied.

The admiral snapped her fingers. "Never mind about that. Where is the raider headed, do you know?"

"There are three possibilities," he said.

"Name them."

He did so in order of preference.

"You have made thorough notes of your mission?" she asked.

Clack nodded.

"Splendid," the admiral said. "Radio those to me and hurry back. I want to study the notes before I speak with you about the journey."

"Yes, Admiral," he said, trying for his former emotionless voice.

He wondered if she had lied to him about the extra time. He knew it on good authority that the Chairman's daughter had a morbid sense of humor. He could not trust her. Could he hold the notes over her as insurance regarding the cortex bomb? Should he tell her she would have the notes the minute the bomb was removed from his skull?

No. He didn't dare. He would be disobeying a direct order if he failed to send the notes now. Then, she could legally destroy him. He would have to take a dreadful risk.

"I'm waiting, Interrogator," she said.

Did he detect a hint of mockery in her voice? He was sure he did. With the greatest trepidation, Clack tapped the transmission button. Then he waited, staring at the chrono, wondering just how much longer he really had left to live.

-36-

Tanner fell into the deep sleep of utter exhaustion. His body was thoroughly beat. Perhaps his conscience might have bothered him about flying the *Dark Star* through the asteroid base, but something about the Innoo Flaam halted that.

The centurion slept with the ancient blaster cradled in his arms as a child might hug a teddy bear. He shifted every few hours, and a groan escaped his pressed together lips from time to time. He dreamed about an eerie land of rusted towers and glowing pits. The dream horizon pulsed with purplish-orange colors. Metallic screeches sounded like soulless bats. In the dream, Tanner crept through the land with the blaster ready and glowing. Something watched. Something waited. It desired his soul, to devour him, to transform him into a murderous thing that hunted humans.

After what seemed like an eternity of walking, the dream Tanner came upon a huge hole in the ground. Steel tracks led into the gloom. It was dark down there. Tanner gripped the blaster harder than ever, and in a slow tread, he entered the cavern of steel.

He could feel the hungering things wanting to devour him. They called to him in his sleep, pleading, promising and beseeching that he hurry it up already. They had been slumbering for too long as it was. Their ancient enemy might find them. Before that one came, they must rearm and re-train for another gigantic conflict.

As Tanner set foot into the cavern, an all-encompassing horn blasted. The ground trembled. The skies shook and the horn-noise intensified. What did it mean?

Tanner looked around wildly. Would the ground split open? Would cyborgs emerge?

"No!" Tanner shouted, bolting upright in his room on the *Dark Star*. Sweat drenched him. His blanket was in disarray and he clutched the heavy blaster against his chest.

Once again, the hatch buzzer sounded.

Tanner stared at it. Had the noise entered his dream? With a grunt, he set the blaster on the nightstand and went to the hatch, opening it.

Greco stood there looking worried. When the apeman saw Tanner, he stepped back, his gaze going up and down.

"What happened to you?" Greco asked. "Are you feverish?"

"I don't think so."

"You're soaked with sweat."

"Bad dreams," Tanner said.

"Those don't make you sweat like that."

"Forget it," Tanner said. "What's the problem? Why are you buzzing me?"

"Oh. You've been out for days."

"What? Two whole days? Big deal. I was beat."

"No," Greco said, "try four and half days."

"Come on. That's not possible."

"Lord Acton suggested I wake you up."

Tanner rubbed his face. He felt worse than ever and famished, and his garments stuck to him. He hadn't even taken them off…four and half days ago. Could that be right?

"Okay," he said. "Let me rinse off, eat and meet you in the control room."

Greco nodded.

"Is anything wrong?" Tanner asked.

"I'll tell you later."

"Sure. Fine. My head is sore. Let me get some chow in my belly and I'll start to feel better."

***

Tanner sat down at the controls beside Greco. The apeman grinned at him. The centurion studied the sensor board.

"The Coalition fleet is moving out-system," Tanner said. "That means they came in-system."

Greco told him about a Coalition raider that had gone all the way into the asteroid belt. "But this is even more interesting." The apeman tapped a control.

Tanner listened to intercepted messages going between the raider and the flagship. "I thought the Coalition encrypted everything."

"They do."

"But I'm hearing the actual words," Tanner said.

"Isn't it great?" Greco said. "For once, we have the advanced gadgets. A guy could get used to this."

Tanner rubbed his jaw.

"You don't like it?" Greco asked.

"Of course I do," Tanner said. "I'm just curious. This is high-grade equipment, maybe some of the best in the Backus Cluster. How come Magnus Shelly had it lying around to sell to us?"

Greco shrugged.

"Doesn't that strike you as a little too coincidental?"

The apeman became thoughtful. "Do you think Magnus Shelly was in this from the beginning? Is she working for Acton? That hardly seems possible. Why would Acton have boarded our old raider if he had access to better all this time? No. You're too pessimistic. We got a break for once. Maybe we should just leave it at that."

"Yeah," Tanner said. "Our big break is what troubles me. We've never had one before. Why should we get one now? It makes me suspicious."

"The sleep didn't do you any good, boss."

Tanner kept rubbing his jaw. All those bad dreams had soured his mood. "Acton did bargain with triton, more than I've ever heard of anyone having in one place. We should have received ten raiders like this for the amount he paid, not just one."

"Shelly didn't have to be in cahoots with Acton," Greco said. "She just had to have the equipment to sell. Maybe she'd been saving some of this stuff for a long time, wondering if she'd ever find someone with the money to buy it off her."

"Maybe I'm just being paranoid," Tanner muttered.

He watched the Coalition fleet for a time, listening to the various exchanges. The *Dark Star* was a super-raider now. Yet, would that be enough against the worst scourge in the galaxy? The Old Federation had left powerful sentinels in the system while the cyborgs might have even worse defenses on and under the planetary surface. What waited for them on Planet Zero, on the last planet on the galactic rim?

Tanner brooded for half a day, finally running into Acton.

"Sleep well?" the Shand asked.

Was it Tanner's imagination, or did Acton seem too interested in his sleep? "It felt awesome." Tanner slapped his chest. "I've never felt better or more refreshed."

"That's odd. Your features don't show it."

"Looks can be deceiving," Tanner said.

"I forgot to warn you about one, hmm, strange phenomenon regarding the blaster." Acton paused before saying, "It has an effect on one's subconscious over time. In some people, it produces a murderous desire to kill. In others, it brings on bouts of depression. You didn't sleep with the blaster near you, did you?"

"Nope," Tanner said.

Acton eyed him sidelong. "I hope you're telling me the truth."

"You hope I'm telling you the truth," Tanner nearly shouted. "You're the one who's always spinning tales or, or—"

"I see," Acton said. "You slept with the blaster near. I should have remembered to tell you about that tiny drawback. The ancient weapon has obviously affected you. I have a theory as to the process involved. I believe it has something to do with the energy beings. Some of their essence drained into the blaster to give it a harmful aura."

"How's that even possible?" Tanner scoffed.

"The force field, of course," Acton said. "That's the obvious method. As the energy creatures attempted to breach the force field, some of their essence must have drained into the gun. You must beware of keeping the blaster around you too long at any one time. You're wearing it even now. I don't think you should keep it near when we enter hibernation."

"Ha!" Tanner said. "I know your plan. You'll swipe the blaster while we're all asleep."

Acton eyed him, nodding, but saying no more about the blaster.

***

Tanner hit a heavy bag, landing solid thuds with his wrapped fists. The *Dark Star* would have to begin dumping gravity waves soon in a stealth deceleration. He'd been doing some thinking while waiting for that.

WHAM, WHAM, he hit the bag particularly hard with two right hooks. It felt good, but if he kept it up like this, his wrists would throb later.

Tanner saw motion out of the corner of his eye. He turned. It was Patrician Ursa.

"Lady," he called.

She paused in the hall, finally retraced her steps and peeked into the small fitness chamber—it was more a fitness closet.

"Patrician," he said, as he began to unwrap one of his fists. "Do you...do you think a force field could contain the, ah, essence of ancient energy beings?"

She smiled. "What a quaint notion. Why would you ever think of such a thing?"

"I'll give you one guess."

"Ah. Yes, the Shand must have told you a tale about your blaster."

"That's a highly accurate guess. Do you think Acton lied to me?"

"What did he say exactly?"

Tanner told Ursa the story about the Innoo Flaam versus the energy beings.

"I suppose it could be true," Ursa said. "Yet, I don't see what that has to do with force fields and ancient essences."

"All right," Tanner said. "Here's what Acton told me an hour ago." He told her about the blaster's ill effects upon people.

"That's interesting," Ursa said. "Do you feel any different since handling it?"

"Maybe," Tanner admitted.

"But you didn't tell the Shand that?"

"I'm sick of his smugness."

"And sick of his always being right?" she asked.

"Maybe that too," Tanner said with a shrug. "But it's more than that. The meeting with the other Shand in the weapon shop showed me what they really think of us. It wasn't an enchanting picture. The other Shand thought Acton should castrate me in order to make a more docile slave."

Ursa nodded thoughtfully. "I'm not sure we can judge Lord Acton by human standards."

"So we allow him to act like a tyrant against us?"

"When has he done that?"

"You're kidding me, right?" Tanner said. "What do you call his treatment of the Lithians? He's put controls in their minds. That's wretched. He drugs people and fiddles with their thoughts when it suits him. I don't trust him."

Ursa was nodding.

"We're about to make a vast leap through hyperspace while everyone sleeps," Tanner said. "We're heading all the way to the edge of the galactic rim. What's waiting for us on Planet Zero?"

She grew thoughtful. "This is a strange voyage, very strange." She stared at him. "You remind me of my uncle. I only had one. He was a military man and could be quite stern. He was also fun when he was in the right mood playing games with Marcus and me. Once, though, a lion slipped past our dogs. The beast was mad. It padded onto our yard as blood dripped from bloody cuts. My uncle saw it, and I saw his knees quiver with dread. He must have known what was going to happen. Very quietly, he told Marcus and me to begin walking to the house. We were to walk slowly. He would go talk to the lion in the meantime."

"What happened?" Tanner asked.

Ursa shook her head as she looked down the corridor. "I turned and looked at the lion. It yawned then, exposing horrid teeth. I couldn't help myself. I screamed. It was shrill and loud, and I ran as fast as my little legs could carry me. Marcus ran after me, shouting in fear."

Ursa shivered while closing her eyes. "My uncle had a knife. He'd left his service pistol in the house so he wouldn't accidently shoot us. That's what he said whenever he took off his gun belt. When we saw that, Marcus and I always knew we were going to have fun.

"Naturally, the lion saw us as prey, and it bounded after us. My uncle shouted at the top of his lungs, drew his knife and charged the great cat. He fought it, Tanner. He forced the beast to turn toward him. My uncle got in the first strike, but it was his only one. The beast mauled him with its razor-sharp claws. Then, the lion bit his throat to choke him to death as great cats do to their larger prey. That's how the servants found my uncle. The lion roared, crouched on his corpse, warning the servants to leave it with its catch. They shot the beast. I never did get to look at my uncle again."

Ursa opened her eyes, staring at Tanner. "When you fought Lupus that's what I saw for just a moment. Instead of thinking of you as my uncle, I saw Lupus as my protector, as my uncle. You killed Lupus just like a lion would. Now…now I think that maybe you were like my uncle, only you won the battle instead of losing it."

"Lady," Tanner whispered.

"We're off to face more lions, Centurion. We might all die, but we must face the beast in order to save humanity. Don't you see?"

"Lady," Tanner said, stepping up, daring to take her hands in his.

She stared into his eyes as her lower lip trembled. Tanner smiled, moving instinctively closer to hug her.

"No," she said. "You must not. We must maintain our decorum. I hope you understand." She tore her hands from his and raced down the corridor.

Tanner watched her go. She was beautiful, and she had been hurt before. A powerful sense of protection filled Tanner. He never wanted to see Ursa hurt again. He never wanted to be the cause of any hurt to her again either. He would protect her if he could.

Slowly, Tanner unwound the other wrap. He studied the blaster, which lay on his folded shirt in the corner. Maybe he would keep the blaster hidden in his room during the hibernation. If it could truly cause him to become murderous or depressed—

Tanner shook his head ruefully. Why did nothing seem to be what it appeared to be on this trip? A feeling of unease touched him. It would soon be time to lay down for the long sleep.

***

The *Dark Star* left the Petrus System and reached hyperspace territory. The raider then came to an all stop.

The Coalition fleet was headed in this direction. It wasn't on an intercept course with them, but it would be in the general area soon.

Tanner donned the special crinkly, silver fabric. It was cool to his skin. The others did likewise, including the Lithians. He'd left the blaster hidden in the engine room. If the ancient gun caused bad dreams, he didn't want it near him during the long sleep.

Once he donned the strange garment, Tanner lay down in a special cubicle. Tubes led from it to a hibernation tank. He was going to trust the Shand, and he was going to trust that Greco's fail saves would kick into gear if Acton tried anything while they remained in hibernation.

Trust was good. A few backups were even better.

They'd debated about racing into hyperspace at high velocity in order to travel faster through hyperspace. Maybe getting to Planet Zero faster was better. If the Coalition fleet followed them there, wouldn't getting to the star system several days earlier prove advantageous?

That was one possibility. Acton gave them a powerful reason for forgoing that advantage. The Old Federation defensive devices in the star system might spot them more easily if they dropped out of hyperspace at speed. Those powerful devices might spot them anyway, although they were going to come out of hyperspace quite some distance from the system for just that reason.

"Stealth is our great power," Acton said. "We must do everything we can to save it."

"And if the Coalition beats us down to the planet?" Marcus asked.

Acton smiled strangely. "I seriously doubt they shall win that race. If the Coalition fleet shows up, they will have to fight their way to the planet. That, I think, they will not find easy."

As a cover slid over Tanner, he hoped the Shand was right. After listening in to some of the Coalition messages, he knew those people were dead serious.

What if Acton gets up while we're all sleep? What will he do? Those were the centurion's last thoughts before hibernation took over.

-37-

The *Dark Star* slipped through hyperspace, traveling from the Petrus star to one on the edge of the galactic rim. Hours passed, days, and finally several weeks. The small raider followed the same path used long ago when the last Old Federation fleet had headed for the last stronghold of the deadly cyborgs.

Everyone aboard the modified raider hibernated. The various ship systems purred along smoothly. The computer watched until finally a time unit clicked a relay.

A hibernation unit warmed as oxygen puffed into the cubicle. The woman under the glass stirred, moving the crinkly garment she wore. Finally, she pushed up, sliding the glass open.

Particles of hibernation gases leaked into the greater compartment. It was the former insulation chamber, made bigger to allow for the two Lithians.

Ursa Varus had wakened first. She'd been a computer hacker during the war and had slipped a coded sequence into the computer to adjust her hibernation unit to her new schedule.

Ursa shivered. She hadn't told anyone about this little hack. It was her secret. Not even Marcus knew. She gazed at each sleeper in turn, lingering on Centurion Tanner. He was handsome, and he seemed devil-may-care much of the time. She loved that about him even as she realized he was too abrasive, too given to impulses. Still, she found him attractive. It was too bad he was a plebian in almost all his habits.

Lastly, she studied Lord Acton. *I can kill him. Should I do it?* She didn't think so. They needed him. For years, she had learned all she could about Planet Zero. Most people regarded it as a legend. Oh, no, the planet was quite real and very dangerous. Would it hold weapons to help a handful of desperate patriots free their world from foreign tyranny?

Ursa dearly hoped so, as she didn't know what else to do if this failed.

Shivering again, wanting to get back into hibernation, Ursa decided to get this over with.

She walked through silent corridors, listening to the ship's thrum. The modifications were amazing. Even in hyperspace, they had gravity.

Ursa changed clothes in her room, picked up tools and a weapon. She hurried to what had been Lacy's quarters. It took an hour to break in. Finally, Ursa entered the room with a gun in hand.

What had she expected, a cyborg to jump her? Yes, probably. Instead, she found what looked like a hibernation cubicle. In it lay a partly constructed cyborg.

Ursa debated about what to do. Finally, she opened the tube, and closed it even faster. The cyborg stank to high heaven. The flesh had rotted, or some of the flesh had. Could that thing ever walk and talk again? She didn't see how.

The patrician debated again. Finally, she searched the room, finding a keyboard. After several minutes, she realized it was connected by wireless to the cyborg brain, or whatever passed for a brain in that steel cranium.

Ursa worked nonstop for two hours. She put a destruct loop in the brain. A set of code words would set the annihilating loop into action and destroy the connections. That in effect would kill the brain.

Afterward, Ursa wiped her fingers on her pants. She typed faster, attempting to erase any evidence of her tampering. If the Shand didn't search for tampering, it shouldn't automatically be obvious.

Ursa retraced her steps. She showered, scrubbing herself. Even though her stomach growled, she did not eat. That would interrupt the hibernation process. She put on the crinkling garment and returned to the hibernation room.

"Lion Maximums Remus," she said into a microphone.

The computer went into action.

She settled back into the cubicle, put the mask over her face and breathed the long-sleep gases. The glass slid into place and her eyelids fluttered.

The computer would erase its steps. No one would know she'd been up. This might cost her on Planet Zero, as she wouldn't have slept as soundly as the others had. But she needed an ace card against the Shand. He would want something at odds with them. When he tried to enforce his will, Ursa knew she would have to strike out of the blue in order to beat a creature few had bested.

***

The small spacecraft continued its journey through hyperspace. It carried living beings through a strange and lifeless realm. As it traveled, a special clock inside a hibernation unit slowly went tick-tock, tick-tock. At a precisely numbered tock, revival gases hissed inside the first cubicle.

The *Dark Star* still had several subjective days left in hyperspace before it dropped back into normal space. The others would not revive for one hundred and fifty hours. Lord Acton stirred in his chamber, however. After a time, the glass plate slid back. He rose in a mechanical fashion, feeling stiff.

He had lived for so long now, so very long, and there were still so many projects yet to complete. After climbing out of the hibernation cubicle, he stood there like a weak vampire, simply enduring until his heart began to beat faster and with greater rhythm.

Moving stiffly, Acton headed for the engine room. As he took one step after another, the process became easier. He did not want to stay up long. This shouldn't take more than fifteen minutes' swift work. The key to doing it now was that it would be unrecorded.

These humans were a cagey group. The apeman was most unusual. Acton debated if Greco should have a hibernation accident. In the end, he decided against it. The centurion wouldn't listen to reason or allow any *faint* to touch his skin. He'd been surprised the first time at the creature's strength of will. The centurion was uncommonly stubborn. Acton had never met anyone more so. No. He would let the apeman live. Otherwise, he would have to kill the centurion too, and he needed Tanner on the horrible planet.

In the engine room, Acton went to a small station. He had explained this as a cooling unit for the venter. It was nothing of the sort. This could act as an emergency control unit for the entire ship.

Acton crouched over the unit, programming fast. When the time came, he could override any automated command. It would only work once, he suspected, but once was all he needed.

Afterward, the Shand headed back to the hibernation room. He hadn't even taken off his crinkly garment.

Lying down, Lord Acton waited. Soon, the plate slid into place and the gases hissed. He fell back into hibernated slumber, knowing that he would wake up soon to the most dangerous enterprise of his exceedingly long life.

***

Once again, the small spacecraft continued through hyperspace with all its passengers asleep in a mechanical womb. The computer processed. The hibernation unit kept the frail creatures of flesh and blood alive and the support systems functioned without fail.

As the end of the journey neared, a hidden program in the computer slithered into prominence. Greco had written it for Centurion Tanner.

"Acton might know you woke up early," the apeman had warned.

"What do I care about that?" Tanner had replied. "If he plots devilry, this might trump him. I hate the idea of lying supine, killed in my sleep."

"It would be better killed face to face?" Greco had asked.

265

"Yes! I want all my wounds in the front, none in my back."

The apeman had scratched his head. "What difference does that make?"

"All," Tanner had said, "all the difference in the universe."

The program ran, switching relays in a hibernation unit. The centurion's cubicle began waking its occupant.

Like the others before him, the young legionnaire stirred, soon opening his eyes. In slow motion, he removed the mask, slid back the glass and climbed like an old man from the sleeping tube.

Two phrases kept recurring: *I'm alive. I made it. I'm alive. I made it.* Finally, he had a new one: *Acton didn't kill me. Well, well, well, how about that?*

Tanner managed a slow grin. He felt ancient, as if his blood barely stirred. He tore off the crinkly garment, staggering nude from the hibernation chamber to his quarters.

It took him longer to feel normal than it had taken the other two. He showered, ate sparsely and put on his uniform.

He felt better afterward, slapping his chest and taking a deep breath. Was it time to get the Innoo Flaam? He didn't think so. Let the blaster stay where it was, brooding as it must have brooded for centuries, maybe even for millennia.

Tanner stopped. Was that right? Did the blaster brood? *You know what? Maybe it did.* Could it be alive? No. It was an object. It was stupid to believe it lived.

What's wrong with me?

Tanner moved to the hatch to get into the control room. As he did, he paused. The gun couldn't be alive. It wasn't a cyborg. But if it was haunted, how had it become haunted? Acton had said it was through the force field. Might the blaster have trapped the essence of ancient energy creatures?

Tanner snapped his fingers. There was the answer. The energy creature or creatures would do the brooding, a living entity. Could he communicate with it or them?

The centurion laughed hoarsely. He already had been communicating with them or they with him. He felt…what— emanations from an ancient energy creature?

That sounded about right.

Could he tap into fuller communications with the beings?

Tanner shook his head. He highly doubted that. The energy beings likely would have gone mad by this time. Besides, this was all conjecture. He had more important things to worry about.

The centurion hurried. He kept looking over his shoulder as he went. He didn't like the empty raider. He especially didn't like it with a haunted Innoo Flaam with him.

"Get a hold of yourself, man. Acton has freaked you out. You're a legionnaire of the AirSpace Service. Remember that."

Shortly thereafter, Tanner slid into his seat. He looked at the bleak hyperspace world with its dark streaks. It felt desolate. He wanted out of this realm, the sooner the better.

In order to take his mind off hyperspace and off ancient energy beings stuck on a spaceship with him, Tanner made diagnostic checks of the ship's systems. Everything was looking good. He became so absorbed with the checking that he forgot to keep track of the time.

Suddenly, a klaxon began to wail. Tanner's head snapped up. He checked the chrono. "Right," he said, jumping up, hurrying to the hibernation chamber.

-38-

Tanner stepped into the hibernation chamber as Acton's upper glass slid open. As the Shand sat up, the centurion leaned against the hatch, pretending to pant.

With the sound of his crinkly garment, Acton sat up.

Tanner watched him out of the corner of his eye.

The lean alien used his arms to lift himself from the tube. Acton seemed stronger coming out of hibernation than Tanner remembered being.

The Shand began to cough as he climbed out all the way.

"You're up," Acton said in a dry whisper.

"Yeah," Tanner whispered.

"And you are pretending to have hibernation sickness," Acton said. "Why is that? Ah. I understand. You're practicing deceit."

"How do you figure?" Tanner asked.

"You rigged your unit to let you out before everyone else. That shows a lack of trust."

Tanner felt guilty, and he nodded. "I guess I underestimated you. I thought you would try to do something to me."

"You were wrong."

"It appears so," Tanner said.

"And...?"

Tanner scowled. Why did everyone want him to apologize? He was getting sick of it. "Don't you have things to do?"

"Yes," Acton said. "There is much to do before we drop out of hyperspace. We cannot afford any mistakes, any missteps. I suggest everyone undergo a physical to make sure nothing is wrong with him or her."

"What do you think is going to be our worst danger?"

"That is an excellent question," Acton said. "I do not know, probably when we go underground on Planet Zero."

Tanner instantly recalled his dream. "What did you say?"

"The underground search will probably be the most dangerous."

"Great," Tanner muttered. "I had to ask."

A new klaxon began to blare. The two looked up.

"We'd better find out what's wrong," Acton said. "It could be critical."

* * *

Tanner and Acton sat in the control chamber, the Shand still wearing his crinkly garment.

"I've discovered the problem," Acton said. "We are about to drop out of hyperspace."

"It's too soon," Tanner said.

"Yes. I haven't yet found the reason for the early drop. This is strange. I would— Emergency!" Acton shouted. "Hang on, Captain."

Tanner watched in amazement as Acton began emergency procedures to bring them back into normal space. He studied the board and finally saw it. The *Dark Star* headed straight toward a gravity-well anomaly. If they got too close to the anomaly, the ship would implode.

"We're crossing into normal space…" Acton said. "Now."

Tanner felt a bump, and the universe seemed to flare into existence. He closed his eyes fast. Everyone knew that watching during the switch from hyperspace to normal could drive a man mad.

Yet another klaxon began to shriek. Tanner heard Acton tap the controls, shutting down the noise.

"It's safe to look," the Shand said.

With the scanner, Tanner began searching for the anomaly that had almost killed them. He found it right away.

A huge rogue gas giant was dead ahead a billion kilometers or so. Far beyond the planet was a single star. Was that Planet Zero's star?

"What you're seeing," Acton said, "is a wild planet."

"I never heard of such a thing."

"It simply means the gas giant does not belong to a star system. This planet is free, wild, unaffected by any star's gravitational pull."

"It has to feel some pull from that star out there," Tanner said.

"I am running a scan and an analysis of the gas giant's path. Give me a few minutes."

"Sure," Tanner said. He studied other ship's sensors, searching for anything that might be trying to lock onto them and fire weapons. Once he satisfied himself that the *Dark Star* was safe from immediate danger, he began to study the distant star.

"It's a Spectral type F star," the centurion said. "It has a yellow-white hue and a surface temperature of seven thousand K. Does that match with Planet Zero's star?"

"Yes, yes," Acton said. "Please, allow me to work in peace."

Tanner kept studying the star system. It was still the length of several normal star systems away. That meant they would be traveling for a while to reach it. He doubted they would burn at high Gs. They wanted to go in stealthily, not in a blaze of velocity that any sensor could spot.

He found three gas giants in the outer system and one terrestrial planet in the inner system. The terrestrial planet was in a Remus-like orbit. Given the F-type star, it would probably be hotter than Remus but not as jungle-like as Avernus. That was something at least.

"Oh, this is interesting," Acton said low under his breath.

Tanner waited. When the Shand didn't say anything more, the centurion leaned over to look at Acton's board.

"What's that?" Tanner said. He saw huge objects orbiting the wild gas giant.

270

"Those are gigantic laser platforms," Acton replied. "On one of them, ancient sensors are sweeping outward in our direction, searching. The others appear to be inactive."

"Shouldn't the platform have pinpointed us, then? We just came out of hyperdrive. That usually shows up as a splash."

"Our raider no longer does anything in the usual manner. It has become a highly unusual vessel."

Tanner ingested the idea.

"I'm curious," Acton said. His long fingers played upon the controls. For a time, he stared at new readings.

"Well?" Tanner said.

"The laser platforms are of Old Federation design," Acton said. "I have seen models of those before. That would imply the laser platforms are several thousand years old."

"Maye that's why the thing doesn't sense us," Tanner said. "The sensors don't work like they used to."

"That is a possibility," Acton said quietly. "But that also presents a problem. How did the platforms get into orbit around a wild planet?"

"Uh...the Old Federation guys put them in orbit. That's the only thing that makes sense, right?"

Acton shook his head. "You do not understand. The wild gas giant wasn't there last time I was out here."

"That's it," Tanner said, "time out. You've been here before?"

"Why would that be surprising to you?"

"Ursa said she's been here before as well. If the two of you have already been here, why did you need me to take you back?"

"I was here..." Acton let his words fade.

"Yeah? You were...what?"

"Quite some time ago," Acton said, dryly.

"Twenty years, thirty years, what?" Tanner asked.

Acton resumed tapping the board.

"Longer than that?" Tanner asked.

The Shand still didn't respond.

"Are you going to tell me the last time you were out here was longer than fifty years ago?"

Acton seemed to become absorbed in his work.

271

"Just how old are you, Lord?"

Acton's head whipped about so he stared at Tanner. "Don't ever ask me that again."

"What? Why not? Oh, I get it. Are you saying that asking you your age is like Ursa and me rutting on the floor?"

"It is."

"Okay. I supposed what you're also saying is that you and Ursa weren't together here a few months ago, or whenever it was that she was."

"Correct," Acton said. He pulled out his slate and began to tap on it. He stood abruptly. "I must be alone in order to consider this."

"Consider the wild planet or the laser platforms?" asked Tanner.

"I will be in my quarters, Captain. Unless it is an emergency, do not interrupt me." The Shand stalked out of the chamber, absorbed with his slate.

Tanner watched him go, wondering. Then, he went back to studying the gas giant, the orbital laser platforms and the star system shining in the distance. That was their destination, and once they landed on the freaking planet, they would have to go underground *just like in his dream.*

-39-

The others revived at their leisure.

In time, Greco joined Tanner on the raider's tiny bridge. They spoke for a time concerning the wild gas giant. It had three laser platforms in crisscrossing orbits. Every so often, sensor signals blipped outward from the working one.

"As far as I can tell," Greco said, "we're invisible to it."

"The old *Dark Star* wouldn't have been invisible," Tanner said.

The raider sailed serenely through the dark. Every so often, Tanner tapped squirts of gravity waves, minutely increasing the ship's velocity.

Two days later, Greco made a discovery. "You're not going to believe this. I'm not sure I believe it myself. I've found a gigantic battleship in the gas giant's upper atmosphere."

"An active battleship?" Tanner asked.

"Its fusion engine is idling," Greco replied, "so I'd call that active. Various signs show extreme age, well over one thousand years."

"Why do you think it's down there?"

"The reason appears obvious to me," Greco said. "Given the right situation, I believe the battleship will fully power up and charge any intruder."

"Are there any more battleships down there?"

"I've only detected the one," Greco said.

"One could be trouble," Tanner said, "but at least it isn't a flotilla."

The hours passed as the *Dark Star* invisibly crawled past the wild gas giant and its deadly arsenal. Tanner sipped coffee in the galley with Ursa. They talked about the wandering planet, mulling over the Shand's theory about its not being here before.

"He must be right," Ursa said. "I don't remember a wild gas giant the last time I was here either. Yet, that seems impossible. Gas giants don't travel like spaceships. No one could have cloaked it."

"Maybe it was on the other side of the star as your raider," Tanner said.

Ursa shook her head. "We still should have detected it, especially with the platform making sensor sweeps."

They didn't come up with any workable theories as to how the gas giant had gotten here. It was an unbelievable mystery.

Every hour, Tanner slightly increased the *Dark Star's* velocity. By now, they were traveling considerably faster than before, but it was still slow in relative terms.

All the while, Tanner or Greco watched for the Coalition fleet dropping out of hyperspace.

"If the Coalition followed our path," Greco said later, "maybe we'll get lucky and they'll miss spotting the gravity-well danger. Boom, boom," the apeman said while clapping his hands. "They're gone, imploded one by one."

"That would be nice," Tanner agreed.

As the wandering gas giant fell behind them and the star drew closer, Tanner spent more time searching the approaching system.

It was different with no other nearby stars. After the F-type sun, there was empty space, a vast gulf before the next galaxy. The Local Galactic Group contained 54 different galaxies: most of those were dwarf galaxies. A dwarf galaxy was small, often with several billion stars. The Milky Way contained as many as 400 billion stars. Most dwarf galaxies orbited the larger ones like the Milky Way or Andromeda Galaxy. The distance between normal galaxies was incredible, far beyond what anyone could hope to travel in a lifetime even in hyperspace.

"It's like our galaxy is an island," Greco said one day.

Tanner shuddered, not liking that for some reason he couldn't figure out. It lingered back in his mind, refusing to show itself. He scowled. What was going on? Why would he care if his galaxy were an island or not? Whatever the problem, it remained unfocused but present like a stealthy raider.

By diligent work, he built up a map of the approaching star system. He'd already spotted a few laser platforms in a close orbit around the most outer gas giant.

"Study the different moons, too," Ursa suggested. "I believe the Old Federation people built heavy turrets on some of them."

By this time, the *Dark Star* had finally worked up a reasonable velocity given the distance of travel left.

"I wouldn't build up any more velocity," Ursa said. "One of those sensors will spot us later if we have to brake too hard. If just one of them sees us, we're dead. You know that, right?"

"Perfectly," Tanner said. The huge platforms could undoubtedly generate far-striking lasers.

Bit by bit, Tanner and Greco discovered ancient turrets on the various moons. They also found mines coated with black ice drifting in random patterns. Perhaps as bad, there were over one hundred sensor buoys scattered throughout the outer system.

"The system itself is a fortress," Tanner told Ursa in the rec room. "How did Majorian ever figure he could slip past all that?"

"Easy," the patrician said. "None of us saw *all that* the last time we were here. No one knew we had to be so careful."

Tanner was bent over the pool table, readying a shot. He paused and straightened. "What do you mean?"

"Exactly what I said," Ursa told him. "Don't you realize yet how advanced our new sensor systems are?"

Tanner scowled. He hadn't realized. He'd known they were better, but not fantastically so.

"I've only realized it myself lately," Ursa said. "In five frantic days, Lord Acton completely changed our raider—your raider. It was more than a mere upgrade. In truth, he made the *Dark Star* something different. We're like a ghost out here, one that can see much better than before."

275

"It's like a man in a nighttime forest," Tanner said. "And suddenly he can see as well in the dark as an owl."

Ursa nodded.

"I hadn't realized the extreme difference, but it makes sense now. Yes. I've been so preoccupied with Acton, with worrying…"

"Worrying about his motives?" Ursa asked.

Tanner grunted. He'd become more and more worried about the blaster and the ancient energy beings. He hadn't handled the gun since hiding it before entering hyperspace. Was that why Acton had given the Innoo Flaam to him instead of handling the weapon himself? Tanner had almost become convinced that it was because the blaster was too dangerous to handle, which meant the Shand would have played him yet again.

"It's strange being way out here," Tanner said. "We're alone with the Shand, with his enslaved Lithians and who knows what he has in Lacy's room."

"You have the blaster," Ursa said.

"Yes…"

"Is something wrong with the gun?"

"Maybe."

"What?" Ursa asked.

Tanner glanced around the chamber. Acton must have installed listening bugs in here. Should he have let the Shand know he doubted the blaster? That might have been a mistake, one he should fix this instant.

"I'll tell you what's wrong with the blaster," Tanner said. "I don't dare shoot it in the ship."

"Oh. I thought you meant something else."

"Like what?" asked Tanner.

"Maybe there was a failsafe so it wouldn't shoot if aimed at Acton," Ursa said.

"I don't see how he could do something like that," Tanner said. But in reality he did. He saw it right away. It made him wonder about the weapon even more. How did Acton know so much about it and the energy beings? That seemed simple. He'd met the energy beings sometime in the past. Maybe the energy creatures powered the blaster. Maybe Acton knew the energy being in this particular gun and they had an agreement.

Was that crazy?

Tanner had begun to believe that nothing was crazy on this voyage.

"What are you thinking?" Ursa asked. "You seem so solemn, so preoccupied."

Tanner smiled. "The pressure of the trip is getting to me. The hibernation…I'm still trying to shake off the aftereffects."

"Yes," Ursa said. "I know what you mean."

"Let's finish the game," Tanner said suddenly. "But let's make it more fun. We'll wager."

"What should we wager?"

"That's easy. If I win, I kiss you."

Ursa blushed, blinking faster. She shook her head. "Please, Centurion…let's be friends. I…I can't manage more than that."

Tanner was silent for a moment. Then, he forced another smile. "Of course, Lady." Without another word, he bent over the table, lining up a shot.

Thus, he failed to see Ursa studying him closely as she brushed her fingertips across her lips. Was she wondering what it would have felt like kissing him? Maybe she was.

***

The next few days were tedious and long. Tanner and Greco continued to catalog the approaching star system. They continued to find more equipment, but hadn't spotted any spaceships anywhere.

"I have a theory involving the gas giants," Greco said. "I wonder if waiting spaceships are hiding under the methane clouds like on the wandering planet."

"Seems like a bad spot to hide a ship for a long time," Tanner said. "The atmosphere would corrupt the outer hull given enough time. It would be better to leave them in space."

"Agreed," Greco said. "But the methane clouds would keep the ships hidden better."

Tanner shrugged. "Why would that matter? All these laser platforms and sensor buoys are watching Planet Zero, right?"

"We've seen more than one sensor sweeping out-system," Greco said. "That means some of the sensors are making sure no one outside comes in."

"This is all very confusing," Tanner said. "Why did the Old Federation people leave so much hardware behind? Why wouldn't they have taken it home with them?"

"Lord Acton told us why. They're guarding—"

"Look," Tanner said, interrupting. "I know what everyone is saying, but it doesn't add up. If people were truly worried about hidden cyborgs, why not go down to the planet and scrub them? I mean, at the very least plant a hundred nuclear bombs on the planet. If cyborgs crawl up from somewhere deep, boom, a nuke goes off, scratching those cyborgs. In my opinion, the Old Federation people could have finished the menace forever. Instead, they let cyborgs linger down on the surface and leave all this precious hardware behind. Why would the Federation do that? Does that make sense to you?"

"We should ask Acton," Greco said.

"What for?" Tanner said. "He likes his secrets too much to spill them to us. Besides, he has his own agenda." Tanner scratched his scalp as he stared into space. "There must be something more down there than just cyborgs. Something Acton doesn't want to tell us about."

The apeman searched the centurion's features. "You should question Ursa. She's the one who would know more."

Tanner stared into Greco's eyes. He didn't nod, not even in the slightest. But he saw that his friend understood him. Tanner did know something, and when the time was right, Greco now knew that he'd tell him what.

Soon, the two of them continued to study the nearing star system.

***

In his quarters, Acton sat back. He tapped his slate so the centurion's face zoomed larger. It was clear the others knew he had planted listening devices throughout the ship. What they didn't realize was that many of the devices gave him visuals as well.

Lord Acton reviewed every one of the centurion's features as he spoke. He tapped the slate, overlaying the man's normal responses.

Yes… Tanner of Remus was sharper than his fighting man's features should warrant. The young legionnaire was dangerous. Giving him the Innoo Flaam might have been a mistake. Could…?

Acton shook his head. He wouldn't even allow himself to think that, not now, not here confined to the spaceship with…

The Shand frowned. He must control his thoughts. This was his most dangerous mission ever. Still, the odds of success should be good as long as the Coalition fleet stayed away. If it arrived too soon…all his long preparation might go to naught.

Stay the course, Acton told himself. *See this through. If you fail…all sentient life might be in danger of extinction.*

He closed his eyes, gathering new energy. Soon, now, he and the humans would have to take the fatal step. He hoped he had the courage to see this through, by Rull he did.

-40-

By slow degrees, the *Dark Star* dumped gravity waves, slowing its velocity. Two weeks had passed since dropping out of hyperspace. The stealth ship neared the outer edge of the last star system in the galaxy.

Beyond was open space into the grand reaches of the cosmos. A vast loneliness waited out there, the cold of deepest space. Yet that wasn't the *Dark Star's* problem. Could the stealth raider slip unnoticed past ancient waiting sensor buoys, past dangerous laser platforms and sniffing moon turrets?

If the *Dark Star* could, that was merely the first layer of defenses to worm past. Worrying about what waited beyond was too much now and for some time to come.

The tiny vessel slipped past the imaginary line, entering the unnamed star system. The F type star shined with a yellow-white hue as it had for millennia. The terrestrial planet of the star orbited in its slow circuit with perhaps the last remnants of the once mighty Cyborg Empire down there, rusting for ages.

"We are the ghost," Tanner said.

Greco grinned at him.

"What are you getting so toothy about?" Tanner asked. They were in the control room.

"Your analogy is backward," the apeman said. "We're the living breathing beings passing into the graveyard of an ancient conflict. Those ancients still hunt for their enemy."

"No. They hunt to make sure no one helps their ancient enemy get a start over."

"We don't know that," Greco said. "It's just what our special passenger has told us."

For the hundredth time this trip, Tanner wished Nelly Jordan had joined them. He wondered how she was doing on the Calisto Grandee gigahab. Had she beaten her Rigellian Fever? She could have helped them outsmart Acton despite his Shand toys.

The days passed with endless waiting and watching. Tanner or Greco made slight course corrections, trying to evade yet another black ice-coated mine. They used the new ship sensors, searching each passing gas giant. At no time, did Tanner or Greco detect waiting battleships inside the methane atmospheres.

Once the raider passed the halfway point, they stopped searching the gas giants and trained the sensors solely on Planet Zero and its orbital space.

Orbital space there held hundreds of devices.

"Those are orbiting nuclear missiles," Greco declared one day.

Tanner searched for Acton, telling him the news. "Hundreds of orbiting missiles," the centurion said, "possibly five hundred or more."

"Daunting," Acton said.

"Yeah, there's that. But I have two other words for you, *Lord*: too much."

"We can nullify the orbital threats," Acton said.

"Sure, by going to each missile in turn and deactivating it. Now, that might take some time, don't you think? Do we have the time, though?"

"We will not have to go to each missile," Acton said.

"No? How come? What's your genius plan this time?"

"The same as always," Acton said. "We shall insert down onto the planet—"

Tanner grew alert. "Insert? What do you mean insert? You're not talking about taking the *Dark Star* down onto the planet?"

"That would be ridiculous," the Shand said. "The many sensors on and around the planet would detect the raider's heat

281

shield. By the time we reached the surface, the missiles would already have begun dropping."

"Right," Tanner said. "That's what I was thinking. So when you mean insert…?"

"I do not understand your coy manner," Acton said. "You have inserted before. I have a record of your time in Remus's elite space-strike team."

Tanner smiled. He even laughed. "Are you kidding me?"

"In what particular?"

"Enough already," Tanner said. "I'm not inserting onto that freak world. It's bleak, a desert planet with vast electrical storms. Winds howl at three hundred kilometers per hour in places. With the fine sand down there, that could tear off our skin."

"We won't stay down there long."

"Oh? You're inserting too?"

"I am, my Lithians, Lacy—"

"Whoa, whoa, whoa," Tanner said. "I'm not inserting with the cyborg princess. Do you think I'm stupid?"

"I have noted your distrust, but it is unwarranted. I have proven a faithful companion—"

"Until you start talking about inserting onto a planet no one can leave. Why do I want to spend the rest of my life down there? I forgot. Oh, that's right, no one ever told me about that until this moment."

"We will find cyborg vessels and lift off," Acton said.

"Uh, how do these cyborg vessels get out of the star system? You are seeing all these black ice mines, right? You do know laser platforms and gun turrets will shred anything trying to leave?"

"They will not remain there," Acton said.

"Oh no? Care to tell me how you figure that?"

"Captain, the Coalition is coming after us. They shall clear our way."

Tanner shook his head. "What? You never said any of this before. How do you know they're coming?"

"I know through logical deduction, of course," Acton said.

Tanner rubbed his face, turning away. How had he ever gotten into this mess? This star system daunted him, preyed on his spirit.

"You should look upon this as a grand adventure," Aton said. "It is the mission of a lifetime."

Tanner's nostrils flared as he began to count to ten. Once he reached it, he spun around. "Why don't you level with me, Acton? What's your purpose for coming? Do you plan on letting any of us leave?"

"You have a clear purpose," Acton said in lieu of an answer. "You wish to free Remus from tyranny, from foreign occupation. You have come to acquire a powerful weapon."

"I did. But dying on fool's quest doesn't seem to be the brightest move. I mean, I'll even grant you tremendous weapons lie hidden down there. But the hardware in the star system is just too much. What can fight past all that? It would take a huge star fleet. I doubt a handful of people are going to raise something of that caliber. Otherwise, the cyborgs of long ago would have done just that after the Old Federation people left. The cyborgs would have fought free and gone into hibernation elsewhere."

"That is soundly reasoned, I grant you."

"Now, you're trying to sell me on an idea that we'll come up with this superweapon to fight our way free. But it gets better. You're going to give me this superweapon to keep. You're going to do this while the Lithians are there to help you stop me."

"You will possess the Innoo Flaam," Acton said.

"Right, that's going to trump all your Shand secret knowledge about how everything works. Somehow, I doubt that."

"You are not a trusting creature."

"Wrong!" Tanner said, as heat built up. "I'm not a trusting *man*. Do you get that, Acton? I'm a man, not some brain-scrubbed, gelded creature wired to do your bidding."

"You are overwrought."

"Maybe because you're a sneaking liar planning to double-cross us at the worst moment," Tanner said. "Why, I ought to—"

Acton leapt back. They were in the rec room. The Shand leapt back as he raised both hands, palms outward, aimed at the centurion.

The hands didn't glisten. Instead, Tanner had the impression Acton aimed unseen weapons at him.

Slowly, Tanner released the hilt of his monofilament blade. The knife was secured under his arm by its harness.

As fast as the Shand had taken the stance, he lowered his hands, standing normally.

Tanner flexed his hands and grew uneasy. He had a temper. It didn't show that often, though. Not like this. He'd been like a dog working itself up. He frowned. Is that what had happened to Lupus?

"What just happened, Acton?" he asked.

The Shand seemed to become even more alert than previously. "I would appreciate it if you told me what you meant."

"I was ready to stab you," Tanner said.

"I noticed."

"Why did I get so mad?"

"I am not a mind reader, although I have studied the human species for a long—"

"No," Tanner said, waving his hand through the air. "You know that's not what I'm talking about. Something else happened." He tapped his head. "It's like a pressure against my mind. I don't know why I haven't noticed it before this. Something pushed me, making me edgy. What have you brought onto the ship, Shand?"

"I have warned you about the blaster."

Tanner laughed bleakly. "It has nothing to do with the blaster. Lupus went crazy before we ever brought the Innoo Flaam aboard. This is something else, although maybe it's similar to..." The centurion's eyes grew wide.

"If—"

"You filthy bastard," Tanner whispered. "You brought one of those energy beings onto my ship, didn't you?"

"What energy beings?" Acton said.

"All your boxes—the triton has something to do with them, I bet. That's where you got all the triton. You lied to me about

284

them. You said you didn't know if they'd survived their ancient war. But they've survived all right. That's why I've been so edgy all this time. That's what pushed Lupus over the edge and me to gut him like that."

Tanner took several steps back, panting, shaking his head. "What's the plan? How are you going to get an energy being to insert onto the surface? That's doesn't make sense."

Acton watched him closely. "I underestimated you, Captain."

"Do you plan on killing all of us before this is through?"

"By no means," Acton said. "I require your help and that of your companions. I do not think I can do this by myself. Given that, I am not so ungrateful as to plot your deaths. That would be beneath my dignity."

"What are you hoping to do? What's the big plan?"

"I desire to destroy a monstrous danger to all life."

"Do you mean the cyborgs or something more?"

"I won't know precisely until I go down to see what happened."

Tanner shook his head. "What does that even mean? Why won't you let us in on the exact mission?"

Acton froze. Even his breathing stilled. He remained like that for thirty seconds. Finally, he relaxed, stepping back.

"You make intuitive leaps," the Shand said. "I do not believe you reasoned that out. I am impressed, and that surprises me. I did not think you could surprise me in a positive manner, Centurion. I wonder… Yes. That must be it."

"It being what exactly?" Tanner asked.

Acton smiled coolly. "I will have to retreat to my quarters and consider this. I may have to adjust the plan. I salute you, man. You have penetrated…well, never mind. I must retreat and think about this carefully.

-41-

Tanner spoke to the others in the rec room. First, he went over the room in meticulous detail. He found listening devices, a visual scanner and one other tiny microphone that defied their best efforts to understand.

Afterward, Ursa placed a small device on the green felt of the pool table. It made a soft buzzing noise. Greco complained about a pain in his forehead.

"This is an anti-bug device," Ursa explained. "It creates vibrations harmful to microphones. Perhaps you are sensitive to them."

"To vibrations," the apeman affirmed.

"I am sorry for that." Ursa appeared thoughtful. "I think it's wise to keep it in place. Can you endure for a little while?"

Greco nodded.

Ursa gripped his forearm. "Every precaution might be the most important one."

"Agreed," Greco said.

Ursa regarded the others as she released his arm. "Despite the device, I suggest we speak in soft tones to be on the safe side."

Tanner told them what he knew, although he didn't say anything about his bad dream. An inner voice told him to keep quiet about that.

"This is amazing," Ursa said after he'd finished. "I had no idea. I also have to admit that the last time I was near this star system, neither I nor the others spotted even a portion of what we're seeing with the *Dark Star*. I've never heard of a star system secured like this. Remus would have demolished the Coalition invasion if we'd had half this system's resources."

"I'll tell you what I want to know," Tanner said. "This other stuff is important—our stealth sheathing and fantastic sensors—but I understand that more or less. Shands, though, I know very little about them."

"That's puts you in the same category as everyone else," Ursa said. "Shands are a mystery."

Tanner smiled softly, not altogether believing her. "The more I learn about you, Patrician, the more I suspect you used to work for Remus Intelligence. I think you know more about Shands than you let on."

Ursa chewed on an inner cheek. "Maybe I know a little more than you concerning Shands. Still, it's little enough. They're supposed to be old. How old, I don't know. More than two hundred years old, that's for sure. Unfortunately, that's the limit of my knowledge about them."

Tanner still wasn't convinced. "What about your best guesses, then?"

Brother and sister traded glances. Marcus gave her the slightest of nods.

Ursa drew a slow breath, saying, "A few times, I had a feeling of antiquity concerning Lord Acton. Does that mean one thousand years or simply five hundred? I honestly don't know. He has vast knowledge of many things. He can make deep plans often fifty years in advance of the actual attempt. A Shand is rational beyond our understanding of the word. To date, they have seemed benevolent toward humanity, although there are a few hints that some Shands have been involved in planetary genocides."

"What hints?" Tanner said.

"They're old," Ursa said, shrugging, "going back to humanity's earliest explorations. I doubt they would make any sense to you."

"What about energy beings? Do you know anything about them?"

"I do not."

Tanner looked around the table. "What are we going to do now? Do we play along with Acton? Primarily, should I insert onto Planet Zero with him?"

Greco had his elbows on the table as he clutched his forehead. "What choice do we have? We've counted the orbital missiles. We know they have nuclear payloads. It would take weeks, maybe months to dismantle each one. By that time, the Coalition will have shown up."

"I've been thinking about that," Ursa said. "Does the Coalition fleet matter anymore?"

"What?" Tanner said. "Oh. I get it. Let's say they show up tomorrow. How do they hurt us, as they would be too far out for weeks, at least, to fire any weapons at us? At least, too far out if they travel at our speeds."

"It's more than that," Ursa said. "We saw the Coalition fleet in the Petrus System. Their biggest warship was a cruiser. How could a small fleet of cruisers and destroyers battle their way through the star system? The mines alone would obliterate them long before they reached the inner system. If the entire Coalition battlefleet appeared, we might still be safe."

"Will we be safe if the Coalition launches missiles into the star system?" Greco asked. "Might that cause the Old Federation equipment to become fully alert? Maybe the sensors would sweep with greater power or sensitivity then."

"That might be a problem," Ursa admitted. "Although I doubt it, and I'll tell you why. I think Acton has foreseen that happening and planned accordingly."

"Fine," Tanner said. "That brings us back to the central problem. Should I insert with Acton onto the planet?"

Each of them looked at the other, including Greco who removed his hands from his forehead.

"Maybe you should," Ursa said, "but with a caveat. Acton will have to tell us his exact motives. He'll have to spell out his escape plan off the surface."

"If he's so old," Marcus said, "maybe he plans to wait out the problem. What's ten years of waiting to a being who has lived one thousand?"

No one had an answer for the Varus heir.

"I like your idea," Tanner told Ursa. "We have to know more before we agree. Let's stick with that. Until then, let's continue cataloging everything we can find about the star system. As we do, Greco and I will try to figure out more about the surface and any cyborgs...or other creatures waiting down there."

"Do you suspect energy creatures?" Ursa asked.

"If such things exit," Tanner said. After his bad dream, he had little doubt about that. Still, he was hedging his bets, making sure he didn't say too much about them.

***

The *Dark Star* coasted toward an intercept point with the approaching planet.

At various intervals, Tanner dumped gravity waves, slowing the craft a little more. Each time, Greco trained the ship's sensors on the closest Old Federation equipment. So far, no energy blip had appeared on those structures or ice-coated mines to show they'd spotted the *Dark Star*.

"I've lost weight," Greco said after a raider-slowing process.

Tanner looked up, stretched and eyed his hairy friend. "Not just a little weight," the centurion said. "You've lost a lot."

"I'm too worried all the time," Greco said. "I'm not used to that."

"I thought apemen were carefree."

"Compared to you Remus men we are," Greco said. "But that's due to our lifestyle. Being cooped up in a spaceship for an extended period and with all this responsibility pressing down on me...my appetite disappears for days at a time."

"What do you do with apemen like that back on Avernus?"

"Throw a party," Greco said. "Get him a female, maybe several. Stay drunk for a week, the obvious remedies."

"We don't have any booze on board."

"Although there is a woman," Greco said.

Tanner found himself frowning.

"You don't want to share her?" Greco asked.

"Is that a serious question? Are apemen leaches?"

"No and no," Greco said, smiling. Both of them looked at his stomach as it rumbled. "I needed that," the apeman said. "I'm heading to the galley."

Tanner nodded as his friend got up and left. When the sounds of the apeman's footfalls faded, the centurion leaned forward, focused on the sensor scope.

The star system's terrestrial planet neared. It was a barren world lacking any oceans or large bodies of water. Tanner had a found a few lakes filled with water. There were greater volumes of liquid underground. By the indications, hell-burners and greater had once pounded the planet. Much of the water had boiled away into space at that time. That seemed beyond reason, yet the indications were there. Two giant craters showed on the rocky continents. Someone had rained at least two asteroids onto Planet Zero. It amazed Tanner the planet still had an atmosphere. Then, it had surprised him it was a breathable atmosphere.

Finding a colossal terraforming plant had changed the equation. For days, Tanner had scanned the vast structure. Processes worked down there, fueled by fusion engines. There was no sign of life, however. There was no sign of weaponry or defensive equipment. Even so, hour after hour, day by day, the giant plant scrubbed the atmosphere, making it more breathable. Despite its size and the volume of air passing through, it would have taken the terraforming plant hundreds of years to have gotten the atmosphere to this point.

Tanner had questions concerning the terraforming plant. If the cyborgs had built it, why hadn't the Old Federation people destroyed it? If the cyborgs hadn't built it, who had? The indications showed great age. Was the age great enough to match the Old Federation equipment?

For some reason, Tanner doubted that. Building the terraforming plant would have taken massive work in a short amount of time or hard work over a massive amount of time. Yet, the time couldn't have been too long or the process wouldn't have turned the atmosphere breathable by now.

If someone had built the plant after the Old Federation people left, why hadn't the orbital nukes obliterated it?

There were too many mysteries concerning Planet Zero. The longer he studied the world, the more Magnus Shelly's modifications to the raider amazed him. Tanner doubted the notable had just happened to have these various techs on hand. It seemed more reasonable that she'd gathered them over time, saving them for the day a Shand offered an outrageous amount of triton for them.

What had Ursa said? A Shand often made plans fifty years in advance. That might be long enough to gather the equipment to make the raider a super stealth craft.

Tanner bent down, tapping adjustments to the scope. The planet possessed few lakes and no oceans. In their place were desert oceans and endless mountain chains. They were not jagged mountains ranging into the sky, but rounded ranges low to earth. Endless grit and wind must have worn down the peaks.

The sensor began to beep. Tanner's fingers moved fast over the board. He focused, narrowing the observed territory. The beeping lessened. He adjusted again. The beeping quickened and Tanner soon found another hole.

So far, he had counted six giant holes that led underground. None of those holes had metal tracks leading down like the ones in his dream.

Tanner swallowed uneasily. He didn't like searching the surface while alone. It was easier, more comfortable, when Greco sat beside him, cracking jokes or just yakking it up.

By the analysis, the hole led to an underground depot of some kind. The scope indicated lots of high-grade metal in the hole. He wondered if that meant an army of waiting cyborgs. Could it also mean cyborg warships?

Tanner sat back. If they had come to gain a warship for Remus's coming freedom, why hadn't they tried to commandeer the Old Federation battleship in the wandering gas giant? He bet the colossal craft would give Coalition warships a deadly fight. Yet, could one Old Federation battleship, even a giant one, take on an entire Coalition fleet? He didn't think so. If that was the case, was there a greater weapon down there under the planet? What could he find here to drive the Coalition off Remus?

Being here made Tanner doubt. If Remus patriots had gotten here before the war, maybe adding several battleships would have made Remus too hard a nut to crack. Now, though, with the Coalition occupation forces already in place...

Is this a fool's errand? Had Maximus been wrong all along?

That was a galling thought, one too bitter to contemplate for long. That would mean his life after the war had been in vain. He would have fought all those war years in vain, too. No! This wasn't in vain. There had to be a weapon down there that would change everything. Whey else had the Coalition hunted them so hard? That must prove the weapon existed.

Tanner exhaled, continuing the laborious scan. An hour passed, two. He leaned back, stretched and—

A klaxon rang, causing him to jump.

With gritty, wide-open eyes, he tapped the panel. His stomach knotted. What had they tripped? The Old Federation equipment must have finally penetrated their stealthy hull. That would be a disaster.

He saw it and a small laugh escaped him. None of the Old Federation equipment in the star system had moved or reacted to the *Dark Star*. Instead, a laser platform on the distant, wild gas giant had just fired at something even farther away.

Tanner refocused the scanning scope away from Planet Zero. He used the longest range, finding the distant orbital platform as it fired another laser and followed the direction of the beam. He saw them then.

The Coalition fleet was dropping out of hyperspace in the general area the *Dark Star* first had. One of the Coalition ships exploded, raining debris everywhere.

The Old Federation laser platform had begun to destroy the new socialist conquerors of the Backus Cluster. Tanner laughed with delight. Maybe this would be reason enough to have come here: to lure a Coalition fleet to its destruction.

-42-

Interrogator Prime Clack Urbis sprinted for the bridge as the red alert alarm rang through the CBN Cruiser *Bela Kun*.

He had already been on his way to the bridge. They had unexpectedly dropped out of hyperspace. The deputy superior had explained that over the ship's comm a short time ago. An unforeseen gravity-well danger had forced them to abort out of hyperdrive.

Clack reached a lift, panting as it zipped up to the bridge. In a moment, doors opened. He staggered onto the bridge, staring at the main screen.

A huge laser beam burned through a destroyer's hull armor. Molten drops of metal drifted through space. The laser must already be smashing through the destroyer's interior decks, causing inner explosions and boiling water. Red flames blew out of the hull breach. The destroyer shuddered as hull plates tumbled away into space. Then, the destroyer exploded, half the ship disappearing in an internal nuclear blast.

"Is our force screen holding?" the deputy superior shouted in a shrill voice.

Clack watched in dazed awe, his usual reserve momentarily forgotten. Who had fired on the destroyer? Could the Remus renegades have led them into a trap? The fleet had already been to one star system with nothing to show for it. This one—

Another laser reached out. This one burned a Coalition raider out of existence. Metal, vapor and human beings dissolved in the horrendous heat. It was sickening and devastating.

"Deputy Superior," an officer shouted. "I have spotted the attacker."

"Show me, show me," she shouted.

The main screen wavered. In place of a nearly blank star field was a dark gas giant. From an orbital position, another laser fired.

"What is that?" the deputy superior shouted. "What am I looking at?"

"An orbital laser platform," the officer said. He was a small man focused on his sensor scope. He tapped his panel. "It's a giant platform, the only working one. Deputy Superior, this is a lone attacker."

"Launch missiles!" she shouted. "Focus our lasers. We must hit it. We must destroy it before it annihilates the fleet."

Clack sat at his location, turning to his board. He saw the laser beam destroy another raider. Whoever ran the platform over there was merciless.

"Move people, move!" the deputy superior shouted. "Our survival depends on it."

One of the other cruisers reacted faster than the *Bela Kun* did. A laser beamed the platform.

Immediately, the platform laser stopped beaming a destroyer. It switched targets swiftly, focusing on the attacking cruiser.

Clack rubbed his fingertips together. If the *Bela Kun* fired, might not the platform target them next? Maybe the best thing would be to turn and run. The platform's laser was too powerful. It was annihilating the fleet. Yet, they might not have time to escape. Maybe the only way to win was to hit the platform harder than it hit the fleet.

"Faster!" the deputy superior shrieked. "We're all going to die because you're so slow. I'll put everyone before the firing squad. I'll—"

Clack stood and said firmly, "That is enough, Deputy Superior. Collect yourself and command with calm. Our survival might depend on it."

The deputy superior wasn't listening. She stared at the main screen as her face mottled purple and red. With her fists clenched, she screamed for more speed.

"We're all going to die!" she shrieked. "This is it. This is—"

A shot rang out. The deputy superior toppled dead onto the deck, her head a gory ruin.

Smoke trickled from Clack's sidearm. He waved the gun from side to side before holstering it.

"Steady as she goes," Clack said. He snapped his fingers, motioning two security men to remove the twitching body from the bridge. He went to the superior's chair, sitting down. Without taking a deep breath, with no noticeable reaction, he said, "We will destroy the platform at once. Thus, you will carry on with speed. But remember this, keep your head. We are the Coalition's first line of defense."

The officers of the bridge turned back to their boards.

As Clack sat, as he put his hands on the armrests, his stomach tightened with fear. He didn't want to die. Yet, he didn't intend to lose it the way the deputy superior had. He would give orders until the giant laser—

"Sir," propulsion said.

"Yes?" Clack asked.

"I suggest we jink hard, sir. Evading the beam seems like the best defense."

"Do so immediately," Clack said.

Propulsion turned to his task.

"Let that be a lesson for the rest of you," Clack said. "If you have a good piece of advice, let me hear it at once. Propulsion has just received a mark of excellence for his comment and quick thinking."

Now, finally, the other ships of the Coalition fleet began to react as well. Cruiser lasers, destroyer particle beams and masses of missiles from the rest clawed at the giant platform. At the same time, it continued to annihilate the expeditionary fleet.

"It's too big for us, too well shielded," weapons said.

"The enemy has a force screen?" Clack asked.

"Yes," weapons said. "Its wattage is incredible."

"Keep pounding it just the same."

"We are, sir, but—"

"No defeatism on my watch, mister," Clack said. "I don't want to hear anything but 'yes, sir, we're taking care of it, sir.'"

Outside in space, an escort vessel exploded, hurling debris around it like a huge grenade. That took out a raider that hadn't moved far enough away. A spinning chunk of escort literally ripped through the raider, spilling humans into space.

"Who made the platform way out here?" weapons asked.

"We'll find out soon enough," Clack said.

"Sir, it appears the gas giant is a wandering planet. I don't understand that."

"First, we must destroy the platform," Clack said. "We will worry about mysteries after that."

"I'm taking evasive maneuvers," propulsion shouted.

"I can hear you just fine," Clack said. "Therefore, speak in a normal tone."

"Yes, Interrogator," propulsion said in a calmer voice.

The giant laser flashed past the *Bela Kun*. The cruiser was still alive, pounding the incredible force screen over there.

"I've spotted an enemy vessel, sir," weapons said.

"What kind of vessel? Clack asked. His stomach tightened more painfully than before.

"It's huge, sir, massive, unlike anything I've ever actually seen. I studied about ships like that in the Academy."

"Yes?"

"It's a Doom Star, sir," weapons said in an amazed tone.

"What is a Doom Star?" Clack asked.

"It's ancient, sir, from the Old Federation. They modeled it from the first space era, sir." Weapons studied his scope. "Sir, its tonnage is greater than our entire fleet combined. If the laser platform doesn't wipe us out, the Doom Star surely will."

"Belay that kind of talk, mister," Clack said. "The Coalition always survives. Our socialist morale overcomes any obstacle."

The weapons officer didn't reply.

Half the Coalition fleet was gone. The rest jinked wildly even as they poured fire at the distant platform. Then, the laser platform found another ship. The destruction of the fleet had slowed, but it was still remorselessly happening.

"How long until our first missiles reach the platform?" Clack asked.

Weapons ran a quick analysis. "Thirty-two minutes, sir."

Clack closed his eyes in despair. They would all be dead by then. He had to think of something. He had to—yes! "Hail the—what did you call it?"

"Doom Star, sir," weapons said.

"Yes, yes, hail it at once, communications," Clack said. He didn't know what else to do. Maybe they could surrender.

Slow, agonizing seconds turned into minutes. A cruiser died this time. The Coalition lasers hardly seemed to dent the enemy force screen. Would even the missiles be able to breach it?

"Haven't they replied yet?" Clack said, his voice straining.

Communications shook her head.

"Try harder," Clack said. "Our lives may depend on it."

A few bridge officers glanced at him.

Clack shoved knuckles against his teeth, biting them. He wanted to keep control of himself. The remorselessness of death shook him.

No! He tried to focus on the Golden Path. He didn't need emotions just now. They just got in the way of true thought. He used the Stalin mind trick, and almost shouted at the pain of his teeth digging into his flesh. He removed the fist from his mouth.

"Sir," communications said. "I may have something."

"Put it on the main screen," Clack ordered.

A second later, the dark gas giant disappeared. In its place appeared a tall woman with stern features. She wore a strange uniform.

"Old Federation," weapons said. "She's a rear admiral."

None of them could understand her.

"Communications—" Clack said.

"I'm working on a translation, sir," she said. "If you'll give me a moment, I might have it."

Clack's stomach twisted. He tried the Stalin mind trick again, but his brain felt sluggish. He wondered if he would scream soon. Who would shoot him and take command if he did that?

The woman on the screen looked at them expectantly. Something happened then, and the image flickered. She began the process over from the beginning.

"I've got it," communications said.

Clack listened. The entire bridge crew did. The Old Federation woman asked them to identify themselves.

"Do so at once," Clack said.

Communications complied. As she did, a Coalition escort blew into its component atoms.

The image flickered once more. The woman nodded and smiled. "I have waited a long, long time," she said. "I am a replica. No. That isn't right. I am an image. I don't know how much time has passed. But I have remained at this post to guard the terrible cyborg graveyard. You must not let them out. You must keep watch as I have watched. They are a terror to humanity. We have destroyed their empire, but we fear some may have tunneled too deeply for us to detect. It is your turn now. I pray you have the strength of will to see this through. I welcome you to a frightful and lonely task."

"Sir," weapons said. "The laser platform has ceased firing. Sir, it's dropped its force screen. What's happened?"

"Is the platform out of power?" Clack asked.

"The platform must be linked to the rear admiral," communications said. "Once she welcomed us…"

Clack hit the armrest of his command chair. "We did it," he said. "I don't know exactly how we did it, but we stopped the platform from firing."

"The Doom Star is still lifting out of the planet's gravity well, sir," communications said. "I think it plans to come out and meet us."

"Hit!" weapons shouted. "Our lasers are chewing into the platform. We're going to destroy it."

"Stop firing!" Clack shouted. "Stop! If we destroy it, maybe the Doom Star will destroy what's left of our fleet."

"Sir?" weapons asked.

"Stop!" Clack shouted, standing. He whirled on communications. "Give me open channels with all the remaining ships. Do it now!"

"Done, sir," she said.

"Stop firing," Clack ordered. "I have made contact with the last Old Federation commander. Stop firing or the platform will resume its attack on us. This is a class one order. I demand every ship to obey me at once."

Clack dropped back into his chair, waiting. "Are they listening?"

"Yes, sir," weapons said. "Everyone has ceased firing. What about the missiles?"

"Self-destruct them," Clack said.

"Sir," communications said. "You might want to wait on that order."

Clack scowled, stepping toward her.

"Admiral Sensei May is on a closed line, sir," communications said. "She sounds angry."

In the pit of Clack's stomach, it felt as if someone had just punched him. He had given a fleet wide order. Maybe he'd saved them all, but he'd also assumed command authority. What would Admiral "Hatchet" think about that?

Clack tried to swallow in a dry mouth. "Thank you," he said hoarsely. "I'm taking her call…"

***

Two hours later, Clack sat in the conference chamber aboard the admiral's cruiser. Her ship had survived, meaning the expeditionary fleet had two cruisers, three destroyers, three escort ships and seven raiders. The laser platform had smashed the fleet, giving them devastating losses. Maybe it would have destroyed the entire fleet if Clack hadn't acted fast enough. It was the only thing that had kept him alive. Despite his quick thinking, the admiral had put him on probation. It meant he had one demerit. If he gained three demerits, he would die an excruciating death. Of this, the admiral had assured him.

The admiral entered with several security guards. Everyone around the table rose. She ordered them to sit.

The meeting opened with questions. Where had the wandering gas giant come from? What did anyone know about Doom Stars?

Answers flooded the chamber regarding the last question. Doom Stars were the mightiest combat vessels constructed

299

during the Old Federation. Like the one accelerating to what remained of the fleet, a Doom Star was curricular in shape. It had collapsium hull armor thicker than any ship ever built. The weapons systems could pour out terrific, annihilating energy that would swamp most force screen in seconds.

"And this monster ship is heading toward us," the admiral said. "It is clear the Doom Star is empty, run by computers. My analysts tell me the rear admiral who spoke to our illustrious interrogator is but a holoimage. Do any of you have any suggestions about what we should do with the ghost ship?"

Clack looked around. To his eye, it seemed as if everyone intended on remaining silent. Admiral Sensei May intimidated all of them, and for good reason.

"What?" the admiral said. "I don't have any takers? This is interesting. Are you also silent, Interrogator?"

"No, Admiral," Clack said. "I have a definite idea."

"Ah. How wonderful, how truly wonderful. Please, share it with us."

Clack wondered if he was about to earn his second demerit. He decided to speak anyway. As far as he could tell, it was the only rational move. His Stalin mind trick had allowed him to use his intellect to see the truth.

"Admiral, I think we should commandeer the Doom Star," Clack said. "My sensor officers tell me there are more laser platforms in the nearby star system."

"And, and," she said. "Don't stop now."

"I presume our adversaries are heading even now for the cyborg planet," Clack said. "We must go there and defeat them, lest they gain an extraordinary weapon."

"Forgive me if I lack your breadth of insight," the admiral said, "but aren't we about to acquire an extraordinary weapon?"

Clack nodded, feeling sick. He should have kept his mouth shut.

"Plus," the admiral said. "My sensor officers have failed to spot any adversary nearing the cyborg planet. It stands to reason the laser platform destroyed the enemy raider, if it ever reached here."

Clack dared to clear his throat.

"You wish to say more?" the admiral asked, watching him with reptilian eyes.

"If you would permit me to speak," he barely managed to say.

"Ah, now you have grown tepid? Please, Interrogator, do not blow hot and cold. First, you order everyone to stand down. Now, you feel as if only you have the intellect to see the correct course. But now you've become like a shy maiden. I do not approve, Interrogator."

Clack put his hands under the table, as they had begun to shake.

"Speak!" Sensei May said sternly.

"Um, Admiral," Clack said meekly, "we failed to stop the stealth raider in the Petrus System. Perhaps we have failed again because they now possess a superior stealth craft."

The admiral eyed him scornfully.

"Maybe the Doom Star will have superior sensors," Clack said. "These will allow us to spot the raider—if it exists at all."

The admiral continued to stare at him. The security personnel were watching Clack Urbis with hungry eyes.

He began to sweat.

"Do you think you could learn how to operate the old Doom Star?" the admiral asked suddenly.

Clack blinked. "Admiral?" he asked.

"You heard the question," she said. "Now, answer it. Can you or can't you?"

"I could," Clack said, not knowing either way. He realized he had no other choice.

"I dislike risking any more lives in this fantastic adventure," the admiral said. "We have lost too many good Social Unity people. But since you have guessed correctly several times already, perhaps you are the perfect choice to send to the Doom Star."

Clack nodded meekly.

"I will give you a handful of officers. If the Doom Star has run on automated for so long, maybe it can for a little longer. You will lead the way, Interrogator."

"Yes, Admiral," he said.

301

She stroked her chin, eyeing him. Then, she regarded the others. "On another point…" she began.

-43-

Tanner stood as he fiddled with the controls of the holographic projector. Lord Acton was still in his quarters, working on something. The rest of them were in the rec room.

"This is fresh," Tanner said, "and it's also long-range."

He showed them the gigantic battleship that had come up out of the wandering planet's atmosphere. Around it like tiny bees swarmed what remained of the Coalition fleet.

They had watched the fleet being destroyed and became deflated when the laser platform had quit firing. Then, the fleet quit destroying the undefended orbital structure.

"I can't tell for sure," Tanner said. He speeded up the images. "But it seems as if some of them entered the Old Federation battleship. Now, the new fleet is headed here, accelerating at three gravities. Will the big old battleship stop the moon turrets, mines and laser platforms from annihilating our enemy or have the Coalition bastards just signed their death warrant?"

"We must assume the worst," Marcus said.

Tanner nodded. "That's my thinking too."

"Acton knows the answer," Ursa said. "We must confront him with this. Confront him with a united front. Unless and until we know exactly what it is that we're attempting, I vote we stop helping him."

"He's helping us, I thought," Tanner said.

"We all thought that," Ursa said. "I believe the evidence shows we were deluded."

Tanner studied the others. "Okay then, I guess it's time I tell you what I think." He told them his thought about Acton having an energy creature in one of those metal boxes. He told them of his certainty that this thing fiddled with their emotions, particularly anger.

"It's why Lupus went wild, I think," the centurion said. "And it's also what…pushed me to react equally wildly in return against the underman."

Silence filled the room.

"That is an interesting theory," Ursa said. "What brought it about?"

Under the table, Tanner shuffled his feet. Then, he told them about his bad dream concerning the planet. "I don't know if there's the essence of an energy creature in the Innoo Flaam or not or it's something else. But the bad dream seemed too real. Something has been pushing our thoughts. I think if you consider yourselves these past weeks, you'll notice it in yourselves, too."

Marcus and Ursa traded glances. She nodded.

"What is it?" Tanner asked. "You've been holding back, haven't you?"

"Not holding back," Marcus said. "Ursa noticed at the beginning of our voyage that the undermen acted moodily. That is unlike them. We've suspected for some time it had to do with Acton."

"That's what I'm saying," Tanner replied.

"No," Marcus said. "We mean directly with Acton. We believed the undermen didn't like Acton's scent or something similar. Now, your idea of energy creatures—it's interesting. Why would they negatively effect our moods, though?"

"I haven't the slightest idea," Tanner said.

"I find your theory about the triton fascinating," Ursa said. "We know triton is related to high-energy states in nature. Maybe that's why Acton has so much and is willing to spend it so freely."

"The ancient blaster could cause uneasiness or bad dreams for other reasons," Greco said. "Are you sure the blaster could be related to the changes?"

"Acton warned me against keeping the gun too close when I'm asleep," Tanner said.

"Maybe he did that as a screen," the apeman said, "a diversion."

"That's the problem," Tanner said. "We don't know how to judge or test the validity of his words. He could be telling us anything and as long as it sounds plausible, we believe him. He has too many advantages."

"He primarily has the one," Ursa said, "knowledge. That one, however, often trumps everything else." She shrugged. "We must force a showdown. I suggest you retrieve the blaster."

"Why?" Tanner asked. "So I can threaten to shoot him?"

"Do you have a better idea?" Ursa asked.

Tanner shook his head.

"Why are you troubled?" she asked.

Tanner chewed on his lower lip. "I don't understand Acton. I'd like to know what a Shand is exactly. How alien is he?"

"What kind of question is that?" Ursa asked. "An alien—"

"I'll tell you," Tanner said. He pointed at Greco. "One could argue apemen are alien. One could even make a point that undermen are alien from humans. They're a different species, are they not?"

"It depends on what you mean by species," Ursa said.

"Yeah," Tanner said. "That's my point. Why can Acton mimic humanity so well? Maybe he's part human. I mean, maybe far in the past humans went too far in their genetic experiments. Maybe the scientists made Shands."

"From your observation," Ursa said, "does that seem likely?"

"I have no idea," Tanner said. "I've seen him do strange things. The way he folded into a corner when we fought the pirate gunmen—that was freaky. Does he sweat the drug he uses on people? It seemed like he did with Ottokar. That's the other thing. Why does the drug work so well on people? Maybe because whatever Acton is, it is similar to humans."

"Whatever he really is," Ursa said, "it's time for a showdown with him. We're almost in orbit. The Coalition is still coming after us and they've found a new weapon. Maybe

305

we should have gone for the giant battleship ourselves. Maybe that was the real prize all along instead of whatever is on the cyborg haunted planet."

"Right," Tanner said. "Let me get my gun."

***

Tanner made a pit stop in his quarters. He put on his Remus uniform and buckled on the special holster for the Innoo Flaam. Then, resolutely, he marched to the engine room. He feared suddenly that Acton had found the hidden weapon and put it somewhere else.

His heart pounding, he entered the engine room and hurried to the fixture. With a powerdrill, he undid the screws. Finally, he pulled off the grille. The gun was gone.

Tanner's heart beat faster yet. The bastard had—

Just a minute, he told himself. He leaned in and smiled like an idiot. The big blaster had moved at some point in the journey. He reached in, and hesitated.

Tanner held his palm over the gun. Could he feel anything different about it? He wasn't sure.

The centurion gripped the heavy, longish blaster, drawing it out of the duct. With a decisive shove, he put it into the holster. Then, he put the grille back in place and drilled the screws into their spots.

Tanner drew the blaster, looking at the weapon. He—

Wait. He moved the gun near his face. He felt something stir against his skin. It was…a vibration. Would a hidden energy being cause that?

Tanner inhaled, flexing his chest. He marched for the exit. As he strode through the ship's corridors, he thought about the voyage.

The *Dark Star* had been a different ship at the beginning. Maybe he'd changed, too. At the beginning, he had simply been Centurion Tanner, the bounty hunter waiting for Consul Maximus to find a plan to free Remus. Now, he was supposed to stop a terrible menace, the cyborgs from ancient times. Yet, if the menace simply was cyborgs, why had the Old Federation gone to such insane lengths to fortify this star system? It

306

seemed like far too much of an effort. It would have been much easier to just land and dig out the cyborgs.

This is something else, isn't it?

They all knew that somewhere inside themselves. The *Dark Star* was something else, too. Tanner never would have thought to build a super stealth craft like this. He had the feeling they could go anywhere in the super-modified raider.

The tiptoeing through this star system had been an education. Acton had done more—

Tanner stopped as the hairs on the back of his neck lifted. His gun hand darted to the blaster. He flipped the switch so it vibrated and made an audible sound. At the same time, he threw himself to the side.

Something tiny like a mosquito hissed past.

Tanner backpedalled, drawing the blaster. "If you try that again, I'm going to shoot. I've switched it to the highest setting, as well."

His back bumped against a hatch. He scanned the corridor ahead. Acton stepped into view. He put a small needler into a holster under his suit jacket.

"That was a remarkable, intuitive leap," the Shand said. "A pity, though, because now you're making everything more difficult."

"Where are the others?" Tanner said, with the blaster aimed at Acton's chest.

The Shand nodded. "You have surmised correctly. I have put them to sleep for the moment. They are otherwise unharmed."

"You listened in to our meeting."

"Well done, Captain, you have deduced another truth. I used a directional listening device, training it on the chamber. The apeman and you discovered all the hidden microphones in the rec room. Ursa's anti-bug device made the directional listening difficult, though. Still, I heard enough."

"I want to see my friends."

"In time, in time," Acton said.

"If you try anything—"

"Captain," the Shand said. "Do you see my hands? There are in plain sight, yes?"

307

"I see them. I want you to put them down at once. I believe you have hidden weapons in your palms. I don't know if they can breach my blaster shield, but I don't feel like testing it just now."

Acton hesitated for just a fraction. Then, he lowered his hands.

"If the Lithians try for me while we're talking, I'm firing at you."

"You will kill us all if you fire the blaster in the ship."

"That I will," Tanner agreed.

Acton cocked his head. "I'm not sure you're suicidal enough to fulfill the threat."

"That's funny, because I was just thinking the same thing about you. I don't think you're suicidal enough to test me, especially as I have an activated Innoo Flaam pointed at you."

Acton smiled, and it seemed genuine. "I've never met anyone like you, Captain. You are elemental and stubborn. Despite my vastly superior intellect, I find myself stumped more than I should be by you. By you, Captain, an inferior being. Such a role switch is beyond my understanding."

Tanner didn't just fixate on Acton. He kept aware of his surroundings. He wasn't sure what the Shand planned next. If Acton had gone to such lengths to keep everything secret, why should he change all of a sudden?

"Let us bargain," Acton suggested.

"Nope," Tanner said. "Either you wake my friends and rearm them or I'm shooting you. Those are all the choices you have left."

"If you do that, the human race has a greater than fifty percent chance of perishing."

"I'm supposed to take your word on that?"

"That would be easiest and in the end wisest move," Acton said.

"I'm too elemental for that, too stubborn, remember?"

"That's true," Acton said. "Just a moment, please." He made a harsh, loud and guttural sound.

Tanner's hackles rose. He heard a grunt through the hatch coming from the room behind him. He didn't turn around, though.

308

"A Lithian was getting ready to surprise you," Acton said. "He hid there a while ago. I told him to hold just now. Very well, Captain. I will wake your companions. In truth, I probably shouldn't have incapacitated them. I do so hate anyone coercing me. In that way, you and I are alike. I struck out of force of habit, a very old habit, but one just the same. Can we agree to a truce?"

"We can, provided you tell us the truth for once."

"Yes," Acton said. "Let us make this a marvelous exception to my normal rule of thumb. That might even prove interesting, eh?"

-44-

They met in the rec room around the pool table. Everyone aboard the *Dark Star* had packed into the chamber.

The two Lithians crouched near the hatch. They were too big for the raider. Under natural conditions, they would have panicked and started smashing things. Several taps on a brown control unit had been all Acton needed to do to soothe them.

Seeing that had caused Tanner to wonder about Acton's words earlier, saying he had instructed the one to stand down. Had that been true or another misdirection? Why shout when a tap on a control unit could make the Lithian obey?

Vulpus stood behind Ursa. The underman watched the Lithians, his right hand tight around his sheathed baton.

Tanner doubted the baton would slow down the big uglies. Maybe the underman battling the Lithians would give him time to draw and activate the blaster.

Marcus also wore a gun, one of the new ones from the weapons shop on the hideaway. Greco and Tanner completed the crew. The four of them with Vulpus were on one side of the pool table. Acton with his Lithians was on the other side.

"I hope you're all feeling better," Acton said.

Tanner had helped the others after they'd woken up. The Shand had darted each with the little gun he'd fired at Tanner in the corridor. The spring-driven gun had fired needle-thin knockout darts.

"Are you frightened of us?" Ursa asked. "Is that why you acted as you did?"

310

"Frightened of you, my dear?" Acton said. He shook his head. "Of him," he pointed at Tanner. "Yes."

"Because of the blaster?" Marcus asked.

"That amplifies his strengths," Acton said. "I'm not sure it's the critical reason, though."

"None of that matters here," Tanner said. "We want to know the truth."

"The truth," Acton said. "He wants to know the truth. Is that all?" he asked the centurion.

"No more evasions," Tanner said. "Why did you come here? What's on the planet? It has to be more than just cyborgs."

"It is more," the Shand said. "They also amplify the original problem."

"There's something more than cyborgs?" Ursa asked in disbelief. "Then all the old legends about the Old Federation battling the cyborgs—"

"Are perfectly true," Acton said, interrupting her. "The Old Federation fought a terrible war against the cyborgs. It brought about savage destruction and sapped the strength of the Old Federation. The Great Breakup took place soon after the end of the war, with endless years of barbarism all over the galaxy. Granted, there were a few points of light, but far too few. Now, at last, the galaxy, or this part of the galaxy, anyway, is stirring again."

"Were you really born on Manhome?" Ursa asked.

"That is not at all germane to the situation," Acton told her.

"But still—"

The Shand raised a hand. "I will not submit myself to further scrutiny. You want to know about the planet, about the terrible danger threatening all of us. That will suffice for the present. I will tell you that."

"It would be good to know who you really are, Lord Acton," Ursa said.

"I am humanity's benefactor against a terrible event that will soon sweep upon you with a frightful vengeance," Acton said. "It has been a long, long time coming, believe you me. It has taken delicate timing on my part. Now, I suspect, it is too late for them to retreat elsewhere. If we had come too soon,

311

that's what would have happened. The secret enemy would have drawn back, possibly evaded the blow. I suspect there are other transfer nodes in our galaxy they could use. This is a known one, though, and that will hopefully make all the difference."

"Transfer nodes?" Ursa said. "Delicate timing and retreat? What in the world are you talking about?"

"Phazes," Acton said. "They are the energy beings Centurion Tanner keeps wondering about. We don't know what the Phazes call themselves, but it is what we call them."

"By 'we,'" Ursa said, "you're referring to other Shands?"

"Obviously," Acton said.

"What are the Phazes and what do they have to do with cyborgs and this dreadfully bleak planet?" Ursa asked.

Acton put his elbows on the edge of the pool table and pressed the fingertips of his right hand against the fingertips of his left.

"The cyborg Web Minds are among the vainest entities in the universe," Acton began. "Please, hold your questions, Patrician, I am about to tell what a Web Mind is and how it bears on our present peril."

The Shand paused as if collecting his thoughts. "The cyborgs were a terrible danger. Each of their victories allowed them to grow rapidly as they absorbed the defeated into their ranks. It was a wretched process. A captured human found himself strapped onto a conveyer belt. Often wide awake, he went through the skin choppers, which peeled away his epidermis. It was a ghastly procedure. I won't go into further details how certain organs were removed and old muscles replaced with new and more powerful fibers. Graphite reinforced bones, steel plates in places, the additions changed the poor wretch. Circuitry found its way into many places, most of all in the defeated human brain.

"Those mechanical-human creatures weren't the main, carefully constructed cyborgs of legend. Machines made those in a different way. I'm taking about the cannon fodder that did the majority of the dying. We—meaning the Shands—have calculated that many of the hastily constructed cyborgs had dim recollections of their former humanity. To be precise, they suffered cruelly as they fought for the Web Minds under mental compulsion.

"The Cyborg Empire was a monstrosity, a curse against life even as it mimicked life. With remorseless, logical brutality, they conquered wide swathes of stellar territory. If we fail to stop those down on the planet, the same awful conquering system will launch anew into our galaxy."

"Wait a minute," Tanner said. "You said the great danger was something else, though."

"I did."

"But if the something else wins, it or they will still unleash the cyborgs on us?"

"That is correct," Acton said.

"What does any of that have to do with Web Minds?" Ursa asked. "Whatever they're supposed to be."

"I'm getting to that," Acton said. "You are all remarkably impatient. The most simian looking of you has the greatest capacity to wait. That is ironic, don't you think?"

Greco stirred. "Why do you insult us at every turn? I have never fathomed the need. The truly superior don't need that as a crutch to their ego. It shows weakness in you, Lord Acton."

The Shand paused, his eyes tightening. "Hmm, well, we shall see, shan't we?"

Greco said nothing more. For the moment, neither did the others.

Acton finally nodded. "So then, let us talk about the Web Minds, a remarkably gruesome fixation to every cyborg manifestation. Many have likened the cyborgs to ants or bees. They are a hive creature, often linked by wireless servers to each other and to a controller. The first creators of the cyborgs also constructed Web Minds. First, many kilograms of brain tissues found themselves teased from various brain masses, from slain humans. Those tissues were eventually layered in sheets and placed in a green computing solution. Electrical and other impulses stimulated the mass. It contained hundreds of human brains meshed into one. Most of the old memories were scrubbed. In their places, new memories and synapse links emerged. This mass mind was smarter and could think faster and more deeply than any single human could."

313

Acton sat back as he picked up his cane. It had rested against his chair. He used the lion head to scratch the underside of his chin.

"The Web Minds concocted marvelous strategies. They could on occasion outthink the greatest computers and the wisest Shand. That was the true feat."

Ursa glanced at Tanner and rolled her eyes.

The centurion grinned. He was thinking the same thing. Shands apparently loved to boast.

"The problem with this incredible brain power was arrogance," Acton said in a musing tone. "Almost to a one, each Web Mind became extraordinarily vain and even pompous. This seldom occurred right away. It took time for the fatal flaw to assert itself. Truthfully, it caused the cyborgs to make mistakes. It's what allowed the Old Federation a fighting chance against the Cyborg Empire. Often, various Web Minds came into conflict with each other. They logically saw the flaw in that, but considered themselves above such pettiness. In that way, they became blind."

"Yet, even an *arrogant* Web Mind must have been dangerous," Ursa said.

"Oh, yes," Acton replied, "but as I said, it gave the Old Federation with Shand help a chance. And over the many years, those chances added up to victory time and again. In the end, it led to the cyborg defeat. The problem was that as these Web Minds died, new, less pompous ones took over, and their cyborg minions became more dangerous again for a time."

"What does any of this have to do with Phazes?" Tanner asked.

"I'm getting to that," Acton said. He set the cane on his lap and put his elbows back on the edge of the pool table.

"I don't know which Web Mind did so," Acton said, "but one of them learned about the Innoo Flaam and the energy beings. The Innoo Flaam fought the first Phaze Invasion twenty thousand years ago. The Innoo Flaam won, but at great cost to themselves as I've said before. Somehow, the Web Mind learned of this ancient conflict.

"During the Cyborg-Old Federation War, this Web Mind searched for every clue, every hint about the Phazes. In its arrogance, it must have believed the cyborgs could harness their incredible energy. Linked together, the two would prove invincible. Unfortunately for life in our galaxy, this Web Mind had cunning with its pompous arrogance. It survived the last years of war. Carried by its workers in various pieces, it went down to Planet Zero and burrowed deeper than any Old Federation device could follow."

"That part seems hard to believe," Tanner said.

"Oh, the Old Federation people tried," Acton said. "They went to great lengths to follow and destroy the cyborgs. The Federation people took catastrophic losses, and they never could be sure they'd gotten the damnable Web Mind."

"It's still alive down there on the planet?" Tanner asked.

"That seems more than possible," Acton said.

The four humans traded glances.

"What does any of that have to do with energy beings?" Tanner asked.

"Yes, that is the point now, isn't it?" Acton said. "The evidence suggests the Web Mind constructed a transfer node, an interstellar transporter. It dug up the specs long ago on an old, formerly Phaze-controlled planet from the first invasion."

"Wait," Tanner said, "a transporter like one that reaches across space to move someone from A to B?"

"Across a vast gulf of space," Acton said. "We Shands have long studied the ancient war between the Phazes and the Innoo Flaam. The energy beings did not originate in our galaxy. They originated far, far away."

"How do you know that?" Tanner asked.

"I'm not going to delve into details," Acton said. "It would take too long to relate and it isn't germane to the point at hand. It is sufficient to say that in their eternal hunger, the Phazes came to our galaxy twenty thousand years ago."

"What do you mean by eternal hunger?" Tanner asked

"The Phazes appear to be a devouring species," Acton said. "They demolish life at a fantastic rate. Perhaps as bad, most weapons have little to no effect on them."

"Hold it," Tanner said, loud enough to cause the Lithians to snap their heads up.

"What now?" Acton asked.

315

"Our raider has a gun that can kill Phazes, right?" Tanner asked.

"It does."

"And I carry a blaster than can kill them, too."

"Indeed," the Shand said.

"So we're going down onto Planet Zero to kill Phazes?"

"If they have come over, and if they attack us," Acton said.

"What do you mean 'if'?"

"That is the tricky bit," Acton said. "The transfer node doesn't work as we would think it should. It doesn't bring the Phaze over in once piece at one moment of time. Instead, it brings over photon and electrical particles year by year as each 'piece' travels the incredible distance."

Acton continued, with a far-off expression, "A normal Phaze can travel through space, allowing it to go from planet to planet. They have proven that on more than one occasion. But they cannot travel across the depths of interstellar space between galaxies and survive. That is why they need a transfer node or interstellar transporter. They will never build spacecraft as we think of them, so—"

"What galaxy are they coming from?" Tanner asked, interrupting. "The Andromeda Galaxy?"

"No," Acton said, "the Triangulum."

Tanner frowned. "I've never heard of it."

Ursa spoke up. "I have. It's in our Local Galactic Group. The Andromeda Galaxy is nearer at two point five million light years. The Triangulum Galaxy is three million light years away."

"Is that the only difference between them?" Tanner asked, bemused.

"No," Ursa said. "The Triangulum is much smaller than the Andromeda Galaxy. The first has approximately 40 billion stars, while the Andromeda has one trillion."

"That is all correct," Acton said, impatiently. "Over time, this transporter has gathered several Phazes into our galaxy. The half-formed Phaze inhabits a cyborg in much the same way a caterpillar transforms in a cocoon. The crossing drains the Phaze as its energy body is stretched and separated making the journey. Somehow, possessing the mechanical construct

316

protects the incubating Phase. The last particle to make the great journey is the intellect or soul of the Phaze. It also needs time to incubate in its host as it restores its energy body.

"That means if we had moved too soon, the final part of the Phaze would have remained in the Triangulum Galaxy. There, it could begin the process anew." Acton nodded. "Yes, these Phazes would surely try to cross the great gulf again but in a new, perhaps hidden location over here." Acton coughed gently. "We have reason to believe they have devoured all possible life in their galaxy. That is why they strain to come to ours and feed."

"That doesn't make sense," Ursa said. "I mean, I don't see why photon-electrical creatures would or could feed off living beings such as ourselves. I'd think they'd eat something else."

"It doesn't matter what we *think* is true," Acton said, "but what is true. The why and how is the province of others. I am telling you what is, not what should be."

"Okay," Tanner said. "You're saying Phazes have come over."

"Yes,"

"And they're streaking around the planet down there as energy beings?"

"They might soon enough after their incubation period in the various cyborgs they've entered," Acton said.

Tanner shook his head. "What the heck? Can Phazes possess people like demons?"

"If you're referring to supernatural beings," Acton said, "the answer is no. In some fashion we don't understand yet, a Phaze can lodge itself in certain kinds of machines, such as a cyborg, and these machines can serve as incubation hosts as the Phaze gains coherence and power."

"I think I'm beginning to see," Ursa said. "A transporting Phaze goes through life-cycles as it were. Before it can freely dart about as an energy being, it gathers its power while residing in a cyborg-like machine."

"That is correct," Acton said.

"So...how long is the host phase of their existence here within a cyborg?" Ursa said.

317

"A year, ten years or one hundred years," Acton said. "It depends on which school of Shand thought is accurate regarding ancient Innoo Flaam text."

Ursa laughed bleakly.

"How do the Phazes combine with the cyborgs?" Tanner asked. "I mean, how does the entire process work?"

"This is a fundamental question," Acton said. "It is my belief the Phazes use the cyborgs as tools. Once they 'hatch,' as it were, we think the Phazes will wield the cyborg mass as if they were the machine-men's gods. This new cyborg menace will be much worse than the old, as the Phazes will be behind them instead of the arrogant and eventually pompous Web Minds."

"Oh," Ursa said. "Yes, I understand. Before, the cyborgs had a built-in weakness with the pompous Web Minds. This time…"

"This time," Acton said, "there will be no known weaknesses. This time, an alien intelligence will direct the cyborgs in the most ruthless assault upon life that this galaxy has ever faced."

Ursa turned to Tanner. "We have to go down. We have to kill the Phazes or destroy the transfer node."

Tanner rubbed his jaw. His dream was beginning to seem more like a possibility every moment. He said as much.

Acton frowned, looking troubled.

"Do I have a Phaze in my blaster?" Tanner asked.

"No," Acton said. "But you do have a link of some kind to them. It is one of the processes allowing the gun its power. In effect, the blaster senses the Phazes and the Phazes in turn sense the gun."

"Great," Tanner said. "That means they know we're coming."

"I'm afraid you're right," Acton said.

"What about in your room," Tanner said. "You have something there that affects our moods."

"True," Acton said.

"Is it a living thing?"

"No, but it is another ancient device the Innoo Flaam invented. I will take it down with us when we go."

318

"Are there any working cyborgs down there?" Tanner asked.

"That is an unknown," Acton said. "You're talking about activated cyborgs. Certainly, there are scads of them waiting in storage. Still, I would suspect functional cyborgs are on the planet. The Web Mind could also be down there, perhaps having become insane with rage or maybe infested with a Phaze for all I know."

"This is sounding worse by the second," Tanner said.

"This is a terrible mission," Acton agreed. "It is why I came."

"I have a question," Greco asked. "What weapon do we get for our troubles? What is on the planet that will help Centurion Tanner and the tribune to free Remus from the Coalition? Is it a secret cyborg vessel?"

Tanner, Marcus, Ursa and Greco all watched the Shand closely.

"I have already given you a secret vessel," Acton said. "This is an unusual raider. There isn't a spaceship in the Backus Cluster like it."

"That doesn't answer the question," Greco said.

"I know," Acton said. "There is something on the planet that will aid you against the Coalition."

"What?" Greco asked, "A cyborg ship?"

"No," Acton said, "a nullifier. It is yours if we survive."

"What is a nullifier?" Greco asked.

Acton smiled. "First, help me in my task. Then, I will surrender my claim to the nullifier. On this, I give you my solemn word as a Shand."

None of the four said a word. Finally, however, Tanner stirred.

"I want to know more soon," the centurion said. "But I've heard enough to give you my answer regarding my help."

"Yes?" Acton said.

"I'm in," Tanner said.

"So am I," Marcus said.

"I'm reluctant," Ursa said, "but I shall fight with the others."

319

Greco sighed. "I'm not much of a soldier, but whatever I can do, I will do it."

"Excellent," Acton said. "Then it is time to begin planning for the insertion. We have a few more days until we reach orbit. Once we do, we should act at once."

-45-

Tanner and Acton worked in tandem in the control room. When the centurion became too tired, Greco spelled him. Over the next three days, the trio worked the *Dark Star* into an exceedingly gentle orbit around Planet Zero.

A feather couldn't have done it lighter. They had to ease into this. Otherwise, Old Federation or hidden cyborg sensors might detect them. There were more than just orbital warheads up here with the ship, but lasers systems that looked like missiles.

"The Old Federation people were cunning," Greco said. "I wouldn't have suspected that."

"They feared that they hadn't done enough," Acton said. "If we Shands are right, they didn't. The Phazes will be able to deactivate all of the orbital missiles and lasers given enough time."

"Could they make it past the mines, turrets and laser platforms in the outer system?" Greco asked.

"Not fast and while keeping the cyborgs intact," Acton said. "But it is possible."

The two continued the orbital parking procedure. During it, Tanner returned to the control room. A sleepy-eyed Greco nodded in greeting before departing.

"This is historic," Acton said. "This is the softest, gentlest, sneakiest insertion in galactic history."

Tanner eyed the Shand. He couldn't remember the last time Acton had slept. So he asked, "Have you rested lately?"

321

"I am fine."

"Shands don't need sleep?"

"That is an old wife's tale. We need sleep like every biological organism does."

A flare of light on Tanner's screen switched his interest. He adjusted the scope. "Look," he said. "The Coalition fleet is separating. The Doom Star has increased gravities." He studied the screen. "Six G's acceleration—they're moving fast."

Acton examined the readings. Finally, he shook himself. "They will arrive sooner than I had expected."

"You think the Doom Star can smash through the defensive equipment at speed?"

"Possibly," Acton said. "Yet, we can't worry about that now. You and I and my Lithians have an engagement on the planet."

"What happened to your idea of taking Lacy, your cyborg key?"

"She has degenerated beyond my repair, I'm afraid. I have tried, but…" He shrugged.

Tanner glanced at the scope, frowning at the image. "Can a Doom Star defeat all the proximity mines, the lasers and moon turrets?"

"If the Coalition people have figured out how to control the Doom Star," Acton said, "maybe they have override codes for those items, as well."

"Oh," Tanner said. "Yeah. That's bad. Maybe we can sabotage them, eh? Maybe we can figure out how to activate the proximity mines at least."

"If I have enough time later," Acton said, "that is a possibility. First, we must find and destroy the Phazes."

"And the Web Mind," Tanner added.

"That is secondary."

"Not to the people of Remus. My world will be among the first to feel the new cyborg wrath. Isn't that true?"

"That does seem like a logical deduction."

Tanner blew out his breath. "How much longer until we insert?"

"That depends. We must pinpoint the Phazes and the location of the interstellar transporter. I don't know how long that will take."

"Can you do it from up here?"

"I believe so," Acton said. He took out the slate and began to tap.

***

It took three orbital passes around Planet Zero. Finally, Acton straightened, lowering the slate. "I have it. I believe this is the critical location."

"Where's that?" Tanner asked.

In lieu of answering, the Shand put away the slate and began to type on a panel. Soon, he zoomed in on a mountain range. At the bottom of a granite peak was a large hole in the ground. High-level magnification showed tracks leading into the hole.

"It's just like my dream," Tanner whispered.

"That confirms it, then. I doubt the hole will lead directly to the transporter, but that is the beginning trail."

"The hole doesn't make sense," Tanner said. "Why didn't the Old Federation people go down the holes back in the day and destroy everything they found?"

"I doubt the holes were there then. They are a more recent phenomenon."

"I don't understand. Wouldn't their sudden appearance have sent a few missiles raining down on them?"

"Not if the holes appeared during a natural disaster, for instance. The orbital AIs first had to calculate the holes as a cyborg directed phenomenon."

"That seems like a kind of obvious deduction to me," Tanner said. "Big hole with tracks—the cyborgs did it. Launch the nukes."

"On the face of it, you're right. You must take into account, however, that the cyborgs are exceedingly clever concerning computer systems and artificial intelligences. It's possible the Web Mind developed viruses over the centuries, inserting them into orbital AIs one at a time. Eventually, the AIs became—"

"Stupid enough to ignore obvious evidence," Tanner finished. "Okay. I suppose that's possible. It makes sense after a fashion. I guess it's another thing we don't know for sure. But I just had a thought. Why not do the same thing but in reverse. We'll take over a few missiles and order them to slam into the hole? Let the nuclear explosions take care of the problem for us."

Acton tapped his chin. "Let me put into a perspective you can understand. That would be like trying to drown out a gopher infestation with a water hose. It seems like it should work but never does. The gophers always know how to block the water or have dug much farther than the small amount of water can reach. The same would likely be true here. That would have two disadvantages. One, the cyborgs would know someone is coming. Two, mere nuclear warheads aren't going to destroy any Phazes. It takes a different kind of force to do that."

Tanner appeared mulish but finally replied, "So what you're telling me is that we're going down into the depths of Planet Zero?"

"That is correct. Are you ready?"

Tanner laughed. "How does one get ready for that? To tell you the truth, I'm terrified."

"That is the proper response, as this is a terrifying mission. But we have the tools, Centurion. Perhaps if you focus on this it will help: if you succeed, you will gain the resources you need to finally free Remus."

Tanner eyed the Shand. "You'd better not be lying to me."

"I wouldn't have said if it wasn't true." Acton checked his slate. "You have an hour to get ready. Then, you and I are heading down."

"How are we going to do it?"

"Thankfully, I have a gravity sled. We shall use it. One hour, Centurion, and then the four of us shall head downstairs to the planet."

***

One hour and twenty minutes later, Tanner waited in the airlock. He'd shaken hands with Marcus and Greco and had

324

hugged Ursa. He wore an armored spacesuit, listening to the harsh sound of his own breathing. It had been several years since he'd done something like this. He hadn't missed it in the slightest.

One problem with doing this was that there would be no verbal communications until they touched down on the planetary surface. The two of them wouldn't communicate with those in the *Dark Star,* either. They wouldn't give the orbital sensors any transmissions to pick up and lock onto.

Thus, the outer hatch's opening caught Tanner by surprise. He squawked as it slid up, the noise reverberating in his helmet.

Take it easy. You can do this. You used to be a space-strike specialist, remember?

He eased to the edge of the hatch. The darkness of the outer void greeted him. He looked around until he saw the stars of the Milky Way Galaxy. He didn't like the galactic rim, its bleakness. He sure didn't want to go down onto the last planet.

"No one ever asks a centurion what he wants. He gets his orders and then he follows them."

Tanner wasn't sure why saying that comforted him, but it did. He spied the contraption then, and it didn't look like a sled. It was a disc with a central upright control in the middle. Radiating out from the control unit were bars fanning to the edge of the disc. They looked like nothing more than playground bars he used to grab as his friends spun a merry-go-round faster and faster.

The lean being in a spacesuit had to be Lord Acton. The other two were the Lithians, giants in spacesuits with mirrored visors. How did the Shand keep them under control out here?

Tanner shoved off the *Dark Star.* As he did, weightlessness took over. He drifted toward the "sled".

Various metal boxes had been bolted to the disc. Tanner had no idea what they held.

The centurion floated until his gloved hands grasped a bar. He pulled himself onto the sled. Acton's mirrored visor glanced his way, going up and down. Otherwise, there was no communication between them.

Tanner looked around. He saw lines attached to the Lithians' spacesuits and a line for him. Finding it difficult to do with his gloves, he finally managed to hook himself to the sled. Afterward, he waited.

The waiting took too long, so Tanner began looking around. He spied the star field behind them. That was home. That was Remus. Go long enough up the spiral arm and one would reach Manhome—Earth. Had Acton really traveled that far to get here?

Tanner studied the stars. It was strange, this star system was filled with deadly devices, but he didn't see any of them from here.

Motion caught his eye. He glanced at the *Dark Star.* The sled had floated so he could spy the main port window. Greco waved to him from inside.

Tanner felt a keen sense of loneliness. He raised his right arm, waving back. Would he ever see Greco again? Would he ever get back into the *Dark Star*? Would he return and pick up his quest to kiss Ursa Varus. She was a patrician. He was a plebian.

"What's that matter when boys meets girl?" Tanner snorted to himself. Who was he kidding? Sometimes, that meant everything.

The sled lurched under him. Grabbing one of the bars harder than ever, Tanner looked at the Shand. Acton stood at the central control, tapping. Tanner looked at the *Dark Star.* They had moved farther away from it. Acton's crazy sled worked after all. Now, could it get them down onto Planet Zero?

They drifted slowly, leaving the raider behind. As they moved, Tanner sidled toward the edge. He looked down at the dusty planet. It had few clouds, wispy white forms. Most of the world looked yellowish and bleak. There were touches of blue, the few lakes. Somewhere down in that mass was the monstrous terraforming plant. Acton had never gotten around to telling them who had built it and when. For that matter, the Shand hadn't told them the true story about the wandering gas giant outside the system. Tanner bet Acton knew how those things had happened. The Shand said he was being honest, but he wasn't telling them all his secrets. Maybe he'd left out some key tidbits about Phazes and Web Minds.

Tanner shook his head. He shouldn't worry about that now. He should enjoy this. He floated down toward the planet of destiny. Would he survive the fall? Would the nuclear-tipped missiles rain down while he was exploring underground?

Despite his best efforts, Tanner shivered. This was different than facing Coalition soldiers. It was different than hunting down Keg and other ruffians as a bounty hunter. This was grand. It was impossible and it was terrifying rather than exciting.

Tanner chuckled suddenly. He knew how to overcome his fear. He would force himself to accept the mission. He would decide to fight like a warrior, a centurion. He would live or die, but he would do it courageously. He would laugh at death and danger.

As Tanner told himself these things, the disc continued its steady descent toward the surface. This was unlike the plunge onto Avernus. Nothing went by fast.

I can take time to enjoy the ride.

Tanner grinned inside his helmet. He was doing it. He was getting into this. He had a weapon made to kill Phazes. He would find these galaxy invaders and—

The disc shuddered. Tanner felt the vibration in his hands. He looked at Acton. The Shand blew backward, his boots leaving the deck as he headed upward. The leash snapped tight, and that yanked Acton back down toward the deck.

Reacting without thinking, Tanner leaped for the alien. His own line played out, and it was longer than Acton's. He reached the Shand, caught him and helped absorb some of the blow as the two of them struck the central column.

Tanner managed to grasp a bar. So did Acton. At that point, the sled began to plummet toward the distant surface far below.

-46-

Tanner felt the slightest tug of gravity. He didn't believe it was his imagination. The disc went down, although there was nothing yet to let him see that. Maybe it was his old space-strike training kicking in.

This isn't going to be anything like the dive down onto Avernus.

Faster than he could believe, the disc would begin to wobble from air resistance. Then, it would tumble end over end. Soon after that, they would spin. Likely, the blood would rush out of his head, rendering him unconscious. He wouldn't realize they'd failed. He'd just—

Do something, damnit! You're paralyzed with fear or indecision. What good is that?

Tanner reached down, grabbing Acton by the shoulders. He shook the Shand. When nothing happened, he shook the Shand harder. He would make Acton's head rattle back and forth in the helmet.

Suddenly, with a start, Acton reached up. Had the Shand been unconscious? Had the sailing up, down and hitting hard done that? Since they were keeping communication silence, Tanner didn't dare ask.

Acton clawed his way up the control column. He stood there, tapping, searching the screen and tapping more.

How long until we begin heating up? Tanner wondered. Would the orbital sensors pick them up then? Would that be

328

enough to cause a few nukes to drop or would a laser platform take them out?

Tanner watched the Shand work frantically. It wound Tanner up inside, and he didn't see how that was going to help him. Why should he spend his last few minutes in life fretting? Maybe he should think about all the wonderful times in his life. He should—

The gravity sled wobbled.

"It's beginning," Tanner told himself. He found himself gripping a bar with all his strength. With an act of will, he let go. Shuffling his boots, he worked to the edge.

The disc wobbled worse than before.

Motion at the corner of his eye caused Tanner to turn all the way around. A Lithian stumbled. The big man staggered backward. Had he lost his balance? The disc wobbled again, violently. That pitched the Lithian upward.

Tanner had grabbed a bar before the same thing happened to him.

Gravity must have taken hold of their craft. They'd fallen far enough now to reach the slightest wind resistance. The Lithian shot outward and then down. At that point, his safety line snapped, the end disappearing as it slithered over the edge.

Tanner frowned. That didn't seem right. He felt bad for the big fellow, certainly, but they were all dead, right? This was the end. They had failed because the sled had proven a bust.

Why did the Lithian fall like that? We're both falling at the same velocity, aren't we? Yet, the giant plunged over the edge.

It finally struck the centurion. They weren't falling at the same velocity. That meant Acton had brought the gravity sled under control, or at least partial control.

The Lithian—

Tanner leaned over, searching. The Lithian had almost become a dot. He could see the giant's flailing limbs.

If the sled is working, that means the Lithian need not have died.

The realization brought a pang of grief for the Lithian. Was it the one who had bumped his head on the corridor ceiling what seemed like a lifetime ago now? With the grief came another shock. Would a sensor pick up his falling body? Acton

329

had said before some sensors could pick up a flesh and blood creature doing a planet dive. If that was true—

"We may all be dead and just don't know it yet," Tanner muttered.

He breathed sharply through his nostrils. He used his bar, gripping hand-over-hand to the center control column. He tapped Acton on the shoulder.

The Shand turned a mirrored visor to him.

Tanner pointed where the Lithian used to be. Acton turned that way, staring for a time. Finally, the Shand regarded him, moving the helmet up and down. Afterward, Acton hunched over the controls, manipulating them with a will.

Tanner still hung on. At the beginning, it had been dark around them, with the world spreading out in a hazy curvature. Now, the darkness had begun to lighten. The centurion could no longer see the curve of the planet. Instead, a vast dusky field spread from one end of the horizon to the other.

They were coming down onto Planet Zero. After all this time, he was doing it. Now, finally, fear, worry and the other accompanying emotions fought for his attention. Tanner struggled to compose himself. It was harder than it should be.

He studied the boxes bolted onto the gravity sled. One of them must hold whatever it was that Acton hoped to use against a Phaze.

Could they kill a thing that took centuries to cross between galaxies? It seemed incredible. What did the Phaze eat during all that time? How did it sustain itself? Or did the act of passage occur in some sort of timeless stasis?

Tanner gave a humorless chuckle and fixed his thoughts on the mission. He stood there, enduring, as the Shand guided the gravity sled onto the last planet in their galaxy.

***

What seemed a long, long time later, the gravity sled gently lowered toward toy-like mountains. This was like riding a slow-moving elevator. The dark of space had long ago departed. Now, a blazing orange color filled the sky. Greco had mentioned the phenomenon a few days ago.

330

Tiny rusty particles filled the air. They gave the world the orange color. Remus's sky used to look like this during certain sunsets. Here, the entire sky was a blaze of gold and orange. It seemed right, somehow.

Tanner looked everywhere. The sky was devoid of clouds. High above them, the *Dark Star* waited. How many times would the others orbit Planet Zero before they learned whether he and Acton had won or lost?

For the hundredth time, Tanner studied the approaching mountains. They were bare. Not a single blade of grass grew on Planet Zero, at least, none that he had seen. He saw dust devils, rust-colored grit swirling across a lifeless landscape.

How long ago had it been since the Old Federation had walked on the planet's surface? Despite himself, despite the grimness of the mission and the craziness of the situation, Tanner grinned. This was stunning.

Then, the gravity sled shifted with a lurch. It began moving faster, but to the left this time instead of straight down.

Tanner kept his eyes on the nearest mountain. They were circling it. Then he saw the hole. It wasn't just a large hole. It was as big as the mountain. The hole could have swallowed a small town. How far down did it go?

Tanner moaned involuntarily. He wasn't proud of it, but he had seen the tracks. They were large, like train tracks, and gleamed silvery in the orange light.

The gravity sled no longer slid to the side. It was over the giant hole. Worse, to Tanner's horror, the disc began dropping again. It did so faster than before, although it wasn't quite plunging. Without a doubt, they headed straight down for the hole.

Are we going to go into it?

Tanner looked up as the last Lithian tore at the buckles of his helmet. The man-creature seemed frantic. The centurion glanced at Acton. The Shand motioned with his gloved hand, making the move of drawing a gun and firing at the Lithian.

Was that right, though?

Acton repeated the gesture more urgently than before.

331

Tanner would have to dig into his spacesuit to get his blaster. Not only did he not want to kill the Lithian. He didn't want to open himself to the elements yet.

The blue-skinned Lithian succeeded. He tore off the helmet and roared at Acton. Tanner could hear the sound through his helmet. The creature's skin shined, literally shined, as if alight.

The Shand watched the Lithian closely and ducked. The helmet whizzed past the lean Acton, to sail over the edge of the disc and curve down toward the hole.

The Lithian roared again. It was a lonesome cry, filled with poignancy. Grabbing its safety line, the Lithian tore it free. Then, it lurched toward the boxes. With a fixed gaze, the Lithian went for the nearest one.

The gravity sled tilted to one side. That threw Tanner, catching him by surprise. His helmet conked against a bar. Fortunately, he had padding in the helmet. He flailed and grabbed a bar, barely did it in time.

The sled flipped in the other direction. Was Acton trying to catapult the Lithian off the sled? Tanner managed to look up. The blue giant clung to a bar, bawling in terror.

Tanner looked over. Acton didn't pay him the slightest heed. The Shand had hooked himself to the control column. With his gloved fingers, he manipulated the panel.

The gravity sled straightened and plunged down. Tanner felt his boots and then his body lifting from the disc. Looking over, the saw the same had happened to the Lithian. The giant clung on grimly even as huge tears streamed from his eyes.

Abruptly, the disc slowed and seemed to wobble. Were they losing power? No. The wobbling stopped. They continued down under power.

Tanner held onto the bar even as he studied the Lithian. The blue giant clung to his bar. He no longer wept nor did his skin shine like before. Still, he eyed the nearest box with almost total fixation. A glance in Acton's direction showed Tanner the Shand watched his creature.

What was going on with the Lithian?

For the next little while, each of them maintained the same pose. Finally, though, the Lithian dared to loosen his grip. He began working toward the box.

Tanner held on tight.

Abruptly, the gravity sled tilted. The Lithian bawled like a calf, a loud and dreadful sound unlike any sound Tanner had ever heard the Lithians make.

At that point, the sled dropped faster than ever. Sparks flew from the control column and smoke billowed. The craft wobbled violently because it was anything but aerodynamic. The Lithian cried out, tears flying once more.

Acton worked the controls desperately—

Once more, the wobbling quit, the gravity sled began floating and they entered the giant hole.

We did it. We've reached Planet Zero. Now, we're going underground to hunt the energy beings and to kill the cyborgs waiting under the earth for us.

-47-

Clack Urbis plotted in his mind.

The germ of the idea had begun some time ago. He had risked himself several times on this assignment. Entering the Doom Star had been the greatest dare, and it gave him nominal control over the greatest starship in the Backus Cluster. Certainly, the Doom Star was greater than any warship in Coalition service.

He sat in the command webbing in the center of the vast vessel. It was several kilometers in diameter, stocked with awesome weaponry. On the screen, the dusty planet showed its bleakness.

That was the target. After the search teams had studied the ship's records these past days, everyone agreed the cyborgs had landed there.

Clack glanced at the bridge crew. Many had come from the *Bela Kun*. He trusted those the most, but he wasn't sure yet that they would...

Dare I even say the word to myself? Mutiny. Not mutiny against the Coalition or Social Unity, but mutiny against the monster in charge of the expeditionary fleet.

Clack had brought an interrogation team with him on the sly, sure that Admiral "Hatchet" hadn't noticed. His team would help him convince the others. The true resister would be the commodore, one of the admiral's henchmen who had joined the ship party. The commodore controlled the security team of hard-eyed combat veterans.

334

The Doom Star was vast. Clack had come across to it with seventy-three people. Most were technicians, experts in their field. It helped that Old Federation ways were similar to Coalition warship methods.

"I've detected another cluster of mines, sir," weapons said. It was the same weapons man as had been aboard the *Bela Kun*.

"Did you give these mines the coded signal yet?" Clack asked.

"Yes, sir."

"Did the mines respond?"

"All but one, sir. That one's protocol seems to be off."

"Shoot it."

Weapons nervously licked his lips. "Uh..."

"You have a comment you wish to make?" Clack said.

"I'm not sure firing on the mine would be wise, sir. That might begin a chain-reaction among the other mines."

"Oh. Yes. Well, keep working on the protocol code. We're not going to stop now."

"Yes, sir," weapons said.

Clack studied the main screen. They had passed the last outer system gas giant. None of the orbital laser platforms there had fired upon the Doom Star. No moon turret had washed them with radar. Each had responded to the Old Federation codes to stand down.

It had been the second thing the search parties had looked for. The first had been ship controls.

Now, the Doom Star zoomed through the system at a fantastic velocity. It had left the other ships far behind on the edge of the system. Admiral "Hatchet" played it safe. She had decided on the maneuver quite some time ago. Clack had already decided how to play this part of it. The Doom Star would continue to plow through the system, deactivating the various weapons platforms and turrets.

None of the sensor people had found the *Dark Star* yet. In spite of that, Clack still believed they were here. His people had spotted the orbital missiles circling the last planet. They had discovered sensor devices among the missiles. And to add to—

"Sir," sensors said. "I'm picking up an anomaly on the planet."

Clack sat up. "On the planet, is that what you said?"

"Yes, sir," sensors said.

"Tell me. What is it?"

"A metallic object, sir," sensors said. "This is unbelievable. I've never seen sensor readings like this. I do believe I'm detecting three life-forms on the object."

"On the planet?" Clack said.

"Oh!" sensors said in surprise.

"What now?"

"They're gone, sir. The object and the life forms have vanished from my board."

"Was there a malfunction in your equipment?"

"No, sir. They're just gone."

"Objects don't just disappear, mister."

"I'm aware of that, sir." Sensors turned around to face him. "Maybe they have a teleportation device."

Clack scoffed. "Have you ever heard of such a thing?"

"No, sir, but this Doom Star makes anything seem possible."

Clack blinked several times. That was an interesting phrase: "anything seem possible". Would these people join him in permanently taking over the Doom Star? It was a heady thought. How could he accomplish that, though? Admiral "Hatchet" waited back there, ready to order him off the Doom Star. The commodore with his security men would squash any mutiny by drawing guns and threatening first and then blasting.

"Increase our velocity," Clack heard himself saying.

Propulsion turned to him. "Sir…"

"Do you have something to add, Propulsion?" Clack asked.

"We're already moving faster than I would advise, sir."

"Are we indeed," Clack said. "May I inform you that sensors just picked up enemy readings?"

"We lost them right away, sir. Maybe they were ghost images."

"Do you believe that, Sensors?" Clack asked.

"Oh, no, sir, we saw the real thing. I'm checking my recording of them. The thing and life forms were definitely there."

Clack raised an eyebrow at propulsion.

"Even so, sir," propulsion said, stubbornly. "Our velocity will demand an intense burn near the planet. I suggest we begin decelerating already."

Clack shook his head.

"Sir, may I ask why we need to get there so quickly?" propulsion asked.

Clack tapped his heart. "Something huge is taking place over there. We have to get there and stop the people from Remus, stop the Shand, from doing whatever they're intending to do."

Propulsion glanced at a security man standing with his legs spread near the hatch. "Uh…I'm not sure I understand, sir."

Clack scratched the fabric of his command chair armrest. He caught propulsion's glancing gesture. He understood its significance. Why did he have this certainty of destiny playing out on the planet's surface? He wasn't sure, to be honest. But the feeling had been growing in him. The closer they came to the planet, the more he understood the reality of the situation. This was the biggest thing ever. The Remus fanatics and the crazy Shand would do something on the surface—

"I know what happened to the strange object," Clack told sensors.

"What's that, sir?" sensors asked.

"They plunged into a hole. They're heading deep underground."

Sensors frowned. "That might explain why I lost contact. Yet…how could you know that, sir?"

Clack chuckled as more of the bridge officers glanced at him. "Know is too strong of a word. It was the most logical deduction. Don't you agree?"

Sensors rubbed the bridge of his long nose. "Yes. I suppose I would. That makes perfect sense. If I may say so, sir, that is some fine deductive work."

Clack felt inordinately proud of himself, sitting straighter in the command chair. One could get used to running a starship. It was different, almost cleaner, than having to tear down a person's personality in order to dig at the truth.

The interrogator leaned toward the main screen, which aimed in the same direction as the approaching planet. He felt a sense of purpose building in him. A growing rightness demanded that he increase velocity even more. They were going too slow.

"Propulsion," Clack said in a stern voice. "You will increase another gravity in speed."

The woman stared at him. "Sir, our speed—"

"I'm not here to listen to your excuses," Clack said.

"Sir...I don't know how to say this delicately."

"Then don't say it," Clack said. "Obey my order."

Sweat had begun to glisten on propulsion's forehead. "I must point out, sir, that you're not a regular starship captain. You're a jumped up Special Intelligence operative who has gained the admiral's ire. She hates you, sir. Now, I wonder if she hates the rest of us as well. We don't belong on this ship, sir. It's haunted and..." Propulsion looked around the bridge, seeing everyone eyeing her. Their faces seemed brighter than she remembered. It almost seemed as if their skin glowed. On a few, their hair stirred as if static electricity moved strands.

"Add another gravity of acceleration to the ship immediately," Clack said slowly.

"Sir..." propulsion said. "That's madness. Don't you see? I feel—"

"You what?" Clack said, enraged with the bridge officer. "You are spouting off to me after failing to obey a direct order. How dare you?"

Propulsion was frowning. She looked around, and seemed frantic. "Doesn't anyone else hear it in the interrogator's voice? He's not right. He's—"

"Silence!" Clack roared, pointing at finger at propulsion. "You will be silent or I will have you shot."

Propulsion hunched her shoulders. She looked at the security man. He had his hands on his belt, glaring at her. "Sir—"

"Kill her," Clack said.

The security man unsnapped his holster. In a smooth move, he drew his sidearm, beginning to aim—

"Wait!" propulsion shouted. "Please, wait, sir. I realize—I was having a panic attack. Yes, sir, I'll add a gravity of acceleration at once, sir."

Clack glared at the offensive officer.

"Should I shoot her, sir?" the security man asked.

"Let us see if she can follow orders," Clack said.

Propulsion swallowed so her throat convulsed. Her long fingers played upon her controls. A hum went through the bridge.

"We have increased speed, sir," propulsion said weakly.

Clack motioned to the security man. He seemed reluctant as he holstered his sidearm. With a renewed sense of purpose, the interrogator resumed his seat.

Fifteen minutes later, communications spoke up. "Sir, I have the admiral on the line."

"Do you indeed?" Clack asked.

"She is requesting information. She wants to know why we're heading so fast toward the planet."

"The reason should be obvious to her," Clack said.

Several bridge personnel chuckled. Propulsion wasn't among them. Instead, her hands shook as she looked at her neighbors nervously.

"How should I reply to her, sir?" communications asked.

"Don't," Clack said. He decided his former idea regarding mutiny was senseless and needless. It occurred to him that most of the bridge crew already agreed with his inner thoughts. A few, like propulsion, didn't understand, but that didn't matter. In fact, watching propulsion had become entertaining. He found her lack of understanding strangely humorous.

Clack Urbis frowned as he rubbed his head. In truth, he didn't feel quite himself. It felt as if...as if...

The interrogator shrugged. Propulsion didn't understand the need for urgency, but almost everyone else did.

"Don't send the admiral a reply, sir?" communications asked. "Is that your decision, sir?"

Clack cocked his head. Was that his decision? That was an interesting question. It almost felt as if something spoke to him, telling him what to say, maybe even telling him what to think. He smiled crookedly. That was a foolish thought, wasn't it?

"Sir?" communications asked.

"Yes," Clack said. "That is my decision. It takes too long for messages to travel back and forth. We shall go in and investigate the planet. The admiral can study our reports later at her leisure. We don't have time to worry about her. We have to get to the planet with all haste in order to forestall the greatest tragedy in the galaxy."

For some reason, Clack found that uproariously funny. He began to laugh. Others took up his laughter, as it was quite infectious. Soon, everyone on the bridge was laughing, including the security man. The only one who didn't laugh was poor little propulsion, who hunched her shoulders, casting nervous glances all around her.

She acted as if the rest of them were mad or possessed. It was most amusing, most amusing indeed.

-48-

The gravity sled slid through a giant cavern under the earth. Floodlights from the sled shined all around them. Old rusted beams braced the rock. Below, two iron rails stretched into the darkness.

The shaft no longer went down, but parallel with the surface. The cavern was so huge that the *Dark Star* could have easily traveled through it instead of the comparatively tiny gravity sled.

Tanner had pulled out the Innoo Flaam and holster. He'd also removed his helmet. He continued to wonder if that was a good idea or not. There was a powerful metallic odor down here, while a copper taste in his mouth made him spit constantly. Deep, metallic groaning sounds made it seem as if the cavern would collapse at any moment. The worst groans made Tanner's nape hairs stir. He hated this place.

Acton was also bareheaded. He'd taken off his helmet when he'd dug out the brown control unit. By that time, the Lithian had madly pried at a box's lid. Due to his incredible strength, fingermark imprints dented the metal box. Several taps on the control unit had changed everything. The Lithian presently snored beside the bolted down, half crumpled box.

Action stood at the control column, guiding the disc as they slowly moved through the vast subterranean cavern. "We're close," he shouted.

Tanner nodded. He felt it, too, a presence drawing nearer or their coming closer to it. The presence wanted them to come but it also feared them.

The centurion realized the presence had manipulated the Lithian earlier. It had to be a Phaze, right?

Moving closer to the Shand, Tanner raised his voice. "I thought Phazes could only control certain kinds of machines like cyborgs."

"They can only *inhabit* such machines," Acton said. "Control or manipulation is a different process."

"You had something on the *Dark Star* that blunts their mind control power, didn't you?" Tanner asked.

Acton nodded, keeping his focus on the gloomy path ahead.

"Did you bring that with us?" Tanner asked.

Acton shook his head.

"Why am I still in control of myself then?"

Acton laughed. It was a harsh sound. "Don't you remember me saying you are incredibly stubborn?"

"I figured you were insulting me."

"Far from it," Acton said. "Your stubbornness is an aid in our mission. I don't believe another mind can control yours. For better or worse, you are your own person."

"That's why I'm carrying the blaster, isn't it?"

"To a large degree," Acton said.

"It knows we're coming, right?"

Acton nodded.

"Why doesn't it just run away?"

"Because we're heading toward something it wants to protect," Acton said.

"You mean the transporter."

"I do indeed," Acton said.

"Why did you bring your Lithians if you knew the Phazes can control minds?"

"I know less than you surmise," Acton shouted. "Besides, I didn't think they would bother. Now, please, shut the hell up. You're driving me crazy. I have to do this right or—hang on!"

Tanner barely grabbed a bar in time. The sled sank fast. At that moment, a flash of blazing light appeared up the tunnel. It sped at them like a comet. It had a large glowing section that crackled like a fireball. The tail waggled. The thing flew overhead, passing the sled at speed.

"What's that?" Tanner shouted.

"A pure Phaze," Acton said. "We may be too late. That one no longer needs to inhabit anything to gain strength. It is free to move anywhere. Keep hanging on, and get ready to use the blaster. I don't think I can ready my own surprise in time."

The sled slowed hard at the last moment. Even so, the landing was jarring. Tanner lost his grip, flew up and slammed down onto his back.

"It's coming," Acton shouted. "Draw your blaster."

Tanner fumbled for his gun as he sat up. He drew it, flicked on the switch and shouted, "What setting should I use?"

"The highest, you fool. You want to kill it."

Tanner climbed to his feet and focused on the blaster as he switched it to its highest setting. The gun vibrated as the end of the barrel began to glow pink.

Do not do this thing, the Phaze spoke directly into his head. *I am a god, come to give you power unlimited. I can grant you every desire your heart beats to possess. Lower your gun. Turn it off. I am your god. I am your best friend.*

Tanner heard the thoughts in his head. He didn't think this was telepathy, though. It had to be energy flowing through his synapses, speaking directly into his brain. It made his face feel hot.

Maybe the blaster's force screen helped him some. Maybe it linked him more directly into the Phaze's mind. He didn't know which.

Gripping the heavy, longish blaster with both hands, Tanner looked up. The comet blazed at him. It didn't have eyes, but he sensed the thing studying him. With a jerk, Tanner raised the gun.

"Let it get in close," Acton shouted. "It can dodge the shot if you fire too soon."

Tanner licked dry lips, making a rasping sound. He wanted to scream. Instead, he focused on this photon-electrical creature from the Triangulum Galaxy. Who had ever heard of something so crazy? That little pipsqueak galaxy only had 40 billion stars. Who did it think it was, sending over freak aliens to a much bigger, badder and better galaxy?

Tanner squeezed the trigger.

"Fire!" Acton shouted at almost the same time.

The blaster took a half beat. It vibrated harder, and a red beam flashed from the Third Period Innoo Flaam. The beam slashed into the blazing comet thing.

Tanner flinched as a horrible mind-scream gave him a blinding headache. His flinch took the beam off target. Then, Tanner's trigger finger lost strength.

A subdued comet zoomed overhead. Flashing motes of light spilled out of it like phantasmal blood. The beam wound seemed to be bleeding the flashing motes. The comet thing didn't swerve and come back at them. It kept barreling down the tunnel as if trying to flee. After leaving the comet-shaped creature, the flashing motes almost immediately lost color, soon disappearing altogether.

Finally, the scream no longer sounded in Tanner's head. The aftereffect left splotches in his eyesight, though. He blinked, wiping tears from his eyes.

The distant Phaze darted around a corner, no longer visible.

"You flinched," Acton said. "You could have killed it. Instead, you merely wounded it. If the Phaze had known better, it would have attacked while your blaster recharged."

"Hey," Tanner said, "you never told me it could scream like a banshee in my head."

"That's because I didn't know."

"Fine. Next time—"

"There may not be a next time!" Acton shouted. "You've only wounded it. Now, it can tell the others about your blaster. They'll be smarter next time, provided they even dare to face us again."

Tanner nodded curtly to himself. They would know better what to do next time, but so would he.

"Let's go, Acton. We have some Phazes to hunt. Why are we just standing here like idiots?"

The Shand glanced at him before he manipulated the controls, taking the sled up and heading deeper into the underworld.

***

They traveled in silence for a time.

Tanner studied the tunnel bracing, the spotlights washing over them. He couldn't fathom how the cyborgs or Phaze-controlled cyborgs had built these vast structures without the orbital AI sensors detecting the work. The Web Mind must have written viruses long ago, infiltrating them up there. Did those AIs and missiles even work anymore? Maybe Acton and he had gone to all this trouble of sneaking into orbit for nothing. Maybe nothing worked right in this star system anymore.

"This doesn't make sense," Tanner said aloud.

"You must particularize your complaint," Acton said. "If it's too broad, how can I interpret it?"

"The Old Federation orbital sensors had to pick up this internal activity—I mean cyborgs digging or building these vast tunnels."

The Shand nodded after a moment. "I agree with your analysis."

"So…?"

"Perhaps the Phazes have already tampered with the orbital equipment," Acton said. "This is the most logical answer."

"Either that or the Web Mind developed viruses."

"That would suffice as a cause as well," Acton agreed.

"Does that mean the Web Mind or the Phazes could send the orbital warheads down on us?"

"What would be their motivation to do such a thing?" Acton asked.

"Are you serious? So they could stop us, of course."

"I see your reasoning, but it might complicate matters for them to drop all those warheads. It would possibly harm their efforts to leave the planet in the near future. No. I doubt they will think of raining the nukes on us immediately. I suspect they believe they can easily kill us."

"Even after the first Phaze buzzed us and failed to do diddly against us?" Tanner asked.

Acton studied his board. "We will not get many more chances to kill Phazes. Either we strike hard and fast, and win…"

"Or we lose," Tanner finished for him.

"That is the most logical outcome if we do not win the next round."

"You're full of logic today, aren't you?"

"I am always full of logic," Acton said.

"Full of something," Tanner muttered to himself. He had become uneasy. The weight of the earth above pressed down on his spirit. At least the feeling wasn't another Phaze-attack on his mind.

Tanner grinned. After all this time, his stubbornness had finally come in handy. An easily convinced person would have already folded to the Phazes. A person who would give up after only a few tries would fail down here. Only a stubborn, donkey of a man had a chance to save humanity. Tanner decided he liked that. He would remember that the next time someone told him he was too stubborn.

Provided there ever is a next time, he told himself.

"Ah," Acton said.

Tanner glanced up. "What's wrong now?"

"Notice the tunnel walls."

Tanner squinted as the light flashed on the metal bracing and rock. "What about them?" he asked.

"They're sweating."

Tanner saw it, then. Water slicked the rock. In places, droplets slid down the wall. He studied the ceiling. It was wet. Were they passing under a lake or maybe an underground stream? If the tunnel above collapsed, would a wave wash over them, smashing them onto the floor?

"How far are we underground?" Tanner said.

"Approximately a kilometer," Acton said.

"Why isn't it hotter, then? I thought the deeper one went, the hotter it became."

"It is hotter, quite a bit, in fact. I'm surprised you haven't noticed. Ah!" the Shand said. He tapped his board, studying it. "Cyborgs approach. Let me amend that. We're approaching a cyborg battalion, or whatever they call the formation."

346

"Moving living breathing cyborgs?" Tanner asked.

"That is correct."

Tanner cursed under his breath. "Should I ready my blaster?"

"Negative," Acton said. "I have a different surprise for them."

"Your surprise will work, right?"

"We will find out shortly." Without warning, Acton walked away from the control stanchion He went to a metal box, knelt, inspected the top and stood. He knelt at a second and then a third box. By this time, he was near the edge of the flying sled.

That made Tanner nervous. "Do you want me at the controls?"

Acton looked up. "On no account," the Shand said. "You would tip us. They are delicate controls and take a master's hand."

"Yeah? Well, how are we staying on course without you at them?"

"Cease your yammering at once. I must concentrate and ready this before we reach the next bend."

Tanner shut up. He kept his hand on the blaster butt as it rested in his holster. His stomach roiled as Acton removed the box's top. The lean alien reached inside, adjusting the equipment.

"Acton!" Tanner shouted. "A bend is coming up. We're heading straight for a wall."

"Yes, yes, give me a moment's peace, will you. I hadn't realized your need for useless chatter. It is quite annoying and at the worst possible moments."

"Acton! Hurry up, will you?"

The Shand looked up. He hurried then, looking down and typing faster. At the last moment, he jumped up and ran back to the control unit.

To Tanner's horror, his running made the gravity sled wobble. He gulped down any noise he might have made.

"Grab a bar!" Acton shouted.

Tanner had already done so. Then, he remembered the sleeping Lithian. "What about your blue giant?"

347

Acton clipped his suit to the control, and he manipulated fast. He looked up at Tanner, staring blankly. Then, he shot an agonizing glance at the sleeping giant.

A line secured the Lithian. Would it hold during a tight turn?

The gravity sled wobbled again, and it turned, leaning one way. Tanner felt himself slipping. He groaned, hanging on tight.

The Lithian jerked to a halt, stopped by his line. Then, the line snapped. The blue giant shot toward the edge. He hit a bar, spun around it and shot off the sled against rock, smacking with a meaty sound before falling toward the floor.

"We lost him!" Tanner shouted.

"That will cost us," Acton said. "That could cost us dearly. I'm going to need his strength before this is through."

"He just flew off," Tanner shouted. This last death shook him. They were deep underground flying through sweaty walls with a possible lake over them and a cyborg battalion ready to kill them and more of the horrible Phazes plotting who knew what.

"I miscalculated," Acton said.

Tanner laughed harshly.

"Maintain your decorum," the alien said. "It is critical." They flew farther. The Shand cocked his head. "Why did you laugh just now? I do not understand."

"You bastard," Tanner said. "You called it a miscalculation. What you mean is your mistake cost the Lithian—your man—his life."

"He was my creature. I am not convinced he was fully human."

"Whatever he was, he was your responsibility to protect."

"Are you accusing me?" Acton said.

"Yeah! That's right. That's what I'm doing. Don't you have any feelings?"

"Not if I can help it," Acton said. "I am on an eternal quest to expunge them."

"What's that mean?"

"I rid myself of emotions because they hinder my success."

"Why did the Phazes control the Lithians' minds? I thought you had something to block that."

"I already told you I do."

"Apparently your device was as useless as your emotions."

Acton scowled. "That is incorrect. The unit is still aboard the *Dark Star*. I have already told you as much."

"A fat lot of good the unit does us up there. We just lost a Lithian because of your forgetfulness."

"On the contrary," Acton said. "The unit is critical to our survival. Without it onboard, your friends would possibly succumb to Phaze mind suggestion. We would not have a means of leaving this place if the Phazes succeeded on the raider, causing it to crash on the planet, for instance."

Tanner stared at Acton, the Shand's words sinking in. "This is a hellhole of a planet."

"That is an apt description."

"Why did you think the Lithians could out-stubborn the Phazes like me?"

"That was my miscalculation. Now, desist from your accusations. We're nearing the cyborgs. Tell me if you spot one."

"Can't your sensor see them?"

"The general vicinity of them," Acton said. "There could be a few—"

Before Acton could finish, a bullet smashed against the control station. They were under attack.

-49-

Tanner threw himself flat onto the gravity sled. He slid a pair of goggles over his eyes, adjusting them. Immediately, he saw a silvery humanoid creature down the vast corridor. It had shimmering garments and bounded across the floor at them.

The thing moved fast like a machine, and its eyes glowed with an eerie red color. Each bound took it twenty meters or more. Nothing manlike should be so quick.

"Shoot it," Acton said. "But grab a rifle. Don't use the blaster."

Tanner slid to a duffel bag, tearing it open. He slid a heavy combat rifle from it. It was a Remus rifle from the *Dark Star's* gun locker.

The cyborg fired more shots. It had a long-barreled pistol, the barrel lifting at each shot with flames shooting out the end. The exploding slugs *whanged* off the bottom of the gravity sled.

Acton had begun taking evasive action, lifting the front from time to time.

Tanner cursed, telling the Shand to keep it level a moment. He targeted the bounding monstrosity and fired in rapid succession, missing each time.

"I'm going to have to get lucky," Tanner shouted. "It can actually dodge my bullets."

"Fire!" Acton shouted. "It's jumped. It's airborne. It can't dodge now."

Tanner had looked back at the Shand to complain. Now, he whipped his head around. In the wash of powerful beams, the centurion saw the cyborg. It had leapt off the floor thirty meters below and sailed toward them. How could it do that? It was better than a powered-armored space marine was.

Something happened to Tanner then. Something cold and urgent washed through him. He targeted the approaching cyborg, and he fired. His bullets smashed against armored body parts, shredding metal and graphite muscles from it. Unfortunately, that didn't stop the cyborg. With a clang, it landed on the sled.

Tanner instinctively raised his aim, shooting rapid-fire at the brainpan. The head snapped back at each slug. Finally, the steel braincase cracked open, and a slug tore into the human gray matter, the brain inside.

Abruptly, the cyborg lost coherence, toppling from the edge of the sled and dropping toward the floor.

"Excellent shooting, Centurion," Acton said. "I congratulate you."

Tanner used the back of his hand to wipe his dry mouth. His heart was hammering, but his mind was clear with combat intensity.

"I've spotted two more," Acton said, as he studied his board.

"These guys are creeps. I need something better." Tanner slid on his belly to the duffel bag. This time, he extracted a grenade launcher.

In seconds, he peeked over the edge of the sled. He didn't have long to wait. Two more cyborgs bounded into view. Like the first one, they fired long-barreled pistols. Tanner didn't launch any grenades just yet. Instead, he let Acton manipulate the disc, using it as a shield. Tanner worried about one of those shots doing something critical to the sled's underbelly. If the sled began to drop, he'd realize the cyborgs had succeeded.

"Now," Acton said.

Tanner tracked and fired, launching a grenade at an airborne creature. The grenade struck an armored chest, destroying it in the blast. The blast also knocked the cyborg off target just enough. As a lifeless husk, it went sailing past them to slam against a rock wall.

The next cyborg fared no better, the grenade blasting off its head.

"You are a rare soldier," Acton said.

"I'm a legionnaire of Remus."

"Yes," Acton said. "You are, and a splendid one, I might add. Few humans could have bested three cyborgs in a row. Now, we're approaching the battalion."

"How many do you think that is?"

"A little more than six hundred cyborgs," Acton said.

Tanner paled. "That's great. How are we supposed to kill six hundred of those things?"

"We are not," Acton said. "I am."

Tanner studied the Shand, finally grinning. "You're a royal pain in the ass; do you know that, Acton? But man alive, you do have style. You're all right despite what everyone says about you."

"You have no idea how much that gratifies me hearing you say so."

Tanner's grin grew into a genuine smile. "Not a bit, huh, Acton?"

"Correct."

"Okay. I'm watching you. Let's see what you have, old son. Show me how it's done."

Acton closed his eyes, and it seemed to Tanner that the alien mumbled low under his breath. This was interesting. The Shand bowed his head, and the mumbling increased in speed and volume. It was in a language Tanner had only heard once before. That was when Acton had spoken to the other Shand in the weapons shop. Finally, his eyes snapped open. There was a new intensity to Acton. It made him seem like a lord indeed.

"What was that?" Tanner asked. "What did you just do?"

Acton ignored him.

"Did you just pray?" the centurion asked.

"What else should I do when nearing the possible end of my long existence? Now, please, I must insist, give me silence."

Acton hunched his head, and his long fingers played on the controls. The gravity sled angled toward the floor, zooming lower. Soon, they skimmed the surface by a bare meter.

Tanner heard the ground rushing past. They were going faster than at any time earlier. The rushing wind brought tears to the centurion's squinting eyes. He'd shoved up the goggles so they sat on his head. Because of the increased speed, he pushed them back over his eyes.

Acton stood tall as he moved from the controls to the open box. He paused there, knelt and pressed something. Then, he fairly leapt back to the controls. With a fixed gaze, he watched their progression.

The disc flew into a large cavernous area. With his special goggles, Tanner saw the waiting cyborgs. Some gripped long-barreled pistols. Others cradled heavy rifles. Still others stood by crew-serviced weapons, heavy machine guns and plasma tubes.

Tanner kept watching as the gravity sled slid toward certain destruction. Any second, he expected a devastating barrage to blast them out of the air. Instead, nothing happened. The battalion of machine-men waited in perfect poise.

"Why aren't they attacking?" Tanner finally asked.

"They cannot," Acton said. "They are caught in a stasis field. My nullifier is old and worn, but it is still working. I doubt its capacity, however. All we need is a few more seconds and we shall be past them."

"What about the return voyage?" Tanner asked. "Will the stasis field work then?"

"It is not called a stasis field. That is what a nullifier projects."

"Got it," Tanner said. "I have to tell you I like the name."

The gravity sled swept past the frozen battalion of cyborgs, heading deeper underground.

The box began to beep, and a flashing blue light emanated from it.

"What's happening now?" Tanner asked.

"The nullifier is reaching its limit. Quick, turn it off. I cannot leave my station now. You will see a big red button. Press it three times in quick succession."

Tanner got up and did just that. After the third click, the blue glow stopped shining from the freaky gauges.

"Hang on," Acton said.

Tanner dove, hitting the deck, wrapping his arms around a bar.

The gravity sled sped out of the giant cavern back into a large hall. It moments, the sled slowed as if trying to pitch the centurion off. He wouldn't let go of his bar.

"We have reached the great entrance," Acton shouted. "Now, we shall descend for a time."

"What do you mean?"

Instead of hearing Acton's answer, Tanner felt the sled dropping fast, plummeting. They no longer sped parallel with the floor, but dropped down what appeared to be another hole, this one much smaller than the original. As they dropped, the temperature rose rapidly.

Just how deep were they going to go?

-50-

As they dropped, the air began to shimmer strangely. Tanner noticed motes of pulsating light. It reminded him of the wounded Phaze. He pointed, trying to bring it to Acton's attention. For some reason, the centurion found that he couldn't form the words. He wanted to, he thought them, but he couldn't shape his mouth to eject them.

The motes became thicker and the air itself seemed hazy. Tanner no longer noticed any heat. Instead, it cooled, soon becoming cold and then frigid. It didn't seem to be just his imagination. Mist jetted from his mouth or nostrils every time he exhaled.

Tanner flexed his fingers. They had become stiff as if with disuse. That seemed more than odd. Why would they stiffen right away? He scratched his cheek, trying to figure it out. To his shock, his fingernails scratched more than stubble, but an actual growth of beard, almost several days' growth. That made no sense whatsoever.

That stirred Tanner's mind. The motes had thickened again. He could feel stabs of heat every time his skin moved through a mote. That quickened his energy.

He looked around, and he noticed the tunnel had changed dramatically. They didn't plunge through a hole in the earth, but through a vast energy field. This energy didn't have walls. Instead, it felt as if the gulfs of interstellar space spread out in all directions around them.

Now, Tanner stared significantly at Lord Acton. The Shand stood frozen. Was the alien in a stasis field? If that was true, was it their stasis field or the enemy's field?

Tanner swallowed, moving his fingers again. They were even stiffer than before. He checked his face. His beard had grown. In some fashion, time moved differently in the hole in the ground, in the energy flux between galaxies, if that's what this was.

Eyes widening, Tanner wondered if they had entered the transporter. That must be it. What had he expected an interstellar transporter to be, a disc on the ground that would shimmer with light when someone crossed over? Something that brought photon-electrical Phazes from the Triangulum Galaxy would have to be quite different, right? This fit the bill of weird. Did that mean he was correct in his assessment?

The gravity sled shuddered, and the motes of light vanished in a flash. The frigid chill evaporated in a blast of heat. It made Tanner choke, unable to draw a breath.

"We're inside," Acton said in a wheezing voice. "Quickly, Centurion, draw your blaster. It is time to hunt Phazes."

"Did we just go through a time warp or something?"

"We went through something," Acton said. "I wonder if we are still on Planet Zero."

Fear stabbed Tanner in the heart. "Where else could we be? Why is it so hot, then?"

"Yes, yes, you are correct," Acton said. "We are on Planet Zero. Look, you, do you see that over there?"

The gravity sled had slowed considerably. Below them spread out a vast panorama, a giant cavern. A lava stream flowed past pulsating energy fields. Inside one field was a large dome with brain sheets and green computing gels. Cables of various colors and sizes snaked from the dome to eccentric machines of bizarre, hexagonal shapes. The machines hummed and pulsated with squiggles snaking across them at weird intervals. There were even larger machines there, but they were black as if they no longer ran.

"That is the heart of the transporter," Acton said. "It is run by the Web Mind. We have arrived. This is the transfer node.

The Phazes must defend it or we shall destroy their bridge, destroy their link."

Tanner found it hard to move. He was sluggish and stiff. It felt as if his body fought to betray him. He wasn't sure if it was the time warp or if hidden Phazes tried to manipulate him.

Why resist? something said in his mind. *It is useless. Turn your weapon on the alien traitor. He means to cheat you. Surely, you realize that.*

With his hand on the blaster butt, Tanner glanced sidelong at the traitorous Shand. The alien had screwed with them from the beginning.

Yes, that's right. He is a cheating Shand. He pretends to be your friend. In the end, he wants the treasure all for himself.

Treasure? That didn't seem right. Tanner scowled. The treasure was a nullifier of his own. If he had one, he could go back to Remus and defeat the Coalition, the socialist meddlers that had killed his sister during her wedding.

Anger turned into rage as Tanner thought about that.

Direct your anger at the alien beside you. He is the cheater. He is the Coalition—

"No. He's. Not." Tanner said. "You alien freaks from the Triangulum Galaxy are the cheaters. You want to devour humanity. Well, guess what? I'm here to stop you, me, Tanner of Remus."

Saying that made Tanner feel better. He drew the blaster. With his thumb, he flicked it on so it purred with power.

Tanner checked the barrel, liking the red glow.

No! the thing shouted in his mind. *I do not allow you to live. I will require your life from you, pest. You cannot come into our nest, not at the great moment of my awakening. I am the Radiant Sigil, the First Rarified of Excellence!*

Tanner saw an angry comet rise from behind a shimmering force field. Only a small trickle of golden motes bled from it. The thing began to pulsate, and it charged, a comet-like tail growing behind it. It weaved strangely. Tanner realized it was trying to time and thereby dodge his shot.

I am too quick for you. I am too powerful. I am the Radiant One. I am your god.

"Yeah, I don't think so, buddy," Tanner said. He gripped the blaster in both hands. He wondered if this was how the Innoo Flaam and the Phazes had duked it out in the old days twenty thousand years ago.

Closing one eye, Tanner tracked the creature with the other.

"Careful," Acton said from behind. "There are more than one here. I believe they plan to swarm you."

Tanner glanced around. He saw three more of the comet-like aliens. They were coming low, trying to catch him unawares.

"Sneaky little tykes, aren't you?" Tanner said under this breath. Instead of training the blaster on the others, he kept the gun fixed on the first Phaze, the one calling itself the Radiant One.   ·

Four Phazes converged upon Tanner. He stepped to the edge of the gravity sled. "Get ready," he said over his shoulder. "We're going to have to dance for thirty seconds after my first shot."

Suddenly, the Radiant One rushed him. Tanner tracked it more tightly, and the thing veered hard. Whirling to his right, Tanner saw a different Phaze rushing upward at him. He pulled the trigger. A gout of red power flowed from the blaster. The beam struck the Phaze directly.

The thing screamed into Tanner's mind. He was ready and hunched his shoulders. With everything in him, he kept pulling the trigger and kept the beam on target.

Suddenly, a mindless shriek sounded in his head. The comet-thing exploded in a flash of golden motes. Electrical discharges flashed in every direction.

Tanner flattened onto the disc floor. At the same time, Acton tapped the controls. They went up fast, the gravity sled humming with power.

Come back, murderer. You will face our wrath. We will torment you for an existence.

"Keep moving," Tanner shouted. "They're pissed." He stared at the heavy blaster. It vibrated, with the barest of pink color at the barrel.

For thirty seconds, Acton dodged the Phazes. At twenty seconds, a comet flashed hard at them. Tanner raised the gun. The thing veered at the last moment.

"They don't like playing chicken," Tanner said.

"I don't understand the idiom," Acton said.

A click sounded. Tanner checked his gun. "You don't have to, my friend. Let's go back to hunting. I want to kill me more of these galaxy murderers."

"May I suggest something else?" Acton said.

"What's that?"

"We will continue to flee."

"That doesn't make sense—oh, yes, draw them in. Good thinking, Acton."

As Tanner spoke, the Shand manipulated the controls. The gravity sled began to climb.

Tanner peeked over the edge. "They're coming after us, all three of them."

"I will switch direction at your word."

"Got it," Tanner said.

You flee too soon, mortal. You were presumptuous to come into our place of power. You—

"Switch!" shouted Tanner.

Acton tapped the controls. The gravity sled shuddered, and instead of going up, it went down.

As soon as Tanner adjusted to that, he stood up.

What is this? Why is the machine descending? I suspect a trick, my brothers.

The first Phaze blazed into sight. Tanner aimed and fired. A second later, a hot beam poured square against the photon-electrical creature.

It screamed in Tanner's mind, and it exploded in a blaze of multiple colors. If it hadn't been such a deadly game, Tanner might have enjoyed the display.

Dropping to his stomach, hooking an arm around a bar, Tanner shouted, "Start jinking. We have thirty seconds to go again."

The disc did exactly that. Instead of seeing the remaining two Phazes come after them, the two comet-like beings shot straight up.

359

"Where are they going?" Tanner asked. "Are they going to get reinforcements?"

"I do not know," Acton said. "But now that they have fled, even if momentarily, let us destroy the great machine, the heart of the transporter. In this way, no more Phazes can come through and those that are still charging up inside a cyborg will be left without their intellects."

"Sounds good to me," Tanner said. "What do we have to do?"

"My box is a special kind of bomb. That is what the Lithian attempted to destroy before. As soon as we land over there, I will set it. Then, we must flee before the Phazes return with reinforcements."

-51-

The gravity sled began to float toward the shimmering force fields below. Acton trained the majority of the spotlights there. Thousands, maybe tens of thousands of cyborgs began to stir in vast incubation tubes. Beside the large tubes—many of them holding a hundred or more cyborgs—were stockpiles of plasma tubes, X-ray mortars and heavy rifles.

"What is this place?" Tanner shouted.

"I have no more time to explain. According to my instruments, the last two Phazes are heading through the time field."

"So?"

"It must mean they plan something else than facing us," Acton said. "We don't know how much time we lost coming through the warp."

"I hate this place," Tanner said. "I especially hate that big old thing over there." He pointed out the glass dome with brain sheets in green computing gel.

"That is the Web Mind. It must sense us, even though I have the feeling the Phazes have blinded it."

"How would they do that?"

"The easiest way, I'd imagine," Acton said, "by unhooking its video feeds. Sensory deprivation is a cruel tactic against any human-like organism."

Tanner stared at the Web Mind dome. He spun around. "I have an idea. Can we talk to the Web Mind?"

"Why would we want to?"

361

"You said they were arrogant and pompous."

"To an intense degree," Acton said.

"Then maybe we can use that," Tanner said. "If the Phazes have taken over, won't the Web Mind hate that?"

"Ah, yes, that is subtle and quick. And it may be our best hope. The heat coming from the lava stream is too much. I cannot take the sled much lower or risk our never rising."

Without further ado, Acton went to another box. With a few taps, the cover slid off. He worked frantically inside it. Soon, the dome down there glowed with an eerie color.

"I have gained contact," Acton said. "It is a crude link, but we should be able to talk to it. I suggest you do the talking. I am too logical. The Web Mind is sure to have reverted into an emotional wreck. You are therefore better suited to communicate with it."

"Thanks, I guess," Tanner said. He took the microphone Acton handed him. "Hello," he said.

A strange mechanical voice replied from a speaker in the nearby box. "Who is this? Who dares to address the Supreme Majesty of the Galaxy?"

"I am an enemy of the Phazes," Tanner said.

"What are Phazes? Make your meaning clear before I obliterate you."

"Yes, Great One," Tanner said. "I will gladly do that. I have come a long way to speak with you."

"That is logical," the Web Mind said. "I am the greatest and most supreme intellect alive. And yet, if you can fathom the horror of this, my allies have betrayed me. They are ravenous devils without gratitude—"

"They are fleeing, Great One," Tanner said.

"Never interrupt me again. That is the supreme sacrilege. Surely, you must realize that."

"I do," Tanner said. "I am in gross error. I thought you didn't realize that the Phazes, your allies, rush to escape your wrath."

There was a pause. Then, the Web Mind asked, "How do you know this?"

"They race through a time warp to reach the surface. I believe they mean to leave the planet."

"Without me?" the Web Mind asked.

"That is why I wanted to speak with you. Since I know you are the greatest living intellect, I yearned for your aid. If I aid you, Great One, would you help me with a problem?"

There was another pause before the Web Mind said, "Yes, of course, of course I will aid you. You are human, are you not?"

"I am, Great One. Will that be a problem?"

"No, no, I love humans. Perhaps after this is over you can show me your homeworld—if it is near."

"It is very near," Tanner said. "Oh, this is marvelous. I'm hoping you'll aid me regain my throne."

"Yes, of course I will, of course. You can trust me implicitly."

"Thank you, Great One. But what shall we do about the time warp?"

"Silly human, I will deactivate it. If you will simply hook me up to the machines over there…"

The Web Mind gave Tanner instructions about what to do to the black, powerless machines he'd seen earlier.

"I will gladly do what you say, Great One, but the heat from the lava stream—"

"Yes, yes," the Web Mind said impatiently. "I already understand your problem. Simple biomasses such as you are very weak. That is one of my greatest defense mechanisms. Now, listen closely while I tell you how to do this. Are you listening?"

"I am," Tanner said.

"Good," and the Web Mind proceeded to tell them how to blanket the heat from the lava stream. "Once you have landed, you can hook me to the power core. I can do everything else then."

"You are kind to aid me like this," Tanner said.

"I realize that," the Web Mind said. "Now, enough talking, hurry and obey me or…"

"Or?" Tanner asked.

"We will speak of that later. First, do I as say and all will go well with you. You have my solemn word on this, and my word is golden."

363

"I'm glad to hear it," Tanner said. "I'm signing off, Great One, to go and do your will."

***

Soon, Tanner watched the shimmering shielded ground draw nearer.

"What's powering all this, by the way?" the centurion asked.

Acton didn't answer. He was too busy bringing the sled closer by degrees. Finally, they hovered over the humming, shimmering mass. Below a newly strengthened force screen, the lava stream continued its sluggish flow. They only felt a little of its intense heat now.

Tanner licked his lips. From this low height, he could see that the Web Mind dome was huge, two-stories and three acres of brain mass pulsating with thought. How many humans had been mind-stripped to feed the beast?

"Look," Tanner whispered. "More cyborgs stir. Some of them are watching us through their tubes."

"The Web Mind will surely release the cyborgs once you hook the foul creature to its machines," Acton said.

"He or it had no compunction about lying to me," Tanner said.

"Of course not," Acton said. "To the Web Mind, you are a gnat, less than gnat. Would you keep your agreement with an ant?"

"If the ant bargained in good faith, I would."

Acton grinned. "Perhaps that is so. Now comes another tricky bit. You will have to jump down."

"I know."

Acton nodded, left his station and went to the nullifier box. "If this breaks down..."

"I know," Tanner said, wiping sweat from his face. "How about you find out where their nullifier is. It's my prize, remember?"

Acton did not respond.

Tanner decided to drop it for the moment. Either the Shand had honor or he didn't. If he didn't...Tanner hadn't decided yet

364

if he would shoot Acton if he broke his word. The centurion would improvise when the moment came.

"There," Acton said, standing. "I have set it. "Now..." He hurried to the control, dropping them lower yet as the sled headed to the dome.

A click sounded. Power flooded from the nullifier, and a small portion of the force screen disappeared. Heat billowed from that spot, but not the former lava heat.

"Here we go," Tanner muttered. He knelt, slid over the edge, hung on as he looked down and let go. He dropped and hit rock. With an intense longing, Tanner looked up at the hovering sled. That was his ticket home. If something happened to the gravity sled, he would be stuck down here with the waiting cyborgs.

Time to move, he told himself.

With a feeling of growing dread, Tanner trotted away from the sled. He reached huge optic fiber cables. Bending his knees, he grabbed a coupling, grunting as he lifted. Dragging, sweating, straining, he brought it to a port. He could have used the Lithian's strength. Had Acton foreseen this moment? Tanner couldn't see how.

For the next few minutes, the centurion worked with a will, huffing, puffing and sweating harder each second. Around him, the larger dark machines whirred with power. That created more light as they turned on. Video lenses soon swung around, watching him. He stopped for a moment and waved. He couldn't help himself. After that, he worked faster.

Soon, entire sections of machines snapped on with lights and power. The Web Mind was getting its senses back and maybe more control. This seemed like a grim gamble. What else could they do, though?

Huge generators roared into life. Other machines powered up. More force screens shimmered into existence. Out of the corner of his eye, Tanner noticed cyborgs climbing out of a big tube. Several of the vile creatures glanced at him.

They gave Tanner the creeps.

Instead of dashing at him, instead of going for heavy rifles, the cyborgs raced to work on repairing the Web Mind.

Tanner blinked sweat out of his eyes. He looked up. The gravity sled was higher than he remembered. Was Acton cutting out on him?

The sled began lowering. "Get ready," the Shand shouted, with his voice coming over the edge.

Tanner walked to the lowering sled, even though he wanted to sprint. The cyborgs felt like beasts, Remus lions perhaps. They would surely look up if he moved too fast.

Finally, Tanner jumped up. He grabbed hold of the sled and chinned himself onto the top. "You have no idea how good it feels to be back on board," he said.

"It has been an adventure, Centurion. I will not soon forget you."

Tanner stared at Acton. "What does that mean? Are you double-crossing me?"

"How do you gain that understanding from my words? I am impressed with you. We have one more risk, and then we shall discover how cunning the Web Mind is."

"What risk? What are you talking about?"

"Over there," Acton said. He manipulated the sled. It slid across the shimmering floor.

"Humans!" the Web Mind boomed, speaking through vast speakers.

"Can you hear me, Great One?" Tanner asked.

"I can pick up any audio signal I desire down here," the Web Mind boomed. "My capacities are returning. The star lords have acted faithlessly. They are attempting to escape. I will alert the orbital lasers."

"Uh…" Tanner said. "Can lasers hurt these star lords?"

"This is incredible," the Web Mind said. "The lasers do not harm such creatures. I do not understand. I should have known that. How can a mite like you have understood such a thing before me?"

"I think it's the warp up there doing that," Tanner said.

"Silly mite," the Web Mind boomed. "That is not a warp. It is part of the interstellar bridge, the link between our galaxies. The star lords derive power from there. They have turned their entire galaxy—never mind. You don't need to know about that. I have learned so much. Yes, the star lords are traveling through what you refer to as a warp. Do they seek to escape me? I will depower the bridge for a span."

"Down there," Acton whispered. The sled was over a storage area. "Jump down and grab that black unit. Slide it here as fast as you can."

Tanner breathed deeply. Nearby, two or three hundred cyborgs worked like ants, repairing various things. They seemed grotesque in a manner Tanner couldn't explain.

The sled lowered. Tanner jumped down and walked fast to the storage unit. As he did, several cyborgs let go of a heavy line and began striding toward him.

"I know what you are doing," the Web Mind said. "I do not approve of anyone stealing from me. My servants will bring you to the vats. You will amuse me until the bridge collapses. I have already begun the process."

"You said you'd help me if I helped you," Tanner said.

"I will help you," the Web Mind boomed. "I will help you leave your senseless existence and enter one of worth."

"Doing what?" Tanner asked. He'd reached the storage unit. Now, he tugged and pulled, dragging a nullifier across the floor.

"You will serve me," the Web Mind replied. "Nothing could be greater or mightier than that."

"I think you have a point," Tanner said, breathing heavily.

"You are attempting to mollify me. It won't work. Stand aside from the unit. I do not want my servants to harm you unnecessarily."

Tanner didn't know what Acton was doing. He could hear the servomotors in the approaching cyborgs. Three of them drew near. They must have weighed a lot more than him, as they clanked heavily with each step. Their strength and likely speed would dwarf his own.

"I want to remain human," Tanner said.

"I am the master here," the Web Mind said. "It is only my will that matters. Your will is meaningless. You will soon understand this much better than you could ever conceive."

The first cyborg reached for Tanner. The centurion stepped in toward it, swinging his monofilament blade. The knife-edge one molecule in thickness, easily sliced through the titanium

367

body parts and granite muscles. In a thrice, he chopped up the three cyborgs, dismembering them. Each of the parts clanked heavily onto the rock floor.

When Tanner was finished with them, he found himself shaking with dread. He sheathed the knife and heard a thud. He whirled around and found Acton beside him.

The two dragged the cyborg nullifier to the landed sled. As more cyborgs began striding toward them, the two huffed and puffed, straining to get the heavy nullifier onto the gravity sled.

As they struggled, a curious phenomenon began. Forces of power that stretched toward the Triangulum Galaxy began to dim. The web of energy up in the passage started shrinking toward the Web Mind and its interstellar transporter machines.

"Push," Tanner grunted. "Push before the cyborgs get here."

Acton pushed. Then a croaking cry escaped the Shand's throat. He shoved harder, and the nullifier lifted as they tumbled it onto the gravity sled.

Man and Shand climbed aboard the purring disc.

"Help me right it," Acton said.

Tanner threw himself at the nullifier, shoving, straining so sweat popped onto his forehead. Slowly, the heavy unit tipped upright.

Acton stood, inspecting it.

Tanner glanced at the approaching cyborgs, around fifty of them. He couldn't chop up that many quickly enough. He drew his blaster.

"Put that away," Acton said. The Shand knelt beside the nullifier and began manipulating bizarre controls. His long fingers moved fast. Suddenly, the nullifier began to hum, to vibrate.

Tanner saw the cyborgs freeze. A few were off-balance because they'd just raised a leg. Most of those toppled onto the rocky floor.

Acton rose with a grunt, staggering to the sled's controls. He worked the panel and they began to rise.

"Why didn't we do that sooner?" Tanner wheezed.

"The nullifier has to be on the instrument you wish to keep working," Acton said. "Otherwise, we would have put the sled in the stasis field, too."

Now, the sled shuddered as it lifted faster, gaining speed.

At the same time, gauzy lines of power sped toward the Web Mind's transporter machines. Looking up, Tanner spied a vast hole. No more motes floated up there, just normal Planet Zero air.

"Is the interstellar transporter off?" Tanner asked.

"For the moment," Acton said. "Soon, the nullifier will be out of range. The Web Mind will begin to think and act again. It will likely begin waking all the cyborgs on the planet."

"Do the cyborgs have spaceships hidden down here?"

"I deem that very likely," Acton said.

"And the Web Mind now controls the orbital missiles, right?"

"It seems more than possible, especially given its words a few minutes ago."

"Where does that leave us?" Tanner asked. "We haven't stopped the menace at all. Two Phazes are up there. Can the Web Mind kill them?"

"I doubt that."

"So what's the plan?" Tanner shouted. "I don't want to have done all this for nothing."

"We have temporarily broken the star bridge between galaxies. That will harm any incubating Phazes, as it will keep their intellects from crossing over and joining their energy bodies."

"Provided we find a way to destroy the interstellar transporter forever," Tanner said.

"That is correct."

Tanner rubbed his face, feeling useless.

"Don't forget you've already slain two Phazes. It appears that only four have fully incubated."

"Okay, okay," Tanner said. "That's right. That's good to remember. Where did the last two go to?"

Acton looked upward as the sled continued to climb. "That, my friend, is what we're attempting to find out."

369

-52-

Ursa sat at the controls of the *Dark Star.* The centurion and the Shand had been gone for days. She hadn't heard a thing from them, not one peep. Surely, the two were dead.

Greco had thought otherwise until this morning, a subjective ship-time morning. What did a hairy apeman know about such things anyway? No orbital missiles had stirred. No Old Federation sensors had turned around. No orbital laser missiles had activated. The gravity sled had disappeared into a giant hole. That had been the last she'd seen of Tanner and Acton as she'd watched on the scope.

After that, the days went by in lonely orbits as the *Dark Star* circled Planet Zero.

Greco hadn't come out of his room today. No doubt, he mourned the captain. Her brother Marcus was in a funk, brooding, lying on his bed with an arm across his eyes. Vulpus had caught the mood. The underman frowned as he rolled dice. He and Lupus used to gamble hour after hour. After Lupus had died, Vulpus had played for the two of them. Now, the underman didn't even keep score.

This was too much, too bitter. What was she supposed to do now? This had been the big plan. Not only had they failed, but how long would it be before cyborgs and Phazes boiled out in a tide of conquest, starting at their end of the galaxy.

What is my responsibility?

Sure, she could watch the Coalition being ground into dust. That would be something. Yet, would it feel good as Coalition soldiers turned into cyborgs? Somehow, she doubted that. Maybe it was time to sink their differences with Social Unity. Remus might have to join in a Grand Crusade against the Phaze-run cyborgs.

To that end, Ursa had debated for days about what to do with the approaching Doom Star. The giant battlewagon braked hard now. It would be in orbit in less than an hour. Should she make contact with their commander? Should she try to convince them that all humanity was at stake? Could she get the Coalition people to scour the planet, to burn away as many cyborgs as possible?

Why had the Doom Star come in so fast? Why had the rest of the Coalition fleet stayed far behind at the edge of the star system? Did the Doom Star hunt their raider? Or did the Coalition people know more? Maybe they came to grab cyborg equipment. Could they be so stupid as to land on the planet?

Ursa kept rubbing her hands together, trying to figure out the best move. *It's all up to me. I'm the one. I have to make the right decision. I just wish I knew what it was.*

She frowned at the comm. Several times now, she'd reached out to tap the controls to hail the vast Doom Star. The gigantic battlewagon daunted her. How had the Coalition people figured out how to run it? She'd heard Admiral May attempt to communicate with the Doom Star. As far as Ursa could tell, the people on the Old Federation battlewagon hadn't answered their own admiral.

That had given Ursa pause. It meant something, she was sure of that. She just couldn't figure out what that something was.

Ursa kept rubbing her hands together. As she had many times before, she tore her hands apart, using one to rub the scowl lines out of her forehead. If she frowned too much, the lines would remain. She didn't want lines. She wanted smooth features, pretty features.

I should have kissed Tanner. Why didn't I? Why am I always so shy?

She scoffed at herself. Kisses didn't matter at a time like this. Kisses meant nothing at the end of everything. Ursa

371

frowned and began rubbing her hands again. Maybe kisses meant everything at the end.

She reached out. She had to call the Doom Star—

Ursa Varus blinked in surprise. The scope blinked. She saw something on it. After all these days, was this them? Had Tanner and Acton made it after all?

Ursa began tapping furiously. She studied the scope. Her features fell a second later. That wasn't Tanner. It wasn't even the sled. It was two energy blips. It was two—

"Energy," she said. "Are those Phazes?"

Suddenly alert and frightened, with her heart beginning to jackhammer, Ursa studied the scope more carefully. If those weren't Phazes, they would have to be plasma blasts. She couldn't see any discharge mechanism on the surface, though.

Her heart beat faster yet. The energy blips rocketed upward. They came straight for the *Dark Star.*

Ursa moaned in dread. What did that mean? Why would Phazes attack the raider? Did it—

Her eyes widened. The blips separated. One still headed here. The other—

She tapped the scope. The other one headed out on an intercept course for the Doom Star. Why did the Phaze do that?

Ursa tapped the comm, opening intra-ship communications. "This is an emergency," she said. "A Phaze is heading toward us. I have no idea what I should do. Please, Marcus, please, Greco, I need some help to figure this out."

***

Ursa sat transfixed. She felt a pressure against her head. She almost thought she heard something in her mind. If she listened very carefully—

"Patrician, what did you say?"

Slowly, Ursa turned. Greco stared at her from the hatch. He seemed far away. He seemed—

Ursa forced herself to blink. She didn't know what was wrong with her, but something was.

Greco stepped forward, grabbing her shoulders with his hairy paws for hands. He shook her gently. "Can you hear me, Patrician? You called on the comm."

"Phazes," Ursa heard herself say. "They're coming."

"You've seen them?"

"Look," Ursa said, indicating the scope.

Greco let go of her, stepping around. He froze as if frightened.

"What's wrong?" Ursa said. She turned too, and she saw it then through the port window. A blazing comet-thing headed straight for the *Dark Star*. She saw it outside the ship. She sensed it watching her, and she sensed rage, incredible rage.

Ursa screamed and Greco hooted with terror. The Phaze came at them, hitting the port window and oozing through the glass. Ursa's knees gave way. She crumpled onto the floor as the Phaze came through the port window and entered the *Dark Star*.

Greco also fell away. Ursa heard the apeman thump down near her. Then, the Phaze was in the control room with them. She felt it turn and glance at her. It seemed to be studying her, maybe reading her mind.

A moment of delight filled Ursa. The Phaze flew away, heading down a corridor.

"What was that?" Greco croaked.

"A Phaze," Ursa said.

"I know that," Greco said. "I just sensed vast delight. Did you feel that, too?"

"I did. The feeling must have come from the Phaze."

"That's what I thought," Greco said. "Why would the Phaze feel delight on our ship?"

"The cyborg!" shouted Ursa. "Maybe it wants to possess something. Maybe it needs to get inside a machine thing like a cyborg. Did it read about Lacy in my thoughts?"

"We're doomed," Greco said.

"No," Ursa said, "maybe not."

***

The patrician of House Varus ran down a corridor. She shouted for Vulpus. She hoped she was in time. She had never expected it to come down to this.

Greco spoke through the intra-ship comm. He was alerting Marcus. An enemy creature was inside the ship. It seemed the Phaze was heading for Lacy's room.

Ursa heard metal groan and shriek. The pit of her stomach twisted. This reminded her of the day her uncle died. She had to face her own lion today instead of shrieking in terror as her family and friends died.

Ursa slid to a halt. Oh, no, this was sick and terrifying. The cyborg lurched down the corridor. Rotted flesh dripped from it. How was that thing moving?

It turned. The eyes glowed with an eerie color. The cyborg raised an arm with a rotted, metallic finger pointing at her.

"Name," the cyborg said.

Ursa shivered. She realized a creature from another galaxy spoke to her. What did it want?

"Ursa Varus," she told it.

"This," the cyborg, or the Phaze inside it said. "This one is crippled."

Ursa nodded. She was horrified to be having this conversation.

"You…obey me," the thing said.

Ursa found herself nodding. She couldn't help it. Yes, she could feel the Phaze crawling inside her mind, touching levers, as it were.

That's when Vulpus hit the thing from the side. The underman clubbed it with his baton. The cyborg staggered, but that was it. Vulpus howled, beating at the cyborg head, making it bend to the side at each blow.

Before Ursa could warn the underman, the cyborg got its hands on him. With a wrench, the cyborg cranked Vulpus's head to one side. Then, the thing slammed the underman against a bulkhead. It did so three times, finally dropping the dying Vulpus onto the decking.

"What are you?" Ursa screamed. She shook her fists at it. Tears flowed freely. It had killed Vulpus. It was a monster.

"Quiet," the thing told her.

"No!" Ursa shouted. Finally, she remembered the code words, the one she had put in the cyborg's head after waking

374

up alone during the hyperspace journey. Ursa shouted the code words at the thing.

Those horrible shining eyes blinked at her. A second later, the cyborg lurched toward her, the eyes burning more brightly.

"What did you say?" the cyborg asked.

Ursa stepped back, wondering why it wasn't working Maybe the Phaze had fixed her damage. Maybe—

The cyborg croaked horribly. It shuddered. The head lifted. The mouth opened. Then, the cyborg body smashed against the left bulkhead. A moment later, it struck the other bulkhead. It was as if the cyborg had forgotten how to walk. It tried to focus on her. Then, it fell face first and began to shudder and writhe as if in terrible agony.

As that happened, the Phaze oozed out of the cyborg. It expanded into its comet shape and size. How had the thing squeezed inside the cyborg in the first place?

The comet shape had orange lines zigzagging through it. The process of leaving the now dead cyborg seemed to have troubled it.

The Phaze, seemed to focus on Ursa. Slowly, it drifted after her as if to hurt her badly.

Ursa turned around with a start and sprinted away from the trailing Phaze.

Now began a strange set of circumstances. Ursa ran. The Phaze followed. Ursa ran harder, panting. The comet shape gained speed. Finally, Ursa reached the control room. Greco sat at the controls. The apeman trembled as if he watched a ghost chase the patrician.

"The gun, the gun," Ursa shrieked.

Even as the apeman continued to shiver, Greco turned around, tapping controls. At the last second, he dove onto the floor.

It seemed as if the Phaze charged them. Yet, it also seemed as if it wasn't in full control of itself. Perhaps being in a dying machine thing hurt or dazed a Phaze. How that could be, Ursa had no idea. She had felt the thing's rambling accusations against her, though. That's what had given her the idea. She remembered what Acton had told Tanner. Only a few kinds of weapons would hurt these other-galaxy beings. Centurion

Tanner wore one on his hip. Notable Magnus Shelly had installed another into the *Dark Star*.

Ursa rolled to a halt against the controls. She had dove onto the floor. Greco had also ducked. They both saw the comet thing, the Phaze, glide over them. As easily as if moving through a curtain of falling water, the energy creature passed through the front of the ship. It kept going in space.

"Now!" Ursa screamed. "We have to do it now."

Greco was up, but he shook too horribly to do anything. In agony, he looked at Ursa.

She sat in a seat, targeted the Phaze.

Maybe it understood its danger at the last moment.

Let us bargain, Ursa Varus. You are a great lady. I am very impressed with you. I will make you the greatest bargain in the universe. You will be amazed.

"Die!" Ursa said, as she tapped the firing control.

A beam lanced, hitting the Phaze. Ursa heard screaming in her mind. It caused her to shiver, but she kept her finger on the tab.

The beam burned long enough. The comet-shaped Phaze exploded into a scintillating shower of multicolored motes. It was amazing, beautiful and meant this Phaze, at least, was dead and gone.

-53-

Clack Urbis knew a new and powerful sense of rightness. The Doom Star approached the wonderful planet of promise. He sensed a grand and glorious purpose building in him, and he felt that most of the rest of the crew did as well.

There were a few holdouts in the crew. One could tell by the stooped way they walked. They were constantly glancing over their shoulder in a sneaky manner. Propulsion did that even now. She was here on the bridge with him.

Clack smiled behind his hand as he watched her. It seemed obvious that she was a secret admirer of Admiral May. No doubt, the woman kept a dairy, jotting down notes that she hoped someday to hand to Admiral "Hatchet." Only—that day—would never come. Clack believed that more than he believed in Social Unity.

A pang of unease touched him. Something could be better to him than Social Unity? That seemed...

The secret smile slipped as he lowered the shielding hand. That was an odd thought. He'd grown up in the crèches. He had gone to every hum-a-long held by his hall leaders. In school, he'd received high marks for his correct thinking. In fact, he was a zealous defender of the Party and an upholder of the Chairman's rule. Thus, to think the planet, a dull ball of sand, rock and hidden cyborg treasures, should be more important than Social Unity was heresy of the rankest sort. He should be the last person to think it.

Clack rubbed his neck. Was something wrong with him? He glanced around the bridge at the others. They worked their controls urgently. He'd hardly ever seen them work harder. Why were they being so diligent?

The interrogator prime frowned, rubbing his neck harder. He loved Social Unity. Mass humanity needed guidance. That was a pure truth. Left to himself, man was a destroyer, a glutton that forgot his neighbor in order to stuff his own pie hole. Social Unity made certain everyone thought and acted together for the good of the greatest number of people. That was right. That was good. That was wholesome.

Why would a rocky, windblown, cyborg-infested planet be more important than the truths of his life? Should he commit violence against himself?

Clack continued to rub his neck, beginning to hunch his shoulders. Something was definitely wrong aboard the Doom Star. He couldn't pinpoint it, though.

Clack stood, frowning. The skin of his neck had begun to chaff from all the rubbing. He paused a moment, glancing around before approaching propulsion. The bridge officers were busy at their tasks, too busy to look up at him.

That was good. Clack didn't want anyone to get the wrong idea. He kept turning until his gaze met the security man near the hatch.

The security officer had thick shoulders and a big chest. The man clearly worked out with weights. His hand rested on the butt of his holstered sidearm. Worse, though, the man frowned as he stared into Clack's eyes.

He knows, Clack realized. That was quickly followed by: *What does he know?*

Without realizing it, Clack hunched his shoulders more than before and turned away from the security officer's glare.

Less sure of himself, Clack moved near propulsion. She hadn't noticed him. She didn't attend to her controls. Instead, she had a book. It was small and red, and it was open. She appeared to be secretly reading it while on duty.

Clack cleared his throat.

The woman snapped the book shut, sliding it under a leg. Her hands shook, but she looked up bravely nonetheless.

378

Clack wanted to ask her about the book. It must be worth credits. Was it an ancient relic perhaps? Why would she be reading it while she was on duty?

Propulsion met his gaze. She had blue eyes. He'd never noticed that before. Instead of looking away as she had before, she held his gaze. She frowned. This frown was unlike the others the past few days.

"What...?" Clack said, and then he didn't know what else to say.

Her frown deepened. "I think you know," she whispered.

Instead of asking her, "What do I know?" He nodded slowly. He did know.

"You're the first one who has come out of it," she whispered.

"The rest of the crews' minds are controlled, aren't they?" Clack asked in a soft voice.

She nodded as she kept staring at him.

"Who's controlling them?" Clack asked.

"I have no idea, sir."

He glanced at her board. It showed the approaching planet. "We're just about in orbit," he said.

She nodded.

"What's on the planet that could cause this?" he asked.

"I don't know," she whispered. "But I think you're right, sir. Something on the planet has drawn us here."

With his shoulders stooped, as he rubbed his sore neck, Clack moved back to the commander's chair. The joy he'd known only a short time ago had vanished. He didn't dare look up at the security officer. He couldn't stand to see those watchful eyes again. The security officer seemed to have realized that Clack was no longer one of them. How long would whoever controlled most of the ship's personnel allow him to remain in nominal charge?

Should I merge back under with the others? Clack wondered. Maybe it was better to be part of the mass mind than to be one of the few in charge of his own thoughts. *No. I can't do that in good conscience. I am an interrogator prime. I have a duty to the Party. I will do whatever I can to deliver this mighty warship back into Coalition hands.*

***

The Doom Star orbited Planet Zero. Ship's sensors swept the surface. No one had spotted the *Dark Star*. The rest of the Coalition fleet waited or would soon reach Admiral "Hatchet." The ships that had originally joined the Doom Star had turned back some time ago. Admiral May had ordered them to return.

Clack gnawed on a knuckle. He no longer delighted sitting in the commander's chair. He was a Special Intelligence officer. He had a duty to find this new enemy. The enemy was hidden and he, she or it controlled most of the crew.

Should he try to reason this out with those controlled?

Clack sneered at himself. That would be the height of folly. The mind control seemed to operate on an emotional level. Trying to reason with an emotional person was always a mistake. He must appeal to other, hopefully, stronger emotions.

It struck him, then. He knew what to do.

"I have an announcement to make," Clack said. "It is the most important announcement of this trip."

One by one, the bridge officers turned from their boards to stare at him.

"We belong to Social Unity," Clack said. "Does anyone disagree with this?"

No one did. Good. He could proceed.

"We are servants of the State. More than that, we owe the State everything because it has given us life, our education, our rank and worth. Once we reach old age, the State will give us health benefits and—"

"Why are you saying this?" the security officer shouted. "This is a trick. You're trying to trick us. You're no longer one of us, Interrogator."

"That is a lie," Clack said, with heat. "I am the most loyal person on the ship. I serve the Party. Who do you serve?"

The security officer opened his mouth to reply. Before he could finish, a red alert began to wail on the bridge.

Clack snapped forward. "What's going on? What caused the alarm?"

"Sir," sensors said, "I'm picking up an unusual life form reading. It appears to be..." He looked up, "Sir, the

380

approaching life form appears to be made of photons and electricity."

"Have you pinpointed it?"

"I have, sir."

"Put it on the main screen," Clack said.

Sensors' fingered blurred on his board. Seconds later, an image appeared on the screen. Everyone on the bridge saw a comet-shaped thing heading for the Doom Star.

"It appears to have come up from the planet," Clack said, "not from space."

"Yes, sir," sensors said.

"Is it hostile?" Clack said.

The security officer laughed harshly. "It's friendly. It's our friend. You should know that, Interrogator."

Clack regarded the man. The security officer's skin shined and his hair kept rising as if with static electricity. The interrogator sensed a violent intent in the security officer.

"Weapons," Clack said, as he stared at the security man. "Ready the plasma ejector. As soon as the plasma is ready, you will fire at the approaching comet."

"You will not do that," the security officer said. The man drew his gun, aiming at Clack.

"Look at his shiny skin," Clack said in a rush. At the same time, he stood, ducking behind the commander's chair.

The security officer's gun went off, a bullet smashing into the chair.

"Countermand your order," the security officer shouted.

"Weapons," Clack said.

"Sir?" Weapons asked, as if confused.

Clack darted up. The security officer stared at weapons. Clack used his sidearm, pumping one bullet after another into the security officer. The muscled man staggered backward. As he did, the shine on his skin lessened and finally disappeared. At that point, the security man hit the deck, dead.

Clack stood, with a smoking pistol in his hand. "Fire the plasma ejector. Do it now."

Weapons sat hunched over his board.

"Did you hear me?" Clack shouted.

Weapons didn't reply as his hair began to rise.

"Fire the plasma ejector!" Clack shouted, striding toward weapons.

The man continued to sit at his station as if frozen. Clack put a hand on the man's shoulder. It was hot, very hot. He spun the man around just the same. Weapons' facial skin shined eerily.

Clack shoved the barrel of the firearm against the man's head and fired. The body jerked and collapsed. Clack stared at the weapons board, having no idea how to use it.

"I'll do it," propulsion told him.

The rest of the bridge crew stared at them with hostility.

Propulsion sat on weapons' chair, her fingers blurring. "I'm targeting the thing," she said. She glanced at Clack. "The plasma is almost ready, sir."

Clack looked up at the main screen. It showed the comet creature. It was almost to the Doom Star. "Fire," he whispered, "fire at once."

Propulsion nodded, tapping her board. Nothing happened. "It will be ready to fire in another two seconds."

Clack glanced at the main screen. The thing had already reached them. To his astonishment, the comet creature oozed into the viewing screen and then disappeared from sight.

"The ejector is ready to fire," propulsion said.

Clack said nothing.

Propulsion looked at the scope. "Where did it go, sir?" she asked.

"Yes," Clack said. "That is an excellent question."

-54-

As the Phaze entered the Doom Star, the gravity sled lifted from the giant hole beside the mountain. It began to climb into the heavens.

Tanner locked the buckles of his helmet. He'd secured it to his armored spacesuit. He couldn't believe they'd actually managed to leave the horrible underworld. Seeing the sun again was glorious. The red sky looked like the most beautiful thing in the world. He smiled so hard that his mouth began to hurt.

They'd slain Phazes, but two had escaped. Cyborgs revived underground. A Web Mind had regained control. Had it activated the star bridge again? Did it have a way to battle the Phazes?

As the sled lifted like an elevator, Tanner had an overwhelming desire to contact the *Dark Star.* Several thoughts kept him from doing so. One of the Web Mind's comments earlier indicated it controlled the orbital missiles. That would imply it also controlled the orbital sensors and lasers. If he communicated with the raider, that would surely give away their location. Still, if the Web Mind knew what to look for, why wouldn't it use the orbital sensors to find them?

Tanner stared into the heavens as they floated upward. What was the right choice? Surely, the Web Mind had regained control of the situation after the nullifier had gone far enough from it. A laser missile could be aiming at the sled right now.

Using his chin against an inner helmet control caused the visor to *whirr* upward. He approached Acton. The Shand soon did likewise, rising his visor.

"We have to contact the raider," Tanner said.

"That would be unwise at this junction."

Tanner told Acton his reasoning.

"I cannot believe this," Acton said. "Yes. I agree with you. I will contact the raider at once."

***

Ursa and Greco were in the control room, having just spoken to Lord Acton. The apeman piloted the *Dark Star* down into the atmosphere as the patrician studied the nearest orbital missiles.

"Oh-oh," Ursa said. "The nearest orbital is moving as if to target us."

"I thought one might." Greco glanced at her board as his simian forehead furrowed. "We'll have to be tricky."

"Whatever we have to do, let's do it now."

Greco's hairy fingers played across the board. The *Dark Star* pivoted as it plunged into the atmosphere so the front faced the back. Targeting the orbital, Greco activated the same weapon used to slay the Phaze. It was a short-ranged weapon, but short-ranged in space terms, easily able to reach the laser-firing missile. A powerful beam blew the ancient missile apart. Unfortunately, that alerted more of them.

"This could be an impossible situation," Ursa said. "What if for every missile we destroy, two more start targeting us?"

Greco scratched his head. "We still have some tricks left, new ones from the hideaway. We'll try chaff first."

"What's that?"

"Strips of tinfoil," Greco said. "We're going to put out so much it might cause the targeting systems headaches."

"How does one give a computer a headache?"

"Perhaps the better way to say it is that we'll gain a few more minutes, at best," Greco replied. "We have superior decoys to those Acton used in the Nostradamus System. If we use everything we have, maybe we can reach Tanner in time."

"Then what will we do?" Ursa demanded.

Greco gave her a critical glance. "The best way to defeat these situations is to tackle one element at a time, preferably the most troubling first. Then, we will move to the next element, but not before the problem occurs."

"Good thinking," Ursa said.

The two of them concentrated on the difficult task as the *Dark Star* kept heading down.

***

Tanner pointed up. He saw flashes high above them. He knew those couldn't be lasers, because almost all lasers were invisible to the naked eye.

As the gravity sled strained to gain height, Tanner felt exceptionally exposed. His back crawled with a burning sensation. Something targeted them. Could the Web Mind see them through orbital sensors? The desire to flip off the multi-brained cyborg was nearly overpowering.

Then, a long streak burned to his left high in the atmosphere. What was that? It seemed like a falling star. Was it a nuclear-tipped missile coming down? If so, why did it blaze like that? No. He didn't think it was a missile.

Swallowing uneasily, Tanner watched the streak go farther and farther away. A sense of dread began to build in him. For some reason, he believed the streak had something to do with the last Phaze. Ursa had told him how Greco and she had slain one. That was incredible.

As Tanner watched the shooting star, the feeling of being targeted lessened. That was interesting. Did the Web Mind fixate on the shooting star instead of them? He dearly wanted to know what the falling object was.

***

"The Doom Star is going down," Ursa said.

Greco glanced at her board. "Does it plan to land on the surface?"

"I have no idea."

"This bodes ill for us and likely for humanity, too," Greco said.

"What does that mean in Basic?"

385

"I don't like this," Greco said. "Why would the Coalition people land on the planet?"

"You do remember I saw two Phazes, don't you? One of them headed for the Doom Star. Do you think it's taken over somehow?"

The apeman and patrician traded worried glances.

"It appears the situation has become more complex," Greco said.

"We should head down faster," Ursa said. "The sooner we get the others, the sooner we can leave this godforsaken place."

"Leave the planet with its waking cyborgs?" Greco asked.

"That wouldn't be optimal, I realize."

"No."

"Maybe Acton has an idea what we should do."

Greco scratched his head as he continued to pilot the *Dark Star* toward the gravity sled. He had the germ of an idea. He would have to think this through carefully, although he'd have to do so quickly.

"Only one orbital is beaming at our chaff," Ursa said.

"I wonder what happened underground," Greco mused. "What did Tanner and Acton accomplish down there?"

"The sooner we reach the others," Ursa said, "the sooner we'll hear the whole story."

"Yes," Greco said. "The orbital attack against us has lessened. Perhaps you have the right idea. We should do this while we have an opening. Hang on, Patrician. We will attempt the retrieval at combat speed."

***

The *Dark Star* reached the gravity sled before Tanner and Acton had left the red-colored atmosphere.

· The raider hovered in place as Acton maneuvered the sled on top of it. As soon as the sled clanked down, the two grappled with the nullifier, trying to push it onto the raider.

As they worked, an upper hatch opened. Marcus stuck his head out. "Here!" he shouted, tossing them a towline.

The three of them worked fast, emptying the sled of useful items.

"I'll strap the sled onto the raider," Acton said.

"Wrong," Tanner told him.

"This is an ancient heirloom," the Shand said. "I cannot simply abandon it."

"The sled isn't worth our lives," Tanner said. "Look. We may have to disappear again. If the gravity sled is on top, the sensor-resistant hull plating won't do us any good. The Doom Star will be able to target us."

"He has a point, Lord," Marcus said. The wind up here had picked up, tousling the big man's hair.

Acton gazed at the gravity sled. "I must launch it then. The least it can do is act as a decoy."

"Good thinking," Tanner said. "That might help us escape unnoticed."

"The Doom Star is landing on the planet," Marcus told them.

"That is ill news," Acton said. "I don't understand it—unless the last Phaze has taken control of the ship."

"Why would it do that?" Marcus said.

"At the very least," Acton said, "to gather a ship full of cyborgs."

"Hurry up with your sled," Tanner snarled. "We still have a lot of work to do before we've defeated this menace."

Acton ran to comply.

Soon, the three of them watched the gravity sled begin to climb again.

"Let's go," Tanner shouted.

The three of them hurried to the hatch, and Tanner closed it with a *clang* after them. Immediately, the raider began to race in a different direction as the sled.

-55-

"I don't understand," Ursa said. "Before, the orbital sensors hunted us diligently. Now, it's as if they don't care about us anymore."

She rose from her seat in the control room. Tanner took her place as Acton slid into the other chair.

Tanner checked the board. He could still hardly believe he'd made it back onto the *Dark Star*. He never wanted to go underground again for as long as he lived.

He sensed Ursa bending low. She pecked him on the cheek. "Welcome back, Centurion," she whispered.

Tanner looked up in astonishment. Then, he grinned. "It's good to be back, Lady. I missed you," he added, before he could stop himself.

She smiled, clearly liking that.

"This is all very well," Acton said. "But I believe it is time to act, not to gush affectionately over each other."

Ursa blushed as Tanner's grin widened.

"Right you are, Lord Acton," Tanner said, turning to his board. "What do you suggest?"

"That we lift into high orbit," Acton said. "That we go around to the other side of the planet from the Doom Star."

"Why's that?" Tanner asked. "The Coalition people aren't the ones who have pinpointed the raider."

"If the Phaze has taken control of the Doom Star, we're no longer worried about the Coalition here."

"Okay, but how does that—"

"The Doom Star has entered the planet's atmosphere," Acton said, interrupting. "The vessel has gone dangerously low, almost to the surface. The warship wasn't constructed for heavy atmospherics. One possibility for taking the vessel so low is so the Phaze can be within mind control range of the Web Mind."

"The Phaze doesn't need the Doom Star near for that. The energy creature could go itself at any time."

"Maybe the Phaze wishes to remain on the Doom Star in order to control the crew."

"Oh," Tanner said. "We don't know enough, do we? But that's still not…" Tanner fell silent, thinking. "Is that why the orbital sensors have stopped searching for us? Is there a contest of wills taking place between the Web Mind and Phaze? Maybe the Web Mind can't control the orbitals while it's fighting to keep its will intact."

"That is my belief," Acton said.

Tanner nodded. "One way or the other, though, our time to act is surely limited."

"Maybe limited just enough for us to go out far enough to render ourselves invisible from the orbital sensors. Once we're hidden as before, we shall be hard to find again."

"Right," Tanner said.

The *Dark Star* continued upward, leaving the red sky as it entered the darkness of space. By slow degrees, it went from low to high orbit. It soared far above the countless devices circling the planet.

"Now what should we do?" Tanner asked.

Ursa had departed the control room. She'd been beat and said she'd needed a few moments to herself.

"It is time to go around onto the same side as the Doom Star," Acton said. "We must discover exactly what it is doing."

"Got it," Tanner said, as he piloted the raider.

Thirty-seven minutes later, Tanner spied the mighty Doom Star on his scope. It hovered less than a quarter of a kilometer from the surface. That was daringly low indeed for a deep space vessel.

"I see a string of shuttles," the centurion said. "They're entering huge hangar bays to land inside the Doom Star. I see other vehicles, too. They have a strange design. I wonder if they're cyborg craft."

"Put what you see on the screen," Acton said.

Tanner did so, sitting back. The possible cyborg craft had swept back wings and narrow fuselages.

"Those are space superiority fighters," Acton said. "I have seen such craft in history texts. Those are cyborgs vessels. Can you zoom in more tightly?"

Tanner did. They saw cyborg pilots in the cockpits as the space fighters headed for the giant hangar bays.

Without a word, Tanner changed focus, soon zeroing in on the surface. There, cyborg soldiers milled in their thousands. When a shuttle landed, a section of cyborgs marched up a landing ramp into the shuttle. Some carried cargo, most just had rifles and ammo packs. The various shuttles lifted and went directly to the Doom Star.

"They're loading up on cyborgs and cyborg tech," Tanner said.

"That would indicate the Phaze has gained control of the Doom Star," Acton said.

Tanner scowled. "We failed then, right? The Phaze controls cyborgs. It would seem it has an entire planet of them at its disposal. The great assault will soon begin upon humanity. If the Phaze has regained control of the Web Mind, that means it can bring through more Phazes to our galaxy. It can also link the intellects of the ones who have fully incubated here."

"Your conclusion is obvious and correct," Acton said.

"So...what do we do now?"

"What can we do?" Acton asked.

Tanner snapped his fingers. "You're a super genius, right? Why can't you use the Web Mind's viruses? Surely, if it took over all the orbitals, you can do likewise."

"I doubt it would make any difference. The Doom Star is an Old Federation warship. Surely, it has the correct codes for the orbital missiles and sensors. If I rip control of them from the Web Mind—no, the Phaze controls the Web Mind and the Phaze appears to control the Doom Star. What is your plan?"

"Nuke the Doom Star."

"That might make a slight difference," Acton said. "It still leaves all the cyborgs and their hidden equipment under the planet. They have clearly awoken. It is merely a matter of time before the great assault begins."

"So we're finished?" Tanner asked.

"No!"

Tanner and Acton turned around. Ursa had returned.

"The centurion should speak to Greco," Ursa said.

"That does not explain your 'no,'" Acton said, seeming puzzled.

Tanner stood up. "Maybe not, but if someone has an idea, I want to hear it. I haven't come all this way and gone underground and back to give up this easily."

***

Tanner buzzed Greco's room. There was no reply. He made a fist and hammered on the metal hatch.

"It's open," Greco said through the closed door.

Tanner entered a smoky, hazy room. The place was a mess with the bed unmade, clothes and junk strewn on the floor and half-filled containers sitting here and there.

Greco leaned back, balancing himself on the rear legs of a chair. His feet were on a computer desk, the toes wiggling. An open bottle of brandy sat on the desk beside a tumbler with a splash of alcohol on the bottom. The smoke came from Greco's big, nasty, black cigar. It stuck out of his simian lips. He puffed lustily, making the end glow red as he put more smoke into the air.

"What is this?" Tanner asked, coughing, waving smoke from his face.

Greco plucked the stogie from his mouth. The apeman waved the cigar in the air, making a trail of smoke. "This, my fine friend, is me lubricating my mind. I need brandy and a cigar to help me think deeply. I have been doing that ever since you boarded. I have a reached a fantastic conclusion."

Something about the way Greco said that convinced Tanner the apeman knew what he was talking about.

"Do you remember what I told you about a *koholmany*?" Greco asked.

391

Tanner shook his head.

The apeman puffed some more. Then, he bent forward, picked up the glass and threw its remaining brandy into his mouth. He smacked his lips afterward, giving a hoot of delight.

"This is my best stuff," Greco said. "I tell you, my friend, my thoughts have percolated into high gear. I am near my dream, and all because of you. I cannot believe this day is coming. It is the reason why I left Avernus long ago to join you."

"You're drunk," Tanner said.

"I am, I am," Greco said, "on the possibilities that lie before me. I am giddy with delight."

"Does this have anything to do with the cyborgs?"

"A small part of it does, I admit. You will gain your desire as I gain mine."

"Okay…" Tanner said.

"A *koholmany* is an Avernite's great dream," Greco said solemnly. "You know I love vibrations."

Tanner glanced at the drums in the corner.

"My dream has always been—let me amend that. For a long time, I have wished to fulfill Tesla's boast of being able to split a planet apart by applying a small amount of force at precisely the right locations."

Tanner scowled. "Why don't you spell it out for me so I can understand?"

"It is simple. My *koholmany* is an invention, a device to fulfill my dream quest. If we can gain control of the orbital missiles, I have developed a precise pattern of impacts and explosions." Greco used the cigar to point at the computer screen.

Tanner saw an image of Planet Zero on it. The planet had thousands of lines on it.

"Those are fault lines," Greco said. "During your long absence, I plotted them."

"Okay. So what?"

"So…if you can gain control of the missiles for me, I can show you where to hit and explode them in such a way that it will split the planet. Will that not destroy the vast majority of the cyborgs?"

"Yes!" Tanner said. He stared at the screen more closely. Then, he studied the apeman. "Can you really do this?"

"Can Acton gain control of the orbital missiles? I happened to be listening in on you two a few moments ago."

Tanner paused, thinking. "Let's go find out."

-56-

Clack shuddered. The last few hours had been one horror piled upon another.

He had been powerless as his officers brought the Doom Star down into the deep atmosphere. Everyone had obeyed the image of the Old Federation rear admiral. She had first appeared to them from the Doom Star as it climbed out of the wandering gas giant. It was just an image, an ancient replica of a former living person. Now, though, something had changed dramatically. He didn't know how, what or why, but the comet thing that had entered the Doom Star had combined with the ancient image. It had been the thing controlling their thoughts.

The image of the Old Federation rear admiral had appeared on the main screen from time to time. She'd spoken arrogantly, giving orders. Clack had watched helplessly from the commander's chair. The image had eyed him several times, grinning malevolently. He had the distinct impression that it toyed with him.

He knew cyborgs boarded the Doom Star. They had been for some time. He could not allow that. It was time to do something, the only thing that made sense.

Willing himself to act, Clack pressed a special tab on one of his armrests. "This is the acting captain," he whispered.

He waited. Finally, a signal showed on the armrest.

Clack had discovered the self-destruct sequence during his journey to the planet. He'd memorized it and now began to press armrest buttons in an exact manner.

394

Sweat beaded his forehead. He didn't want to die. He yearned to live a long time. It had been his goal to climb high enough in Special Intelligence to win extended life. He'd made many plans. Now, those plans meant nothing.

With a sleeve, he blotted his forehead. All the while, he continued the self-destruct sequence. He did not dare glance at the new security officer or see if the Old Federation image watched him. That would be the worst. He had to concentrate on his task. He had to act natural. He did not want to go down in history as the worst traitor to humanity. Surely, someone somewhere would discover that he had commanded the Doom Star that went down to the cyborg-infested planet. This was his sacrifice to Social Unity. He could pay his debts. For the good of humanity, he must.

Clack paused, rubbing his fingertips. He could feel a burning sensation in his back. He knew. He just knew that someone watched him.

Don't do it, he told himself.

Despite the desire to continue with the self-destruct, Clack raised his head and dared to peek at the main screen.

His life seemed to catch in his throat. The rear admiral stared into his eyes. She grinned evilly, as if enjoying this.

"What do you think you're doing?" the image in the screen asked him.

Clack's mouth became dry. He couldn't swallow, although he began to shiver. If he could finish the sequence, he could escape whatever horror the thing in the screen planned for him. He knew that look. He had seen it a hundred times in a mirror.

"Do you think I don't know what you're doing?" the image asked.

Clack's shivering became trembling. It hurt his stomach to clench it so tightly. He opened his mouth, but no words came out.

"Do you not realize that I am your new overlord?" the image asked. "In time, I will control the entire galaxy. From here, we star lords shall continue our enteral conquest."

Confusion filled Clack. What had the image said? He frowned, and his curiosity helped to quench some of the growing terror. He managed to moisten his tongue. That seemed like a minor miracle.

"S-S-Star lords?" Clack stammered.

"It is what you shall call me for the short term remaining of your pathetic humanity."

"I-I do not understand."

"When you do, you will wish you did not."

The hatch opened and the most wicked-looking creatures clanked onto the bridge. They gleamed metallically in places while graphite-strengthened muscles bulged in others. They had horrible faces, part metal and part flesh. Clack had seen the cyborgs milling on the surface. He hadn't gotten the opportunity to see one up close until now.

"Clack Urbis," the image said, the supposed star lord.

He looked up at the main screen.

"It is time for you to begin life anew," the star lord said.

"Please," he whispered. "D-Don't do this. I-I'll serve you."

"By destroying this lovely warship?" the star lord asked.

"No. That was a mistake, a terrible misunderstanding. I can...I can show you things."

The star lord smiled. "I do not think so. I prefer that you become a cyborg, too. I wish to test the convertor my minions have brought aboard. You will be the test subject. Afterward, you will join their ranks and serve me faithfully for the rest of your miserable existence."

Clack's eyes widened with horror.

"Yes," the image in the screen said. "I will also test your companion in disobedience. The two of you shall become cyborgs together."

Clack tried to finish the self-destruct sequence, but none of the responses worked anymore.

"No," propulsion said. "Let go of me. I don't want to go with you."

It felt surreal as Clack turned to see two monstrously strong cyborgs pluck poor propulsion from her seat. She struggled to no avail. Her weak human muscles couldn't compare to the cyborgs.

Sweat slid down the interrogator's face. This was the end, wasn't it? Nothing could save him. It was over.

"Please," propulsion wailed. "Don't hurt me."

Clack stood as other cyborgs approached him. He drew his gun, and in an act of mercy, he fired two shots into propulsion. She went limp in their grip, although she managed to turn to him with pain and gratitude in her eyes.

"Thank you," she mouthed, too quiet for him to hear the words.

Feeling more surreal than ever, Clack turned the gun on himself, but he wasn't fast enough. A cyborg ripped the weapon from him, hurling it across the bridge.

"No," Clack said, struggling.

"I have changed my mind," the star lord said from the screen. "Now, I will save you for last. I want you to see what you are going to become."

Clack struggled harder as two cyborgs hauled him toward the bridge's exit.

***

Deep underground, the Web Mind worked furiously. Its vast brain could think with lightning speed, playing out thousands of scenarios in seconds. It had regrouped at speed, its workers repairing more of its extended substance as it gave them wireless instructions.

At first, it had directed a few orbital sensors to look for the gravity sled and the two interlopers. Then, it had found their space vehicle. For a time, the Web Mind had toyed with them, enjoying the limited attack. Oh, how they had tried one thing after another.

Then, the Doom Star descended into the atmosphere. A quick calculation and several thousand possibilities later, it reasoned that one of the star lords from the Triangulum Galaxy had gained control of the Federation vessel. The Web Mind well understood the awesome powers of a Doom Star. It had faced them in battle a lifetime ago.

The Web Mind was certain the star lord returned in order to control it again. On no account would the Web Mind ever submit to dominance again. Yet, it realized that it had no good defense against the photon-electrical creature.

397

Thus, the Web Mind strained to turn on the interstellar transporter. It succeeded. The time warp came back online. It would give the Web Mind time to recalculate, as it would be several days before even a star lord could work its way through the protective field. Turning on the interstellar transporter had momentarily cut it off from the orbitals as well. That didn't matter much, as the Web Mind wasn't worried about the paltry humans with their tiny spacecraft. The star lord and Doom Star were the true concern.

Now, the Web Mind discovered its secret lines to other locations on the planet. It had laid them long ago, a way to thwart the limiting time effects of the surrounding warp.

What the Web Mind found was infuriating. The star lord loaded up the Doom Star with its cyborg creatures. The energy being also stole cyborg equipment.

Oh no, this was too much, far too much. The Web Mind wasn't going to stand for this theft. Yes, the star lord controlled those cyborgs. But there were other cyborgs in other locations on the planet that would still obey the true cyborg lord.

Now, the star lord would learn its folly of double-crossing the greatest, most supreme intellect in the universe, which was the Web Mind, of course.

You are about to die, Star Lord, and I am the one who is going to destroy you. No one betrays me and gains from it, absolutely no one.

-57-

Lord Acton's eyes gleamed. "Without the Web Mind's viruses, this would have been impossible. I am amazed at the Old Federation equipment. I also have a new appreciation for the cyborgs, for the Web Minds in particular. They may indeed be arrogant and even pompous, but there is a reason for that. They are the super geniuses. I am a mite, as the one called you earlier, Centurion, compared to it."

"I remember," Tanner said, working hard to control his impatience. It was difficult, at times, interacting with the highly intelligent. Both Greco and Acton liked to spout off when they should have been working as hard as possible to complete the project.

"The only problem I foresee will be following the apeman's strict procedure," Acton said.

"It must be done exactly as I have outlined," Greco said. "Otherwise, the planet will not split in two. Then, I will have failed. This is my supreme moment. You cannot let me down, Lord Acton."

"I am not attempting this for the sake of your *koholmany*," Acton said. "I am doing this in order to halt the cyborgs."

"Yes, yes," Greco said. "I understand. But this is my moment of glory. I have always believed planet-splitting possible. The centurion once said such splitting could be a weapon. Now, I understand what he meant. Before, by pure concentration—"

"Enough!" Tanner shouted. "Will you two eggheads finish this? We're almost out of time. Surely, the Doom Star is filled to capacity by now. It will lift off before we start. We won't destroy it then in the coming inferno."

Greco scowled.

Acton nodded slowly. "The centurion could have a point. We might also take the Doom Star down with the planet. Should we begin?" he asked Greco.

"Yes, your lordship," the apeman said, "I would love to start. I am giddy with the possibilities."

The three of them were jammed in the control room. Tanner stood behind Greco and Acton. The *Dark Star* was in midlevel orbit around Planet Zero.

Acton took a deep breath. Once finished, he began to manipulate his slate. A secret war now took place as the Shand attempted to activate the takeover of hundreds of orbital missiles and sensors. At the same time, he tried to force the laser missiles to target the Doom Star.

He had worked at this for hours, setting everything up for a mass cyber-assault. Greco and he had infiltrated the orbital AIs and computers. At this precise moment of time, the takeover began in earnest.

"Something is fighting back," Acton said. The glowing slate shined on his face. He put the slate on his lap and began tapping faster, like a man possessed.

Tanner leaned over the seat, looking down. He didn't understand the constantly changing schematics he saw.

"Oh, clever, clever," the Shand muttered. "But that isn't going to foil me. It might stall a few missiles, nothing more."

"No," Greco said. "The missiles must all hit in the exact sequence I've outlined. Everything will be ruined if they fail to act precisely. Then, we might as well not have tried this."

Tanner had never seen Greco so worked up. The intensity was something to behold.

"Ah," Acton said. "I have a breakthrough. The missiles should begin to head down soon. The lasers will give the Doom Star and maybe the Phaze something to think about."

Tanner waited, anxious, wondering if they could actually pull this off.

"No," Acton hissed. "No, I will not allow you to do that."

"Do what?" Tanner asked. "What's going on?"

Acton didn't answer. His fingers blurred furiously, the tips tapping the slate. Tanner had never seen anyone type like that.

Acton must have entered the zone of his mental concentration. He no longer spoke, but typed, paused and typed so the schematics changed one right after the other on the slate. Soon, it seemed as if the schematics blurred on top of each other.

Tanner looked out the port window. He saw a missile burn hot as it angled down toward the planet.

"Oh, yes, oh yes, yes, yes," Greco said. He began to hop up and down, hooting with delight. "It is happening. The great moment has come. I have made my *koholmany*. I understand vibrations better than anyone, even better than the legendary Tesla."

***

All around Planet Zero, the orbital missiles began to streak down toward the surface. Each missile had exact coordinates. Each moved in a perfect sequence.

At the same time, orbital lasers moved into position high above the Doom Star. A cannon poked out of each nosecone. Then, ancient fusion drives thrummed, building up energy. At once, several orbital lasers beamed the mighty warship.

The first attacks seemed to have caught the Doom Star by surprise. Heat boiled against collapsium armor, doing nothing destructive at first.

More laser missiles slid above the giant battlewagon. They, too, beamed into the atmosphere, losing some strength but not much. Like the others, the beams boiled against the thick collapsium. While Doom Star armor was fantastic, even it couldn't sustain this ravenous assault for long.

Shuttles racing for the hangar bays veered off. Cyborg fighters began to climb for the stratosphere, afterburners roaring as flames lengthened. Clearly, they went after the orbital lasers.

Still, the orbitals beamed their combined rays against the Doom Star.

Now, the Old Federation battlewagon began to rise. As it did, mighty laser and particle beam cannons poked from its hull. It spat fire at its attackers.

An orbital laser missile exploded. So did another and a third. The Doom Star began to annihilate its tormentors. Orbital lasers continued to heat the hull armor, though. Now, many of the beams combined on one location. The first particles of collapsium burned away.

The cyborg space fighters began to target the orbital lasers.

At that point, low over the horizon from every point on the compass appeared more cyborg fighters. There were larger ships, as well. They converged on the Doom Star.

These cyborg vessels responded to the Web Mind deep underground. It had given them special instructions. Afterward, each cyborg pilot would maintain radio silence, not accepting any further instructions from anyone.

Time passed as the Doom Star gained speed. Yet, it was a giant vessel, never made to operate in an atmosphere. That made it more sluggish than it would have been otherwise.

The last of the orbital lasers slid into position above, adding their beams. The Doom Star had obliterated most of them. The Phaze's cyborg fighters would finish the rest.

That's when the first air-to-air missiles launched from the wave of new cyborg vessels that streaked at the great battlewagon.

Abruptly, the Doom Star's lasers, particle beams and point defense guns began to blaze at the new threat. It was a testament to the Old Federation. The Doom Star was an engine of destruction. It wiped a wide swath of destruction through the approaching air-to-air missiles, but not a total obliteration of them.

At that point, the Phaze-controlled cyborg fighters reached low orbit. The fighter cannons smashed the remaining orbital lasers.

Those lasers no longer burned against the now pitted collapsium armor. They had weakened the hull in many places, though. Those places glowed red, throbbing like bleeding wounds.

The masses of Web Mind-controlled fighters and heavier attack vessels zoomed at the great Doom Star. It was like thousands of bees swarming a lion, stinging it repeatedly.

Thousands of Web Mind fighters and attack vessels exploded, raining metallic debris onto the ground. Fires raged on the surface. All the while, little missiles, big missiles and anti-ship laser streaked against the hull. A few missiles hit. Some of those were nuclear.

Finally, a crack appeared in the great hull. The Doom Star seemed to stagger.

The mass now aimed there, pounding the crack with more missiles, gushing lasers into the widening gap. One missile made it into the level behind the hull. It exploded, ripping bulkheads with a nuclear explosion. That caused coolants to bubble and froth, spilling onto laser coils. A hiss of steam rose, water boiled and a secondary explosion ripped into a battery storage area. Acid bubbled, burning through a deck.

The Doom Star stopped its upward motion, lowered a fraction and then resumed its flight into space.

***

Clack staggered once more. He had no idea what was going on outside. He was in the convertor chamber, a nightmare from Hell.

He'd witnessed too many crewmembers strapped onto the terrible conveyor. He had often closed his eyes, moaning, vomiting more than once. It was a terrible process, the skin choppers, the new muscles and the circuits inserted into each brain.

Soon, it would be his turn. There were only a few others left now. What would it feel like? What—

A muffled explosion shook the chamber. Clack staggered. He looked up. The bulkhead nearest the explosion blew apart. For a second, Clack could see the atmosphere outside. That didn't seem right. What could break through a Doom Star's armor?

The next moment, he saw a missile. It was a big thing. It sailed into the convertor chamber and exploded. The blazing white was the last thing Clack Urbis saw before the nuclear blast reached him.

***

Outside, the great Doom Star rolled as it began to sink. One too many explosions had destroyed its propulsion and gravity control. Still, the last cyborg fighters and attack vessels threw themselves at the giant battlewagon from a lost era.

Now, the Phaze's fighters struck back.

It seemed impossible the Doom Star could survive this pounding. Yet, the masses of attackers had dwindled. Those left ignored the space fighters hitting their flanks. They had one order, and one order only: *hit the Doom Star*. That was the order they were going to obey as long as they breathed.

-58-

Aboard the *Dark Star*, Tanner stood transfixed by the images on the main screen. This was awesome. It was clear the Web Mind was in the fight, throwing its resources at the Phaze-controlled Doom Star. The great battlewagon staggered with its hull ruptured in places.

At the same time, hundreds of Old Federation orbital missiles all over the planet raced to reach their detonation points on the surface. The orbital satellites that had circled Planet Zero for so long finally came down.

The first hit sandy surface and exploded, sending up a giant mushroom cloud. At the same time, the force traveled into the earth and struck a fault line. That caused an interior vibration. It wasn't a great vibration in the scheme of things, but it was the first of many.

More nuclear explosions went off around the planet. More mushroom clouds climbed into the heavens. The continuous and precise strikes made the planet vibrate more than before. Continental pressure points slipped, causing further earthquakes. This happened to every fault line on the surface. Every pressure point slipped. Every tectonic plate moved. A vast, worldwide earthquake began to take place. It shook greater than the day the twin asteroids had struck the planet.

The entirety of Planet Zero quivered. Under the surface, caverns and halls fell, crushing millions of cyborgs and their military equipment. The Web Mind more than a kilometer underground did not escape the destruction. The time warp around it merely meant that its death would occur a little later, but it was as good as destroyed.

The vibrations shook the planet harder and harder. Vast cracks appeared on the surface. Those cracks zigzagged with ominous intent.

On the *Dark Star*, in the control room, Greco hooted wildly as he jumped up and down.

Tanner couldn't believe this. It was working. Would he see the planet split apart before his eyes?

The quakes intensified...and began weakening. The zigzags grew still. Underground water fountained into the air. Then, the vibrations all around the world lessened. The cracking surface no longer splintered. The earthquakes and vibrations quit.

On the *Dark Star* Greco stopped hopping up and down. Instead of smiling, he frowned at the main screen

"What happened?" the apeman asked.

"We've succeeded against the hidden cyborgs," Tanner shouted. "You did it, Greco. My instruments show planet-wide, massive destruction. Those quakes surely crushed the cyborgs out of existence. We only have the Doom Star to worry about now. Everything else is gone."

Greco looked dejected. "My *koholmany*," he muttered. "My *koholmany* failed. I don't understand. The planet should have splintered apart."

"You defeated the underground cyborgs," Acton said. "Isn't that good enough?"

Greco stared at the Shand. Finally, the apeman shook his head, saying, "No, it isn't good enough. I can't believe it. I failed."

"No," Tanner said, slapping his friend on the shoulder. "You're the greatest success ever." He turned to Acton. "Now we're going to have to figure out what to do with the Doom Star."

***

The Doom Star seemed like a smaller version of the planet. Giant cracks split the hull, but the ancient battlewagon was somehow still intact. It continued to roll, though, and it lost height.

No more orbital lasers beamed at it. Those were all dead. The last cyborg attackers either succumbed to the Phaze's fighters or tumbled in the howling, nuclear-created winds that had begun sweeping the planet. That cyclone also swept Phaze fighters end over end.

"Is it finished?" Tanner asked.

"Look," Acton said. "Do you see that?"

Tanner tapped his board. He saw it all right. A comet-shaped thing with a glowing tail flew out of the Doom Star. The Phaze headed for space.

Tanner looked at Acton. "Are you thinking what I'm thinking?"

"Enlighten me," Acton said.

"It's time to hunt the last Phaze."

"Then, the answer is yes. That is what I was thinking."

Tanner nodded curtly, tapping the controls. It was time to head down and catch the Phaze by surprise if they could.

As the Phaze rose, as the *Dark Star* plummeted, the great and ancient Doom Star rolled around and around. As it did, the Old Federation battlewagon gained speed. Wind shrieked around it. The ball rolled faster.

Then, the Doom Star smashed against the surface. Billions of tons of metal crumbled and pushed against rock and sand. It created a mighty boom. Metallic shrieks tore into the air. Rock splintered and sand rose in geyser after geyser.

The cyborgs new and old, all the humans on the craft, smashed and bounced, shattered and died. Everyone aboard the Doom Star perished even as the giant battlewagon continued to crumple onto the barren surface.

✳✳✳

Tanner laughed. "It's about time. I wondered when the Phaze would get wise to us."

Acton nodded.

The comet-shaped Phaze abruptly changed direction. Instead of traveling for space, it headed down.

"That's what it should have done in the first place," Tanner said. "If I were it, I'd ooze into the ground. What could we have done then?"

"Nothing," Acton said.

"Right," Tanner said. "That's what I'm saying. It was stupid."

"Or it miscalculated," Acton said.

On the screen, the comet zoomed for the radioactive surface. The tail wriggled madly.

"Target acquired," Tanner said.

"The gun is ready."

Tanner waited, waited, and then pressed the tab. The *Dark Star's* special cannon fired, hitting the Phaze.

The familiar scream sounded in Tanner's head. He didn't like it even though he desperately wanted to finish this creature. Then, outside the raider, the Phaze from the Triangulum Galaxy exploded with a multitude of colors.

The energy being was dead.

-59-

Everything should have been over then. The Phazes were dead and by now, so was the Web Mind. The people aboard the *Dark Star* had thwarted the terrible calamity of revived cyborgs with photon-electrical allies. Planet Zero couldn't hurt anyone anymore.

The new menace was the old menace, although it wasn't critical to them at the moment. After all this, the Coalition admiral had decided to begin heading for Planet Zero. Every surviving ship of the Coalition expeditionary fleet was coming this way. Unfortunately, it appeared Admiral May had the codes to the system's Old Federation sensors, mines and moon turrets. A few drones were also headed this way. That meant the *Dark Star* would not go out the way it had come in.

"Even if we can sneak past the drones and fleet," Tanner said, "why take any risks at this point?"

The centurion presently squirted gravity waves from the raider. He piloted the *Dark Star* toward the system's F type star.

It had been a day now since the Phaze's death, the Doom Star's destruction, the missile barrage and the planetary earthquake that had smashed the hidden cyborgs and their ancient equipment. Greco was still in a blue funk at what he saw as his own failure to split the planet. Tesla's ancient boast still stood unfulfilled.

Tanner sighed. The apeman reminded him of the smart kid in class who was always deflated if he got an A- instead of an A+.

The days merged into each other as the *Dark Star* left the last planet behind. For the first time in a long time, Planet Zero was truly a dead world.

For hours, Tanner or Acton sat at the controls, listening for signals from Planet Zero. Nothing ever blipped. Could even cyborgs survive beneath trillions of tons of sand and rock? Somehow, Tanner doubted that.

The raider passed the star, swinging wide around it. Now, they no longer sped toward the interstellar gulf. They went to the side, as it were, to ride along the galactic rim.

That meant more delay, but it switched their direction as they drifted through velocity alone. Tanner could have squirted more gravity waves, but after all they had been through, he decided to play it safe. "What's another week after our ordeals?"

No one liked it, but no one disagreed. Old Federation drones launched by the Coalition continued to search for them. The various devices in the systems had joined in the hunt. It didn't matter, though, not against their fantastic stealth equipment.

"We can go anywhere we want," Tanner said. "This is the stealthiest vessel in the Backus Cluster."

"It might be the stealthiest in the Orion and Perseus Spiral Arms," Acton said.

At last, the day came when the raider reached hyperspace territory. Now, they had to decide where to go next. Everyone agreed that the Nostradamus System was a good choice. What helped was that it was a straight shot from here, with no interstellar objects between them and their destination.

The *Dark Star* entered hyperspace without a hitch, leaving the hunting drones and the Coalition fleet behind in the star system.

Before entering hibernation for the long journey to the Nostradamus System, Tanner went to Greco's quarters. He knocked on the door.

"Come in," the apeman said.

410

Tanner did, finding Greco lying on his bed. "Mind if I sit down?"

"Help yourself, brother," Greco said listlessly.

Tanner took a seat. He scratched his cheek. "So what do you think?"

Greco kept staring up at the ceiling. "About what?" the apeman asked.

"We tried Consul Maximus' great plan. We went to an impossible world and picked up a nullifier. While there, we took care of some problems. I'm not sure yet how the nullifier is going to help us free Remus and Avernus."

Greco turned to him. "This has nothing to do with my people. They're already free. I doubt the Coalition has been able to subjugate them."

"You don't know that."

"Last time we checked, that was the case. Why would it be any different now?"

Tanner nodded slowly. "Maybe you're right."

Greco put his hands over his chest and twiddled his thumbs as he went back to staring at the ceiling.

Tanner looked around. The room was still a sty. He got up and went to the desk. Out of the corner of his eye, he noticed that Greco didn't respond to that. So, the centurion began opening drawers.

"Do you mind?" Greco said. "That's an invasion of privacy."

Tanner ignored the apeman, opening the bottom drawer and extracting a bottle of brandy.

Greco finally sat up. "Put that back. It's my special—"

Tanner broke the seal, opening it.

Greco's eyes nearly bulged.

"This is to your victory," Tanner said. He poured into a glass, handing it to the apeman."

"I should hit you for doing that," Greco said. "I could whip you in a fight if I wanted to. I'm far stronger than you are."

Tanner continued to hold out the glass. Finally, Greco took it, cradling it sullenly.

"Why the long face, my friend?"

"You had no right to open my brandy," Greco said.

411

"We're celebrating. Don't you want to celebrate?"

"Why? I failed. I tried to split the planet—"

Tanner put his head back and laughed.

Greco scowled as his fingers tightened around the glass. "It isn't right to mock me, especially in my own room."

"Are you kidding me? I'm not mocking you. You did a great thing."

"Do you mean by destroying the cyborgs?"

"No," Tanner said. "I don't mean that at all."

The scowl became a frown. "I don't understand."

"You're trying to make a *koholmany*, right? You want to split a planet in two."

"I've said that many times," Greco said.

"Well, you came very close the other day," Tanner said.

"Which is not the same as success," the apeman pointed out.

"I'm surprised at you. Surely, you know the ways of great inventors."

"What ways?"

"An attempt that doesn't work isn't a failure. It simply means that that exact method doesn't work. So, you're one step closer to finding the step that *does* work. So you try again and get closer each time until you succeed. Doesn't that make sense?"

Greco stared at the centurion. Suddenly, he exposed his teeth. It could have been a grimace, but Tanner knew it was a toothy apeman smile.

"Say, that's right," Greco said. "I've thought for a long time that the system we used would work. Clearly, it didn't. But that doesn't mean—well, as you said, I've crossed out a false way. That means I'm closer to the truth, I'm closer to making my *koholmany*."

"Exactly," Tanner said.

"Yes," Greco said. "That *is* worthy of a drink."

"A toast then," Tanner said, as he clinked the bottle of brandy against the apeman's glass. "To finding the vibration that will split a planet in half."

"Indeed, indeed," Greco said. He slugged back his brandy, holding out his glass for more.

After first taking a moderate sip, Tanner poured his friend more. It was good to see the apeman upbeat again.

"Let's get victory drunk," Greco said.

"I'll drink to that," Tanner said.

***

The next day, as Tanner massaged his aching head, he sat down in the galley with Lord Acton. The Shand ate a sparse salad, chewing each bite thoroughly.

"We should enter hibernation soon," Acton said.

Tanner didn't respond right away. He opened a bottle of water, guzzling it. He was still dehydrated from getting drunk with Greco.

"I have decided to give you the newer nullifier," Acton said. "By rights, I should give you my old one and keep the new one. Yet, I suspect you would be upset if I took the better one."

"You never miss a beat, do you, Acton?" Tanner muttered.

"Hmm, yes," Acton said, taking another forkful of salad. He chewed for a time. "We have accomplished a marvel. What is more, what you did underground was magnificent."

Tanner eyed the Shand.

"Is something wrong?" Acton asked.

"No, no, it's simply that I'm not used to receiving compliments from you. I'm sure it doesn't mean you're trying to butter me up for something else. I would never suspect such a thing from you, Lord."

"Sarcasm is not your strong suit," Acton said.

Tanner considered his next words while studying his water bottle. Finally, he looked at Acton. "Thanks for the Innoo Flaam. Thanks for the incredible stealth ship. But most of all, thanks for aiding humanity. We really did need your help. You know what, Acton? You take the good nullifier and I'll take the poor one. I don't really know what good a nullifier will do me anyway."

"You continue to surprise me," Acton said. "You must realize I want you to have the better nullifier. Thus, you throw my compliment in my teeth. Well done, Centurion."

"Lord Acton," Tanner said. "For once, you have miscalculated my intent. I really am thankful for all you've done. I can be a pain at times. I know that. But you stuck with us. I'm being fully honest. But I'll take the better nullifier. And you know what?"

Acton shook his head.

"I'm hoping you'll stay with us for a while."

The Shand set down his fork. "I will hire you, Captain, if you're willing."

"Hire?"

"A Shand must work according to the codes of our species."

"What do you have in mind?"

Acton hesitated, finally saying, "Surely you recall what Ursa told you. A Shand has many plans, often fifty years in the making. The patrician is essentially correct concerning that. I will have to consider my priorities as I take into account your particular skill sets. I'm sure I have an idea or two that could use a fellow like you with a ship like this."

"You know I plan on freeing Remus, right?" Tanner said.

Acton stared at him. "What I have in mind will help with your objective."

Tanner thought about that. "Count me in then, Lord, for a reasonable fee. I also want to get Nelly Jordan from Calisto Grandee. First, though, let's all take a well-deserved rest in hibernation."

"Agreed. I will head there shortly."

"Me, too," Tanner said. "Before I do that, though, I need to talk to Lady Varus."

***

Tanner raised his hand to knock on Ursa's hatch. He figured pressing the buzzer would be too—

The hatch opened before Tanner knocked. Marcus was there. The tribune stepped out and stopped abruptly upon seeing Tanner. The bigger man eyed him. Some of the former friendliness had departed.

Tanner didn't know why.

"My sister is the heiress of House Varus," Marcus said in a stern voice. "It is good for you to remember that."

Tanner nodded.

"She—"

"Marcus," Ursa said from her room.

Marcus glanced back into the room. "Remember your high station, sister. We must go home one day. We must free our world. It may be that we will be the highest nobility left. Shouldn't we—"

"Thank you, Marcus," she said. "I appreciate your concern. I really do."

Marcus wouldn't look at Tanner now. Finally, he brushed past the centurion to march down the corridor.

Tanner watched him go. He thought Marcus and he were friends. Why had the man suddenly decided to act like this?

Ursa stepped up, giving him a troubled smile. She wore a sweater he'd never seen before, set in such a way that one of her shoulders was bare. He noticed her hair next. She must have taken some time to do it up like that. She also wore a touch of makeup.

Tanner had a good idea now why Marcus had become angry. "You're beautiful," he said.

Ursa looked down, smiling.

He stepped closer, taking her hands. "Ursa Varus," he said.

She looked up. "I have a bottle of wine. I thought we might celebrate our victory."

Tanner grinned. She looked so beautiful, and she had clearly made herself up for him. A few sips of wine, some soft talk—

Impulsively, Tanner leaned in, kissing her. She kissed him back. He let go of her hands, holding her face as he continued to kiss her.

Suddenly, she pulled free, staring at him with wide eyes. She looked more beautiful than ever. "I'm sorry. I-I can't do this. I want to. I thought I could. I know you don't understand. But Marcus is right about this. I have to think about our world's future."

Tanner knew what Marcus must have just told her. Ursa was a patrician of the highest blood and the highest house. He

415

was just a lowly plebian. While he might have done much to save humanity, the centurion still needed to know his place in the order of Remus society. Someday, they would all go home again, and Ursa could well be Remus's new leader.

"I..." Ursa said, frowning in obvious self-torment.

"Lady," Tanner said.

She looked up at him.

He touched her cheek. She leaned into his hand a moment before drawing back.

"You're beautiful, Ursa. But you're also a patrician of House Varus. Your brother's right, as you say. You must remember your high station."

"Tanner," she said, staring at him as if across a great gulf.

Tanner recalled the promise he'd made to himself about her. He never wanted to see her hurt. Marcus did not yet approve of him for his sister. The tribune recalled Remus values. Maybe Marcus had just helped his sister remember those values as well.

Inwardly, Tanner shrugged. So be it. He liked a challenge. Winning Ursa was worth convincing Marcus the he, Tanner, was more than just a plebian. Maybe...maybe if the centurion freed Remus, Tanner of Vesuvius would be the one to rule the planet with Ursa beside him.

"We're going to enter hibernation soon," Tanner said.

Ursa nodded wordlessly.

"We're heading for the Nostradamus System."

"Oh."

"After I get my computer specialist, I plan to continue my mission to free Remus. Lord Acton might be helping us."

"Us?" Ursa said.

"If you're going to be staying..." Tanner said.

Ursa stared into his eyes. "Do you want me to stay?"

"Yes."

"I will," she whispered.

"Good. You should get ready then."

She raised her eyebrows.

"Unless you plan to wear that outfit to the hibernation chamber," he said.

She blushed, smiled shyly and closed the hatch.

Tanner stared at the hatch. Then, he turned, doing so just in time to see Marcus dart behind a corner far down the corridor. Her brother had been watching.

Tanner smiled as he headed in the opposite direction. The road to Remus's freedom might still be long and winding. He was going to need all the allies he could get.

Now, it was time to prepare. They had acquired a great tool in the nullifier. He also had this super stealth vessel and an Innoo Flaam gun. He would drive the Coalition off Remus just as he had vowed.

Tanner smiled wider. It was time to rest. The good guys had won a round. That was rare in this galaxy. He should enjoy it while he could.

The End

Made in the USA
Middletown, DE
07 July 2020

12082665R00236